T0385301

# MURDER AT THE PALACE

**N.R. Daws** spent thirty years as a civil servant, mostly in security and counter-terrorism. He is a hiker, skier, lover of history and travel, as well as a long-standing fellow of the Royal Geographical Society. He was awarded an MBE for charitable services in 2006. An alumnus of the Curtis Brown Creative writing school, he achieved Highly Commended in the Blue Pencil Agency First Novel Award 2019, where he met his agent, Nelle Andrew. His first novel, *A Quiet Place to Kill*, was published by Thomas & Mercer in 2021.

## *Also by N.R. Daws*

### KEMBER AND HAYES SERIES

A Quiet Place to Kill
A Silent Way to Die
A Perfect Time to Murder

# MURDER AT THE PALACE

## N.R. DAWS

ORION

First published in Great Britain in 2025 by Orion Fiction,
an imprint of The Orion Publishing Group Ltd
Carmelite House, 50 Victoria Embankment
London EC4Y ODZ

An Hachette UK company

The authorised representative in the EEA is Hachette Ireland,
8 Castlecourt Centre, Dublin 15, D15 XTP3, Ireland (email: info@hbgi.ie)

1 3 5 7 9 10 8 6 4 2

A CIP catalogue record for this book
is available from the British Library.

ISBN (Hardback) 9781 4091 9979 3
ISBN (Trade Paperback) 9781 4091 9980 9
ISBN (eBook) 9781 4091 9982 3
ISBN (Audio) 9781 4091 9983 0

Typeset by Deltatype Ltd, Birkenhead, Merseyside

Printed in Great Britain by Clays Ltd, Elcograf S.p.A.

MIX
Paper | Supporting
responsible forestry
FSC
www.fsc.org    FSC® C104740

www.orionbooks.co.uk

For Jane.
Wife, proud mother to our two daughters,
best friend and loyal supporter.

Please note that while the notable locations in this story are real, the characters and events are fictional.

# Cast of Characters

**Base Court**

Ground Floor, South-West

    Mrs Lydia Bramble – Lady Housekeeper to Hampton Court
      Palace

    Kitty – her loyal housemaid

Anne Boleyn's Gateway

    Lady Ives (widow)

**Seymour Gate**

    Reverend Thomas Weaver – Chaplain of the Chapel Royal
      at Hampton Court Palace

**Master Carpenter's Court**

Ground Floor, North Side

    Mrs Gertrude McGowan (widow)

    Miss Sarah Cameron-Banks – companion to Mrs McGowan

First Floor, North Side

    Mrs Flora Woodruff (widow of Commander Algernon
      Woodruff RN)

    Miss Alice Woodruff – Mrs Woodruff's unmarried
      daughter

    Mildred – housemaid

Ground Floor, South Side
    Lady Madeleine Whalley (widow)
    Sunny – her cockatoo
First Floor, South Side
    Mrs Catherine Ewan (widow of Major Richard Ewan DCM)
    Lady Emelia Chafford (widow of Sir Philip Chafford KCB)
    Miss Philomena Franklin – Lady Emelia's unmarried sister
    Rosie Hawkins – housemaid
    Mrs Joan Marsh – cook

**Fountain Court**
Third Floor, South-West
    Lady Venetia Merritt (widow) – and her ward

**Police**
    Detective Inspector Cole – of Scotland Yard
    The sergeant – Hampton Court Palace police

**Hampton Court Palace staff**
    Billy – Gardener

# 1

Mrs Bramble, holding the title of Lady Housekeeper of the grace-and-favour apartments at Hampton Court Palace, was a creature of habit. Two slices of toast with thick butter and a smear of marmalade, always accompanied by a hot cup of Earl Grey tea, constituted her usual breakfast. It may have been the morning after a long shift supervising at a gala entertainments evening but that did not require any special deviation from her routine. On occasion, she might veer towards a soft-boiled egg with toast soldiers, but anything more elaborate was confined to special occasions and yearly events such as Christmas and Easter. That's not to say she didn't enjoy fancy food when she could get it, but she wasn't about to pay fancy prices for it, thank you very much.

Mrs Bramble broke off the corner of a crust, deposited a blob of butter on top and placed it on the floor next to her chair.

'There you go, Dodger,' she said to the jet-black cat giving her his full attention through big green eyes.

Dodger by name and dodger by nature, named after Mr Dickens's slippery character in *Oliver Twist*, he was also a creature of habit and insisted on licking butter from a cube of toast every morning, after his main breakfast provided by Mrs

Bramble's housemaid, Kitty, of course. Mrs Bramble did not begrudge this particular extravagance, it being a small price to pay for his mousing duties and the company he afforded her of an evening. She watched him for a moment before raising her head to look out of the window, trying to let her mind wander in peace before the rigours of the day intruded. She failed, unable to stop herself from noting the early-morning comings and goings across the bridge over the moat and on Outer Green Court.

Mrs Bramble loved her job, believing it as rewarding and satisfying as anything she had ever done but a lot less dangerous – she had seen more than her fair share of death – and not nearly as traumatic, although never boring. In general, society life at the palace was pleasant and enjoyed by most. However, a number of petty disputes had blighted palace life of late, the recollection of which left a sour taste beneath the sweet marmalade on Mrs Bramble's tongue.

Even so, she revelled in her chief role of overseeing the staff whose work ensured all areas of the centuries-old palace were kept as spotless and presentable as possible for everyone who lived in, used or visited its hallowed rooms. Residents given tenancy by royal grace and favour, members of the public arriving for the purpose of visiting residents or delivering goods, the humble domestic servants within each household and staff in the public areas dealing with the hordes of tourists who descended on a daily basis all had the same expectation. Every apartment, chamber, corridor, cloister and court had to be maintained to the highest standard and Mrs Bramble prided herself on achieving this day in, day out, all year, every year.

'I forgot to ask,' said Mrs Bramble as Kitty appeared in the doorway looking as presentable as always in her uniform of a long-sleeved black dress, white apron and crocheted white

2

cap. 'Was the disagreement between the two housemaids serving at the gala resolved last night?'

'They had a bit of a set-to, but it seemed like something and nothing to me,' said Kitty.

'Hmm,' said Mrs Bramble, aware of a past frostiness between the pair.

Then she noticed the envelope Kitty hesitated to deliver and guessed the identity of the sender before even seeing the writing on the front. Kitty took a few steps towards the table and propped the envelope against the marmalade pot before taking a step backwards.

'Do you need a top-up of tea, Mrs B?' she asked, glancing down at the envelope. 'To fortify you?'

'No, thank you,' said Mrs Bramble with a smile. 'I believe I'm used to these by now.'

'Yes, Mrs B,' said Kitty, leaving the room.

Mrs Bramble looked at the unopened letter and sighed at the sight of the printing on the outside declaring it had been despatched from the Lord Chamberlain's Office. As neither he nor his office were in the habit of sending her pleasantries in the post, or by any other means, for that matter, the envelope could contain nothing good. Most likely, one of the many feuds involving the palace residents had taken another turn, hence Kitty's hesitancy.

Mrs Bramble, having married an infantryman in the British Army and taken his name, had travelled with him and, being childless, had trained as a military nurse to be useful and to occupy her time. Her experience had taught her how to cope with those who were frightened or in pain, and to engage on equal terms with pompous officers and the rambunctious rank and file, skills that often came in useful in her current position.

She thought now of her husband, a much-missed brave man who, having risen to the rank of sergeant, lost his life from

3

cholera. The outbreak in Bengal that had claimed him became a pandemic that even now, all these years later, still swept the globe. She had been posted back to England but left nursing a year later because her heart was no longer in it and she wanted to get away from the army and the memories it evoked. Stints as a housekeeper in hotels of various quality and private houses of dubious repute had further honed her ability to deal with bumptious owners, colleagues and guests alike.

And now, here she was at Hampton Court Palace.

Mrs Bramble cleaned her butter knife and prepared to bite the bullet. She slid the knife under the envelope flap, slit it along its length, removed and unfolded the headed notepaper, and read the short missive.

Her lips pursed. Another complaint from Mrs Gertrude McGowan about the unfair allocation of apartments at the palace.

And people thought her job an easy one.

Mrs Bramble shook her head and closed her eyes for a moment. Yes, she loved her job but conceded she would love it even more if it did not involve daily interaction with some of the more challenging residents.

She took a final mouthful of tea and Kitty reappeared at the sound of the clink as she replaced her cup on its saucer.

'All done, Mrs B?' said Kitty.

Mrs Bramble had employed Kitty for the last three years and enjoyed a rapport that facilitated a certain amount of social information and intelligence being fed back via the residents' servants. In return, she had come to entrust her innermost thoughts to the young woman.

'I almost can't bear to go out there today,' Mrs Bramble confided. 'That dreadful woman's gala carried on way past the bedtime of anyone decent.' She looked down at Dodger, who looked up when she paused. 'Yes, all right, I know,' she conceded. 'I'd better go see whether the Great Hall has been tidied properly, but you mark my words, there'll be hell to pay if the superintendent or I find one stick of furniture out of place or one unsightly mark. Paying visitors have a right to expect cleanliness if nothing else.'

Dodger left his toast, now licked clean of butter, and sauntered away, unconcerned by the problems of people.

'I'm sure it won't be too bad,' said Kitty. 'I know most of the staff around here. We have our own get-togethers, as you know, and they're quick smart about mopping a spillage or sweeping up a breakage. It'll all be shipshape and Bristol fashion, you mark my words.'

Kitty loaded the breakfast things onto a tray and disappeared towards the kitchen.

Mrs Bramble had been Lady Housekeeper for five years and prided herself on running a tight ship. That meant she needed to know every resident's business, and she did, but it didn't mean she had to like all of them all of the time. On her travels, she had sometimes found the higher up the political, military, financial or social scale one existed, the more intolerable they could be, but she always played fair and now took her roles as confidante, facilitator, adjudicator, allocator, protector and gatekeeper to each and every resident as seriously as her duties as guardian of the grace-and-favour apartments.

Mrs Bramble enjoyed living in her own comfortable ground-floor apartment and found its spaciousness and understated elegance most satisfactory. In addition, its position on the south side of the tower that formed the main entrance of the Great West Gatehouse afforded her the satisfaction of being able to look out first thing in the morning and last thing at night to reassure herself all was well. She did so now, watching while a chestnut horse that had seen better days brought a milk cart to a halt as the local postman who had borne the fateful

5

letter strolled away from the palace. Others went about their business, but nothing seemed untoward. And so, the sudden bell-ringing and banging on her front door made her heart beat faster, and in unison with the knuckle rapping.

'Mrs Bramble, Mrs Bramble, come quickly!' came a muffled call from outside.

Mrs Bramble wiped her mouth on her napkin and rushed into the hallway, stepping on Dodger's discarded toast in the process, in time to see Kitty unlock the door.

'Oh, Kitty—' A young woman fell forwards as the door opened.

'Calm yourself, Rosie,' said Kitty, holding up her hand to quieten her. 'Where's the fire?'

Rosie Hawkins, housemaid to Lady Emelia Chafford and her spinster sister, Miss Philomena Franklin, stood in the doorway, shaking.

'Ain't no fire, Kitty. It's—it's—'

Kitty put her hands on Rosie's arms for reassurance. 'Breathe, dear,' she instructed, and Rosie took gulps of air. 'Now, take your time and tell us what's happened.'

She seemed to realise all of a sudden that Mrs Bramble was standing nearby and looked at her with wide eyes. 'Lady Emelia needs your spare keys urgently,' said Rosie, taking another gasp. 'It's Miss Franklin. Her Ladyship thinks she's dead!'

# 2

'Kitty, fetch Dr Kemp at once,' said Mrs Bramble as she hurried along the hallway to the next room.

Kitty complied without hesitation, almost tripping over Dodger as he got caught up in the commotion.

Mrs Bramble unlocked a wooden cupboard set against one wall, unhooked the bunch of spare keys to the Chaffords' apartment from where it hung alongside many others and returned to usher the distraught Rosie out of the apartment. She locked the door before hastening along the cloister on the west side of Base Court, the largest of the courtyards in the palace, with Rosie scurrying after her. Easing past dawdlers in a narrow passage leading to the much smaller Master Carpenter's Court, they emerged into the open and reached a painted oak door, left unlocked by Rosie, which gave access to a small, plain entrance hall, lit at night by an ornate chandelier. Winding steps led to the first-floor apartment shared by Lady Emelia and her sister, and Mrs Bramble took these two at a time, leaving the much younger Rosie holding her stomach, breathing heavily and lagging behind.

Lady Emelia met them inside, standing solemn-faced with fluttering fingers worrying the amber-hued opal pendant hanging from a delicate chain around her neck.

'Mrs Bramble, thank God,' said Lady Emelia, rattling the knob of the door beside her. 'My sister's in the study but not answering, and it's locked.'

'I'm afraid I won't be able to open it if the key is in the lock,' said Mrs Bramble.

'It's not, I checked.'

Mrs Bramble cocked an eyebrow. 'Rosie said you think Miss Franklin is dead.' She sorted through the apartment's spare keys for the one that fitted the study. 'How do you know?'

'I, er, looked through the keyhole ... and saw her slumped over the bureau.' Lady Emelia clutched her pendant again. 'I fear she's had a heart attack.'

'Is Miss Franklin in the habit of locking the door while inside?' Mrs Bramble found the right key and inserted it in the lock.

'Not usually, no.'

The lock clicked and the door opened with ease. Lady Emelia gasped and Rosie cried out behind them. Mrs Bramble's heart gave a leap as she caught her breath. Miss Philomena Franklin was indeed slumped forwards on the open writing flap of the bureau, with a silver letter opener protruding from her back between her shoulder blades.

'Rosie, make some tea,' said Mrs Bramble, but Rosie stood ashen-faced. 'Now, girl.'

Rosie turned away, leaving Mrs Bramble to hold Lady Emelia back from rushing into the study.

'Is she ...?'

Mrs Bramble gestured for the woman to stay outside and stepped forwards herself, onto something hard underfoot. She bent down and found the key to the study door. 'Must have fallen out,' she said and moved over to Miss Franklin. Having been a military nurse dealing with death every day, she knew a dead body when she saw one, knife or no knife, and a quick check of Miss Franklin's neck above a string of pearls that matched her earrings and bracelet confirmed the absence of a pulse. She shook her head at Lady Emelia and the woman slumped against the door frame with a cry before retreating to the hallway.

Mrs Bramble's keen eye noticed a fountain pen lying on the blotting pad rather than replaced in its inkwell. Green blotches stained the paper. A half-eaten beef salad sandwich and full glass of water stood discarded on a tray placed on a low, spindly-legged table between two over-stuffed easy chairs. An expensive-looking drinks cabinet against the far wall displayed bottles labelled as dry gin, dry sherry, a gin flavoured with sloe berries, a single malt whisky and ruby port. A decanter of golden liquid suggesting it might contain a different spirit such as brandy stood alongside several glasses.

The chill air in the room held a slight smokiness and Mrs Bramble moved across to the wide-open window to look out, a floorboard below creaking in protest. A few chimneys showed evidence of early-morning fires lit in sitting-room grates, but even though the study's hearth held the cold ashes of an old fire, the smell in the study was not of wood or coal. She shivered and closed the window before turning back to the room with a thoughtful expression. Not being familiar with how the two women liked to keep their study, she could not say whether anything had been moved or taken. That would be something for the police to look into.

'Good Lord,' said Dr Edward Kemp from just inside the doorway.

At a glance, Mrs Bramble took in his dark, unbuttoned overcoat, striped shirt with every second button undone and a bluish-green stain at the edge of one cuff. Braces held up his black trousers and garish embroidery decorated his house shoes, all suggesting he hadn't expected an early-morning emergency call-out. Rosie stood by his side, wide-eyed and still looking pale. She clamped a hand over her mouth as she retched and ran along the hallway.

Dr Kemp put his medical bag beside Miss Franklin's chair and checked for a pulse at her wrist before paying close attention to her head and neck.

'Somebody's definitely done for the poor lady,' he said.

Mrs Bramble sighed. 'I was once a nurse, Doctor. I thought you might shed a little more light on the matter, other than the obvious.'

'Pardon?' Kemp threw her a confused look. 'Oh, yes. The knife in her back would do it. Sad to say, I saw a lot of this as a young army surgeon in Africa and India. Not often in the back, of course, but stab wounds generally.'

'As did I.' Mrs Bramble stepped closer and frowned. 'That's why the small amount of blood around the entry wound seems a little unusual, wouldn't you say?'

Kemp stood upright, making himself as tall and important-looking as he could. 'Absorbed by the lining of her dress and' – he gave a nervous little twitch of his shoulder – 'her underclothing, I should think. The police have been called?'

'I thought it best to wait for your confirmation before going off half-cocked. We'll need to send for the sergeant right away, although no doubt we'll have to wait for Scotland Yard.'

'Indeed. Quite right.'

She sniffed theatrically, drawing Kemp's attention. 'Do you smell that?'

Kemp sniffed, his nose raised. 'Perhaps Miss Franklin was visited by someone fond of smoking tobacco.'

Mrs Bramble watched him look around as though in search of evidence such as an ashtray.

There wasn't one.

'Hmm,' she said, sounding unconvinced as she followed the

doctor from the room. 'Didn't smell like wood, coal or tobacco smoke to me.' She locked the door, keeping both keys. 'To keep any evidence untainted,' she explained.

'Good thinking,' he said, tapping the side of his nose. 'I'll raise the sergeant forthwith. Good day for now.' He went to tip his hat, realised he'd forgotten to wear one and smiled awkwardly instead. 'Send for me at my surgery when Scotland Yard arrive. They'll want me to remove the body after they've had a poke around.' He turned away, nodded to Lady Emelia and scurried off, apologising over his shoulder.

'What an extraordinary man,' said Lady Emelia, watching the doctor disappear.

'I put his eccentricity down to his time abroad,' said Mrs Bramble. 'He witnessed the aftermath of a lot of fighting in those days, as did my husband and I, and that can change a person. He is reputed to have been in Africa twelve years ago, at the Battle of Rorke's Drift in 1879 during the Anglo–Zulu War, but never speaks of it.' Her mind flicked back to her own experiences that same year on the North-West Frontier of India during what they now called the Second Afghan War. That was the year before she had followed her husband on his ill-fated posting to Bengal. Always so much violence.

'May I ...?' Lady Emelia moved towards the study door and tried the doorknob.

'I'm afraid not. We need to await the sergeant, so I've locked the door.'

'But there are things – papers – I need.'

'I'm afraid everything must remain as it is for now,' said Mrs Bramble in a tone suggesting the topic was closed. 'No doubt Scotland Yard will want to examine the room for evidence. I'm sure you understand.'

The haunted look on Lady Emelia's face implied she did but would still like to get in.

11

'You've had a shock, Lady Emelia. Why don't we sit down and I'll ask Rosie to get you a medicinal brandy with that nice cup of tea?'

'I hate brandy.' She screwed up her nose. 'But I suppose the tea will settle my nerves.'

Mrs Bramble escorted Lady Emelia to the sitting room and went to find Rosie. The housemaid was in the kitchen sipping a glass of water.

'Are you OK, dear?' she asked.

Rosie looked startled. 'Yes, thank you. Just the shock, is all.' She looked at where Mrs Bramble had glanced. A silver teapot with a bone-china cup and saucer decorated with delicate flowers stood on a tray. 'Her Ladyship likes her tea strong and dark.'

'That's as maybe, but it's needed right away.' Mrs Bramble gave her a comforting smile before returning to the sitting room.

Lady Emelia hadn't moved.

'May I?' said Mrs Bramble, indicating a chair with an embroidered cover draped over the back and sitting anyway to forestall any refusal.

Lady Emelia had no choice but to agree. 'What am I to do?' she said, wringing her hands. 'Will I lose this apartment?'

'I shouldn't think so.' Mrs Bramble thought that a strange thing to be considering at a time like this. Then she remembered her own confused feelings at the time her husband had passed away and supposed it was as natural a reaction as any other to losing someone close in traumatic circumstances. 'This is still your home.'

'Who could have done such a terrible thing?'

'And why?' She watched Lady Emelia dab her eyes with a lace handkerchief, noting a flush to her cheeks but the absence of tears. 'Did she have any enemies that you know of?'

Lady Emelia raised her eyebrows. 'That's part and parcel of being in business, isn't it? Rivalry?'

Mrs Bramble frowned at the odd reply. 'I know next to nothing about how business dealings work, but I do know a little about human nature from my time as a nurse. I would suggest ordinary rivals and competitors aren't in the habit of using letter openers as weapons.'

'I couldn't say.' Lady Emelia gave a small shrug. 'Dealing with numbers and money has never been my forte, so my late husband left Philomena in charge of all of our business interests. She and I have never been close, quite the opposite on occasion, but she did have a head for finance. Probably why she could never find a man who would marry her.'

Rosie appeared with the tea and Mrs Bramble waited for her to pour a cup for Lady Emelia, add a splash of milk and leave the sitting room.

'Would it help to tell me what happened?' Mrs Bramble said, curious about what had occurred the previous evening before Miss Franklin had died, and this morning before her body had been found. 'To ease the burden, so to speak.'

'I suppose it wouldn't hurt.' Lady Emelia took a sip of tea, grimaced and set the cup back on its saucer. 'I returned from Lady Venetia Merritt's gala evening in the Great Hall and saw Rosie, who helped out with the serving, knocking on the door of the study. My sister didn't answer but I thought nothing of it. She gets wrapped up in those business affairs of hers, you see.' She paused as though suddenly aware she'd used the present tense. 'This morning, when Rosie brought me my early cup of tea, she told me my sister hadn't taken to her bed. Now that I did find odd and went to find her.

'When I knocked on the study door, I got no reply and the door was locked.' She paused again, to put two lumps of sugar in her tea. 'As I said earlier, she isn't in the habit of doing

that, so I became worried about her health. She's been working hard recently, being a woman moving in a man's sphere,
and I know she had worries she never shared even when I
asked. You hear about so many men, and even women, of a
certain age having heart attacks, don't you? And I thought ...
Anyway, I bent to look through the keyhole on the off chance
I might be able to see something, and that's when I saw her
slumped over the bureau.'

'You saw no one else last night or this morning?'

'No one of consequence, until you arrived with the spare
key.'

'Of consequence?' Mrs Bramble tilted her head.

'One of the other housemaids, from the Woodruffs, I believe,
spoke to Rosie outside about an hour before I left to attend the
gala. Never liked the girl, as you know.'

Mrs Bramble did know because Lady Emelia had accused
Mildred of theft a month ago after she had visited her cook
to borrow a cooking ingredient. At around the same time, a
gold-plated letter opener with a single tiny sapphire set into
the pommel of the rosewood handle had gone missing from
Miss Franklin's study. Before that, the odd pound note had
been 'mislaid' and put down to absent-mindedness, but this
time the obvious but mistaken conclusion had been reached.

The palace police had been called and the sergeant had
searched Mildred's room in the Woodruffs' apartment, much
to Mrs Flora Woodruff's disgust. Nothing had been found to
warrant charging Mildred with theft, but her reputation had
been sullied. If you throw enough mud, some of it sticks, and
Mildred was the one who had argued with Rosie during the
gala.

'Do you suspect Mildred?' asked Mrs Bramble.

'Ah, I'd forgotten her name. I forbade my staff from letting her in ever again,' said Lady Emelia. 'But I would not put it past her to have wheedled her way inside.'

'Miss Franklin was alive when you left for the gala?'

'Definitely.'

'Then I don't see how ...' Mrs Bramble tailed off as Lady Emelia glared at her. 'And your front door is always locked?' she continued.

'Of course.' Lady Emelia frowned. 'Your questions are bordering on the impertinent.'

Mrs Bramble gave her a benign smile. 'Along with the superintendent, it's part of my job as housekeeper to ensure these apartments run as near to clockwork as time and money will allow, and there is often so little of each to go around. All comings and goings are of great importance both to me and the police who guard this palace, and any breach of security is of serious concern if we are to be your protectors.'

Lady Emelia scoffed. 'Security? We have been here three months and look what happens.'

Lady Emelia's household was one of the newest to take up residency in the grace-and-favour apartments, and having never before had a personal run-in with them, Mrs Bramble was inclined towards leniency owing to them still settling in to such a closed community. As such, she chose to ignore the remark as one of the many manifestations of grief.

'Whoever gained access to your sister managed to get inside once and so may try to do so again. I see it as part of my duty to try to ensure that doesn't happen.'

Lady Emelia sipped her tea, the two women eyeing each other suspiciously, too many unanswered questions still swilling around inside Mrs Bramble's head for her to remain silent for long.

'Did Miss Franklin smoke at all?'

15

Lady Emelia looked horrified. 'Are you suggesting she puffed away like a common harlot?'

'Not at all—'

'Refined ladies do not smoke, Mrs Bramble, and neither Philomena nor I have ever touched the filthy stuff.'

'I thought I could smell something in the study, that's all,' said Mrs Bramble, keeping her expression as benign as possible to calm the agitated woman in front of her. 'Did you hear anything at all to suggest there may have been someone in the study with your sister last night, perhaps? A business associate, maybe?'

'My sister sometimes has—' The words caught in Lady Emelia's throat and she paused. '*Had* paperwork to attend to in the evenings but never received visitors late at night. Except when I saw Rosie on my return from the gala, the apartment was as quiet as the whole of this court.' She stood up and Mrs Bramble followed suit. 'If you'll excuse me, I need to lie down for a while until the police arrive. The shock, you understand? I'm sure you have plenty of other issues to attend to. You can see yourself out.'

Mrs Bramble nodded once and watched the back of the retreating woman before ignoring the suggestion to leave and heading for the kitchen. Were Lady Emelia's guarded answers a marker of her grief, station or having something to hide? Time would tell. But of one thing she was absolutely certain: her maid, Rosie, had attempted to reach Miss Franklin on the fateful night of the murder and may have priceless information about what might have befallen the poor woman.

# 3

When Mrs Bramble entered the kitchen, Rosie was sipping from her glass of water again, being fussed over by Mrs Joan Marsh, the Chafford family cook. Mrs Bramble noticed Rosie stiffen and Joan moved back, smoothing the over-apron she had omitted to remove. It was to keep uniform aprons clean while fulfilling chores, but easy to take off when receiving visitors, though the tragedy had thrown all such niceties out of the window.

'This must be a terrible shock for you both,' said Mrs Bramble. 'Especially you, Rosie.'

'It is,' said Rosie. She took another gulp of water.

'After all, you knocked for Miss Franklin last night.'

'Got no answer, did I?' said Rosie, her gaze fixed on her glass.

'Was the door locked at the time?'

'Don't know, Mrs Bramble.' She nodded towards her colleague. 'Joan and I had been serving at Lady Venetia's gala and had to stay behind to help with the clearing up. I was all for my bed, but when I got back, I saw the light under the study door and knocked to see if Miss Franklin needed anything before I turned in. I don't intrude if I'm not called in.'

'But you must go into the study sometimes?' pressed Mrs Bramble.

'Course,' said Rosie, a wariness creeping into her eyes. 'I give it the once-over with a feather duster every morning before the room's needed and sweep around once a week, more if it needs it or I'm told to.'

Mrs Bramble looked at Joan, who snuffled into a handkerchief and shook her head as if to say she never went anywhere but the kitchen. She looked back at Rosie. 'And light a fire?'

'That too.' Rosie gave her a puzzled frown. 'I do it for all the rooms, but only in the morning at the moment. Been too warm of an evening, ain't it?'

'And what about you, Joan?' said Mrs Bramble, looking back to the cook. 'Did you see Miss Franklin last night?'

'No, Mrs Bramble. I went down, as Rosie said, to help with getting the food ready for the others to take into the Great Hall. I came back just before Rosie and went straight to bed. I don't like late nights; not when I've got to get up early to make breakfast.'

'No, of course not. And I suppose neither of you saw Lady Emelia return or noticed anyone loitering around these apartments?'

Both women shook their heads.

'Too busy to notice things that don't concern us,' said Rosie.

Mrs Bramble smiled, knowing from her experience as a housekeeper in hotels and grand houses that staff were rarely too busy to watch and listen, gathering information for regurgitating later in the staff quarters as gossip and tittle-tattle. She'd return to that later. A glance around the kitchen revealed nothing out of the ordinary. Racks of pots and pans, cupboards of ingredients, drawers she supposed contained utensils, a deep square-sided sink and a lit range on which the kettle had been boiled.

'Lady Emelia seems to think the Woodruffs' housemaid called here yesterday.' Mrs Bramble did not follow the statement with a question, preferring to let the two women formulate one themselves.

'Mildred needed sugar,' said Rosie. 'They don't manage their kitchen well enough, so they're always running out of things. I used to let her up to see Joan, but after that time with the letter opener . . .' She sniffed. 'I can't let her past the front door or it would be my job gone.'

Mrs Bramble understood but looked straight at the housemaid. 'Is that what you were arguing about at the gala?'

'Oh.' Rosie's eyes widened in alarm but she composed herself quickly. 'You saw?'

Mrs Bramble said nothing and waited.

'She said it was degrading to be made to stand outside in all weathers when she'd never been charged with anything by the sergeant. I told her there was nothing I could do.'

'Are you sure you did not let her in?'

'Not even to wait downstairs while I fetched the sugar.'

With nothing more to be said, Mrs Bramble voiced her thanks and left them to it. She stepped outside the kitchen and pulled the door to but remained on station, there being no chance she would leave the vicinity while a dead body lay unguarded inside a room within her domain. She listened for sounds coming from elsewhere within the apartment but barely a tap or knock reached her ears. She supposed Lady Emelia had taken to her bed as stated and Rosie, although also shaken, had resumed attending to her duties.

Just fifteen minutes later, the sounds of puffing, panting and creaking wood floated up the staircase and the beetroot-red face of a sergeant from the palace police contingent appeared. The policeman, in his forties with a spreading midriff that bore testament to him having avoided chasing miscreants for several years, gathered his wits while catching his breath. Then he noticed Mrs Bramble standing sentinel, looking at him with a mixture of amusement and disapproval. He smoothed his moustache, straightened his tunic and approached with a reaffixed expression of authority.

'Sergeant,' greeted Mrs Bramble.

'Mrs Bramble,' acknowledged the sergeant. 'Always good to see you, but not under these circumstances. Doctor Kemp alerted me to the, er, problem.'

'A little more than just a problem, I'd say.'

'Ah, yes.' He gave a little cough and wiped the perspiration from his brow with a square of cloth that may once have been white. 'To tell the truth, I don't know whether to be excited or worried. I've sorted out a few nasty bust-ups in my time, but none ever came to this.'

'I'm sure this wasn't the usual kind of bust-up, as you call it, but I wouldn't worry – no doubt Scotland Yard will take matters in hand.'

The sergeant's expression changed, looking as though his face were deflating. 'As it so happens, I've already contacted Scotland Yard and had my instructions. I'm to ensure no one enters the study under any circumstances.'

'That is good to know,' said Mrs Bramble, noticing the sergeant's cheeks colour with embarrassment. She waited, sensing he had more to say.

He cleared his throat. 'Including me.' He cleared his throat again. 'An inspector is on his way. Apparently.'

Mrs Bramble could see the sergeant was in need of a boost. 'I gathered as much.' She nodded. 'Which is why I stood here, to deter any callers. Now you have arrived, I can hand over the duty knowing the scene is in capable hands.' She suspected of all the duties the sergeant might be called upon to discharge in any given situation, standing guard outside a door might be the one he could best fulfil without incident.

The sergeant drew himself up to his full height.

'Off you pop, Mrs Bramble,' he said. 'I have my job to do and I'm sure you have yours.'

Fuming that her good deed had been rewarded with another blunt dismissal, Mrs Bramble bit her tongue as she descended the spiral staircase and exited into Master Carpenter's Court. That was the second time in half an hour someone had suggested she get on with her own work, but protecting the ladies *was* her job and she'd be damned if she was going to let a murderer swan about on her patch without conducting her own thorough investigation.

# 4

Later that morning, with the murder of Miss Franklin still at the forefront of her mind, Mrs Bramble sought out the intrepid Lady Venetia Merritt and her ward. As organisers of annual galas, they were known for their meticulous planning and eagle eyes for detail, and may have seen something interesting the previous evening.

She found them about to enter the stairwell leading to their baroque top-floor apartment, one of several surrounding Fountain Court; some would say the grandest of all the courts at the palace. Unfortunately, Lady Venetia had been engaged in a complicated dispute with Mrs Bramble for several weeks and wished to take her to task over it.

'I would love to remain in our magnificent apartment, but the appalling heating and faulty drainage are becoming intolerable,' said Lady Venetia, her red hair, piled high, seeming to quiver with an indignation of its own.

'I'm not sure I can explain it with any more clarity,' said Mrs Bramble. 'Anything external is the responsibility of the palace, but I'm afraid the onus is deemed to be on residents for pipework inside the apartments.'

'But it's the same pipe,' said Lady Venetia for the fifth time.

'I am aware—'

'My staff do not have the capability to attend to this. Even if I get a little man in to do a repair, it will be just that – a quick fix that may or may not last another winter.'

'Is that not better than nothing?' said Mrs Bramble, not without some sympathy.

'Good heavens, no.' Lady Venetia frowned. 'Wherever do you get your ideas from? No, by far the best solution for all in the long term is to replace the whole of the damaged pipe in one go. This will, by obvious necessity, expose and replace the length of damaged pipe external to my apartment.'

'But therein lies the crux,' Mrs Bramble explained again. She had waited for the argument to come to a head so the solution she wanted to suggest would look more attractive than allowing the dispute to drag on and on. 'As you've intimated, Lady Venetia, you and the palace each have an equal share of and interest in the pipe, so the best I can do is petition the superintendent on your behalf for the costs to be shared equally.'

This seemed to take Lady Venetia by surprise and she wobbled a little, her ward taking her elbow to steady her, before composing herself.

'I suppose that might work,' she said, her surprise now turned to embarrassment; perhaps because she hadn't considered such a compromise herself. 'However, there is still the issue of heating. As you know, Mrs Bramble, the rooms are so large and the ceilings so high they are impossible to keep warm even in the mildest weather. Only during a heatwave does one enjoy a tolerable level of temperature.'

'I *am* sorry to hear that and do not think for one moment I am indifferent to your predicament,' said Mrs Bramble, trying not to let her true feelings show. The constant complaints from residents would normally have run like water off a duck's back, but this particular gripe had surfaced for the umpteenth time that week and she could sense her energy being sapped, especially after the morning's tragic and violent discovery had already taken its toll. 'I assure you I have spoken to the superintendent about this matter. He is as concerned as I am that the Lord Chamberlain's Office is unable to release funds to refurbish apartments and provide hot-water pipes and radiators. If you wish to transfer to another apartment—'

'No, no, no. You misunderstand,' said Lady Venetia's ward, a brief look of horror masking her face until she recovered her composure. 'I believe what Lady Venetia is trying to convey is the difficulty we face in meeting the constant cost of heating, not only during the harshest of winters but throughout the other seasons of the year, given the vagaries of our English weather.'

'I am afraid our climate is something we all have to contend with and is not something against which I can bring my limited influence to bear,' said Mrs Bramble.

'Forgive me,' said Lady Venetia. 'I did not wish to imply you were in any way culpable, but I needed to give voice to a concern I know many of us in these apartments share.'

The conversation, oft repeated in so many words, began to grate on Mrs Bramble's nerves and she decided to end it in a way that would keep the two ladies at bay for perhaps a few weeks. While Lady Venetia had achieved an age where she valued comfort over style, Mrs Bramble decided to employ her ward's pretentiousness against her, knowing she revelled in the kudos she believed living in one of the baroque apartments gave her.

'If I can offer any consolation to you, it is that residents in apartments with smaller rooms and lower ceilings often complain of stifling heat at the height of summer but draught and damp in the winter months,' said Mrs Bramble. 'Oh, that we could enjoy a happy medium, but if you are content to endure a little extra discomfort of a different kind, I could look to move you somewhere' – she paused and looked towards the ceiling as though searching her memory for a suitable vacancy, then looked the young woman straight in the eyes – '*less opulent* and easier to heat.'

'No, no, no,' said the ward, picking up on the deliberate emphasis. 'In no other way are we unhappy with our apartment and we have no wish to relinquish it. We shall have to invest in more shawls, woollens and blankets.' She smiled at Lady Venetia as though that solution had just occurred to her and represented the best outcome.

Mrs Bramble also smiled, but the intensity of the young woman's glare seemed almost tangible, threatening to shatter and project lacerating shards at anyone in her line of sight.

'Come,' said the ward. 'Let us not detain Mrs Bramble any further.' She took Lady Venetia by the elbow and turned her away, whispering urgently in her ear.

'Before you go, Lady Venetia, may I ask about another matter?' said Mrs Bramble.

'If you must.' Lady Venetia turned back and looked at her suspiciously. 'What is it about?'

Mrs Bramble cleared her throat and chose her words with care. 'An incident took place in one of the courtyards during your gala entertainments evening and I wondered whether either of you noticed anything untoward as you returned to your apartment.'

Lady Venetia glanced at her ward, received a blank expression in response and looked back at Mrs Bramble. 'What kind of incident?'

'I'm afraid the palace sergeant has asked me not to say.'

'The sergeant? Criminal then, is it?'

Mrs Bramble said nothing and waited for the woman to answer in her own time.

Lady Venetia's ward obliged. 'We left at the evening's conclusion and came straight home. I didn't notice any strangers
and certainly saw no *incident*, as you called it.' She looked
questioningly at the older woman. 'Did you?'

'I did not,' said Lady Venetia. 'I was too intent on getting to
my bed for a well-earned night's sleep, which I must say has
done me a power of good. Sorry we cannot help, but do let us
know if the *sergeant* wishes to speak to us.'

Mrs Bramble gave a respectful nod, noting the emphasis
suggesting she considered the policeman more worthy of
their time, and kept the inevitable arrival of detectives from
Scotland Yard to herself.

Lady Venetia signalled the end of the audience with a half-
turn to leave. 'Regarding the other matter. Can I leave you to,
er ...?'

'Of course,' said Mrs Bramble. 'And if you do remember
anything—' But the door to their stairwell had already closed
behind them.

She gritted her teeth at the casual rudeness and strode
towards her own apartment, where she hoped for a quick
cup of restorative Earl Grey. Halfway across Base Court, she
heard her name called and turned to see the widowed Mrs
Gertrude McGowan and her lady's companion, Miss Sarah
Cameron-Banks, who lived together on the ground floor of
Master Carpenter's Court, passing through the archway of the
main gate. Her heart sank as the two women, arm in arm, their
voluminous skirts crushed together, waddled towards her, in
step with each other like two geese making a break from their
gaggle.

'Ah, Mrs Bramble,' called Mrs McGowan. 'We'd like a word,
if we may.'

Miss Cameron-Banks repeated 'Bramble' and 'if we may'
like some kind of human echo.

'Ladies, always a pleasure to see you,' Mrs Bramble lied, but in as pleasant a tone as she could muster. An encounter with these two ladies was far from what she needed at this moment. 'I trust you enjoyed the entertainment yester—'

'Yes, yes.' Mrs McGowan waved away the pleasantries and fixed Mrs Bramble with her piercing blue eyes. 'I must inform you that we—'

'—wrote to the Lord Chamberlain.' Miss Cameron-Banks spoke over her, as both ladies were wont to do.

'About the ongoing travesty of justice—'

'—that resulted in us living in a few dark and pokey rooms—'

'—while that brazen wagtail, *Miss* Franklin—'

'—and her shrew of a sister, the so-called *Lady* Emelia—'

'—live in a spacious apartment in relative luxury.'

'Good ladies . . .' Mrs Bramble held up her hands to quieten the women. 'As you are aware, I have but little influence—'

'But there are rules, are there not?' said Mrs McGowan. 'Have we not drawn your attention to their previous—'

'—rule breaking?' Miss Cameron-Banks said over her.

'Miss Franklin brings unsavoury men—'

'—we shall not call them *gentlemen*—'

'—into the palace at all times of the day and night.' Mrs McGowan sniffed. 'Well, the night, at least. Such behaviour is ill-suited to—'

'—a royal palace,' Miss Cameron-Banks finished.

Mrs Bramble couldn't argue with that, although she was well aware much business across the British Empire was conducted in smokey back rooms, bars and clubs at whatever time the interested parties thought most convenient. Having visitors in the apartments was not a rule breach in itself, but receiving excessive callers was discouraged. Not for the first time, the thought occurred to her that one of Miss Franklin's business associates might be involved or, at least, could have seen something. She decided not to mention the presence of a dead body just yet, sure it would distract the two companions and give them an attack of the vapours, while using this opportunity to ask a few questions.

Mrs Bramble put on her best concerned expression. 'When was the last time you saw Miss Franklin with a, um ...'

'Ne'er-do-well?' said Mrs McGowan. 'Two weeks ago.'

'Did either of you see or hear anything untoward or out of the usual around or near the apartments last night?' said Mrs Bramble.

'I did not,' said Mrs McGowan

'Nor I—' her companion offered for confirmation.

'—but we were both at Lady Merritt's gala in the Great Hall and many residents were still abroad until almost midnight.'

Mrs Bramble's experience of army field hospitals had taught her the little tells displayed by wounded officers and men when they lied about their marital status, or how well or unwell they felt. She had soon got wise to them as they tried to flirt with her and secure an assignation or release from the hospital. She saw no such flickering of eyelashes nor flinching in these ladies, which suggested they were telling the truth. She decided to return the conversation to its original topic.

'Ladies, I can confirm I have received a letter from the Lord Chamberlain this morning indicating that applications for any apartment in the palace can only be heard once previous occupants have resigned their residency through formal letter or death.'

'Most unsatisfactory,' said Mrs McGowan.

'Unsatisfactory,' Miss Cameron-Banks echoed.

Mrs McGowan tutted. 'We have brought this to the attention of the Lord Chamberlain on several occasions and cannot fathom why we are placed behind other so-called claimants. Constantly.'

'I agree, it is not an ideal state of affairs.' Mrs Bramble feigned sympathy. 'You know, if it were up to me alone ...' She let the sentence hang, beginning to enjoy the frustration emanating almost visibly from the women.

'Well!' Mrs McGowan pouted. 'What about the mangey ginger tomcat they have cavorting around the place? It prowls around the corridors, scratching wood and drapes alike, and has no respect for personal territory. Does that not breach the rules?'

'I—'

'As far as I can tell, it regards upsetting the pet cockatoo, the one across the courtyard from us, as its life's work. That's another thing. The bird is far too big and loud for anyone's good, and must surely be prohibited. Or is it because you also keep a pet?'

Appreciating neither the accusation nor the sneering nor the glare Mrs McGowan gave her at that moment, Mrs Bramble puffed out her chest and pulled herself up to her full height, like the rising figurehead on the prow of a ship turning into a storm.

Mrs McGowan met her full on. 'It is unsavoury, unsanitary and unfair—'

'Words you have used to describe your own apartment,' interrupted Mrs Bramble, ice lacing her words. 'My Dodger is a mouser employed to keep the rodent population down. The very rodents that are encouraged into the palace in the first place by the lack of cleanliness in many apartments. If the residents looked to their own regimes instead of concentrating on others, we might see wholesale improvement throughout the palace.'

Mrs McGowan's face clouded like a thunderstorm. 'You

would not dare speak to me in such a fashion if my brother, Perry, were here. He would write in the strongest terms to our MP and have this matter settled in a trice. Come on, Sarah.' She pursed her lips before turning away, and in so doing, almost dragged her surprised and stumbling companion to the ground.

Mrs Bramble watched them waddle away, chattering over each other, and her heart sank as she heard Mrs McGowan call back.

'This is not the last you will hear of this!'

# 5

Hearing a clock chime the hour, Mrs Bramble forewent her tea and headed for the passage leading to Master Carpenter's Court. She calculated the Scotland Yard detectives should be arriving at any moment and wanted to be present when they appeared. Hoping she'd left enough time and distance between herself, Mrs McGowan and Miss Cameron-Banks to ensure they had retreated behind their front door, she entered the courtyard as Reverend Thomas Weaver, chaplain of the Chapel Royal at Hampton Court Palace, hurried from the direction of his apartment by the Seymour Gate entrance and cannoned into her.

'I say!' he exclaimed, looking flummoxed. His face broke into a smile when he saw who he had almost bowled over. 'Mrs Bramble, terribly sorry.'

'Good morning, Reverend,' she said, pleased to see her one true friend in the whole palace. 'You always seem to be in such a rush.'

'That's because I'm always late for something or some such. Can't ever seem to take orders from my clocks.'

She chuckled. 'How many do you have now in your collection?'

Weaver looked up and his mouth moved in silent counting. 'Fourteen, at last count,' he said with enthusiasm. 'At least one in every room and none of them appear able to galvanise me into action when action is needed.'

'Well, maybe I can.'

His eyebrows flicked upwards. 'How so?'

She glanced towards the door through which the two women had disappeared. 'Have you heard about the to-do upstairs?'

'To-do?' Weaver lowered his voice conspiratorially. 'What about?'

'I'm afraid Miss Philomena Franklin was murdered last night in her study and policemen from Scotland Yard should be here any time now.'

'Murdered?' His eyes widened. 'Good Lord. What? When? Why? How? By whom?'

'All valid questions, I'm sure, and ones I hope you will assist me in answering.'

'Me?' He looked up at the first-floor windows. 'First and foremost, is Lady Emelia all right?'

'She's fine, as far as I can tell,' said Mrs Bramble. 'Being a bit of a cold fish, if truth be told.'

'Nonetheless, I'd best offer her my condolences and ministrations. Pastoral care and all that.'

'That would be appropriate, and helpful in more ways than one.'

'Oh? How so?'

Mrs Bramble lowered her voice. 'I think Lady Emelia is not letting on as much as she might. While you're attending to her spiritual needs, perhaps you could do me a service.'

'Of course,' said Weaver. 'Anything for you, Mrs Bramble.'

She glanced around to check they could not be overheard and almost laughed when he copied her. 'In that case, the detectives will no doubt undertake interviews once they arrive and I would like you to sit in on as many as you can. You can insist on the basis of ensuring the sensibilities of the interviewees are adequately tended to. That way, you can report back to me and perhaps we can get to the bottom of this.'

'Right, good, right,' said Weaver enthusiastically. Then he frowned. 'Shouldn't that be the job of the detectives?'

'Ha.' She made a screwed-up face. 'They don't know the residents like we do. I have encountered the British police in as far-flung places as Africa, Afghanistan and India. If their counterparts in Scotland Yard are cut from the same cloth, they will make assumptions to clear up the case, accuse and arrest the wrong person for the sake of expediency, and the real perpetrator will get away scot-free.'

'My oh my, that's a damning indictment,' said Weaver, all thoughts of where he'd been hurrying to seemingly forgotten. 'Well, if you think I can help—'

'Good day. I'm looking for someone named Bumble.'

Their heads swivelled to look at the man in an Ulster coat who had entered the courtyard through the passage.

'It's *Mrs Bramble* to you,' she said, her response laden with ice.

'Like the spikey bush?'

That did actually make her feel spikey. 'And you are?'

'Detective Inspector Cole, of Scotland Yard,' said the man, touching the brim of his bowler hat.

'As in the nutty slack I burn in my fireplace?' Mrs Bramble suppressed a smile as a tic twitched at the corner of his eye.

'C–O–L–E,' he spelled out, his voice flat.

'Ah,' she said with as much innocence as she could muster. 'This is Reverend Weaver. Chaplain of the Chapel Royal here at the palace. We've been waiting for you. It's kind of you to make such haste.'

'We're murder detectives, it's our duty,' said Cole.

'Detectives?' She made a show of looking over Cole's

shoulder. 'I see you are alone, but I must say, we did expect more than one of you.'

Cole's eyes flicked a glance to his left as though surprised no sergeant or constable stood at his side. He gave Mrs Bramble and Weaver a suspicious look.

'I can assure you my presence is more than adequate. I was instructed to ask for you on our arrival. Can you take me to where the deceased is at present?'

'Of course.' Mrs Bramble forced a smile. 'This way.'

She wasn't in the habit of letting most people talk to her in such a dismissive manner but she needed the police on her side, or at least amenable to allowing the reverend to sit in. Still biting her tongue, she led the way to the Chaffords' front door. Weaver gave two tugs on the ornate iron handle of the bell pull and a distant tinkle reached their ears. A moment later, Rosie opened the door and led them up the staircase to the first floor, where the sergeant confronted them.

'Nobody in or out, I take it, Sergeant?' said Cole, acknowledging the officer's salute with a nod.

'No, sir,' said the sergeant. 'Just as—'

'Good man. Send for the doctor who pronounced the death.' He stepped around him and rattled the study's doorknob. 'That'll be all. The *Yard* can take it from here.'

Mrs Bramble noticed the emphasis, as though Cole believed himself to be the very essence of Scotland Yard. She often found that those who thought so much of themselves had little about them to warrant it. That said, her opinion counted for little in this case, as the sergeant headed for the staircase, looking round-shouldered and crestfallen.

Mrs Bramble noticed Rosie holding her hand against her midriff and feared she still suffered from shock after seeing one of the ladies of the house with a knife in her back. Not

34

wishing to inflict the scene on her again, she sent her to fetch the mistress while she unlocked the study door.

'Where's the body?' said Cole.

Mrs Bramble ignored the stupid question. The scene inside was as she had left it. The desk stood untouched, the window remained closed and the letter opener protruded starkly from Miss Franklin's back.

'Apart from me closing the window against the cold after we discovered Miss Franklin this morning, this room has remained locked,' said Mrs Bramble.

'Hmm,' said Cole, giving her a sideways glare of disapproval. 'You'll need to stand outside while I have a gander at the room and rootle around in the bureau,' he said, and proceeded to do just that, starting with the window. 'Since Jack the Ripper made his mark three years ago, the ghoulish public seem to expect us to photograph every scene of every crime, even though the newspapers can only publish sketches.' He glanced at Mrs Bramble. 'If they knew how much of their taxes that would cost, they'd think twice. In any case, a photographer was unavailable to travel down with me today. No matter, open-and-shut case on the cause of death, I'd say.'

Cole made a show of inspecting the body and the items both on and in the bureau, including the fountain pen on the blotter, before studying the contents from one of the two main drawers, pulling out a number of invoices and business documents. He removed a diary and a carved wooden box that appeared to have had its simple lock forced.

'No appointments at all for yesterday,' he said, flicking through the pages of the diary.

By the time Lady Emelia arrived at the door, he was on his knees looking under the bureau, having checked the second drawer and found nothing but a hairbrush, a box of matches, a pocket square and two penny coins. Mrs Bramble noted the tell-tale circle of a thin patch on the left sole of his well-worn shoes.

'Ah, Lady Emelia,' said Cole, clambering from beneath the bureau. 'I'm sorry for your loss.' He looked discomfited as her face crumpled and she turned away, consoled by Weaver. 'I'll need to speak to you and your staff, if I may? In the sitting room, perhaps?'

Lady Emelia emitted a sob and headed back along the hallway.

Cole nodded to Mrs Bramble as he stepped from the study, taking the wooden box with him. 'I should be grateful if you would let me know as soon as the doctor gets here. With any luck, he won't be long and we can get the body removed. Where is the key? I wish to secure the room.'

'I have the key and will ensure the door is locked, inspector,' she said.

'I require the key,' he said, holding out his hand while looking her straight in the eye.

She returned his look with steel of her own. 'This is a *royal palace* and I am the appointed Lady Housekeeper. I shall retain the key until told otherwise by the Lord Chamberlain, who can be contacted through his office. If you wish to gain access in the meantime, I am rarely more than a few minutes away.'

Cole hesitated, doubt in his eyes, before he dropped his hand to his side. 'Is there anywhere else I can conduct other interviews? I was told some kind of gala went on last night, so I've sent word that I'll need to speak to the entertainers.'

'You'll find that difficult, seeing as they returned to London first thing this morning,' said Mrs Bramble. 'If it helps, I can attest the entertainers were rather busy during the evening and chaperoned at all times. If you hadn't been so keen to dismiss the sergeant, he would have confirmed that his men escorted them to their accommodation outside the palace after

36

the show.' She saw irritation harden his face but cared little for his bullish attitude.

'I'll also need to knock on doors to ask if anyone saw or heard anything last night,' said Cole.

'My advice would be to visit the residents in their own apartments,' said Mrs Bramble. 'They are mainly genteel ladies of high breeding and good character who won't take kindly to being summoned to speak elsewhere in the palace. Reverend Weaver and I can accompany you to smooth the way.'

'Thank you for the advice, Mrs *Bramble*,' said Cole, emphasising her surname. 'As I told the sergeant, I can handle things from here.'

'I doubt that very much,' she said, not about to cede ground at this early stage. 'After all, you've made requests of everyone you've met and you've only been here ten minutes.' What was it about people with authority and money that gave them the unshakeable belief they could dismiss anyone at will? 'I should point out – the safety and security of the residents of these apartments is part of my responsibility, so I need to *see* all is well.'

Cole's expression displayed obvious surprise at the challenge to his authority by a mere housekeeper.

'I'm afraid you can't be present while I interview the residents or their staff.'

'I must insist *I* am, though,' Weaver piped up, after a nudge in the ribs from Mrs Bramble. 'This is a royal palace and these people are in my pastoral care. I must insist on ministering to their sensibilities during your interviews.'

Cole opened his mouth to reply but seemed to baulk at the resolute expressions on the faces of Mrs Bramble and Reverend Weaver. Mrs Bramble hoped the ruse would work, suspecting he was not au fait with the limitations of royal and ecclesiastical protocol.

37

Cole raised his chin to stretch his neck and said, 'Very well, Reverend, but please sit to one side and don't say a dicky bird.'

'Excellent.' Weaver knocked his elbow on the door frame and gave it a vigorous rub to ease the pain.

Cole tutted and turned to Mrs Bramble. 'You *will* have to wait outside.'

She caught Weaver's wink as he continued to rub his elbow and nodded her acquiescence to Cole. 'Would you like some tea, Inspector?' she said, employing her most sugary smile.

Cole waved away the offer. 'The sooner we get on, the sooner I'll be out of your hair.' He turned to follow Lady Emelia into the sitting room but stopped when a hand touched his elbow.

'Did you notice a certain smokey tinge to the air?' said Mrs Bramble. 'In the study?'

'Can't say I did.'

'Not as much blood around the knife wound as one would expect, either.'

'What relevance is that?'

'You're the detective, Inspector.' She suppressed a smile at his obvious irritation. 'But I used to be a nurse, also trained to notice small details.'

He moved his arm away. 'As you say, I'm the detective, so if you'll excuse me ...'

She watched Cole disappear into the sitting room, followed by Weaver, who gave her another wink.

# 6

Mrs Bramble left Lady Emelia's apartment by the winding staircase and pulled the front door closed behind her in time for Lady Madeleine Whalley to almost bowl her over. At only four inches over five feet tall, the punch delivered seemed slight, but it was the grains dislodged from the cuffs of her sleeves that hurt Mrs Bramble the most. She looked down at her previously pristine black dress speckled with birdseed and winced.

'I'm so sorry,' said Lady Madeleine. 'I cannot see a blessed thing around this dingy place, what with these cataracts and everything.'

'Not to worry, Lady Madeleine,' said Mrs Bramble, brushing pale seeds from her dress and feeling a throb from the big toe that had just been stepped on.

'Dr Kemp has promised to find me a decent surgeon to get them put right, but I'm worried I might not be able to afford it or see anything again afterwards.'

'I'm sure he will do his best and you'll be fine,' Mrs Bramble reassured. 'Shall I walk you to your apartment, Lady Madeleine?' She steered her along the courtyard, the squawking and squealing of an agitated bird increasing with every step. 'I have an issue that needs addressing and now is as good a time as any, I hope.'

'Well, I . . .'

Mrs Bramble helped the flustered woman to unlock the door of her apartment, the volume of noise increasing the moment it swung open, as though someone within were being violently and bloodily attacked. Lady Madeleine hastened straight to a floor-to-ceiling cage standing against one wall of the nearest and largest room, comforting a pure white cockatoo with soothing sounds and quiet words. It calmed in an instant, seemingly pleased to see her, replying with little squeaking noises of its own and poking its beak through the bars.

'My apologies,' said Lady Madeleine, fixing a fresh piece of dark-leaf cabbage to the cage with a clip. 'Sunny gets lonely and misses me when I leave the apartment, in spite of my maid being here, but I only popped into Base Court to see Lady Ives for ten minutes. She does like a tipple, as I'm sure you're aware, and I wanted to ensure she was well after last night.' She chuckled and shook her head. 'Remarkable powers of recovery, I must say.' She glanced at Mrs Bramble. 'What is it you wanted to speak about?'

Mrs Bramble flinched at a particularly raucous squawk. 'I think you can guess.'

'Is it those devil women accusing my poor Sunny again?'

Mrs Bramble sighed. 'If by that you mean Mrs McGowan and her companion, then yes, in part.'

Lady Madeleine adjusted an oval-shaped piece of rough-surfaced bone affixed to Sunny's cage. 'Cuttlefish bone,' she explained. 'Provided for its calcium nutrients and beak-cleansing properties.'

'It's not just those ladies, I'm afraid,' said Mrs Bramble, noticing a cabbage-green tinge to the ends of Lady Madeleine's fingers standing out against the white of the bone. 'It's most of the residents around this court. All of them, in true fact.

Maybe it wouldn't be so bad if your cockatoo sung sweet songs, but it does make quite the commotion. Constantly.'

'They're jealous of my little Sunny.' Lady Madeleine filled the water feeder.

'I'm afraid I must draw your attention to the rules on owning pets—'

'He brings sunshine into my life and does nobody any harm.'

'He shouts random words at passers-by—'

'Gin!' Sunny shouted on cue.

'I don't see how that can upset anyone.' Lady Madeleine reached inside the cage and unhooked a mirror covered in a white residue. 'It's not as if he understands the words he repeats.' She moistened the end of a cloth and began to clean the glass.

'Lady Emelia reported having "rubbish" shouted at her,' said Mrs Bramble.

'Rubbish,' repeated Sunny.

'Mrs Ewan across the way swears blind she heard him call her a "wastrel".'

'Wastrel!'

'Miss Alice Woodruff is threatening to complain to the Lord Chamberlain about being labelled a "strumpet".'

'Strumpet, strumpet!' chorused Sunny.

'Good boy,' said Lady Madeleine, chuckling to herself as the cockatoo bobbed his head up and down maniacally. 'That's my Sunny. Those are the nicknames I assigned to my neighbours.'

Mrs Bramble wasn't amused. She didn't want to make the old woman give up her companion, but ... 'Can you not see rules are rules?'

Lady Madeleine paused as she went to open the cage door again. 'Must I draw your attention to all the other pets in so many of the other apartments? And every one of those so-called lap dogs are far too large to be accommodated on the delicate knees of ladies. Not to mention Lady Emelia's feral creature from upstairs who tries every day to gain access to this apartment, for obvious reasons, and your own beast, Mrs Bramble.' She opened the door and reaffixed the mirror.

'My British shorthair *cat* is not a beast, he is a palace mouser and ratter, Lady Madeleine, as you know,' said Mrs Bramble, peeved that Dodger had come in for scrutiny and unfair criticism once again. Aware that living in one of the apartments without any human companions other than your domestic servants could be lonely sometimes and comforted by the knowledge that her own Dodger kept her company each evening, she decided to be lenient. 'That is not the issue here. Can we not come to some compromise to allow everyone to get along?'

Lady Madeleine squinted at her. 'What do you suggest?'

'I feel the residents may be more amenable to you keeping Sunny if you provided something to keep him amused during the day. I have seen little ladders and swinging perches employed in other cages in such a fashion.' Lady Madeleine pouted, but Mrs Bramble continued. 'I also suggest covering his cage much earlier in the evenings. To quieten his enthusiasm.'

'How early?'

*Four o'clock*, Mrs Bramble wanted to say, but instead said, 'Shall we try nine o'clock to be going on with?'

Lady Madeleine frowned as if considering the offer. 'That's a coincidence. After I left the gala feeling poorly – cheese and I have never agreed with each other – I saw someone in the courtyard around that time yesterday.'

Mrs Bramble's ears pricked up. 'Someone you knew?'

'I couldn't really see. Dressed in dark clothing is all I can tell you.'

'And you thought it odd because ...?'

'Doubly odd. It's quiet in the courtyard that late of an evening, so when I heard footsteps, I went to the window to see who was abroad at that hour. I couldn't see his face, not with my eyes in this state, but he carried an umbrella and we weren't due any rain.'

'Are you willing to make a statement to the police?'

'Police? Whatever for?'

'There is a Scotland Yard detective upstairs as we speak, investigating the murder of Miss Franklin last night, and you might have seen her killer.'

'Murder?' Lady Madeleine's hand flew to her mouth as she emitted a cry that briefly silenced Sunny. Mrs Bramble left Lady Madeleine in conversation of sorts with her chattering cockatoo and issued instructions to the maid to fetch a cup of tea to calm the nerves of her mistress. She then returned to the door of Lady Emelia's apartment and rang the bell. Questions required answers and she needed to ask them before the inspector scared the life out of potential witnesses. Rosie answered the door and confirmed that the inspector and reverend had finished their interviews but remained in the sitting room with her mistress. *Open-and-shut case on the cause of death*, the inspector had said, but perhaps not so much on the who and why.

'Is there somewhere we can talk in private?' said Mrs Bramble from the top of the stairs.

Rosie's eyes widened in alarm. 'I-I don't ...' She looked around. 'M-Miss Franklin's bedroom?'

Mrs Bramble nodded and followed Rosie. Although the room was not lavishly decorated, she acknowledged that some fine pieces adorned the space. A full-length dressing mirror hanging in an ornate free-standing frame huddled against one wall beside a chest of many drawers. An oak wardrobe of some antiquity stood sentinel by a carved wooden dressing table

43

with an oval mirror. While admiring of the ornate hairbrush and matching hand-held vanity mirror, she noticed little else of interest and wasn't there to be a nosey parker. She sat the terrified-looking young woman on the end of the bed.

'Rosie, I've been in this line of work for a long time and I know how invisible us servants can be, more so because we are women. The inspector doesn't want to listen to what the likes of you and I have to say. Oh, he'll hear us, but he won't listen.' She looked into Rosie's frightened eyes. 'I'll listen, if there's anything you want to say to me that may help catch the killer.'

'I dunno what you want ... me to ... say.' Rosie's voice tailed off.

Mrs Bramble smiled. 'You must have been party to some interesting – perhaps even shocking – revelations in your time. I know I have.' The look in Rosie's eyes suggested something withheld and she hoped quiet encouragement might persuade the young woman to open up. 'Were you ever present during some of Miss Franklin's personal meetings, unseen and unheard somewhere in the background, when something pertinent may have been said?'

Rosie's cheeks reddened and she looked near to tears. 'I shouldn't say, Mrs Bramble. Ain't my place.'

'Your loyalty is commendable, but considering what happened to Miss Franklin, I'd urge you to remember anything you can. It may not seem important to you, but it may prove relevant.'

Rosie's gaze dropped to her lap, her fingers worrying a loose thread on the cuff of her left sleeve. 'Miss Franklin was havin' big money troubles and Lady Emelia didn't know,' she muttered.

Mrs Bramble's eyebrows rose. That didn't sound like the family she knew. 'How do *you* know?'

44

Rosie raised her head. 'A couple of weeks ago now, Miss Franklin dismissed me 'cause it was late and she didn't need me no more that night. I hadn't got to my bed, when I heard a visitor arrive with a faint tap-tap knocking at the front door. I didn't hear no bell, so he must've been expected and let in by Miss Franklin. I heard 'em talking – arguing, more like – a few minutes later.'

'If not Lady Emelia, then who?'

Rosie dropped her gaze again. 'Couldn't tell, Mrs Bramble. Miss Franklin shouted, but the other person kept his voice low. A hiss more than a whisper.' She clasped her hands together. 'I tried to listen, but they kept the door shut. All the servants do it.' She looked up defiantly. 'Said so yourself.'

'I didn't recommend it as a pastime, but I'm sure you can be forgiven on this occasion.' Mrs Bramble gave her an encouraging smile. So, Miss Franklin had been visited late at night two weeks ago by a man who refused to raise his voice but sounded menacing nonetheless. 'I appreciate the door was closed, but could you tell what they were arguing about?'

'Some bloke in London,' said Rosie. 'A love triangle, no doubt. Ain't no surprise when it comes to toffs.'

Mrs Bramble detected an edge to Rosie's tone. 'Did you hear anything else or see him leave?'

'I didn't see him go.' Rosie's cheeks coloured again and she swallowed hard, as though trying to keep something inside from bursting forth. 'I almost left 'em to it, when I heard more shouting.'

'About what? Spit it out, girl.'

Rosie took a deep breath. 'A mine. In fact, I posted a letter from Miss Franklin to the family solicitor two weeks ago, the day after the argument. Must've been about that, 'cause I don't think Lady Emelia knew about that either and it didn't sound like it had done very well, from what I could hear.'

Mrs Bramble's eyebrows had risen a little higher. Why wouldn't a coal mine be doing well? The British Empire ran on coal, and money went to money; everyone knew that. She looked to the door, conscious someone might enter at any moment.

'Why did Miss Franklin have money worries if she owned a coal mine, Rosie? And where is this mine?'

'South Africa, they said.' Rosie blinked. 'But it ain't coal, Mrs Bramble. I'm certain o' that. I heard 'em say gold and diamonds.'

The shock hit Mrs Bramble like a tidal wave.

If true, and Lady Emelia had discovered she was being swindled out of a fortune, she had the perfect motive to kill her own sister, the one person with whom she had never really got on. But who had been the other person in the room?

Rosie's face paled and she stood up. 'I'm gonna be sick,' she said, and ran from the bedroom.

And perhaps it was something catching, for Mrs Bramble had a sickly feeling in her stomach, too.

# 7

A knock sounded on the wooden panelling lining the walls on the landing at the top of the stairs. With Rosie indisposed, Mrs Bramble went to investigate and found Dr Kemp standing there, dressed more smartly than before although still looking ruffled and in little better spirits than at their earlier meeting. Behind him waited two men in thick jackets who wouldn't have looked out of place digging graves in the local churchyard, which may have been a sideline to their undisclosed main occupation.

'Come in, Doctor,' said Mrs Bramble, ushering him into the apartment and towards the study. The two men stayed outside. 'Inspector Cole is in the sitting room with Reverend Weaver. I believe they've concluded their interviews with Lady Emelia and her household.'

'It's usually the family who pay the undertaker to collect the deceased, but as this is a murder case ...' Kemp grimaced. 'I have a couple of strong men outside ready to move, er, Miss, um, Franklin for me. Had to pay them myself, of course. Doubt I'll get that back.'

'Comes with the job, I suspect,' said Mrs Bramble. 'Part and parcel, you might say.'

'Yes, well, I'd better *parcel up* Miss Franklin, God rest her soul.'

Rosie reappeared, her face looking drawn.

'Rosie, please inform Inspector Cole that Dr Kemp has arrived to move Miss Franklin,' said Mrs Bramble. 'He should be about finished by now.' She unlocked the study door as the housemaid left to do as instructed. 'The inspector searched this room earlier, so you are free to go in, Doctor.'

Kemp entered and proceeded to check the body once again. His priority during his previous inspection had been the confirmation of a life extinguished. This time he conducted a thorough examination with more diligence and professionalism, while the body remained in situ. Some minutes later, after making notes in a small pocketbook, his appraisal appeared complete. After a few seconds' hesitation, he extracted the letter opener with care and wrapped it in a waxed cloth. With a nod of satisfaction, he called the two men forwards.

'Will you be doing a full post-mortem?' said Mrs Bramble.

Kemp grimaced. 'I'm afraid so.' He gave her a sideways glance. 'It's an aspect of my profession I have little love for, but I do know what I'm doing, Mrs Bramble.'

'I don't doubt it.'

However unkempt Dr Kemp sometimes appeared, he was at least a competent physician, and thorough to boot. It was Cole she doubted, and his willingness to keep an open mind. There could be no question a murder had occurred, but she'd learned another lesson during her long experience as a military nurse – that things were never as obvious or cut and dried as they first appeared. Real life was even more complicated and messy than the sensational stories published in the weekly penny dreadfuls.

The men had wrapped the body with more expertise than she'd expected and were carrying it out through the door by the time Inspector Cole reappeared with Reverend Weaver. She led a round of formal introductions.

'I take it everything is in order, Dr Kemp?' said Cole.

'Yes, Inspector,' said Kemp. 'These gentlemen will take Miss Franklin's body to my surgery, where I shall conduct a thorough examination and take a few necessary samples for analysis. That said, at first and second glance, I have to say it very much looks like how it appears. Stabbed in the back with a letter opener.' He held out the parcel of waxed cloth, the telltale shape confirming the item it contained.

Cole looked satisfied with the summary and took the bundle. 'Thank you, Doctor. I'd be grateful if you could keep the cause of death under wraps for now. I'll be in touch in due course, but if you have need of me, I'm sure Mrs Bramble will do the honours.'

Mrs Bramble gave Cole a friendly look, but her tone held ice. 'I am a royal housekeeper, not a common messenger. I'm sure the good doctor will find you somehow. You will be staying at the inn, no doubt?'

She could see from Cole's tightening of his jaw muscles that the insinuation all coppers liked a drink had not been missed. Behind him, Reverend Weaver's eyes had widened and he was shaking his head. No matter. She did not suffer fools, gladly or otherwise, and it remained to be seen whether or not Inspector Cole proved to be one.

Cole frowned. 'I shall take a room, if need be, but I hope that won't be necessary. The cause of death is not in question and I have a theory in mind about what happened, but I still need to speak to any resident who may have seen something. Lady Emelia is resting in her bedroom and I've finished with her staff.' He looked askance at Mrs Bramble and Reverend Weaver. 'And what of you two? Where were you yesterday evening?'

Reverend Weaver looked flummoxed. 'I-I-I—'

'We both attended Lady Venetia Merritt's soiree.' Mrs

Bramble rescued the bewildered Weaver. 'In the Great Hall, all evening. I, of course, had a supervisory role. The reverend was there by invitation. There will be witnesses aplenty, should you feel the need.'

Cole pondered this and turned to Weaver, whose expression morphed into one of benign interest. 'Who's next?'

'You should speak to Lady Madeleine Whalley,' said Mrs Bramble, annoyed that Cole had turned to a man for advice while in her domain. 'She lives on the ground floor and says she saw the shadowy figure of a man carrying an umbrella passing through the courtyard late yesterday evening. She has cataracts, bless her, so she can't identify who it was.'

'Mrs Bramble,' said Cole. 'Just as you are not a messenger, neither are you a policeman, so I would appreciate you letting me do my job.'

'Gladly,' said Mrs Bramble, with no intention of being brushed aside. 'What have you found out so far?' She looked him straight in the eye.

Cole sighed. 'Lady Emelia confirmed her sister always carried a purse containing about ten pounds and kept a locked box in the bureau drawer with at least another hundred. I don't know why you'd want so much ready cash around you; it's more than most policemen earn in a year. Anyway, the box was empty when I searched the study earlier and the purse is missing. If Lady Madeleine ...?'

'Whalley.'

'Of course,' said Cole. 'If Lady Madeleine Whalley believes she saw something out of the ordinary, I'd better have a word with her for the sake of thoroughness, although I've seen this scenario so many times before that I believe it to be a simple burglary gone awry. It is most likely that a burglar, using the palace's many shadowy corners as cover, got in through the open window but became trapped when he spotted Miss

50

Franklin. Perhaps he was discovered when she entered the study unexpectedly. Either way, he panicked and killed her.

'On the other hand, Lady Emelia said Miss Franklin often had many business and social callers, so a gentleman may have visited Miss Franklin and took umbrage at something she said or did and killed her in a fit of rage. That would be Lady Madeleine's shadowy figure strolling through the courtyard, although if she's almost as blind as a bat, I can't rely on her report as having any bearing on who had a hand in Miss Franklin's death.'

'That's dismissive of you,' said Mrs Bramble, beginning to lose the little faith she'd had in the ability of the so-called Cole of the Yard to uncover the truth with a mind so closed to other possibilities.

'The only other logical explanation is that a housemaid named' – he looked at his notebook – 'Mildred bore a grudge against this household because of a recent accusation of theft by Lady Emelia.' He looked Mrs Bramble in the eye, but it took more than a stare to intimidate her, so he continued. 'A gold letter opener with a solitaire sapphire was taken from the study and now Miss Franklin has been murdered with a similar instrument.' He raised an eyebrow. 'Is that not curious?'

'It is a bit of a stretch to assert such a correlation, and you have no real evidence for any of this, have you?' she said, frowning when Cole didn't contradict her. 'I'd think it more curious as to how Mildred, in her maid's attire – for she would have had no time to change – managed to shin up and down a drainpipe and clamber in and out through a window without the alarm being raised. Even an experienced burglar would have had trouble remaining undetected.'

'That is not an opinion I share.'

'Clearly, but there is no sign of a struggle to indicate a raging or vengeful assailant, with or without a grudge, and

51

Miss Franklin was still wearing her jewellery. Why would Mildred or a burglar, discovered or otherwise disturbed while about their work, leave such valuable items behind?'

No response came from Cole, who seemed disinclined to entertain any more suggestions she might make.

'In my opinion,' ventured Mrs Bramble anyway, 'what remains is suggestive of premeditation, so perhaps there is more to the man with the umbrella than at first meets the eye.'

She also thought there may be more between the residents than had so far been uncovered. Although Miss Franklin was stabbed in the back, it occurred to her that the inspector was attempting to fit his expectations to the so-far scant evidence, instead of looking for other clues that might prove or disprove his hypotheses.

'But then we have the problem of the locked door, which you witnessed,' said Cole with the hint of a smirk. 'Regardless of how the murderer arrived, they must have left by the window, because how on earth could Miss Franklin have locked the door while she lay slumped over her desk with a weapon in her back?'

'That, I should have thought, is what being a detective is all about, Inspector.' Mrs Bramble caught Weaver's eye and flicked a glance at the door, satisfied by seeing understanding illuminate his face.

'I'll take you down, shall I?' said Weaver brightly.

Cole looked relieved at the suggestion, then dismayed as Weaver turned towards the door and clattered into the hall furniture. Weaver righted the coat stand he'd almost knocked flying, apologising to it as though speaking to a sentient being, and Cole allowed him to lead the way from the apartment, seemingly at a safe distance, followed down the stairs by Rosie, who locked the front door after them.

Mrs Bramble waited for Rosie to return and gave her an

encouraging smile. 'You will let me know if Lady Emelia needs anything, won't you?' she requested, but in the tone of a command.

'Yes, Mrs Bramble,' the housemaid replied and returned to the kitchen.

Mrs Bramble turned back to the open study and stepped inside, closing the door behind her in case Lady Emelia reappeared and asked her to leave. The inspector's cursory search played on her mind, and it couldn't hurt to give the room the once-over herself before Lady Emelia had the opportunity to begin her own search for the papers she had mentioned. What could have been urgent enough to cut through the shock and grief of seeing your murdered sister slumped over her writing bureau?

She inspected the window first, grimacing as the creaky floorboard threatened to give her away, and checked the painted frame and sill. Satisfied, she opened the window and poked her head outside to subject the courtyard to thorough scrutiny. After closing the window, she checked the mantelshelf above the fireplace, the table in the middle of the room and along the edges of the floor for anything discarded or dropped. Her attention turned to the bureau, its writing flap still in the open position. The items in the main drawers remained as Cole had left them, except the box with its forced lock, which he had removed.

Mrs Bramble had noted during his search that he'd given the smaller drawers, shelves and cubbyholes no more than a cursory glance, so she checked these now.

Having more than sufficient knowledge of orders, bills and invoices, she could see that the paperwork on display offered no apparent reason as to why they might have interested the murderer, or Lady Emelia. In fact, the bureau was one of the tidier examples she'd seen in her time.

A card dropped from between a sheaf of invoices and fluttered to the floor. She retrieved it and read *The Gunpowder Gentlemen's Club* below the image of three stacked gunpowder barrels. She turned it over in her fingers to reveal the reverse, which displayed an address in London's Pall Mall. She wasn't sure whether that was significant or not, given Miss Franklin's disparate and diverse business dealings and social circle, but she pocketed it just in case.

Her attention returned to the faint smell of smoke she'd detected earlier but which no one else seemed interested in. Lady Emelia and Miss Franklin didn't use tobacco, and she doubted whether Rosie or Joan would have lit up in the study even if they had caught the habit, and neither seemed the type.

It had been but a whiff to begin with, the window having been open all night, and now the merest suggestion of it remained in the air. Any fireplace smoke wafted into a room after drawing flames with a newspaper or as the result of a sudden downdraught tended to leave a different smell.

One of Miss Franklin's callers might have smoked a cigarette, a cigar or even a pipe, but the aroma of combusted tobacco tended to cling to clothes and furnishings with far more resilience, hence the need for smoking rooms, padded jackets and tasselled caps. Also, Mrs Bramble could find no evidence of a smoker's detritus, such as used matches and discarded or dropped ash.

That left only one possibility.

Rosie had said she lit fires in the mornings if required to take the chill off the rooms but not in the evenings because it had been too warm recently. She had not done so today due to the tragic event, so the ashes from yesterday morning had yet to be cleared away. Mrs Bramble took the poker from its stand at the side of the fireplace and prodded the grey ash and charred remains of burned logs and coal with care, not wishing to destroy anything that might prove interesting.

About to give up, she gave it one more go, when the point of the poker flipped the remains of something flat and blackened caught at the rear of the grate. She recognised it as a piece of folded writing paper, with two straight edges and one irregular, burned to a scrap but with light scorching on the remains. It appeared Miss Franklin had been ridding herself of a document, perhaps in a hurry given the incomplete combustion, the result of burning paper being the smell Mrs Bramble had been puzzling over.

She retrieved and carefully unfolded the paper, made brittle by the heat, and gasped.

# 8

Mrs Bramble read the smudged green writing on the paper again, to make sure she'd read it correctly.

The words *failed invest* ... and *ruined lives* painted half a picture, while *I cannot go on* painted the other. However, one phrase leaped out:

*Ending my life.*

Once over the initial shock of finding the scrap in the fireplace, Mrs Bramble realised two things did not fit. Although clearly the remnants of a suicide note, Miss Franklin had never seemed the type to let things get on top of her at all, never mind to such an extent that she would consider ending her own life. If genuine – and no evidence existed to the contrary at this point – burning the note in the grate suggested she must have changed her mind. Secondly, whatever Miss Franklin's original intention, a letter opener protruding from between her shoulder blades contradicted any suggestion she had killed herself.

The note also appeared to confirm Rosie's statement that Miss Franklin had been having financial troubles and at least one of her investments had failed. That begged two questions: could the other person Rosie had heard her talking to in the study two weeks ago be an investor in the failed business and, if so, had that led to murder?

Mrs Bramble took a clean sheet of writing paper from the bureau and folded it in such a way as to keep the charred remains safe. This she pocketed next to the business card before leaving the study and the apartment in search of Cole and Weaver.

'Ah, Mrs Bramble, just the ticket,' came a shrill call along the courtyard.

Mrs Bramble's heart sank in recognition of the voice of Mrs Catherine Ewan, who lived in the first-floor apartment next to the Chaffords. Mrs Ewan had been awarded her apartment on the back of her late husband's achievements. Major Richard Ewan DCM had served in the British Army in India and survived the Anglo–Zulu War in Africa. Later wounded in the leg by a sharpshooter at the Battle of Majuba Hill, during the British conflict with the Boers in southern Africa, he died of blood poisoning.

Mrs Bramble watched the woman approach by degrees, leaning on the cane she tapped on the stone floor, the flouncy sleeves of her colourful robe swaying with each movement, her dress sense stuck in a bygone era. *The Elizabethan era, perhaps*, she mused.

'Mrs Bramble.' Mrs Ewan adjusted the laden basket hanging from the crook of her arm. 'I have been trying to catch you for the last few days but you seem most elusive,' she said, a little wheezy.

This wasn't entirely accidental on Mrs Bramble's part. Mrs Ewan's hearing had deteriorated over the past year or so to the point where conversing in raised voices was necessary, making privacy beyond the confines of the woman's apartment nigh on impossible. Mrs Bramble had avoided her at the gala as much as good manners allowed until Mrs Ewan had stood up, declaring, 'Comedian? Ha! I feel I've had quite enough merriment for one evening.' With that, she had given her dining companions a crooked smile, retrieved her cane and retired with, 'Goodnight to you all.'

Mrs Ewan had taken against the Lord Chamberlain's decision to allow her to install a new bath with running water on the proviso she paid for it herself.

'I'm so sorry, Mrs Ewan. Perhaps we can speak in your apartment now,' said Mrs Bramble, leaning in to keep the required volume to a necessary minimum. 'I've been busy of late.'

'Busy with the gate?' Mrs Ewan looked perplexed. 'Why, what's wrong with it?' She waved away any answer, turning to unlock the painted door that afforded entry to the stairwell to her apartment. 'I received your note relaying the Lord Chamberlain's decision about my request for a new bath, but he cannot have been in full command of all the facts.' Mrs Ewan pursed her lips truculently and rubbed at a greenish tinge on her fingers not unlike the yellow of a smoker. 'I can't afford to purchase a bath when I have little else to sustain me but my husband's pension.'

'I'm sorry,' said Mrs Bramble, having tired of this issue weeks ago. 'I don't see what that has to do with me.'

She caught a waft of something pungent and pine-like. The maid's cleaning fluid?

'To do with fleas? That'll be due to your Dodger and that hairball of Lady Emelia's. It's against the rules, no?'

Mrs Bramble ignored the retort. 'You wrote to the Lord Chamberlain, did you not? About the bath?'

'But-but—'

'Therefore, any facts you feel may have been omitted must have slipped away from your own pen, must they not?'

Mrs Ewan's face crumpled into an angry frown. 'Now look here, Mrs Bramble. I'm not asking for ten, just the one. Given the insanitary arrangements throughout this ancient crumbling edifice, I would have thought even you would have been in favour of any improvements.'

'It is not my place to recommend expenditure to the super-intendent or Lord Chamberlain, Mrs Ewan. I am but a humble servant to all who reside here.' She kept her expression impassive while wishing the woman would simply give in and go up to her apartment ... perhaps for a stand-up wash.

'My apartment is not in a jumble; I keep a tidy home,' she said, sweeping her arm around with indignation to indicate the spotless stairwell, kept in such a condition by her maid. 'I had hoped you would be more understanding and at least try on my behalf. I implore you one last time to throw your support behind my request for a new bath.'

Mrs Bramble sighed, doubting this would be the end of the matter. 'Even if I could,' she said, knowing she could indeed, although her support usually went unheeded, 'I fear there is a sticking point.'

Mrs Ewan looked aghast as Mrs Bramble got closer to her ear.

'You must know to what I am referring?' said Mrs Bramble, fascinated as the woman's face turned scarlet.

'I am a woman living on my own,' said Mrs Ewan through gritted teeth. 'Far be it from you or anyone else to deny me some company from time to time.'

'I deny you nothing, Mrs Ewan. As I have said, it is the Lord Chamberlain who wishes to ensure the numbers of visitors to palace residents are kept within the bounds of propriety.'

'Propriety? Ha!' spat Mrs Ewan. 'How can you talk to me of propriety when she who lives across the courtyard is never at home?'

'Who's never at home?' Mrs Bramble's slow slip into bore-dom arrested with a jolt.

'Miss Alice Woodruff, of course. Lord knows where she

goes and what she gets up to every week leaving her poor mother, Flora, all alone. Would never have been done in my day. Then there's that hideous bird of Lady Madeleine's downstairs. Shouted "wastrel" as I passed and then started squawking "strumpet" continuously yesterday evening after I had returned home from the Great Hall. And that brazen hussy next door receives all sorts at all hours.'

Mrs Bramble's attention snapped back. 'I beg your pardon?'

'Do you not notice or at least hear about the visitors such as the one last night and another, bowler-hatted, this very morning?'

'What visitor last night?' Mrs Bramble was on full alert. 'Did you see who it was?'

Mrs Ewan took a step back at the sharp retort. 'How should I know, when such a parade of strangers beat a path to Miss Franklin's door? You expect it of domestic servants – that is their way – but we should be above such behaviour, should we not?'

'The visitor?' Mrs Bramble prompted.

'He passed beneath my window at about nine o'clock, if you must know,' said Mrs Ewan.

'What did he look like?' said Mrs Bramble, her mind casting back to Lady Madeleine's sighting. 'Did you get a good look?'

'He wasn't carrying a crook. What do you think he was, a shepherd? No. A brief glimpse of a dark cloak, and maybe an umbrella, no more.'

'Probably no more than one of Miss Franklin's usual business associates.' Mrs Bramble eyed the woman, who looked disturbed by the sudden turn of the conversation. 'The gentleman you saw this morning is from Scotland Yard, who no doubt will want to speak to you.'

'Speak to me about Scotland? Whatever for? I don't know any gentlemen from Scotland.'

'An *inspector* from *Scotland Yard*, because Miss Franklin was found murdered in her study this morning,' said Mrs Bramble bluntly, to gauge the woman's reaction.

Mrs Ewan's hand flew to her throat as if in protection against strangulation or having her throat cut. 'Mur ...' Her voice faded, her face beginning to change colour again, adopting an unhealthy pallor.

Her shock appeared genuine and Mrs Bramble softened her stance a little. 'I'd go and have a glass of sweet sherry and a lie-down, if I were you.' She knew very little liquid passed Mrs Ewan's lips that didn't contain some alcohol, even at this time in the morning, and suspected Sunny's cry of 'gin' may also have been aimed at her. 'When I see the inspector again, I'll send him your way.'

Mrs Ewan had a faraway look in her eyes but nodded before she turned away, rubbing her fingers again. Mrs Bramble smiled to herself as the dazed woman started easily up the steps towards her apartment. She seemed to hear perfectly when she wanted to and had forgotten she needed the aid of her cane.

# 9

As the front door leading to Mrs Ewan's apartment clicked shut, another on the opposite side of the courtyard clicked open and the face of Mrs Flora Woodruff, widow of the late Commander Algernon Woodruff, appeared in the opening. His many heroic exploits in the Royal Navy had earned him royal gratitude and her the privilege of residing at Hampton Court Palace after a storm sank his ship in the Bay of Biscay. Despite the free lodgings, Mrs Woodruff was often as sour in spirit as her expression intimated.

'You gave me a start, Mrs Woodruff,' said Mrs Bramble.

Mrs Woodruff glanced along the courtyard. 'Has she gone?'

'If you mean Mrs Ewan, she's returned to her apartment.'

Mrs Bramble raised a peevish eyebrow as the woman beckoned for her to enter, unaccustomed to being gestured to in such a fashion by any resident. She complied out of curiosity and in furtherance of her own investigation, and waited for the door to be locked behind her. Once they'd climbed the winding staircase to the first-floor apartment, Mrs Woodruff invited Mrs Bramble to sit on an overstuffed settee that had seen better days.

After checking out of the window, she too sat on the settee, alternately twiddling a silver ring on the little finger of her right hand and scratching around a large mole above her lip. It was a little claustrophobic, being so close to someone who had often irritated her in the past, and Mrs Bramble wondered why the woman hadn't chosen to sit facing her in one of the high-backed easy chairs. She soon found out, as Mrs Woodruff leaned in conspiratorially.

'Have I heard correctly? Miss Franklin was . . .?'

'Murdered?' Mrs Bramble finished the sentence. If eavesdropping ever became a national sport, Mrs Bramble considered Mrs Woodruff a guaranteed future champion. 'Indeed so, I'm afraid.'

'I'm not surprised in the slightest,' she whispered, and put up her hands in defence. 'Not that I wish to be uncharitable.' She made the sign of the cross and clasped her hands, as though the simple gesture absolved her of anything said or done. 'When Lady Emelia's husband, Sir Philip, passed away, I thought good riddance to bad rubbish, but Lady Emelia and Miss Franklin always were a rum pair, too.'

'I don't know what you mean, I'm sure,' said Mrs Bramble, intrigued and hoping for more.

'You must know, mustn't you? The comings and goings?'

'Their business associates?'

Mrs Woodruff snorted. 'If you say so.'

'Do you know something of their personal affairs?' said Mrs Bramble. Trying to get this woman to open up was like picking winkles from their shells with a pin; a tedious, often painful and sometimes unsatisfactory process.

'Affairs?' She sniffed. 'I never was one for all those complex machinations, and the women were always shuttled off to one room after dinner while the men broke out the cigars and brandy in another. I only knew what I could see with my own eyes and it is no different these days.'

She looked pensive for a moment and Mrs Bramble covered

the woman's hand with her own as a sign of encouragement to unburden herself of whatever she was holding back. Her hand felt cold and bony, in contrast to Mrs Bramble's warm, soft fingers.

Mrs Woodruff relaxed. 'My late husband, Algy, you'd have thought him a lovely man if you'd ever met him, such a charmer. I still have his dress uniform and a business suit in my wardrobe – haven't the heart to part with them. Anyway, he met Lady Emelia's husband, Sir Philip, in some club while on shore leave in London many years ago. Became inseparable for a while and the two families became friends. Sir Philip persuaded Algy to invest in several of his enterprises. Few of them bore fruit, I'm told, and even those that did yielded less than expected.

'Over the years, the relationship soured, especially after my husband tried to recoup some of his capital by selling his shares on, albeit at a loss. Sir Philip saw it as a betrayal of trust and the two men never spoke again, nor did our families. We never got our money back, which is why I find myself ensconced in this place. I presume it is still tied up with that damned family, but I refuse to squander anything I have left on expensive lawyers who would no doubt take everything else from me in fees.'

Greed. Betrayal. Jealousy. Rivalry. Lingering animosity and resentment. Mrs Bramble considered all of these to be motives for murder, but did Mrs Woodruff have it in her to be anything other than an upper-class busybody?

Mrs Woodruff glanced over her shoulder as though someone may have creeped in with them and even now was earwigging behind the settee. 'I might have heard someone, a late-night caller,' she declared, and licked her lips.

'A lot of people milled about last night, Mrs Woodruff, not

64

least those returning from Lady Venetia Merritt's gala evening that you attended.'

'I did attend, but not for long. I stayed for the dinner but I've had better, if truth be told.' She grimaced. 'Too greasy for me. I left before the entertainment with a headache and took to my bed. Mildred came with me and prepared a cold compress.' She touched her forehead theatrically. 'I would have drifted off to sleep had it not been for the tapping.'

Mrs Bramble knew little short of a raging migraine would have forced Mrs Woodruff to absent herself from the rounds of gossip, innuendo and backbiting on offer last night. A condition so debilitating as that would have clouded the senses of any lesser mortal. She watched her twiddling the silver ring again and noticed discolouration on her finger beneath the oversized stone of polished Blue John.

'What do you mean by tapping?' Mrs Bramble asked, knowing the woman still had the eyesight of a hawk, the nose of a bloodhound and the hearing of an owl, despite her advancing years.

'A cane,' said Mrs Woodruff. 'I heard her shuffling along the courtyard, tap-tap-tapping it on the ground like the infantry beating the retreat. The strange thing is, the tapping stopped along from this very apartment, and with a simple knock-knock, a door opened and closed. It was her, clear as day.' She raised her eyebrows and nodded, as if that said it all.

'Who are we talking about?' said Mrs Bramble, wanting Mrs Woodruff to spell it out.

'Old Sourpuss, of course. I heard her tell you someone called on Miss Franklin last night.' She glanced over her shoulder again. 'She's pulling the wool over your eyes. Heard her twice more a while later. If you're looking for an intruder, I say look no further than Mrs Ewan.'

'Why on earth would Mrs Ewan want to kill Miss Franklin?' said Mrs Bramble. The accusation made no sense.

'They are always at each other's throats on that side of the court,' said Mrs Woodruff with a look that suggested such behaviour said it all. 'One has a predatory cat and a big apartment while of the other two, one can't get a new bath for love nor money and the other has a raucous cockatoo. Need I say more?'

Mrs Bramble chose to ignore the insinuations and at that moment, someone attempted to insert a key into the lock of the front door. Finding a key already there on the inside, the caller rapped on the door and a housemaid appeared.

'Mildred, get that, would you?' she said to the maid, and looked at Mrs Bramble. 'Two knocks, then two knocks. In case I have no wish for visitors, it's my daughter's way of announcing herself as a friendly face. I do the same in return, as does Mildred.'

Mildred answered the door and two sets of footsteps ascended the stairs until Mrs Woodruff's daughter entered the room. She placed something in the rack at the base of the coat stand by the door before she shed her coat for Mildred to hang on the pegs.

Mrs Bramble stood in deference.

'Mrs Bramble,' said Miss Alice Woodruff in a surprised tone. 'Do sit.' A dark blue headpiece, piled up with a veil-like mesh of the same colour, quivered atop a tight coil of her hair.

*Quite the modern style*, thought Mrs Bramble.

Extracting the long silver hatpin holding it in position, Miss Woodruff held them out for Mildred to take. With a slight limp, although she tried to disguise it, she moved across to a drinks cabinet and poured herself a large measure of gin and tonic.

'A little early in the day, I'm sure you'll agree, but the hustle and bustle of London followed by a long train journey home shreds the nerves rather.' She took a large mouthful.

'Do me a brandy snifter, dear,' said Mrs Woodruff. 'I may as well keep you company.'

'I'm afraid we're out of brandy, Mother,' said Miss Woodruff, indicating a space on the shelf. 'Here you are, finish this.'

She took another swig and gave the glass to her mother before standing behind one of the easy chairs, holding on to the back with hands still clad in the thin, cream-coloured gloves Mrs Bramble knew she favoured.

'What brings you calling on my mother? Not broken the rules again, has she?' Miss Woodruff smiled.

Mrs Bramble smiled back. Everyone knew Mrs Woodruff never broke the rules, knowingly or unknowingly, although complaints about the number of visitors she received had been increasing of late.

'There's been a murder, dear,' said her mother. 'Miss Franklin, from across the way.' She downed her drink and clinked the glass onto the table.

Miss Woodruff's gaze flicked between her mother and Mrs Bramble. 'Are you sure? Here? In the palace?'

'I'm afraid so.'

'I don't know what to say.' Miss Woodruff clutched the silver crucifix hanging from a delicate chain around her neck. 'Have the police been called? Do they know who did it? Are we safe in our beds tonight?'

Mrs Bramble held up her hands to stop the flow of questions. 'Scotland Yard are on the case and there is no suggestion anyone else is in danger.'

'That's because Old Sourpuss did it,' said Mrs Woodruff.

'Mother!' said Miss Woodruff. She looked at Mrs Bramble and raised her eyebrows. 'Did she? Old Mrs Ewan, that is?'

Mrs Bramble gave a slight shrug. 'I suspect not, but that will be for Detective Inspector Cole to discover.'

'Of course, I'm terribly sorry. Mother hasn't had a good word to say about Mrs Ewan since we had our bath installed.'

'She's adamant her needs are greater than ours and always complains of favouritism,' Mrs Woodruff interjected. 'I'd say her bathless predicament is entirely her own fault due to her being such a curmudgeon. Lady Madeleine is no better, keeping a domestic pet, which like Miss Franklin's cat, is so unnecessary, unclean and against the rules, I'm sure.'

The remark, a snide reference to her own Dodger, was not lost on Mrs Bramble.

'Mother's always loathed a lack of cleanliness,' said Miss Woodruff.

*Everyone seems to be quoting the rules at me without regard to their own breaches*, Mrs Bramble thought. 'I'm sure he'll want to speak to you both at some point,' she said aloud. 'The inspector, that is.'

'Of course, but I don't know I'll have anything to say to the fellow,' said Miss Woodruff. 'I wasn't here last night. I met an old friend in London for dinner, a regular appointment, and stayed over at the Savoy hotel. I've not long arrived back.'

'Then it will be a quick chat, no more.'

'Would you mind, Mrs Bramble? I'd like to get out of these travelling clothes and have a catch-up with my mother. A first-class compartment on the train still requires sitting with strangers and makes one feel grubby.'

'Of course.' Mrs Bramble stood and moved to the door. 'I'll let you get on.'

As she closed the door on her way out of the sitting room, she glanced at the rack at the base of the coat stand and saw a flash of silver embossed with a crest of some kind atop a sturdy cane, almost obscured by an umbrella, before the door was pushed closed from inside. She stood still in the hall for a moment, wondering what Miss Woodruff had really been up to in London. Both women had looked a little cagey but Mrs Bramble couldn't fathom whether that was because her Royal Housekeeper status still meant she *wasn't one of them,* yet she had sat in their drawing room as bold as brass, or because they had something to conceal. You could never tell with most people, whichever class they purported to belong to, because social circumstance and standing had little bearing on one's capacity for untruth.

Mrs Bramble waited for Mildred to escort her downstairs, and at the bottom, she turned to smile at the young woman.

'I'm glad I caught you.'

Mildred looked like a startled doe, her black pupils almost concealing the hazel in her eyes. 'Caught me, Mrs Bramble?'

'You'll have heard about what happened last night?'

'Oh.' Mildred looked down at her clasped hands. 'I'm afraid I did. A dreadful to-do, and no mistake.'

'A little more than a to-do,' said Mrs Bramble. 'Did you see anyone or anything unusual on your way back here from the Great Hall with Mrs Woodruff?'

'No, Mrs Bramble. It were a normal evening and the court-yard was as quiet as anything.'

'You do realise the inspector will want to speak to you, too?'

'Can't be helped, I suppose.' Mildred shook her head. 'Can only tell the truth and say what I saw, which was nothing.'

Mrs Bramble turned the handle and opened the door but stopped in the doorway. 'Your altercation with Rosie last night could better be described as a to-do. The pair of you almost earned yourselves a rebuke.'

'Sorry, Mrs Bramble. Won't happen again.'

'See that it doesn't, at least not in public. What was so urgent it couldn't have waited for privacy?' Mrs Bramble could see

Mildred struggling to look her in the eye and she didn't quite manage it.

'Something and nothing. A little spat between us, is all.'

'Hmm. I don't like spats. They can fester like untreated boils and get out of hand. Try to put this one to rest, yes?'

'Yes, Mrs Bramble.'

Mrs Bramble's gaze remained on Mildred as the housemaid shut the door.

# 10

Mrs Bramble heard a noise further along the courtyard and saw Inspector Cole and Reverend Weaver step out from an apartment. Cole gave a curt nod to the unseen resident as the door closed in his face and he replaced his bowler hat on his head with exaggerated care as if deep in thought.

'Inspector,' called Mrs Bramble. 'How are your inquiries progressing?'

'Slowly, Mrs Bramble,' said Cole as he approached, looking round as Weaver stumbled on what may have been the one loose stone in the whole courtyard. Cole raised his eyebrows and sighed as the reverend regained his balance but not his dignity. 'Many of the residents of this courtyard attended the soiree and returned after the murder had taken place. A few others abroad in the vicinity or at home at the hour in question insist they saw nothing.

'Most of those I've managed to speak to say they take no interest in anything that occurs outside of their social circles, which I find hard to believe. The thing I find most disturbing to my sensibility, which is a hindrance to the investigation, is the plethora of petty resentments some of them harbour towards fellow residents. They run so deep as to render their testimonies unreliable at best.'

Mrs Bramble had known the presence of an outsider, a policeman in particular, would not go down well with those in her charge, even with Reverend Weaver as his chaperone. No matter where in the palace they lived, the residents were once owners or occupiers of large properties in monied areas with ample facilities, staff and privacy. They had financial security and high social standing. Here, however spacious their particular apartments might be and however numerous the members of their households, their social circumstances were much reduced. They lived on top of each other and friction always occurs when people rub against each other every day.

'You'll find Mrs Flora Woodruff and her daughter Miss Alice on the first floor,' said Mrs Bramble, gesturing to the Woodruffs' front door. 'I've not long been speaking with—'

'I told you I was to be the only detective here today,' Cole interrupted, a sharp edge of anger to his words.

'You said yourself, the investigation is dragging—'

'I didn't say drag—'

'And as you dismissed the sergeant earlier, you looked as though you could do with a hand.'

'This is not how things are done, Mrs Br—'

'Yes, yes . . .' She flapped her hand dismissively. Why didn't men listen? 'Anyway, it seems her husband had some bad business dealings with the late Sir Philip Chafford that led to the current cool relationship between the two families.'

'It—'

'That being said, Mrs Woodruff flat out accused Mrs Catherine Ewan, her neighbour on the same floor but across the way, of being the assassin. She said she heard her several times last night, but I'd take that with a pinch of salt if I were you. As you've discovered, each have their own disputes with other residents over who has what bath fitted, who has what pet and who has excessive visitors.'

'I'd appreciate you leave—'

'Mind you, Mrs Ewan did say she saw someone enter the courtyard last night, which might be the same person seen by Lady Madeleine, so no doubt you'll want a word with her as well. Mildred, their housemaid, returned early from Lady Venetia's gala too, escorting Mrs Woodruff home. She says she saw nothing untoward between the Great Hall and their apartment, but it couldn't hurt if you asked her again.'

Cole looked exasperated. 'Kindly leave the detecting to me, Mrs Bramble.'

'Of course, only trying to help,' she said with a smile, and started to turn away. 'Oh, before I go.' She retrieved the note-paper from her pocket. 'As you dismissed the smell of smoke in the apartment and didn't conduct as thorough a search as you might, I thought another look couldn't hurt. After Miss Franklin's body had been removed and you had left, of course.' She held out the paper. 'I found this in the fireplace.'

Cole turned it over in his fingers. 'Writing paper?'

'Handle it with care, Inspector. Inside you'll find the scorched remains of what looks like a suicide note, but we know Miss Franklin couldn't have stabbed herself in the back, don't we?'

She smiled sweetly and left Cole and Weaver as open-mouthed as goldfish prizes at a Mayday funfair.

Mrs Bramble began her usual rounds, neglected since the intervention of the morning's events. It was her responsibility to check that staff under her command fulfilled their duties by keeping the magnificent palace as clean, tidy, habitable for residents and presentable to visitors as possible. Some of the apartments had fewer and smaller rooms, and a few consisted of rabbit warrens spread over two or three floors, linked by narrow passageways, hallways and staircases.

Of course, men and women were shorter in stature in the

Tudor period, but notwithstanding the grand entrance gates and routes to royal apartments, she sometimes wondered whether or not the architects of such buildings considered the provision of general access a necessary evil. Perhaps they thought it detracted from the purity of their vision, something that had to be included, but only once the external aesthetics of the building itself had been accommodated and satisfied.

Some of the apartments provided homes for senior staff in important departments such as the Clerk of the Works, the Keeper of the Great Vine and the Foreman Plumber, who conveniently also doubled as the Superintendent of the Palace Fire Brigade. As far as Mrs Bramble was concerned, that did not mean standards could be allowed to slip. Everyone was expected to do their bit outside of their palace duties towards the upkeep of the royal residence that had become their home, and Mrs Bramble had a keen eye for detail.

Having progressed in fits and starts clockwise around the palace, speaking to many whom she met on the way, she reached the door to the anteroom of the Large Oak Room, where her path crossed that of the Palace Superintendent. She had much to debate with him, not least the various inadequacies of the heating, lighting and sanitation affecting her ladies, but preferred a less public venue to discuss palace business.

Being someone who knew how to keep an ear to the ground, she would not allow herself to be overheard. Nor did she wish to be subject to the attentions of the many eavesdroppers around the palace, and she didn't mean the carved and painted faces listening to the conspiracies below from their vantage points on the hammerbeam ceiling in the Great Hall.

She returned his formal greeting and exchanged pleasantries before spotting Lady Emelia out the corner of her eye, looking in rude health for someone who had taken to her bed after receiving such a devastating shock mere hours ago. For certain, Lady Emelia had made a remarkable recovery, if ever she had been truly laid low before, and she rushed past with a fixed expression of purpose.

Her interest piqued, Mrs Bramble had it in mind to follow Lady Emelia towards the orangery, but that did not deter the superintendent, who proceeded to regale her with details about a minor forthcoming restoration. Not wishing to appear ill-mannered, she feigned interest, nodding at what she hoped were the appropriate points, until he had regurgitated all the plans and bade her good day.

As he strode away, any hope Mrs Bramble had of discovering the reason for Lady Emelia's haste had dissipated. There could be little gained from heading towards the orangery now. It seemed unlikely Lady Emelia would have remained there when she could have been making for the Privy Garden, the Pond Garden or any number of public areas beyond.

The ladies of the palace hurried to and fro daily, if not hourly, always visiting other apartments for coffee mornings, afternoon tea or spiced hot chocolate, swapping anything from local gossip to society news. New residents revealed themselves as fresh arrivals by doing the rounds of dropping off calling cards and invitations, hoping to be taken in on the spot or invited to return. Ladies preferred ambling through the palace with calm, poise and grace before arriving for an appointment, but it wasn't unusual to see someone late for a luncheon striding through the cloisters, appearing to glide on casters because their long dresses hid their feet.

In the hope of acquiring further news, Mrs Bramble resumed her rounds with the intention of finishing in Master Carpenter's Court but got no further than the Wren colonnade adorning the south side of Clock Court. A youth aged about fifteen barred her way, his flat cap scrunched in one hand. She recognised him from the apron wrapped around his middle and the painted sign on the crossbar of his bicycle as a delivery boy from the local fruiterers in the village. That he was under the colonnade at all at this time of day and furthermore had elected to block her progress with his bicycle had taken her aback.

'What on earth are you playing at?' she asked with raised eyebrows. 'You're not supposed to ride your bicycle inside the palace confines, never mind in the cloisters.'

'Sorry, ma'am.' The boy knuckled his forehead in respect. 'I'd just finished my deliveries, when Miss Rosie sent me to look for you. But my employer says I'm not allowed to leave my bike unattended. If I lose it or have it nicked, I'll have to walk my deliveries round until I pay for a new one.'

'Miss Rosie?' Mrs Bramble's heart fell. 'Has something happened?'

'Yes, ma'am. She said to tell you Joan, the Chafford family cook, has been taken poorly and to come quick.'

# 11

On entering Base Court through Anne Boleyn's Gateway, the delivery boy scooted his bicycle with one foot, swung his leg over the saddle and peddled towards the opposite archway of the main gate. Mrs Bramble tutted disapproval at his back and spotted Dr Kemp, almost oblivious to his surroundings, dance out of the bicycle's path at the last second. She altered course, lifting her skirts an inch to prevent dragging them on the ground as she hastened across to intercept him.

'Hello again, Doctor,' she called.

Kemp looked towards her and waved with his free hand, his medical bag clasped in the other.

She caught up and fell into step beside him. 'I hear something is amiss with Mrs Marsh.'

'I should say so,' said Kemp. 'She's come down with stomach pains and vomiting, the poor woman. After everything going on there this morning.' He shook his head sadly.

'Oh dear,' said Mrs Bramble.

As they hurried through the passage to Master Carpenter's Court, her mind remained in turmoil. One of her residents stabbed in the back, word out the police had arrived and now Joan Marsh had succumbed to – what – the outdated state of the grace-and-favour estate? It couldn't be her food; she was a very experienced cook.

An anxious Rosie waited at the front door to admit them to the apartment and was already climbing the stairs when Mrs Bramble spotted something inside the entrance, standing upright against the side of the wooden staircase. People who dropped things and left them there for others to pick up on their behalf annoyed her. It was so unnecessary. Of a mind to mention it to Rosie, she tutted and bent to retrieve it, giving a surprised shriek and grabbing the handrail to save herself from falling as Dr Kemp barrelled into her.

'S-so sorry, Mrs Bramble,' Kemp blurted. 'Change of light and all that. Had me fooled.'

'You'd better go first, Dr Kemp,' said Mrs Bramble, pocketing the offending object that had caused the unfortunate incident and smoothing her dress to compose herself. 'It is a medical emergency, after all.'

Kemp hurried upstairs after Rosie, still apologising over his shoulder as Mrs Bramble followed on his heels.

In the hallway of the apartment, he asked, 'Where is Lady Emelia?'

'Meeting a friend in the Privy Garden for a walk before luncheon,' said Rosie, showing them through to Joan's room.

They found her lying on the bed on her side clutching her stomach, her face pale with obvious pain, a chamber pot placed strategically at the side of the bed, her hair and sheets soaked in sweat.

'Good grief, Mrs Marsh. You look in a right old state, if I may say,' said Kemp.

*Not the best bedside manner*, mused Mrs Bramble as the cook groaned. *That's unlikely to put her at ease.*

Kemp gave Joan a thorough examination, starting with checking her temperature and blood pressure. She gagged when he used a wooden depressor to check her tongue and throat.

He sniffed. 'Have you been drinking, Mrs Marsh?'

'No, Doctor,' she croaked. 'Not unless you count the hot toddy. I made it myself.'

'Ah, that would account for the alcohol on your breath,' said Kemp.

Mrs Bramble rolled her eyes at Rosie.

'I've had a bit of a head cold,' Joan croaked.

'There's been a lot of it about.' Kemp nodded, carrying on with his examination.

He asked questions on bowel habits – much to the embarrassment of the cook – and vomiting, how bad the pain was, where it hurt most and how she felt 'in herself'.

At last, he stood up and declared, 'Gastric fever. Nothing to worry about. I'll prescribe something to settle her stomach and she should drink plenty of fluids.'

But Mrs Bramble did worry. During her time as a nurse, she had heard other ailments diagnosed as gastric fever or influenza by otherwise experienced doctors when the extent of their knowledge left them unsure about what they were dealing with. Some of those ailments had not been brought on by natural causes and the patients had gone on to develop serious complications. After this morning's upset, her suspicious mind wasn't about to let this rest.

'When did this come on, Mrs Marsh?'

'Been coming over a couple of days, but my head's a bit stuffy this morning. Thought a lie down would do me good, so I made a hot toddy about an hour or so ago. Left Rosie to carry on with preparing the vegetables for tonight's dinner.'

'I checked on her and found her doubled up in pain over her chamber pot,' said Rosie.

Mrs Bramble saw a half-empty glass on a stool next to the bed. She picked it up and gave it a sniff. 'Brandy?'

'Yes, Mrs Bramble,' said Joan.

'There used to be a small bottle, but even Miss Franklin had some only now and then,' said Rosie. 'When Lady Emelia found a decanter of it in the study earlier, she had me take it to Joan – Mrs Marsh – because she hates the stuff to drink but doesn't mind it used in cooking.'

'Ah, I see,' said Mrs Bramble, believing she understood what had happened. 'Joan took the opportunity to use some for making the toddy.' She dipped her forefinger in the liquid and, touching sandlike grit at the bottom of the glass, turned to Kemp. 'Can I have a word before you leave, Doctor?'

'Of course.' Kemp snapped his leather bag shut and headed out of the bedroom.

Mrs Bramble disappeared to the kitchen but reappeared a moment later with the decanter of brandy wrapped in newspaper. At the front door, Dr Kemp turned as she approached down the stairs.

'Doctor,' she said, almost in a whisper. 'This is the brandy Mrs Marsh used for her toddy. I'd keep it safe and test it back at your surgery, if I were you. I believe she may have been poisoned.'

'What?' said Kemp, aghast. 'What makes you think that?'

'Because I've seen these symptoms before, when I worked as a nurse. Gastric fever can be caused by many things, as you are aware. If I'm right, you'll find something like arsenic has been mixed with the brandy in this decanter.'

'Arsenic?' Kemp looked incredulous.

Mrs Bramble shushed him and gave him the decanter. 'I found something gritty at the bottom of Mrs Marsh's glass and I'm convinced it is precipitate of white arsenic, caused as the hot drink cooled.'

'But who the blazes would want to poison Mrs Marsh?' Kemp hissed.

'She may not have been the intended victim. I'll have to

tell the inspector as soon as I see him. We can't rule out the possibility the poison was meant for Miss Franklin or even Lady Emelia.'

'Good Lord. I'll get on to it right away.'

'Please be careful with it, Doctor,' she said. 'It could prove to be vital evidence.'

'I will, I will,' Kemp assured. 'And I do hope you're wrong, Mrs Bramble.'

For the safety of the palace residents, she hoped she was, too.

# 12

On returning upstairs, Mrs Bramble instructed Rosie to keep a close eye on Joan and make sure she had plenty of fluids to flush out her system. Having decided to keep hold of the glass containing the remains of the toddy, she also intended to have another look in the study.

She found it curious that nothing had been discovered among the papers in the bureau relating to the kind of serious financial problems the neighbours had suggested. She had given the place the once-over before Inspector Cole's derisory perusal, but she had conducted a proper search thereafter, which had uncovered the suicide note. Of course, the papers might be in the hands of a solicitor or financial advisor, but Miss Franklin did not strike her as the type to relinquish control of such affairs to mercenary men.

One place she hadn't paid much attention to was the bookcase, with its mix of leather-bound tomes containing works of fact and also some fiction. She did so now but dismissed most of the books straight away. Rosie had told her she took a feather duster to the study every day but properly cleaned and swept once a week. Mrs Bramble could see faint lines of dust on the bookshelves close to the spines of the books where a duster wouldn't clean during a 'once-over'. Two of the books appeared to have been removed since Rosie's last weekly clean, the lines of dust being absent. Mrs Bramble took them down.

One was a treatise on the operation of large-scale international businesses, the other an in-depth look at the continent of Africa. Both failed to offer any information by way of bookmarks, annotations, dog-eared pages or even well-thumbed passages. *There must be something I'm missing,* she thought as she put them back. Feeling frustrated and aware that Lady Emelia might return at any time, she had a quick look out of the window to see if she could see her or the inspector approaching. Satisfied she had a few more minutes, she checked behind the bookcase and the bureau, and both beneath and behind each drawer, just in case.

Deciding nothing else could be gleaned from this room, Mrs Bramble walked across to the door with the intention of leaving, but something at the back of her mind made her stop and turn. She'd dismissed it on every occasion she'd heard it — the whole place was ancient, after all — but the noise seemed unusual because she hadn't heard it anywhere else in the room. With this in mind, she went back to the window and heard it again.

A creaky floorboard.

She crouched and pulled back the edge of the rug. A quick check of the few exposed floorboards revealed two loose offenders, which creaked even to the push of her fingers. They appeared to have been cut to make shorter sections, so she prised up the ends and lifted them away. A large cloth bundle had been secreted in the cavity beneath the floorboards, which she now pulled from its hiding place.

The bundle turned out to contain several cardboard files tied together with fabric tape, presumably wrapped in the cloth to keep them from getting dusty. Mrs Bramble suspected

Lady Emelia had no knowledge of the files and she knew their contents would remain a mystery to her, too, if anyone caught her in possession of them. She replaced the floorboards and rug hurriedly, glanced out of the window again as a final check, and made as quick and silent an exit as she could manage from both the study and the apartment.

Praying not to be waylaid by the likes of Mrs McGowan or anyone else, she hurried towards her own apartment. Having almost reached the main gate, she drew back in alarm when Reverend Weaver strode in.

'Are you all right, Mrs Bramble?' asked Weaver, concern lining his face as he looked at the bundle under her arm and the glass of amber liquid in her hand.

'You gave me a start,' she said, with a glance past his shoulder. 'The inspector not with you?'

'He went to find sustenance,' said Weaver. 'His words, not mine. He'd skipped breakfast to get here quicker.'

'Good, come with me,' she said, relaxing.

The perplexed Weaver followed Mrs Bramble to her apartment and she took a glance outside before closing the door behind them.

Kitty appeared, wiping her hands on a cloth. 'Didn't expect you back so early, Mrs B, Reverend Weaver.'

'I didn't expect to be back. May we have tea in the parlour, Kitty?'

Kitty hurried away as Mrs Bramble led Weaver through to the parlour, placed the glass on the windowsill and sat on the edge of an easy chair. Weaver took the one opposite and she positioned the bundle on the table between them, hesitating for a moment before untying the tape and removing the cloth.

'What are these?' said Weaver, staring at the pile of buff and blue cardboard files.

'I'm afraid I'm guilty of a little pilfering,' said Mrs Bramble.

When Weaver frowned, she said, 'But all in a good cause.' She opened the top file to reveal a sheaf of papers held in place with double-crossbar India tags.

'That is Miss Franklin's business.' Weaver sounded horrified. 'Lady Emelia should have those.'

'And she shall.' Mrs Bramble flicked through the papers. 'Once we've had a look and shown them to Inspector Cole.'

'Why would he be interested?'

'Because I found these hidden under the floorboards in the study.'

'You did wha—'

'Look at this,' she interrupted, pointing to a letter headed with the image of an antelope over an outline of the African continent. The words Blue Eland Gold & Diamond Mining Company were printed beneath the emblem in capital letters. 'It's a recent letter from a Dr Peregrine Frizzell, an engineer in charge of managing the mine, reporting that a third tunnel has also failed to yield any gold or diamonds.'

'Gold or diamonds?' echoed Weaver in a squeaky voice, throwing an anxious glance over his shoulder as though being overlooked by policemen about to cart them off for theft. 'Why is that important?'

'Because Mrs Woodruff said the Chaffords had been having business problems, perhaps for many years. This letter confirms whoever had interests in the Blue Eland mines won't have seen a return on their investment. The opposite, in fact.'

'That's not unusual, though. Not in business.'

'Depends how much one has invested. Rich men can write off a moderate sum, but for the less wealthy, putting all of your eggs in one basket can risk ruin.'

'Is that why Miss Franklin may have taken her own life and wrote the note you found?' said Weaver.

'The knife in her back suggests otherwise,' Mrs Bramble reminded him.

She flicked through papers in other files, discovering more letters detailing the trust put in the mining company by investors and the sorry tale of waning hope as shaft after shaft and tunnel after tunnel failed to produce any gemstones or precious metals.

'This is the oldest file, from about ten years ago,' said Mrs Bramble. She showed Weaver more letters, charts and sheets of figures. Some of Sir Philip's investments had borne ripe fruit, but several had turned rotten. 'Look here.' She pointed to a list of investors in all the business schemes, including the Blue Eland Company. Prominent among them were names she recognised. 'In addition to other investments' – she ran her finger down the alphabetical list as she read – 'Sir Philip Chafford KCB held a 51 per cent controlling stake in Blue Eland, Major Richard Ewan DCM (retired) invested 15 per cent, Doctors Peregrine Frizzell (engineer) FRS and Edward Kemp MRCS LRCP had another 5 per cent each, and Commander Algernon Woodruff RN put up 24 per cent of the finance. What do you make of that?'

Weaver glanced heavenwards as though for divine inspiration. 'Apart from Frizzell, who is still in southern Africa, presumably, and the doctor, who is alive and well and still practising in our village, the other three are deceased and all of their widows live at the palace.' He looked at Mrs Bramble. 'Do you think ...?'

'Not at all. As far as I'm aware, they died at separate times of separate causes. There's no suggestion any of them were bumped off. This letter here, though' – she pointed to a solicitor's letter addressed to both Lady Emelia and her sister – 'states Sir Philip left almost everything to Miss Philomena Franklin in his will.'

86

'That must have hurt his wife.'

'Lady Emelia said her sister dealt with all of their financial affairs but didn't mention that everything had been left to her sister,' said Mrs Bramble. 'It appears Sir Philip made a judgement about who had a head for business and who did not, and that's why he left his investments to Philomena. He must have made provision for his wife, though, perhaps in the form of a regular income or some such.' She turned to the next letter. 'It says in this one from the British Union and Empire Insurance Company that although almost twenty years have passed since the Forfeiture Act 1872 renounced the Crown's right to take the estates of felons, including self-murderers, the company will not pay out in the event of the policy holder committing suicide.'

'Not much of a legacy to pass on, is it?' said Weaver. 'A few minor successes bringing in a moderate sum, other investments bought for more than they're now worth, a mining company that seems to be inept at mining and no way out for the family, even by the taking of one's own life. That is still a sin against God, I should add.' He looked at Mrs Bramble. 'Maybe one of the widows took revenge on Miss Franklin.'

She gave a slight shrug. 'Mrs Woodruff is upset at the lack of redress for the huge investments that ruined her late husband and robbed her of a better life, but I don't see her as a murderer. Mrs Ewan hasn't mentioned her personal circumstances, but her husband was an investor, so she might be playing her cards close to her chest, though she also doesn't strike me as the stabbing kind.

'Dr Kemp began his career as an army surgeon and knows his way around sharp instruments, but he swore an oath to save lives and has had a distinguished career doing just that. Lady Emelia could have killed her sister at any time. Why wait until now? They all had motive and opportunity, I'd say, but I can't honestly point the finger at any of them at the moment.'

'What about Lady Madeleine and Miss Woodruff?' Weaver suggested.

'We can rule out Lady Madeleine because she can't see well enough to take anyone by surprise. She's more likely to give herself a paper cut than stab someone with a letter opener.' Mrs Bramble thought for a moment. 'As for Miss Woodruff, she's a bit of an enigma at the moment, but an old friend of mine might be able to shed some light on things.'

Weaver sat back and crossed his arms, as if gastronomically satisfied after clearing his plate of a large lunch. 'You seem to have it all in hand, Mrs Bramble.'

'I wish,' she said, glancing at the toddy glass, which jogged her memory about the object in her pocket.

She brought it into the light and frowned at what she now recognised as a return railway ticket from Waterloo to Hampton Court. The outward portion had been clipped by the conductor, leaving the return portion unclipped and therefore unused. Returning the ticket to her pocket, she called to Kitty to bring her a small empty bottle that had once contained a winter tonic. She had sterilised it with boiling water and put it in the kitchen cupboard herself at the end of last winter, because her stint in the army had taught her never to throw away anything that might come in handy, especially in an emergency. This wasn't the emergency she had envisaged, but she was grateful the bottle would serve for what she had in mind.

Kitty delivered the bottle and Mrs Bramble retrieved the glass. Having removed the cork stopper, she swilled the toddy around the glass to ensure the gritty substance wasn't sticking to the bottom, poured the contents into the tonic bottle and replaced the stopper.

Never took you for a hip-flask woman,' said Weaver, looking on in mild amusement.

Mrs Bramble put the bottle in her pocket next to the ticket, bundled up the files in their cloth and tied it with the tape. 'Could you do me a small favour, Reverend, by finding Inspector Cole and giving him these?' She pushed the bundle across the table to him. 'Don't let anyone else have them, because I'm inclined to think part of the answer is in this bundle and the inspector should have it as soon as possible.'

'Right, good, right,' said Weaver, worry lines creasing his forehead. 'Should I tell him where I got it? I mean, were you supposed to search the study and remove evidence?'

'Tell him I discovered it hidden in the study and gave it to you to give to him straight away, no more,' she said, deciding any proper explanation for Cole could wait for another time.

'Straight away?' said Weaver.

She gave him a look.

'Right, good,' he said.

Mrs Bramble put some chopped mutton down for Dodger (scraped from bones left over from the previous evening's soiree) and ushered Weaver towards the door for him to leave with her. As they stepped outside, Dodger sauntered in with a low meow of thanks.

'He's ready for his lunch and afternoon nap,' she said. 'But I've got an errand to run.'

# 13

Mrs Bramble had known the proprietor of the nearest chemist's shop at the centre of the village for some time. A couple of the oldest and most frail residents had no retained staff to cater for their medical needs and Mrs Bramble had often sent Kitty to the chemist to collect medicines on their behalf, sometimes agreeing to do so herself if she had business to attend to nearby. The pharmacist had chosen his career from an early age and had been intrigued by Mrs Bramble's 'war stories', as he called them.

Her discovery of the financial papers beneath the study's floorboards had thrown her into a quandary. On the one hand, she trusted Dr Kemp's medical knowledge almost without question. On the other, seeing his name among the list of investors in the Blue Eland mining company had shaken her belief that the doctor could have had no part in the death of Miss Franklin, despite what she had told Weaver.

At the moment, she didn't know how he might have gained access and done the deed without being seen. Maybe he had been treating Miss Franklin for some unknown and undisclosed ailment, but surely Rosie would have mentioned that? It was not implausible that such a well-known character may have passed through the palace courtyards unnoticed, almost as part of the background scenery, but his was a face so familiar even Lady Madeleine would have recognised him. Without question, Dr Kemp would have had the means. Maybe he had the opportunity. Now, she knew he had a motive.

A bell above the door tinkled at her arrival and she stood at the counter, taking in the shelves with bottle after bottle of raw ingredients, liquid and powdered preparations, pills, potions, medicines, and all manner of sundry items to assist with general health and common ailments. Lined up neatly on a rear counter, creams and ointments for myriad skin conditions stood alongside pastilles and lozenges for mouth and throat problems, cough linctus and syrups for the common cold, tonics for general malaise and many remedies for digestive disorders. Mrs Bramble counted herself fortunate she'd never had more than a head cold in winter, lasting a few days at most, and touched the wooden counter for luck.

She knew the most dangerous substances remained hidden in the rear room of the shop. Preparations containing laudanum, arsenic and strychnine would be brought out in special circumstances, and the raw ingredients would be kept under lock and key, even though gardeners could acquire the stuff easily for pest control. This small village chemist shop contained enough to cure an entire army, or kill one.

'Ah, Mrs Bramble,' the chemist greeted her. 'Something needed for one of your ladies, or are you feeling a little peaky, requiring a pick-me-up?'

'Good afternoon, Mr Pittman,' said Mrs Bramble. 'It's neither, in fact.'

'Oh?' Pittman raised his eyebrows. 'Intriguing.'

Mrs Bramble glanced over her shoulder as a precaution against eavesdroppers entering the shop and retrieved the bottle from her pocket.

'I'd like you to take a look at this,' she said, placing it on the counter.'

91

Pittman leaned forwards and said, 'Is it a urine sample?'

Mrs Bramble gave him a wry smile. 'No, Mr Pittman, and neither is it the tonic the bottle suggests it is.'

'Then what can I do for you?'

Mrs Bramble pushed the bottle across the counter. 'It purports to be a hot toddy.'

'One of my remedies?' He looked concerned.

'No, Mr Pittman,' she assured. 'The lady in question, a cook up at the palace, made it for herself because she had been under the weather. Drinking this made her worse, with stomach cramps and vomiting.'

'Oh, dear me. If people will try to cure themselves ...' He shook his head sadly.

'If you look at the bottle and tilt it to one side, you'll be able to see something in there that looks like grit or sand.'

Pittman did as instructed. 'Yes. Yes, I can.'

'I have reason to believe it is the remains or precipitate of white arsenic.'

'Good Lord,' said Pittman. 'Arsenic trioxide in a toddy? That'll always do more harm than good. I take it you think it was an accident?'

When Mrs Bramble raised her eyebrows, he looked at the bottle again.

'Are you sure?'

'No,' said Mrs Bramble. 'I can't be sure just by looking at it, but I believe there is a scientific test you can do on whatever that residue is. Would you be able to do me a favour by performing such a test and letting me know the outcome?'

'Of course, of course.' He took the bottle to the back room. 'I'll subject a sample to the simple test when I have time this evening.'

'That would be most kind, although I have no idea what that entails. Is it complicated?'

Pittman returned to the counter. 'Not at all. If you want to come back and watch at about half-past five, you'd be most welcome.'

'Excellent, exactly what I'm after, and I'm sure you know what you're doing. We have a Scotland Yard detective in our midst as we speak, so it goes without saying that discretion is required, and I'll need the bottle and its contents back to give to him in due course.'

'Of course.' He tapped the side of his nose. 'Mum's the word.'

Mrs Bramble walked at a fast pace akin to a march to her next port of call.

The post office was not as empty as Mrs Bramble would have liked for the task she had in hand. The short queue was to be expected, but a couple of nodding acquaintances also stood nearby, although engrossed in conversation. She avoided their eye, looking as stern and purposeful as she could muster, and took a telegram form from the wooden rack. She waited for a quiet spot in the corner to become free so as not to be over-looked and glanced around to ensure she wasn't about to be disturbed. She wrote down the address of the staff quarters at the Savoy hotel in London and composed a message to an old friend who worked there, making it short to keep the cost to a minimum.

Ask Alf. Miss Alice Woodruff seen last night? All details.
Urgent RSVP.

She counted out the pennies and slid them across the counter with her message, hoping it would be understood by her friend at the Savoy, who wouldn't take too long to find the required information and send a reply. The postmaster stamped the form and gave her a receipt, which she managed to secrete in her purse before one of the two women who'd been chatting earlier blocked her exit with a wicker basket.

'Lydia Bramble, as I live and breathe. We don't see much of you these days.'

'And hello to you, too, Harriet Tyler,' said Mrs Bramble. 'I'm a busy woman and seldom have a moment to myself.'

'It's the same for us all,' said Harriet. 'Even private families can be demanding and few of us have the benefit of extra staff to do our work for us. I know I haven't.'

Mrs Bramble bristled at the way the woman looked down her nose at her. Harriet had always had ideas above her station but never the wit she'd been born with to make it happen.

'I'm sorry to hear you're having trouble coping,' Mrs Bramble said in a matter-of-fact tone. 'Perhaps you've taken on too much responsibility.'

Harriet's face clouded and she sidestepped in the way as Mrs Bramble moved to go around her.

'I hear there's a to-do up at the palace,' Harriet said, waiting expectantly for a juicy answer. 'Anything to do with you? You always seem to be in the thick of things.'

Mrs Bramble noticed the woman's fingers smudged with something black and dirty like coal dust and exaggerated a derisive sniff to ensure Harriet knew she had seen.

Embarrassment replaced Harriet's old expression. 'The pen leaked when I was writing my shopping list,' she explained, averting her eyes. 'I've just bought some pencils.' She lowered her basket to hide her hands and looked back at Mrs Bramble, the steel having returned to her eyes. 'Is it true? Has there been a massacre?'

Mrs Bramble sighed. 'What are you talking about? Who told you there'd been a massacre?'

'My sister. A local gardener she knows heard it from the friend of his wife who said the palace had been caught in a massacre.'

Mrs Bramble understood and shook her head. 'No one was "caught in a massacre". Your sister's friend of a friend of a friend must have misheard "Master Carpenter's Court".'

'It's true, then?' said Harriet.

'*One* of the residents passed away last night. That's all.'

Harriet looked put out. 'The police are swarming all over the palace, I heard.'

'Your informants need to stay off the strong drink, Harriet Tyler. A Scotland Yard detective is making *discreet* inquiries into the tragedy.' Mrs Bramble pushed Harriet's basket out of her way and opened the post-office door. 'One policeman. Just one.'

While accepting that word got around, she left the post office in no mood to discuss work affairs with any more outsiders. Gossip was regarded as sport by many who had little else to do with their time, but she had more important things to do, such as getting back to her own investigation.

The railway station awaited.

# 14

Hoping it would be more productive to go to the man at the top in the first instance, Mrs Bramble knocked on the door of the stationmaster's office at Hampton Court railway station, which seemed the logical place to begin her search, and waited for a response. Although anyone could have dropped the train ticket, including a legitimate and innocent visitor of Miss Franklin's, Mrs Bramble hoped it might have belonged to the mysterious caller seen by Lady Madeleine and Mrs Woodruff.

A wiry-looking man wearing a white shirt with a napkin tucked into the collar, dark trousers held up with braces and a peaked cap at a jaunty angle, but no jacket, opened the door with a look of surprise. Seeing Mrs Bramble standing there, he snatched the napkin away and his expression changed as if realising a stray had disturbed his late lunch by coming to beg for scraps, a look she did not appreciate.

Seeing the ticket in her hands, he said, 'Platforms are along the way, madam,' with a curt nod towards them.

'I know, I'm not a fool,' Mrs Bramble snapped.

The stationmaster's eyebrows shot up to meet the peak of his cap.

'I am Lady Housekeeper at Hampton Court Palace and I found this unused ticket in one of our apartment buildings.'

96

'If the date of issue is valid, it can still be used today. Otherwise, no refunds.'

He began to shut the door, but Mrs Bramble stepped forwards, looking him straight in the eye.

'My dear sir, all I wish is for you to tell me whether or not you noticed anyone carrying a cane, in all likelihood hurrying and preoccupied with his own thoughts, late yesterday evening. I believe it might be he who dropped this and I wish to speak with him——'

'Madam,' the stationmaster interjected. 'Are you aware of how many visitors pass through this station every day?'

She wanted to say, *That is not the point*, but instead said, 'I should imagine most passengers amble through the station and the crowds will have thinned considerably by around nine o'clock.' She employed her best benign smile to appear less confrontational. 'If you have no memory, perhaps one of your staff might recall.'

The stationmaster sniffed. 'Perhaps they might. Try the lads on the platforms. If you get no satisfaction there, have a word at the ticket office.'

Mrs Bramble watched him shut the door before turning her attention to the main building. Around the other side lay the main entrance and ticket office, but she had no idea whether or not anything the rest of the staff might say would lead her to an identification or have any bearing on her investigation at all.

'You can't go through without a valid ticket to travel, or a platform ticket if you want to meet someone or see them off on their journey,' said the uniformed guard on the gate.

'But I assure you, the stationmaster said for me to speak to his men on the platforms,' Mrs Bramble complained.

'Well, he can come and tell me himself.' The guard pointed to the unused ticket. 'That there's yesterday's, out of date, and that's an end to it.'

97

Mrs Bramble's smile wore thin and she considered going back to remonstrate with the stationmaster, but she had one more chance, with the man selling tickets. His moustachioed face, thick bottle-bottom glasses obscuring and distorting the upper half, peered back at her across the counter. She asked her questions again and waited patiently as the man said nothing but tilted his head as though dislodging information and passing it through an internal sieve.

After several seconds during which Mrs Bramble feared he might have fallen asleep with his eyes open or expired in front of her, a double toot from the whistle of a departing locomotive seemed to rouse him.

He straightened his head and said, 'I do, as it so happens,' in a slow drawl.

She felt a surge of optimism.

'A woman, maybe a good few years younger than yourself' – she pouted – 'bought a single to Waterloo in time for the ten o'clock yesterday evening. Last train, that is. I have a particular memory of her because she asked whether or not anyone had handed in such a ticket as the one you have there before she purchased a replacement.'

'Did you recognise her?' said Mrs Bramble. 'Does she pass through the station often? Can you remember what she looked like?'

He shook his head. 'Not much good at faces, me. The singular reason I remembered her from her earlier arrival was because she listed to one side like a sinking ship. Most odd.' He wrinkled his nose, which had the effect of pushing his thick glasses back up. 'I don't know if she carried anything, to be frank, but she did have a pronounced limp, so she might have been using a walking stick to prevent her from capsizing.'

Mrs Bramble's mind raced. 'If she left on the ten o'clock, I suppose she must have arrived much earlier. In the morning, perhaps.'

'No,' he said with a slight shake of his head. 'That's another odd thing. 'I noticed her hobble through after the London train arrived at eight forty-five yesterday evening. Most people come to visit the palace, but even those who haven't tend to stay a lot longer than an hour or so.'

The ticket seller declared he had no more information to impart, so Mrs Bramble thanked him and left, more than a little frustrated, to make her way back across the river to the palace, deep in thought. There was no way of verifying whether or not the passenger seen by him had come anywhere near the palace. She could just as soon have been visiting someone in the village, but it all seemed too much to credit to coincidence.

*No*, she thought. *The chances of two tickets being lost by different people coming through the station at the same time must be minuscule, so the woman in question can only have been visiting the Chaffords' apartment, otherwise she couldn't have dropped her ticket on their stairs.*

This woman, having arrived at eight-forty-five in the evening and lost her return ticket at the palace, had concluded her business and bought a replacement in time to return to Waterloo on the ten o'clock train. Enduring the forty-five-minute journey from London and walking across Hampton Court Bridge to spend under an hour at your destination before returning late at night seemed an arduous and expensive undertaking for anyone, let alone an incapacitated woman. Very odd behaviour. There had been no appointment in Miss Franklin's diary for yesterday evening, so the visit had not been pre-arranged. Who was she and what had she done in such a short amount of time? Could her visit have been legitimate, as an old friend or relation of Miss Franklin?

Mrs Bramble shook her head as she walked, oblivious to the

other pedestrians she passed. *The journey and expense would have been justifiable only if setting off early in the morning and spending some time in the company of one's host*, she concluded. Could she have been one of Miss Franklin's business associates?

A short three years ago, Jack the Ripper had terrorised Whitechapel and no one knew what had become of him, so surely that time of night would have been fraught with danger and too late for a meeting, even this far from the centre of London? After all, the mainly female palace residents were far from being arrogant men for whom late-night discussions in the darkened rooms of gentlemen's clubs were not unusual. No, these genteel ladies enjoyed residency at the palace by the grace and favour of Queen Victoria herself.

As Mrs Bramble strode in through the main gate, she realised that without a detailed description, it would be impossible to identify the woman with any certainty. Was she the murderer or a potential witness herself? Whatever she was, finding her might be the key to unlocking the whole case.

'Mrs Bramble!'

She turned at the call and saw Reverend Weaver hurrying towards her across Base Court. He avoided cannoning into her with an emergency stop, panting and clutching his side, his flushed face beaded with sweat.

'I've been hunting high and low for you, Mrs Bramble. I gave the inspector the bundle you entrusted to me this morning and I have to say, he was not best pleased.'

'I thought he might not be,' said Mrs Bramble with a slight smile. 'I knew he'd be peeved at me for taking them from the study, but I suspect he was far more embarrassed at having missed them during his own search in the first place.'

'All true,' said Weaver. 'But you can add your interviews with the resident ladies to that. He gave me a message – a warning – for you to "stop investigating that which is the domain of Scotland Yard". His words.'

'And that's all they are.' She delved in her pocket and produced the train ticket. 'Do you know where Inspector Cole is now?'

'I'm afraid not. Mrs McGowan and Miss Cameron-Banks waylaid him at the other end of Master Carpenter's Court as he finished giving me your message.' He pointed to the far corner of Base Court, where a passage connected the two. 'The ladies were berating him about your conduct and that of the Lord Chamberlain. Quite funny, really.' Weaver emitted a chuckle. 'He tried to convince them he has no jurisdiction over these apartments other than investigating a murder, but they were having none of it. They're adamant your collusion with the Lord Chamberlain amounts to breach of contract.'

Mrs Bramble had pressed her lips together so hard during Weaver's report that they formed no more than a thin line.

'The ladies left him in no doubt,' Weaver continued, now recovered from his dash across the courtyard. 'If he didn't intervene, they would have no choice but to write to the commissioner of the Metropolitan Police about his part in the conspiracy.' He chuckled again.

Mrs Bramble did not.

'As much as I have little time for the inspector at present, I'm sure the commissioner will have even less for the ramblings of high-class ladies who have had their noses put out of joint by an issue of gratis accommodation, if their letter even makes it as far as him.'

'Quite so,' said Weaver, his smile fading. 'He has far too much on his plate.' He gave a nervous cough to clear his throat. 'The inspector made his escape through the old Tudor kitchens after asking me the way to the chapel, but I think that was for the benefit of the ladies so they wouldn't be tempted to follow him.'

Mrs Bramble had some sympathy for Cole. Had she not used avoidance tactics herself in the past to evade the constant clamour for new apartments, fresh facilities and the war between pet owners, all of whom shouldn't have been keeping them in the first place?

She held out the train ticket for Weaver to take. 'I should be grateful if you would track him down again and give him this. Tell him I found it dropped at the bottom of the stairs to the Chaffords' apartment and that the ticket seller at the railway station believes it belonged to a woman who arrived on the eight forty-five from Waterloo yesterday evening and purchased a replacement for the ten o'clock to London last night.'

'So that's where you've been?'

Mrs Bramble nodded. 'Along with the files and the scrap of suicide note, he should know almost as much as me and I hope it will keep him quiet for a while.'

Weaver smiled, then frowned. 'Why do you need to keep him quiet?'

'Because I need to speak to Rosie again.'

# 15

Mrs Bramble kept a sharp lookout for Inspector Cole on her now-familiar journey to the Chaffords' apartment. She had much on her mind and had no desire to engage in discussion or argument while in full sail. Of course, she hoped Cole had made good progress with his own inquiries, because they had the same goal and she thought he might divulge some interesting intelligence at some point, but she wished to avoid interference with her own investigation. At the front door, she yanked the iron bell-pull and waited for Rosie to answer the distant tinkle.

'Mrs Bramble,' said Rosie, clearly taken aback. 'I didn't expect you again so soon.'

'How is Lady Emelia?' said Mrs Bramble, noting a flush to the housemaid's cheeks.

'Her Ladyship's resting in her bedroom. I think she slept for a while, because I knocked earlier to take in some tea and toast but she didn't answer.'

'And what about you?'

'Me?' Rosie looked back, wide-eyed.

'You looked a little unwell this morning and seemed to struggle with the stairs. Even now, you look a little flushed.'

'Oh.' Rosie's hand went to her stomach. 'Under the weather, is all.'

'Did you have any of the hot toddy Mrs Marsh made for herself?

'No, Mrs Bramble.' Rosie shook her head. 'Something I ate from the leftovers last night, I shouldn't wonder. My fault for being greedy, I s'pose.'

Rosie sounded less than convincing but Mrs Bramble decided to let it go. If the girl wanted to eschew her help, so be it. She glanced around to check for eavesdroppers and leaned closer to the housemaid.

'Rosie, dear, do you mind if we have another little chat? Inside?'

'What for? What's happened now?'

'Nothing else has happened, but I thought it might be useful to go over what you said this morning, about you know what.' She flicked her gaze upwards. 'To allow me to understand it a little better myself.'

Rosie looked up the stairs and back to Mrs Bramble. 'I'm not sure . . .' She hesitated, but Mrs Bramble's gaze never wavered. 'Um . . . The sitting room's free. I tidied it this afternoon.'

Mrs Bramble smiled as she stepped into the small hall and waited for Rosie to stick her head out for her own check of the courtyard. She then allowed Rosie to lead the way up the winding staircase, with its central strip of plain carpet held in place by ornate iron stair-rods, and along the apartment's hallway.

Rosie bade Mrs Bramble wait a moment while she padded along to Lady Emelia's bedroom to check her mistress was still asleep, returning to indicate the sitting room. Mrs Bramble sat in an easy chair and gestured for Rosie to sit, too, watching as the nervous housemaid took the chair opposite. The young woman fidgeted as though physically uncomfortable and clutched her hands together so tightly her fingers ought to break at any moment.

'Don't look so worried,' Mrs Bramble soothed. 'All I want is for you to tell me again what you overheard two weeks ago. I know memories can sometimes fade in even a short space of time, but I believe it was something about love affairs and that being typical of ... "toffs", wasn't it?'

'Yes, Mrs Bramble, I remember straight.' Rosie looked relieved to be on familiar ground. 'It sounded like Miss Franklin and her visitor were arguing about a man from London and my first thought was, it's the usual.'

'Usual?'

'Doesn't matter whether you're from upstairs or downstairs, when you get a man and woman together but throw another name in the mixing bowl, you can guarantee it's all about affairs of the heart. All I meant was, there's a lot of it about. Ain't nothing to do with me, what they get up to; I just does my job. Sounded like they got themselves in a right two-and-eight, though.'

'But you heard no names mentioned, of places or people?'

Rosie frowned. 'I did, now I think of it. Not sure it was about the same thing, but I'm sure I heard one of 'em say a bloke's name. "Fritz", it was.' Rosie dropped her gaze to her lap. 'Not a name I've ever heard before, anyway.'

*Fritz.* Mrs Bramble ran the name through her mind. It sounded Germanic, but ... Her mind cast back to the files she'd read earlier with Reverend Weaver and her heart gave a little jolt.

'Could it have been Frizzell, rather than Fritz?' she said.

Rosie looked up, her eyes brighter than before. 'That's it. Frizzell. And I remember now – it weren't nothing about London. It was something to do with that mine in Africa.'

'Very good, Rosie,' said Mrs Bramble, her mind whirring like a fully-wound clockwork train.

Miss Franklin, an investor in the mine, had been arguing

with someone about it and had mentioned Frizzell, who according to the files was another investor. In that case, it seemed reasonable to assume the unknown caller also had a stake of some kind.

'You mentioned earlier about posting a letter to the Chaffords' solicitor.'

'Yes, Mrs Bramble,' said Rosie. 'It were sealed, though, so I don't know for certain what was in it, not that I'd ever look anyway.'

'Of course not, but as you also suggested, could it have been about the mine?'

'Might've been. Might not have been. I couldn't say.'

'No, I suppose not.'

Mrs Bramble paused to consider this new information. What could have been said between Miss Franklin and her visitor that would have resulted in the posting of a letter to the family solicitor and the death of Miss Franklin? And what was the connection to Dr Peregrine Frizzell? Had the late-night caller in fact been Frizzell, the manager of the mine who had relayed frequent reports about the failure to discover any precious metals or gemstones? The very same who would have communicated the financial dire straits the mining company found itself in. But wasn't he in South Africa?

'I said earlier I'd spoken with Lady Emelia and she mentioned in passing that Mildred called on you before you left for the gala. Given the bad feeling between the two of them, I'm surprised she visited you here at all.'

Rosie shrugged. 'She says she won't let one person's prejudice get her down. She still protests her innocence. "You can prove you've got something by holding it up, but how can you prove you haven't?" she said to me once. A fair statement, I'd say.'

106

'Still, is it courage or foolishness to risk a confrontation by coming inside?' said Mrs Bramble, with no evidence that had happened but interested to see any reaction.

Rosie looked up sharply. 'Who said she came inside?'

Her eyes had widened. With fright? Her gaze flicked left and right as though she were struggling to decide what to tell and what not.

'I never let her in, 'cept when it's cold or raining. Wouldn't leave a dog out in that, would you?'

'Did you ever leave her alone while you got her the sugar or other goods?'

'Didn't cross my mind she'd take anything while my back was turned, did it?'

Mrs Bramble nodded. 'Did Mildred come here for anything after Lady Venetia's gala?' she coaxed.

'No, Mrs Bramble.' The formation of tears made Rosie's eyes glisten. 'Not to my knowledge.'

With the young maid looking more uncomfortable by the minute, Mrs Bramble knew no more could be achieved at that moment, so she released her to get a glass of water and continue her duties. The housemaid appeared conflicted by loyalty to her friend and the possibility of . . . what?

Did Rosie suspect Mildred might have had a hand in Miss Franklin's death? Was it such a stretch to imagine a disaffected domestic servant may have come to the end of her tether and sought redress herself? Especially one whose reputation had been tarnished by an unimpeachable society lady without any evidence. Mildred had been accused of taking a letter opener, so was it coincidence that one had been used to kill Miss Franklin? She had left the gala early with Mrs Woodruff and could have had the time, but if that were the case, how had she gained access to the apartment?

107

Mrs Bramble decided there could be no point in searching the study again but found herself at a momentary loss how to continue. Until her friend replied to her telegram, Mr Pittman tested the bottle containing the hot toddy and Dr Kemp had completed his post-mortem on the body of Miss Franklin, there seemed no avenue left to explore at present.

She left the sitting room and descended the stairs with the intention of further attending to the issue of Lady Madeleine's cockatoo, although why anyone would wish to keep a bird so big and so loud was beyond her. She saw nothing wrong with a nice canary, budgerigar or linnet.

Pulling the front door closed behind her, she inhaled cool air and let it out slowly. She would inform the other residents of Master Carpenter's Court about her talk with Lady Madeleine and the measures agreed to mitigate the disruption caused by the raucous bundle of feathers. With any luck, both the bird and the residents would quieten, which would be a blessed relief all round.

Unfortunately, her immediate intentions faded the moment she saw Inspector Cole and Reverend Weaver enter through the archway at the far end. Underneath Cole's arm, Mrs Bramble could see the bundle of files she had found hidden beneath the floorboards of Miss Franklin's study. She had hoped the discovery would please Cole, but his purposeful stride suggested displeasure, confirmed by his clipped tone when he spoke.

'We need to talk, Mrs Bramble. Now, if you please.'

# 16

The expression on Cole's face confirmed Weaver's earlier report about the detective's sour mood. Mrs Bramble found it wholly unsurprising and it didn't bother her in the slightest. She saw their inquiries as separate but complementary, belonging to investigations following different paths that came together occasionally for mutual benefit before veering away again. *Two heads are better than one*, she thought, and their efforts to solve the murder at the palace was a case in point.

Refusing to talk in open forum, she led the men to her front door halfway along the cloister, their footsteps echoing on the red flagstones. Weaver had visited her apartment many times, but Cole had no idea it had several doors through which one could enter or leave quietly and unseen, and she had no wish to enlighten him. Dodger kept up his own form of surveillance from a distance, trying to look unconcerned by the unusual goings-on but clearly intrigued by this departure from normal routine. When Kitty answered the ringing bell, he lost interest and strolled away, leaving the trio to enter the apartment.

'Sorry, dear fellow,' said Weaver as he tried to go through the doorway at the same time as Cole, their shoulders barging together. He looked horrified. 'I-I mean, Inspector.'

Mrs Bramble rolled her eyes as Cole expelled an exasperated

sigh and took a half-step backwards to allow Weaver to enter first.

With an inkling of things to come, she sent Kitty for refreshments and decided to show the men to the room where she had breakfasted a few hours before. Not as comfortable as the parlour, it did contain a large table she believed would come in useful.

With the atmosphere between her and Inspector Cole as frosty as the recent cold mornings, she took up position on one side of the table. Cole, bowler hat placed on the table-cloth, and Reverend Weaver sat on the other. Weaver looked amused by the detective, who fidgeted and seemed somewhat agitated while they waited for Kitty to bring in the tea tray and pour each of them a cup before she withdrew to the kitchen. Between them, and at the centre of the table between the tea tray and the bowler hat, Cole laid down the files relinquished by Mrs Bramble that morning.

'I've been waiting for the opportunity to speak to you, Mrs Bramble,' said Cole at last. He prodded the files with a stubby forefinger. 'You had no right to go snooping around the study and no right to remove this evidence.'

'You agree it is evidence?' said Mrs Bramble, ignoring his rebuke.

'Of course, it's *potential* evidence, relevant or not, but that's beside the point. This is a murder investigation and you are not a detective. How many times must I—'

'Have you looked at the files?'

'What? Of course I have.' Cole looked flustered, caught off-guard. 'A skim through, at least.'

'Then you will know that of the five men who invested in the Blue Eland company, one is the mine manager in South Africa, the widows of three of them live around the same court in this palace and the fifth is Dr Kemp from the village, whom

110

you met this morning. In addition, the major shareholder, the late Sir Philip Chafford, left everything in his will to his sister-in-law, Miss Philomena Franklin.'

'I see.' The intrigued Cole had regained his composure. 'Or rather, I don't see. Your point, I mean.'

'My point, Inspector, is that a failing business threatens to financially embarrass anyone who has invested in the company. The greater the investment, the greater the fall from grace.' She selected a file and opened it at the list of investors. 'Sir Philip had a controlling share in the Blue Eland mining company, but some of his other, more successful ventures provided a cushion in case the mine went bankrupt, as it seems to be on its way to becoming. The others on that list share the risk in proportion to their investment and may or may not have anything to fall back on.'

'As you said, three of them have passed away, leaving their shares to family members; two wives and a sister-in-law,' said Cole. 'I still don't know what you're getting at.'

'It's quite simple,' said Mrs Bramble, for whom facts tended to narrow any focus. 'Although I consider none among the palace ladies to be capable of murder, it has to be said that any one of the current holders of the mine shares may have reached the end of their tether waiting for their investment to earn a favourable return. Perhaps their patience ran out after years of hoping for an opportunity to recoup their stake by refund or resale. The situation would have been exacerbated had it become known that the mine was no more than an interconnected warren of empty shafts and tunnels.'

'Surely you cannot suspect poor Lady Emelia?' Weaver piped up. 'She's just lost her sister in the most horrific fashion.'

Cole shook his head to dismiss Weaver's assertion. 'She had the most to gain if all of Sir Philip's legacy transferred to her in the event of Miss Franklin's death.'

'Not strictly true,' said Mrs Bramble. 'Despite the other investments, Lady Emelia also had the most to lose if the mine went bust. She said her sister dealt with all of their financial affairs because she didn't have a head for numbers and money; that's why her husband left all of his investments to Miss Franklin.'

She turned the pages to find the solicitor's letter and slid the file round for Cole to read.

'It seems to be universally acknowledged that Lady Emelia did not have any business acumen, so killing her sister to take control makes no sense. We don't know the exact terms of any last will and testament left by Sir Philip, but given Lady Emelia's apparent financial buoyancy, I shouldn't be surprised if instructions had been left for a regular allowance to be paid. I also wouldn't be surprised if that allowance left her no better or worse off than before, so what would be the point?'

Cole emitted a brief sardonic chuckle. 'If not Lady Emelia, who do you suspect?'

Mrs Bramble pondered this for a moment before answering.

'Witnesses saw a mysterious figure in the courtyard last night but did not describe him as slinking about in a secretive fashion or running away like a burglar might while making his escape. Add to that the return train ticket dropped in the entrance to the Chaffords' apartment by someone who, according to the railway station's ticket seller, may have been a woman. Then you have the attempt to burn a suicide note in the fireplace. Surely you must admit this case is shaping up to be more complex than a common burglary.'

Mrs Bramble studied Cole's face for any sign of concession but found none.

'I know you favour that as the explanation, but I think it the least likely when you consider he would have needed to sneak into the palace, into the courtyard and into the study through the window, escaping the same way while trying not to be seen or heard. Not an easy task, despite the late hour, because guards patrol the palace and not everyone attended Lady Venetia Merritt's gala entertainments evening in the Great Hall.'

'There you are,' said Weaver, sitting back in his chair as if Mrs Bramble's summary perfectly encapsulated the situation.

Cole glanced at him as though he'd forgotten he was in the room and looked back to Mrs Bramble. 'This is all very interesting, I'm sure, but all it adds up to is an in-tray of circumstantial evidence with no cohesion. The ticket could have been dropped by anyone and the so-called suicide note was not left for anyone to find, so even if Miss Franklin had intended to take her own life, she must have changed her mind.

'The files show nothing more than some lucrative investments, others not so successful, by a husband who had little confidence that his wife possessed the right skills to run a business. Few have, in my opinion. None of this points to a specific murderer, unless you believe Lady Emelia found out about the way Miss Franklin ran the financial affairs and took umbrage at the depth of secrecy and loss of revenue.

'In fact, unless I can identify the suspect in the courtyard who, yes, I still believe to be a burglar who did the heinous deed, the finger must point at Lady Emelia. Don't forget, not all burglars draw attention to themselves by running to and from the scenes of their crimes. She had motive because of the secrecy and mismanagement, opportunity because she lives there, and the letter opener to hand provided the method, which is all the law requires as long as there is supporting evidence.'

'And therein lies the crux,' said Mrs Bramble. 'The scant evidence we have that a burglary may have been committed could be explained away by any barrister worth his salt.'

'And Lady Emelia would be acquitted in an instant,' said Weaver, holding up a finger for emphasis, 'because it's all circumstantial.'

'Exactly,' said Mrs Bramble, not sure whether her friend knew what that meant in legal terms. She closed the file and placed her hand on top. 'I believe this affair is inextricably entangled with the Blue Eland investments. Why else would these documents have been hidden? But we have no hard evidence to point to anyone involved in the South African mine. Or anyone else, for that matter.'

'You seem to be forgetting, Mrs Bramble,' said Cole. 'Despite Miss Franklin's involvement since Sir Philip's death, the initial investments were made by the husbands, not their wives. Is it possible that high-class ladies, most of them widows, would rail at each other to such a degree that it culminates in murder?' He shook his head. 'The more I think of it, the more I fear it may transpire that the burglar is not a burglar, after all, but a man sent to extract payment or exact revenge on behalf of one of the ladies or perhaps some other unknown business associate. Someone for whom a cowardly knife in the back is the only way he can kill.'

Mrs Bramble wondered whether Inspector Cole's mind had begun to embellish the facts because it couldn't make sense of what was in front of him. If so, that was a worry. Many innocent people remained to be eliminated from this investigation and it wouldn't do for one of them to be threatened with the hangman's noose for the want of proper consideration. She interlaced her fingers like a schoolmistress about to scold a pupil and held Cole's gaze.

'I have to say, Lady Emelia seems the most unlikely assailant I could imagine, but your implication that women are incapable of extreme violence is extraordinary, given your profession and experience. Although I have genteel ladies living at the palace, some would resort to almost anything short of murder to get their hands on the best apartments available. I have others who would go to war over the installation of a bath, the keeping of a pet, the frequency of visitors, and myriad other rule breaks, perceived slights and petty gripes. It is only recently that the Woodruffs' housemaid stood falsely accused of theft by Lady Emelia and Miss Franklin, which caused the most awful furore among all of the ladies and their staff.'

'Wait,' said Cole. 'What?'

Mrs Bramble paused, allowing him to digest this new piece of information.

'The poor girl was distraught at the time, and because the accusation came from the ladies and not another domestic servant, her reputation is taking an age to recover,' said Weaver, putting his hands together as though praying for divine rehabilitation.

'Nothing was found to prove guilt?' said Cole, a frown creasing his forehead.

'Nothing at all to suggest a lack of innocence,' said Mrs Bramble.

'Nevertheless, the Woodruffs' girl ... um?' He took out his notebook.

'Mildred,' said Weaver.

'Mildred,' he said as he wrote her name. 'I will need to speak to her anyway, to ensure no stone is left unturned in the pursuit of truth and in the fullness of my investigation.'

'Of course,' said Mrs Bramble, resigned to the fact that Cole would be following in her footsteps again. 'As I was saying, almost all of these ladies have motive and opportunity to remove their adversaries and rivals, perceived or actual, by violent means, but you could no more accuse them of a crime than any of our current suspects. All I'm saying is, the case is getting interesting and we have to keep an open mind.'

'We?' Cole gathered the files and stood. 'There is no *we*. I don't know why I'm even discussing this with you.'

'I suspect that's because you have but five items of physical evidence in your possession, Inspector. The letter opener, these files, a broken cash box, a train ticket and the remains of a suicide note. Three of these are pieces you overlooked and I discovered.'

Cole jammed his bowler hat on his head and winced. 'I have given rein to your imagination and entertained your theories, but I warn you, Mrs Bramble, you must now leave this investigation to me or else I will be forced to take action.' He left the room and called back, 'Good day to you all.'

Kitty appeared in the hallway outside the room and scuttled after Cole. Seconds later, the front door opened and closed as she saw him out.

'Started well but got away from us there, not unlike some of my recent sermons,' said Weaver. 'I suppose we'd better do as he says.'

'The man's short-sighted,' said Mrs Bramble who, like a hound in possession of a juicy bone, had no intention of letting go. 'He seems to have no interest in the list of investors and hasn't bothered to check them all.'

She found a pencil and some paper and wrote a neat note. If Cole wasn't going to check, she considered it her duty to do the honours on his behalf. It would require a little subterfuge on her part, but she wasn't averse to that if it meant uncovering the truth.

'What do you suggest?' said Weaver.

'I still want you to keep close to the inspector, to be his chaperone and keep me abreast of his movements, if you will. If I'm any judge of character, the manner of his departure suggests he'll go for a long walk and a smoke to calm down after our little exchange. Before he returns, could I impose on you to do me another favour, Reverend?'

Weaver's eyebrows twitched in surprise. 'Of course, but—'

'That's kind of you. I've been out of the palace grounds once today and I need to do so again this evening. It will be noticed if I do so for a third time, so I need you to go to the post office for me and send a telegram on my behalf.'

'A telegram?' He frowned. 'To whom?'

Mrs Bramble handed him the note and watched him read.

'Urgently,' she prompted, giving him a half-crown coin as his eyebrows shot up in search of where his hairline used to be.

'Wha . . .' Weaver shook his head. 'The inspector won't like it. I do hope you know what you're doing.'

'So do I,' she said, shooing him from her apartment. 'It hasn't escaped me that each contact we make shows our hand to the murderer. And may prove fatal.'

# 17

Mrs Bramble returned to the room with Dodger threading his way through her legs and those of the table. She bent to stroke his ears, finding the action calming.

Kitty reappeared. 'Can I get you anything else, Mrs B?' she said as she cleared away the tea things.

'No, thank you.'

Kitty hesitated as she went to leave and Mrs Bramble looked at her, expecting a personal request or a suggestion about domestic affairs.

'I couldn't help overhearing ...'

Mrs Bramble smiled. Domestic servants never could.

'I know you've been speaking to the ladies,' Kitty continued, 'but I wondered if you needed help with their servants? Yes, you've spoken to Mrs Woodruff and her daughter, Miss Alice, and to Mildred, their housemaid, but I could see what Mildred has to say for herself, if you'd like? I know you're a kind person, Mrs B, but you're still up the ladder from the likes of us and she might be inclined to say more to me than she would to you.'

Mrs Bramble had already gleaned information from Rosie and Joan in the Chaffords' employ, but Mildred had seemed a little jittery.

'How well do you know her?' she said, thinking the chance to be on the inside at the Woodruffs' seemed too good an opportunity to pass up.

'Not very,' said Kitty, 'but we all work here, so we've got something in common.'

'What is your impression of her?'

'Hard-worker – aren't we all? Down to earth.'

'Do you get on?'

'She's all right. Friendly enough.'

'Just "all right"?'

'I mean, she's a bit of a laugh when the girls get together, but we aren't close friends.'

'That's more than adequate.' Mrs Bramble pondered for a moment. Kitty might have one chance to get Mildred to talk, so the right questions needed asking before the girl buttoned up. 'In that case, could you do a little something for me, as you've volunteered?'

'Anything, Mrs B,' said Kitty.

'I'd like you to get Mildred on her own as you suggest, if you can, and engage her in a little gossip.'

Kitty shrugged. 'We all like a little chinwag from time to time.'

Mrs Bramble smiled. This was far from a chinwag she was suggesting. 'This is very specific gossip, Kitty. About Miss Woodruff's assignations, as well as Mildred being accused of the theft of the letter opener.'

She watched a slight look of worry creeping around the housemaid's eyes and wondered whether or not Alice Woodruff's personal affairs were common currency among the domestic servants. Mrs Bramble disliked the idea of people spying without their full knowledge and consent, but Kitty already kept her ears open and her eyes peeled as a matter of course. Spying, quite apart from subterfuge undertaken in the

119

national interest, was often regarded as an immoral pastime that some had made into unsavoury but lucrative careers. This didn't mean Mrs Bramble could afford to eschew it as an investigative option where murder was concerned.

'Can't be anything to do with Mildred,' said Kitty. 'She's not capable of doing that to Miss Franklin.'

'As I told the inspector, I believe everyone capable in the right circumstances,' said Mrs Bramble.

'Then I don't mind if it helps find who did for Miss Franklin. Could be any one of us next.'

Mrs Bramble didn't think anyone would be next, but Kitty's decision still came as a relief.

'Could you get Mildred to talk about who Miss Woodruff might be stepping out with? Courting, even?'

Kitty pouted. 'I'll try, but some of the servants can be fiercely loyal to their mistresses, as I am.'

*But not all are so conscientious, like Rosie*, thought Mrs Bramble. 'I'm sure you'll do your best.'

'I'll see if I can corner her tomorrow morning. A few of us have arranged to go for a stroll by the river after we've attended to our morning chores, so I should have an opportunity to take her to one side.'

'Perfect, thank you,' said Mrs Bramble.

Kitty gave her usual respectful nod and returned to her duties.

Inspector Cole's offhand dismissal of the mine company and his fixation on Lady Emelia or a random burglar being the murderer had left Mrs Bramble with a sense of deep dissatisfaction. With Mildred now considered a suspect, any other possibility, including the consideration of one or more of the investors being involved, had been pushed to the back of his mind. Despite her own impressions or what anyone else said, not one suspect had been eliminated, but time had begun slipping away for both Lady Emelia and Mildred.

She glanced at the clock. This afternoon was one of the two each week when Dr Kemp brought his medical care to the more delicate ladies of the palace instead of requiring them to attend his surgery in the village. He may have been called to the palace three times today, but he was a creature of habit, although not always punctual, so she assumed he'd commenced his usual rounds about forty minutes ago.

Another glance at the clock.

She wanted to confront him about his investment in the mine before he left for the afternoon to complete the post-mortem on Miss Franklin and test the decanter of brandy, and if she could do that without fuelling the inspector's ire and having him confine her to her apartment, all the better.

She moved to the window, which afforded her the best view of the bridge leading to the Outer Green Court and strained her eyes as she searched. Of Reverend Weaver, there was no sign. This was a good thing, because she hoped it meant he was engaged in the errand she'd set him. Her gaze landed on Inspector Cole, who strolled idly along the path as though engrossed in smoking his cigarette, to the exclusion of all else, sending up billows of white like angry clouds intent on finding someone to rain on.

Of the many doors to her apartment, she took the one leading to the corner of Base Court furthest from the main gate. With work to do, she had no desire to cross swords with the inspector again, at least not yet. Time was getting on, but a party of day trippers chose her moment of egress to troop to that corner and stop right in front of her, their guide launching into an exposition of historical architecture.

She spotted Dr Kemp leave the far passage from Master Carpenter's Court and turn left through Anne Boleyn's Gateway. Eager not to lose sight of him, she politely eased the visitors out of the way like an icebreaker clearing a tentative

121

path through the waters of the Arctic Ocean. Once freed, she strode across in time to see the back of the doctor leaving Clock Court on the far side. By the time she had passed the tall stained-glass windows of the Great Hall on her left, passed through George II's Gateway and entered the cloister along the northern side of Fountain Court, Kemp had almost reached the far end again.

Mrs Bramble increased her pace and followed him as he turned sharp left, shocked to find he'd disappeared.

# 18

Mrs Bramble stared at the empty space between her position and a heavy wooden door that marked the termination of the cloister. When open, this led through to the apartments behind Chapel Court, a small private garden and the grand staircase leading up to the preserved former rooms of the Prince of Wales. Other doors afforded access to yet more apartments and it reminded her of how vast a rabbit warren of rooms – almost fourteen hundred – and cloisters, passageways, courtyards and stairwells the palace contained. Anyone up to no good could slink into the shadows and evade detection or capture, and that's what made the sighting of the shadowy figure so puzzling. Could it have been Mildred, after all?

A door creaked shut further along on the left and she hurried towards it, knowing it must have been the point of entry for Dr Kemp to have disappeared so quickly, and was relieved to be proved correct. A staircase wound up for three floors and footsteps echoed from above. Mrs Bramble looked up and saw the legs of the doctor two flights above.

'Doctor Kemp,' she called, her voice bringing a halt to the footsteps as it echoed its own way upwards.

'Mrs Bramble?' said a voice. 'Is that you?' Kemp's head appeared over the handrail, peering down at her before being withdrawn.

Footsteps descended.

'I'm glad I caught you,' she said as Kemp stumped down the steps, Mrs Bramble trying to sound as though she had come across him by chance meeting and was not out of breath at all.

'What is it?' he said. 'Are you ill? Has one of your ladies taken poorly?'

'No, nothing like that.'

'Well, I haven't tested the brandy, I'm afraid. I've been rushed off my feet today and I've the post-mortem to do as soon as I've finished my rounds.'

'I appreciate that, Doctor,' said Mrs Bramble, aware such a delay might have been engineered by a guilty man. 'I await your findings with interest.' She lowered her voice conspiratorially. 'Inspector Cole spoke to me earlier and it seems he's found some intriguing information.'

'Oh?' said Kemp, his face registering genuine interest.

'You'll correct me if I'm wrong, but I believe you have investments in a gold and diamond mine in South Africa?' She watched for any signs of a guilty conscience but saw only surprise as Kemp's eyebrows rose.

'Good grief,' said Kemp. 'When you said intriguing, I thought you meant in relation to the murder investigation.'

'I do,' she said, suddenly realising being alone with a murder suspect in one of the less frequented areas of the palace carried a risk. 'Alongside the mine's manager and your good self, many shares are now owned by the widows of Sir Philip, Major Ewan and Commander Woodruff.' She decided a white lie was in order. 'The inspector thinks there may be a connection between the failing fortunes of the mine and the death of Miss Franklin.'

'Good Lord,' said Kemp, scratching the back of his neck. 'I wouldn't know anything about that. I retain a small investment in the mine — 5 per cent, I believe — as I have in several other

124

ventures. My broker in London takes care of such things. My father worked in business finance and I learned at an early age that it doesn't pay to put all of your eggs in one basket.'

'A good adage.' Mrs Bramble saw no signs of anxiety, so she decided to press on. 'Do you know anything about the mine manager, Dr Peregrine Frizzell?'

The corners of Kemp's mouth turned down and he shook his head. 'Very little, I'm afraid, other than he has a degree in engineering and was brought in as manager because of his impeccable credentials.'

'A stalwart, trustworthy man?'

'By all accounts, yes. We never met, but Sir Philip and the others all vouched for him. I was assured if he couldn't find gold or diamonds, no one could.'

'And he hasn't.'

'Sadly, no, but not for want of trying, I believe. You win some and you lose some, isn't that what they say these days?'

'I believe it is,' said Mrs Bramble, unsure whether to be convinced or not by the doctor's relaxed attitude to losing his investment.

She wasn't so certain she could be as blasé about such a loss. There again, she didn't have much squirrelled away for a rainy day, let alone enough to warrant gambling any of it on speculation.

'I'm sorry, Mrs Bramble,' said Kemp, making a show of consulting his pocket watch, 'but I must get on with my rounds.'

'Of course.' Mrs Bramble waved away his apology. 'Before you go, may I ask how you knew Sir Philip and came to invest in the mine?'

Kemp gave another facial shrug. 'I suppose it's no secret. I am a member of the same club that Sir Philip and the others used to frequent.'

'The Gunpowder Club?'

'Ah, you've heard of it. It's one of the smaller clubs but well run. We all knew each other in passing and when Sir Philip suggested we dine together at the club because he had a proposition for us, it seemed churlish to refuse. As it transpired, we all became interested in the business opportunity and invested different sums according to our various means.

'I'm a rare visitor to the club these days but have kept my membership because it affords me access to colleagues in the medical profession I perhaps would not otherwise enjoy. On a professional basis, you understand'

'Of course,' said Mrs Bramble. 'I'll let you get on. Sorry to have kept you.'

'Not at all.' Kemp turned away.

'You need to put that in a boil wash.'

'Eh?' Kemp stopped, looking puzzled at the sudden switch.

'Your shirt.' She indicated his shirt cuff, disliking untidiness at the best of times, and certainly not in a professional man.

'Ah, yes.' Kemp glanced at his cuff. 'Got a bit of a mice infestation behind the surgery, so I cadged some Paris Green rodent poison from one of the palace gardeners in exchange for giving him a quick check-up, gratis. A splinter in his eye, as I recall.'

She listened to his receding footsteps as he climbed the many flights of stairs, musing over the revelation that all the investors had met at the Gunpowder Club, making their widows and Kemp turning up at Hampton Court not as much of a coincidence as one might think. Men and women of money, power and influence moved in the same circles and the late husbands of many widowed residents at the palace had once frequented the gentlemen's clubs and finest restaurants of London.

As she left the stairwell and pulled the door closed behind her, Mrs Bramble heard the astronomical clock chiming five

126

o'clock and remembered that Mr Pittman, the chemist, would begin testing the hot toddy mixture for the presence of arsenic in half an hour. The tourist crowds had thinned, a few stragglers being encouraged by palace staff to hasten a little quicker to the exit, making progress back through the palace's courtyards a much easier prospect.

However, despite making it back to Base Court without incident, her onward journey to the village threatened to come to an abrupt halt when she spotted a few of her ladies engaged in a heated debate by the main gate. She groaned and veered to the right on a beeline towards the passageway entrance, taking smaller steps to appear purposeful and occupied but unhurried and unconcerned in the hope of escaping their attention.

Without looking at them directly, she could see Mrs Ewan brandishing her cane, not in a threatening way but more as an aid to drive home her point to Lady Madeleine, who appeared to be countering with her own finger-wagging at Mrs Woodruff. In turn, Mrs Woodruff seemed more than able to hold her own in the altercation. After the day Mrs Bramble had endured, she had neither the time, nor energy, nor inclination to wade into what she knew would be an almighty row about the rules and regulations governing the palace apartments, which the ladies erroneously believed she had a hand in drafting.

As she approached the archway to the right of the gatehouse, strains of the conversation began reaching her ears.

'My visitors do not make as much noise combined as your cockatoo does alone,' said Mrs Ewan. 'You shouldn't even have the thing in the first place.' She gesticulated with her cane again. 'It's far too big. The least you can do is keep it quiet.'

'I do try but it's quite difficult,' said Lady Madeleine, looking as though she might either burst into tears or lash out at any moment. 'Mrs Bramble has asked me to introduce certain measures and I will endeavour to keep Sunny's noise down.'

Hearing her name and eager to know more without becoming embroiled herself, Mrs Bramble swerved on her final approach, using a departing party of visitors as cover. She pressed her back against the wall of the gatehouse, with the group of ladies just in view but blocking the main entrance to her right, and tried to look casual while cocking an ear to listen further. A few seconds later, she noticed an impending interruption approaching in the form of Mrs McGowan and Miss Cameron-Banks. No doubt they would set a cat among the pigeons, or a ginger tom in with a cockatoo, as the case may be.

The waddling, arm-linked pair, even though they could not have failed to notice Mrs Bramble, steamed straight into the fray like a Royal Navy armoured cruiser, their bow wave parting the debating circle.

'Quite right, too, noisy creature,' said Mrs McGowan. 'And I still don't know why Lady Emelia is allowed to keep her ragged beast.'

'Beast,' said Miss Cameron-Banks.

'Especially in an apartment that should rightfully have been ours.'

'Indeed,' said Lady Madeleine, looking grateful for the reinforcements. 'At least my Sunny stays in his cage.'

'Lady Emelia has lost her sister,' said Mrs Woodruff with a sympathetic tilt of her head. 'A little compassion wouldn't go amiss.'

Having heard Mrs Woodruff's uncharitable words about the murder that morning, Mrs Bramble thought this statement a bit rich.

'I'm astonished you think so.' Mrs McGowan's voice pierced the air again, her raised eyebrows adding to the theatrical mask of surprise on her face. 'Considering Miss Franklin entertained many visitors, often late in the evening.' Her expression changed to one of realisation. 'Ah, but I was forgetting, you also enjoy similar privileges, do you not?'

'Casting aspersions has always been most unladylike,' said Mrs Woodruff, without any apparent sense of irony. 'In any case, I'm sure the Lord Chamberlain employs impartiality when allocating residencies befitting one's station.'

Miss Cameron-Banks looked confused, as though unsure whether she had been insulted, and Mrs McGowan clamped her mouth shut, her lips compressed into a thin line.

Mrs Bramble rolled her eyes and walked away from the inevitable confrontation waiting under the archway, diverting instead through the passage behind her. From there she turned left through the Lord Chamberlain's Court, where she found the arched servant's entrance of Seymour Gate had been closed for the day. Frowning, and finding herself next to the rear entrance to Reverend Weaver's apartment, she tugged the iron handle of the bell pull and waited.

The reverend's housemaid, resplendent in her black attire with snow-white apron, answered in a moment.

'I am aware the reverend may not be at home, but I wondered if I could impose on you for a moment?' said Mrs Bramble.

'Of course,' said the housemaid. 'Would you like to come in?'

Mrs Bramble smiled and entered the large stairwell with its winding staircase and iron chandelier. Following through to the hallway, she could see the housemaid's over-apron clutched behind her back. On another occasion, Mrs Bramble might have been flattered that the maid viewed her ladylike enough to receive her in her best apron, but she knew this particular back door to the reverend's apartment had no window to check who the caller might be.

'I don't wish to wait for the reverend,' said Mrs Bramble, putting the waiting maid out of her misery. 'All I need is to leave through the front door.'

'I'm sorry, Mrs Bramble?' The housemaid frowned. 'I don't understand.'

'You will one day, I'm sure. Sometimes there are people you are able to deal with tomorrow who are best avoided today.'

Confusion flitted across the housemaid's face, but she nodded before leading the way along the hallway to open the front door. After a wary glance across at the main entrance and Outer Green Court, and a scan of the path leading to the road, Mrs Bramble left through the front garden, careful to close the gate behind her.

The standstill beneath the archway may have presented a minor inconvenience, but the possibility of the murderer noticing her leaving the grounds once again caused her greater concern. At the back of her mind, she feared such unusual behaviour might provoke them into trying to stop her.

Permanently.

# 19

Mrs Bramble crossed the bridge over the Thames, halting from time to time, keeping an eye out for nosey parkers all the while. She even took a short detour to ensure she remained unnoticed before approaching the chemist's shop. A sign on the door announced it had closed for the day.

She put her face close to the glass and her hand up to shield her eyes to peer inside the darkened shop. She could see Mr Pittman in the illuminated back room through the open door behind the counter, so she rapped three times on the door. This caught his attention and he looked up, smiling when he recognised his caller, and she was soon face to face with the chemist.

'Mrs Bramble,' he said. 'I was just setting up.' He stepped aside to let her in. 'Come in, come in. I shan't be long, and as I said, it's a simple process.'

'It's good of you to allow me to observe,' said Mrs Bramble as she entered the shop and waited for Pittman to shut and lock the door.

A small hanging bell swung and tinkled as he did so.

'Not at all. My pleasure, although I half expected the police to be with you.'

He led the way through to the back room and she took the chair he proffered.

'Inspector Cole from Scotland Yard is a bit of a cold fish, I'm afraid, and I don't believe he trusts our palace sergeant, whom he is keeping at arm's length.'

'How odd, but never mind,' said Pittman. He stopped. 'But where are my manners? Can I get you anything, Mrs Bramble? Tea? A glass of water? I have some fruit cordial left.'

'No, thank you, Mr Pittman,' she assured, eager for the procedure to both begin and conclude.

Although officially on her own time, she could be called to action at any hour, so the quicker the results were known and she could return to the palace, the better.

Pittman turned the lamps up to their full brightness as he left the room and Mrs Bramble noticed he had placed some scientific apparatus on the table in the centre of the room, consisting of a simple spirit burner and a clamp stand. He returned a moment later with the tonic bottle containing the remains of Joan's hot toddy and retrieved a small glass flask from a nearby cupboard.

'To make sure any arsenic is mixed throughout,' he explained, swilling the contents around inside the bottle before transferring a small sample to the flask, 'I need no more than half an inch. If you add some zinc and acid, it produces a mixture of hydrogen and arsine gas if arsenic is present.' He replaced the cork stopper.

'Is it safe?' asked Mrs Bramble as he proceeded to add the new substances to the flask, not so sure she should have accepted his invitation to sit in.

'The window is open and it is a tiny sample so we are at no risk,' he said, fixing a tube to the top of the flask before clamping it in position above the spirit burner. He rattled a box of matches. 'Igniting the gas won't cause any explosion, if that's your worry, but it will oxidise any arsine gas present

132

into arsenic and water vapour.' He struck a match and lit the spirit burner.

'How will you be able to tell if it is there?' said Mrs Bramble, relaxing now she knew there existed no prospect of being gassed or blown to kingdom come.

Pittman retrieved a small ceramic Petri dish from the cupboard and held it up for her to see.

'If this cold dish is held in the jet of the flame and it comes away stained with a silvery-black deposit, it will prove arsenic is present in the toddy. The greater the deposit, the more intense the colour, the more arsenic is present.'

'And the greater the potential for deadly effect,' she said.

Intrigued by the procedure, she watched as the mixture warmed in the flask, causing fogging on the inside of the glass. Pittman struck another match and held it to the end of the tube, a small flame appearing as the invisible gas ignited.

'The moment of truth,' he said, picking up the Petri dish and holding it in the jet of flame.

A silvery-black stain appeared, intensifying a little before Pittman nodded with satisfaction and moved the dish away. He extinguished the spirit burner, allowing the mixture to cool and the gas produced to diminish until the flame at the end of the tube went out of its own accord.

'Proof positive,' said Pittman, displaying the Petri dish triumphantly. 'From the deposit on here, I would say there is enough arsenic in the toddy to kill a person very fast if the whole glass is consumed.' He looked concerned. 'I hope the cook who took a mouthful has recovered?'

Mrs Bramble nodded. 'She is still poorly but, as you say, she took one mouthful, so she should recover in no time.'

'I'm glad to hear it.' Pittman picked up the bottle. 'What would you like me to do with this? Shall I keep hold or dispose of it?'

'Thank you, but I'll take it with me.' Mrs Bramble held out her hand and took the bottle from him. 'I'd also like to take the dish, if I may?'

She watched Pittman hesitate, knowing scientific Petri dishes did not come cheap.

'Of course,' he said at last before opening the cupboard again and rummaging for a few seconds, returning with a tiny box just big enough for the dish.

He removed the contents of glass slides and put the dish inside, face down to avoid disturbing the deposit, and handed it over.

'I must thank you again,' said Mrs Bramble, holding out her hand for him to shake. 'I get the impression I will need these to convince the inspector that something other than a botched burglary took place at the palace last night. 'On her return across the bridge, Mrs Bramble had been fretting about Lady Emelia's cook. Joan had ingested enough arsenic to make her awfully sick and the poor woman would need looking after tonight. According to Rosie, Lady Venetia had said no one could be expected to stay 'in that tiny apartment' after the horror of the morning and had invited Lady Emelia to lodge with her tonight in her large and sumptuous apartment in the baroque Fountain Court.

Unwilling to put herself in the hands of unfamiliar maids, Lady Emelia had insisted on Rosie accompanying her, meaning Joan would be left alone. That hardly seemed appropriate, caring or fair, and Mrs Bramble had it in her mind to do something about it. She took her usual route and gave the bell pull outside Lady Emelia's apartment a hefty tug. Seconds later, Rosie's face appeared around the opening door.

'Ah, Rosie,' said Mrs Bramble. 'I'm glad I caught you.'

'Just in time, Mrs Bramble,' said Rosie. 'I was seeing to Joan before following Lady Emelia over to Lady Venetia's. Her

Ladyship's already gone and I don't like the idea of Joan being on her own while she's ill.'

'That is why I'm here. I don't like it, either. I had an idea – would Joan consider staying with me tonight? With Kitty, I should say.'

Rosie's face lit up. 'Please come in, Mrs Bramble. I'm sure she'd be delighted, and even if she isn't, I'll make her go.'

Mrs Bramble followed her upstairs and along to the bedroom Rosie shared with Joan. The cook seemed a lot better, with natural colour in her cheeks and the earlier perspiration washed from her face. She still looked fatigued and a little delicate, but that was to be expected after being poisoned. Even ordinary accidental food poisoning washed you out and left you drained. At least this wasn't some disease threatening to infect all and sundry. Mrs Bramble had seen enough disease while abroad. Dysentery, malaria, cholera, typhoid; it was worrying what the natural world could do to a so-called civilised person in a few hours.

Joan sat up when she saw she had visitors, but Mrs Bramble urged her to stay in bed for the present.

'I have been told you will be alone tonight and I wish to offer a remedy, if I may,' she said.

Joan looked worried. 'I'll be all right, Mrs Bramble. I'll live.'

'Of that I have no doubt, but you'll come back with me and stay with my Kitty.' She held up her hand to forestall a protest. 'I insist. If Rosie can't be here to care for you after the day you've had, it falls to me to ensure you are not left alone.'

'I-I don't know what to say,' said Joan.

'Yes, would be the best thing. I'm sure you'll be as right as rain in the morning and can return to your duties. I suspect Lady Emelia won't require your services until at least lunchtime, so please don't feel you have to rush. Rosie can ask Mildred, the Woodruffs' housemaid, to look out for deliveries

135

and the postman. If there are any complaints, direct them to me.'

'Thank you, Mrs Bramble. Most kind of you. I'll cook you something nice in the morning ...' She stopped. 'Oh, I don't know what you have in your cupboards.'

Mrs Bramble smiled. 'Kitty has everything in hand and knows exactly what I want for breakfast almost every day, so you can leave that to her. You concentrate on getting well enough for Lady Emelia's return. After a stay at Lady Venetia's, I'm sure she'll be in need of some home comforts.'

Kitty opened the front door to Mrs Bramble's apologies for arriving back at the apartment later than usual.

'Oh, you poor dear,' said Kitty, taking Joan in hand and steering her towards her room.

Mrs Bramble ate her now-cold supper of sardines on toast while Kitty made up the spare bed with fresh sheets and a counterpane and made Joan comfortable. The day's events still churned inside her head and she knew it would take a while for them to stop swirling and coalesce into something she might recognise as a solution. It had been a long, traumatic and tortuous day, the like of which she'd not seen since the Afghan War on the North-West Frontier. She felt she deserved a lie-in herself but knew it would never happen in a month of Sundays.

'Would you like anything else, Mrs B?' asked Kitty as she returned to clear away the empty plate and cutlery. 'A cup of cocoa, perhaps. I'm making one for Joan to settle her stomach and have plenty for another.'

'That would be lovely, thank you,' said Mrs Bramble. 'It might ease my mind and help me to marshal my thoughts.'

Mrs Bramble went through to the parlour and took her leatherbound copy of *Great Expectations* from its place on a shelf. Her favourite easy chair, covered with a delicate chinoiserie design of tiny birds and swirling foliage, second- or third-hand but in beautiful condition, beckoned to her. As she settled down to read the next chapter, she paused when Kitty delivered the cocoa and they bid each other goodnight.

Mrs Bramble opened the book at the place where a postcard from a nursing friend, who now lived in Bridlington on the Yorkshire coast, served as a bookmark. Although one side displayed a black-and-white photograph of the seafront, it brought the Gunpowder Club business card to mind and she patted her pocket to confirm it was still there.

Did it hold any importance for the case, or was it leading her down a blind alley?

Perhaps into danger ...

# 20

Waking in the early hours, it took a few seconds for Mrs Bramble's mind to focus before she remembered where she was. A crocheted blanket had been laid over her, undoubtedly by Kitty, not wishing to disturb her after she'd fallen asleep in the chair, and Dodger lay curled in her lap, weighing her down and keeping her warm.

She watched his chest rise and fall with each tiny breath as she waited for the rest of her own body to awaken. Her book now lay on the occasional table beside the chair, her empty cup having been cleared away. The paraffin lamp next to it that she'd been reading by had been turned to its lowest wick setting, its pale yellowish light creating shadows in the corners of the room.

The small carriage clock presented to her on her wedding day, which had avoided being pilfered from her things while on duty as an army nurse and survived transportation across three continents, ticked like a metronome on the mantelshelf above the fireplace, displaying twenty-five past two in the morning, a time when she was usually curled up in bed. Breakfast remained four hours away and the darkness of night still shrouded everything outside beyond the windows.

Her gaze alighted on the postcard marking her place in the

book, snapping her attention back to the investigation. Nothing could be done and no more questions asked until later, but that didn't stop her mind from slipping its mooring again to head out on a sea of puzzles. Who had dropped the railway ticket? Who was the figure seen in the courtyard? Who had put the arsenic in the brandy? Why had they attempted murder by poison, only to turn to the more violent method of stabbing? Why had those files been hidden under the floorboards and did the information they held really mean anything? Where did the Gunpowder Club fit in? Why had the suicide note been burned in the fireplace, or even written at all? And most importantly, who had disliked Miss Philomena Franklin enough to stab her in the back?

Feeling the pressure of a slight headache forming, Mrs Bramble reluctantly disturbed Dodger, who allowed himself to be lifted, cuddled and replaced on the warm seat of the chair. She moved to the kitchen for a glass of water, intending to go to bed for a few more hours' sleep to stave off fatigue during the approaching day, but her mind had other ideas.

She resigned herself to needing a little exercise to tire herself before attempting to go back to sleep and slipped her coat on before unlocking the door at the end of the hall with as little sound as she could manage. The hinges gave a tiny squeak of protest, nothing remotely loud enough to wake Rosie or Joan, as she slipped outside.

Occasional gas lamps lit the cloisters while Base Court itself enjoyed a lamp over every doorway, shedding bright pools of light separated by stretches of gloom as the night-time fog developed and filled the court with swirling clouds of grey. Although still to be respected, fogs out here occurred in a more natural way, especially this close to the river, and carried few of the toxins blighting Central London.

Confident the murderer had targeted Miss Franklin for a

specific purpose and therefore had no reason to be out and about looking to kill anyone else, Mrs Bramble decided a circuit inside the palace would do her the world of good. It should stave off the headache and set her up for another two or three hours of slumber.

She eased along the south-side cloister, hearing nothing but the faint echo of her own gentle footsteps, and through the short passage to the Wren colonnade in Clock Court, with its sixteen white Ionic columns seeming to glow in the lamplight. Having allowed her mind to wander, Mrs Bramble found herself outside the door leading to the Large Oak Room once again, but no one accosted her this time and she passed through the narrow passage to Fountain Court.

She'd always considered this the most attractive of the courts open to the public because of its fountain, cloistered grandeur and elegant symmetry, but not one person was abroad at this hour. Not even, it seemed, those who were supposed to ensure the palace remained secure at night. That didn't mean they weren't around, but she thought it a little too quiet on her circuit thus far.

She paused awhile, filtering cool night air through the neck scarf pulled up to cover her nose and mouth, her eyes drawn to the light seeming to pulse from the four giant standard lamps standing guard at each corner of the grey-shrouded court. It was a rare occasion for Mrs Bramble to be frightened and now did not represent one of them, although the hairs on her neck prickled when she realised anyone, friend or foe, could be looking down at her from the windows or roofs above, from the cloisters enclosing the courtyard, beyond the fog, or in the shadows cast by the lamps. She ran a hand across the back of her neck for comfort.

Continuing along the cloisters three quarters of the way round the courtyard, she turned right, passed the door to the vestry, and paused outside the Chapel Royal. She had often walked around the palace at this hour when she couldn't sleep, its serenity making it seem somehow at peace with itself and the world. Had often speculated that if a human lump of jelly held up by a bony framework could store the memories of a lifetime, could a grand old edifice such as Hampton Court Palace not do the same? After bearing witness to centuries of history unfolding within its confines, might its own memories be locked in its walls and infused into the very fabric of its being?

Maybe not, she decided. Material things moulded by the hands of men, however beautiful or functional they might be, bore no comparison to the wonders created by the hand of God.

She sighed and followed the lamplit cloister around to the left, hardly noticing the grand wine cellar on one side, the kitchen servery on the other, and doorways leading to more apartments. Like most aspects of the palace, they had become so familiar to her as to be invisible unless on her rounds or she had a specific need to be there, and her frequent nocturnal wanderings did not qualify as special visits. She passed the set of stone steps leading up to the Great Hall, heavy doors barring entry at the top, before reaching the east end of Master Carpenter's Court with the intention of taking her familiar route to the far end, through the passage and back to her apartment.

Then she heard a faint scrape.

She froze and looked up, expecting a roosting pigeon or a patrolling cat on the roof. It occurred to her it could be a person, but the sharp-angled roofs prevented any designs on extensive travel above the apartments, although some residents took tables and chairs up to the spaces in between to enjoy evening drinks in the summer. Some households even kept chickens and grew God only knew what in earthenware pots up there. All against the rules, but Mrs Bramble insisted on keeping her feet firmly on the ground, thank you very much. She was employed to take care of pretty much every other scenario, but not that one, so if anyone wished to police the roofs, they were welcome to do so.

There it was again.

It had come from further along, not up.

Moonlight, such as it was, failed to penetrate as far as the courtyard through the fog, but a gas lamp should have offered some possibility of catching a glimpse of whatever – whoever – had made those sounds. The lamplight only served to give the drifting grey some semblance of solidity and made it difficult to peer through the shadows. She squinted in the hope it would improve her vision. It did not.

It crossed her mind that a vixen, foraging for food to feed her cubs, may have summoned enough courage to enter the human domain in search of easy pickings. Although, she shuddered involuntarily, it could be a rat with the same idea and purpose. Hadn't Dr Kemp said he'd got his Paris Green rodent poison from one of the palace gardeners?

The shadows emitted a hissed curse and Mrs Bramble knew in that moment – it was no four-legged animal abroad in the court. Could she have been mistaken about the murderer not returning to take another victim? Had he come for Lady Emelia, perhaps, unaware she and her household slept elsewhere to-night? Her neck prickled, the blood pounding in her ears as she strained to catch more sounds. She considered ducking through the passage behind her to Fish Court, but it was much smaller and narrower with no way out at the far end and she feared this would leave her cornered with nowhere to run.

She considered screaming but knew it would serve little purpose. The ladies would be too frightened to investigate and

142

there were no guarantees anyone would come running in time to prevent the prowler from either removing her as a threat by claiming her as his next victim or escaping the clutches of justice forever by melting into the night. In any case, Mrs Bramble had never been a screamer. Years as a military nurse had taught her to get on with it and leave the screaming to others.

As much as common sense urged her to edge backwards and flee through the passage to Base Court, her curiosity held her, watching and straining all of her senses to see who had made that sound. Getting closer was the only way she could find out, so, against her better judgement, she edged towards where the building jutted out, trying to look beyond.

A faint scratching came from further along, a sound unfathomable at first before she guessed it must be from trying to pick a lock. Someone was trying to break in to Lady Emelia's apartment!

The lock clicked and all went quiet. Nothing moved for a few seconds until a faint creak of the wooden door being pushed suggested the intruder had succeeded.

*What to do?* she thought, realising the position she found herself in was the result of being far from sensible. Should she run to save herself, but in the hope of finding one of the palace constables? Should she stay put and bear witness, but in fear of being discovered when the intruder re-emerged?

The faint yellow light of a lit candle at an upstairs window caught her attention before the curtain drew across and returned it to darkness. Mrs Bramble frowned. If indeed the murderer had returned, why light a candle? Even on discovering the apartment had been abandoned, why dare? Or did it mean whoever had gone inside knew the household slept elsewhere tonight and had broken in for some other purpose?

But what other purpose could there be, unless damning

evidence remained to be retrieved? Could they be after the decanter of poisoned brandy or the files, or had she and the inspector missed something else entirely?

Something else occurred to her. All the external gates to the palace were locked at night, which meant the intruder searching upstairs must have come from within the palace.

Slow footsteps reached her ears and the elongating shadow of someone approaching the far corner of the courtyard from inside the passage leading to Base Court caught her eye. *An accomplice?* she thought with a jolt. A flare of yellow light followed the crack and sizzle of a match being struck and a single cloud of grey smoke billowed from the archway, rolled forwards like a ghostly apparition and joined the night-time fog. She frowned, waiting for the new arrival to make a move.

After a few minutes, cramp from trying to stand rigid tightened Mrs Bramble's left calf muscle. As the ache extended down her leg to her foot, her toes curled involuntarily and painfully. She feared any need to run would be blighted by being as pigeon-toed as a bird in Trafalgar Square, a possibility made all the more immediate when the front door creaked and the intruder emerged. He did not appear to be carrying anything, so either the quest had failed or he had secreted something about his person.

Mrs Bramble watched the figure turn and bend, and heard the scraping noise again as he appeared to have trouble re-locking the door. With a yelp of apparent pain, the figure froze. Even in the deadened atmosphere of the fog-filled courtyard, the voice sounded small, almost childlike, not masculine at all, and it threw her off track. The figure was too tall for a child. That utterance could not have come from Lady Emelia or Rosie, because they would have used a key, and she doubted the murderer would be concerned about locking the door after breaking in.

144

She started to wonder.

Could it be Mildred?

Could this be one of her other ladies, after all?

If Mildred was the thief Lady Emelia had accused her of being, had she disturbed Miss Franklin in the course of her thieving and killed her? Had she now decided to take advantage of the apartment being empty to go back for more?

The figure resumed its work and the lock gave a faint click. Despite the probability of there being an accomplice staying out of sight in the passageway, Mrs Bramble's curiosity got the better of her.

'Mildred?' she hissed.

Something tinkled as the black shadow's head whipped round and looked her way, unidentifiable behind the scarf covering most of its face. The other figure took one step out from the archway to investigate. This brought it to the edge of the pool of lamplight, revealing itself to be the palace police sergeant smoking a stubby-stemmed clay pipe.

The intruder turned to this new movement, recognised the greater danger and ran from it.

Mrs Bramble slid back into the shadows, her heart thumping with both alarm and excitement, but she need not have worried. The culprit ran straight past, dark clothes billowing and flapping in a vortex of swirling fog, pursued by the sergeant, who shouted, 'Stop, thief,' as the pipe fell from his mouth.

The most prudent thing to do now would be to leave this to the police, return to her apartment and try to snatch an hour or two of sleep before the hustle and bustle that daylight would no doubt bring. But prudence would not provide answers, so she, too, gave chase, keeping the sergeant in sight as he ran through the archway and paused in apparent indecision by Base Court passage.

Two seconds later, his choice made, he crept towards the

Tudor kitchens. Mrs Bramble arrived at the steps to the Great Hall just as he passed the servery. With enough lamplight being cast to deny hiding places in far corners, it should have been easy to follow anyone along this cloister, but the intruder had vanished.

The sergeant stopped to listen. Silence reigned. Although he now gripped a sturdy truncheon in his right hand, he must have recognised the futility of raising the alarm, because his whistle remained in his pocket.

In a rush, the intruder blundered out from behind a stone pillar, barging the policeman in the back as he resumed his escape. By the time the shocked sergeant recovered and set off in pursuit, his quarry had disappeared around the corner. Mrs Bramble had never been a fast runner, undue haste being frowned upon in the corridors and wards of a hospital, but she gained on the overweight and unfit sergeant.

With the cloister lights now supplemented by the standing lamps in Fountain Court, Mrs Bramble saw the sergeant halt, seemingly confused by the possibilities. With his head cocked to one side to listen, his whole body seemed to swell and deflate with each laboured gulp of air. Had the intruder turned left along the north side of Fountain Court or chosen to continue straight on along the west side towards a narrow passage at the far end? Had he turned right through the stairwell containing the Queen's Staircase and on through the passage leading to Clock Court, perhaps?

His head whipped around so fast at the sound of her approaching trot, she deemed him lucky not to have broken his neck. At first surprised, then confused, finally frowning, he went to speak, but a sound echoed from the direction of the far passage. He turned to investigate, Mrs Bramble forgotten in that instant.

The fog, thickening by the minute and even more tangible

than before, now dampened any sound, removing the echo from the sergeant's slow footsteps. Mrs Bramble, standing statue-like and hardly daring to breathe, listened for any sound suggesting the burglar had chosen a different path.

The sergeant stopped and listened, too, turning to look at her but receiving no more than a shrug in response. He tried to wave her away with a sweep of his truncheon, but she wasn't to be removed and stood her ground. He tilted his head as if to say 'on your own head be it' and resumed his slow progress forwards.

With the sound of scuffling feet on stone, a figure detached itself from one of the pillars in a flurry of dark cape and fog and disappeared.

Mrs Bramble didn't wait for the sergeant to recover and disappear into the passage. Instead, in a bizarre re-enactment in reverse of her earlier pursuit of Dr Kemp, she picked up her skirts and set off past the Queen's Staircase. The sound of her shoes reverberated in the stairwell and beyond until she emerged beneath George II's Gateway. Something fell over as her feet kicked it, startling her, and she'd barely registered the words 'Wet Paint' on a board, when she caught sight of the sergeant panting along behind the columns of Wren's colonnade to her left.

Her own boots thudding on the stone floor as she passed through Anne Boleyn's Gateway, Mrs Bramble saw that the intruder had pulled further ahead, running with an unusual gait. The flagging sergeant was losing the diagonal chase across the courtyard, but she wasn't far behind, catching his huffing and puffing bulk as he swerved inside the passage leading back to Master Carpenter's Court. Emerging at the far end, she barrelled into the back of him as he came to a dead stop, almost sending him flying, but he ignored the collision as he peered along the length of the courtyard.

147

Nothing moved. All was quiet. Fog hung like grubby curtains.

The sergeant moved forwards, truncheon still at the ready, placing his feet carefully to avoid the hobnails of his boots giving him away. At the far end of the apartment that jutted into the courtyard, he visibly relaxed and walked back to where Mrs Bramble had remained.

'Lost him,' he said matter-of-factly. 'Not for want of trying, but all the same ...'

'He was somewhat fleet of foot,' said Mrs Bramble. 'This palace is a rabbit warren, so he could be anywhere by now.'

The sergeant holstered his truncheon and bent to retrieve his dropped pipe. 'May I ask what you are doing up at this hour?' He looked in dismay at the two broken pieces of clay and tapped the bowl on the wall, dislodging the spent, still-smouldering tobacco.

'I couldn't sleep, Sergeant. As simple as that. Many a time I've spent roaming the passages and courtyards of this place and I've never experienced anything like this.'

'Nor me,' said the sergeant. 'Not that I habitually indulge in roaming. It was the inspector who asked me to be here tonight. He wanted a good night's sleep in his lodgings at the inn and ordered me to keep an eye on this court until his return "at eight o'clock sharp", he said, although I'll not be required thereafter.' His head dropped a little at the telling of this slight.

'He expected more trouble?' said Mrs Bramble, intrigued the inspector might think so.

'Not so you'd notice, but I suspect the possibility of the criminal returning to the scene of his crime was one he couldn't overlook. I should have apprehended anyone who took an interest in this court tonight, but now I'll have to explain how he escaped and what you were doing out here in the dead of night.'

'Ah, about that.' Mrs Bramble moved closer and put her hand on the sergeant's arm as he pocketed the broken pieces of his pipe. 'The inspector will have enough on his plate and you'd have your work cut out trying to explain my presence, don't you think?'

She hoped the implied suggestion would register, because she had no desire to experience another dressing-down from the Scotland Yard detective, not if it could be avoided.

'After all, whoever it was didn't see me. I didn't get in the way of your pursuit of justice and I kept a discreet distance at all times, except when I ran into the back of you.'

Choosing to omit her calling out of Mildred's name from the list, she looked at his face and saw him weighing up the pros and cons, so she pushed home her point.

'What the inspector needs if he is to solve this case soon is to avoid unnecessary distractions, and telling him about me *will* be a distraction.'

Mrs Bramble looked at the sergeant's face, his complexion appearing yellow in the gaslight, and saw his eyes flicker.

He nodded.

'I'd better get back to bed,' she said, taking her hand away. 'I've had enough excitement for one night.'

'I'll escort you,' he said, offering his arm for her to link. 'The prowler won't return to this court tonight, but there's no telling where he might be.'

She smiled. 'Thank you, Sergeant. There's not much of the night left and tomorrow is going to be another busy day.' Her smile faded. 'I fear another tragedy will befall this palace if the murderer remains at large for much longer.'

# 21

After the unexpected nocturnal activity, Mrs Bramble dressed for bed but could not face lying down. Instead, she returned to her easy chair, feet up on a stool, hoping to doze. Dodger, initially disgusted at being disturbed again, returned to the warmth of her lap and slept contentedly, but her mind remained alert and churning for most of what remained of the night.

Although the burglar had been wearing what looked like trousers, Mrs Bramble was certain she had seen a woman. The cry, the stance, the way of running, it all pointed to the thief being female. The problem was, even though she and the sergeant had not been breaking any records, she doubted most of her ladies could have moved fast, even if their lives depended on it.

What had the thief been looking for? Was she also the murderer? Where had she disappeared to? Who was she?

The woman had looked around at the call of Mildred's name, but that meant nothing. Mrs Bramble conceded she would have reacted the same had she been up to no good on her own in a courtyard in the dead of night and had heard a sudden call, regardless of whether it carried her name or not.

An hour of sleep before the alarm clock clanged her awake left her bleary-eyed, dry-mouthed and with a buzz inside her head.

'I didn't want to wake you last night, Mrs B,' said Kitty as she entered and set a cup of steaming tea on the table. 'But you're looking a little weary this morning, if you don't mind me saying so.'

Mrs Bramble smiled. 'I wish it was the mere product of a disturbed night's sleep, Kitty, but I'm afraid I had some excitement last night.' She sketched out the events of the small hours, with Kitty making sounds of concern in all the appropriate places, and finished with, 'How is Joan?'

'I popped in to see her but she's sleeping. She'll still be under the weather this morning, but I'll get some hot buttered toast inside her and she should be on the mend by this evening.'

'When you see Mildred later, can you find out whether or not anything unusual happened in the Woodruff household last night? I'm not expecting a full confession on the strength of a riverside chat, but she may let slip some detail that will confirm it was her.'

'Or rule her out,' said Kitty.

'Or rule her out,' Mrs Bramble agreed.

'Of course, Mrs B. I can't see it myself, but I'll wheedle out of her anything she knows.'

Mrs Bramble devoured her breakfast of two slices of toast with marmalade and found she needed another cup of Earl Grey tea to wash it down and fortify her. Dodger sat in the corner, licking his lips after his usual treat, but scooted away when Kitty answered a knock at the front door. Seconds later, Reverend Weaver entered the breakfast room and waved away the offer of tea.

'Have you ...' He tripped over the edge of the carpet and caught hold of the back of a chair to steady himself. 'It's these blasted new shoes,' he said by way of explanation for his clumsiness. 'Apologies for my language.' He looked towards the ceiling and made the sign of the cross.

Mrs Bramble smiled back, having heard far worse as an army nurse and knowing his shoes were at least three months old and broken in by now.

'Have you heard about the to-do that went on last night under our noses? Under my nose, to be exact, as I live within earshot, but I didn't see a thing.'

'A lot of senses at work there, Reverend,' said Mrs Bramble.

'Pardon?' said Weaver.

'What I mean to say is, what have you heard?'

'Only that the sergeant chased off a prowler last night.' He tilted his head quizzically. 'Why, what have you heard?'

'I am aware of the kerfuffle that took place.' She gave him a sidelong glance.

The penny did not take long to drop. 'You were there?' Weaver looked perplexed, then concerned. 'I thought you looked a little peaky, but I didn't like to say.'

'I couldn't sleep, so I went for a walk. Finding myself near Lady Emelia's apartment, I saw a figure pick the lock of her front door and enter. I waited and watched, and the intruder emerged minutes later, but I have no idea what she was there for or whether she found it.

'The palace police sergeant appeared at the opportune moment, Inspector Cole having told him to keep watch, and I witnessed the ensuing chase until whoever it was gave him the slip.'

'Witnessed?' Weaver's eyes narrowed. 'Is that all?'

Mrs Bramble smiled; the reverend knew her well. 'All right, took part in,' she admitted. 'Although the sergeant has agreed not to mention that detail. As far as the inspector is concerned, I was never there.'

'Well, I never!' Weaver felt his forehead with the palm of his hand. 'Gives me the sweats just talking about it. Inspector Cole is awaiting Lady Emelia's return to assess whether or not anything is missing. He has sent the poor sergeant packing again because he failed to apprehend the prowler.' He frowned. 'That means he's still out there.' His frown deepened. 'Hold on, you said *she*. You think it's a woman?'

'I'm afraid so,' said Mrs Bramble.

He looked at her askance. 'You must be mistaken, surely?'

'Why must I?'

'A woman? I mean, really?'

'You think women incapable of murder?' she said, slightly amused by his apparent naivety.

'Well . . .' He shrugged.

'I think history tells us otherwise, Reverend, and isn't the Bible littered with female murderers?'

'That may be so, but the genteel ladies of Hampton Court Palace cannot be compared to the likes of Jezebel,' said Weaver. 'I remain to be convinced that any would break into someone's apartment intent on burglary and murder. And I can't imagine any woman here, whether mistress or servant, running through the foggy confines of this palace in the dead of night.'

Mrs Bramble raised one eyebrow.

'Ah, yes, present company excepted,' he said, and looked suddenly horrified at the implication of his words. 'I-I don't mean the murder and burglary, of course, but the running and suchlike . . .' His voice tailed off.

'All I ask is that you keep an open mind, Reverend.' Mrs Bramble suppressed a smile and glanced at the clock. 'We'll have to do a lot better if we're to catch the murderer before she can strike again.'

'You think he, er, *she* will?'

'We can't rule out the possibility that this latest intruder is the murderer and she'd returned for Lady Emelia. After all, we have no way of knowing whether her plan was to kill both sisters, or that Lady Emelia may have been the intended victim all along and Miss Franklin somehow got in the way.'

'Good Lord. I didn't think of that.' His face had paled and taken on a sickly complexion. 'What do we do?'

'There's no doubt we've been lied to somewhere along the line and there must be something we've missed. I need to talk to Lady Emelia again, and most likely everyone else I've spoken to before.'

'What about me? I don't mean me as in talk to me.' He flapped his hand. 'You know what I mean.'

Mrs Bramble thought for a moment, unsure about the reverend's investigative credentials but wishing to avoid interference or rebukes from the inspector.

'I would find it most useful if you could continue to keep an eye on Inspector Cole and let me know the second he decides to arrest Lady Emelia,' she said. 'To my mind, last night's break-in proves neither she nor an opportunist burglar killed Miss Franklin. The murder and break-in were deliberate acts, but it remains to be seen whether or not the same person committed both.

'If I tell the inspector my suspicions, I fear he will take them with a pinch of salt and dismiss the whole incident as another example of the petty crimes committed by the poorest of our nation in areas surrounding the houses of the wealthy. He has been so intent on wrapping up this case in quick order and returning to London that I believe his mind to be closed to other possibilities. If he can't identify a burglar whom he feels might also be capable of committing murder, I'm sure he will arrest Lady Emelia. In the short term, I need him kept at the palace but out of my way so I can unravel the truth of what has gone on here.'

Weaver's face lit up. 'Of course, Mrs Bramble. Glad to be of assistance.' His face fell a little. 'Although, I'm not so sure he appreciates me sticking to him like glue. He said yesterday I'm like his second shadow but he's always been perfectly content with the one he was born with.'

Mrs Bramble gave him reassuring smile. 'I wouldn't worry yourself, Reverend. No doubt the inspector will want to see the route the prowler took last night when fleeing from arrest. Since he's dispensed with the services of our palace sergeant and doesn't know the courtyards and passageways of this palace, I suspect our knowledge will prove invaluable.'

She told him about the telegram she had sent to her friend at the Savoy hotel, her visit to Mr Pittman at the chemist's shop, and outlined her plans for the day, all of which threatened to detach his eyebrows from their moorings as they climbed higher. She glanced at the clock again, seeing the hands close to announcing eight o'clock, and beckoned for the reverend to follow her to the front door. Kitty appeared by their side as if by magic to see them out.

'Kitty, don't forget what we talked about,' said Mrs Bramble, giving her an earnest look.

'No, Mrs B,' said Kitty. 'The walk with the girls is still arranged, so I'll be seeing her later.'

Mrs Bramble waved Weaver through first and stepped out of the apartment to join him in the cloister, ready to be his escort to the main gate. She wanted to make sure she saw him on his way before turning to the task she had set for herself, again wary of meeting anyone who might detain her. Her mind had been full to the brim since her race through the palace and she did not relish the distraction of another day of mundane gripes.

She urged Weaver through the archway to Base Court to scout the lie of the land as Kitty closed the door behind them, but he immediately encountered an obstacle in the form of a small cluster of palace workmen. He tried to negotiate his way around them but sidestepped a split second after one of the men did the same. There followed a comical dance of further sidesteps, shuffles and trips as Weaver's moves mirrored those of the workman's evasive actions.

'Shall we dance?' said Weaver, trying to make light of his embarrassment.

The man emitted a low growl, grasped him by the shoulders, manoeuvred him to one side and strode past before the reverend could impede him again.

Hearing the voice of the approaching Mrs Woodruff in the passage on the other side of the gatehouse, Mrs Bramble hurriedly parted ways with Weaver, emphasising his task of intercepting the inspector, and set a diagonal course across Base Court. Scanning the ground as she went, she arrived at the south-east corner and ducked out of sight, pretending not to hear as Mrs Woodruff called her name. Although she did want to speak to both of the Woodruffs again in due course, now was not the time.

Something about what she had witnessed last night and the route the prowler had taken continued to niggle at her thoughts. Although unsure exactly what she sought, she nevertheless felt an increasingly strong pull to retrace the line of the sergeant's pursuit. That could mean only one thing: information of vital importance waited to be discovered.

# 22

Having successfully avoided Mrs Woodruff, Mrs Bramble continued underneath the Wren colonnade, through the narrow passageway to Fountain Court and along the cloisters. They seemed to be trying to tell her something, but her mind had not yet attuned. Her struggle to untangle the solution was not helped by her failure to avoid the need to address various points and issues raised by other residents living elsewhere in the palace whom she met on this latest expedition. She did so with her usual politeness and good grace, but what she did not need was another interception by Mrs Ewan and Lady Madeleine. Being waylaid by this particular pair outside the doors to the Chapel Royal brought to mind the circle of irate ladies she had evaded the previous day. Her heart sank.

'Mrs Bramble,' said Mrs Ewan as she stepped into the path of the housekeeper. 'I am thinking of lodging another appeal with the Lord Chamberlain. This is the nineteenth century, not the Middle Ages. Ladies of standing should have access to every feature of the modern world.' She tapped the ground with her cane for emphasis.

Mrs Bramble almost smiled at this, given Mrs Ewan's penchant for Elizabethan-style dresses. She became momentarily distracted by what looked like flecks of paint on the arms of

Mrs Ewan's dress, looking not unlike the birdseed on Lady Madeleine's, then realised they were waiting for her to reply.

'Ladies—' she began.

'Forty years ago' – Mrs Ewan spoke over Mrs Bramble – 'the Great Exhibition in Hyde Park made us the envy of the world, so why do so few of us have adequate facilities? The pipes squeak and rattle like a garden gate that hasn't been introduced to an oil can for several months and our apartments are so difficult to keep warm that even our bedtime hot-water flasks need knitted covers.'

'And one cannot acquire sufficient space to expand and move freely for love nor money,' said Lady Madeleine.

'You love honey?' said Mrs Ewan, a puzzled frown lining her forehead.

Mrs Bramble, having clenched her teeth behind a benign smile as she listened, took the opportunity the interruption afforded to speak.

'Mrs Ewan, you are entitled to any service, comfort or invention of the modern world that you desire. Neither the Lord Chamberlain nor I stand in your way.'

'Which begs the obvious question: why am I continually denied?' said Mrs Ewan, incredulous.

'You are not. It is simply the case that the Treasury cannot afford to do everything for everyone, so I'm afraid it falls to persons of breeding, even those of more modest means, to fend for themselves and pay for whatever they need, think they need or merely desire.'

Mrs Ewan looked thunderous at the suggestion they had a limitation of funds in common.

'My dispute is entirely different but no less upsetting,' said Lady Madeleine, elbowing her way in front to take over. She pulled herself up to her full height but still fell a few inches short of looking Mrs Bramble in the eye through her cataract-milky lenses. 'I am constantly taken to task over the keeping of my Sunny but he is part of my family and I will not part with him on any terms.'

'Has someone raised the matter again?' said Mrs Bramble.

'Raised a platter? What is this obsession you two have with food?' Mrs Ewan tapped her cane on the flagstone to focus their attention.

'Lady Emelia accosted me at my door not half-hour since,' said Lady Madeleine, ignoring her companion. 'Apparently, Mrs Woodruff heard a scritch-scratching in the early hours followed by a commotion. To the best of my knowledge, Lady Emelia wasn't even in her apartment last night, yet she accused me of reneging on our agreement to calm Sunny down and demanded I either get rid of him or pluck him for the pot.' She glared at Mrs Bramble as best she could. 'I said she had mice and told her she should get rid of her useless lump of a mangey cat. I'm afraid Sunny called her "rubbish", but she called me names in return I cannot repeat in polite company.'

'I'm sorry to hear that,' said Mrs Bramble. 'I promise to speak to Lady Emelia on your behalf. I'm sure it is just a misunderstanding.'

This was true. The sounds had been made by the prowler picking the lock of Lady Emelia's apartment, but now was not the time to be scaring the genteel residents of the palace. Satisfied for now, the ladies turned away in unison. The speed with which those who detested each other could come together and form an alliance whenever it was in their mutual interest to do so always amazed and amused Mrs Bramble. That they usually allied against her was not so amusing, but the storms in a teacup, for that was what they were most of the time, never proved too serious for her to ride out.

While watching the retreating backs of the women as they continued on their way, whispering with their heads bent towards each other, something they'd said pricked at a memory. Mrs Bramble knew it would niggle her until her mind could complete its work and usher its conclusion to the forefront of her thinking.

Only when Mrs Bramble passed beneath the archway at the east end of Master Carpenter's Court, having not long left her encounter with Lady Madeleine and Mrs Ewan, did something else bother her. She paused for a moment, trying to pin down the elusive thought, and almost nodded in recognition when it slid into her mind like the last tile of a Chinese puzzle.

Her own familiarity with the layout of the palace had allowed her to follow the line of the chase with ease, almost without thinking, despite several encounters and interruptions. Last night, in an effort to catch up with the pursuit, she had taken the most direct route from Fountain Court to Base Court automatically, even as the sergeant had chased his prey along a different course. The fleeing prowler had also taken no wrong turns or blind alleys, had not even hesitated with indecision, and all by the mediocre light of a few gas lamps in the fog. Could the palace be almost as well known to their quarry? If so, what did that tell her about who it might be?

As she moved along the courtyard, she almost ignored the brief glint of something caught between a flagstone and the base of the brick wall, but her natural curiosity and a fleeting memory from last night got the better of her and she bent to retrieve it. Holding and turning what had once been a fine-looking silver hatpin, she inspected a kink in its shaft and a bend near its point, and the leaf-shaped head. Although no longer any good for its intended use, silver was silver and therefore reworkable; not something to be discarded. She wondered what could have caused such damage. Being run over by a cart's wheel, perhaps?

About to move away, she realised whose apartment front

door she had stopped beside. Lady Emelia's. The escutcheon plate surrounding the keyhole displayed several fresh scratches, narrow and sharply defined and not in keeping with the type of natural marks made during hurried absent-minded attempts to insert a key. She looked at the hatpin and came to the obvious conclusion: the prowler seen picking the lock of this door last night must have been using this pin.

A further study of the plate showed a faint smear of dark red. Remembering the cry of pain, might it be blood? That begged four questions. To whom had the hatpin belonged? Was it one and the same who had tried to break into Lady Emelia's apartment? Had the blood been the result of a pricked finger? Why had they sought to gain entry?

Mrs Bramble took a small handkerchief from within the cuff of her sleeve and used the corner to wipe some of the blood to collect a sample. She folded the handkerchief to contain the blood within and wrapped it with care around the sharp end of the pin.

While placing it in her pocket, the local postman, looking hot and flustered and carrying a large mailbag slung across his chest, hastened into the courtyard. He held a bundle of letters and selected one or more to post through letter boxes or slide under doors as he approached where Mrs Bramble stood, oblivious to her presence.

'Good morning,' she said.

A look of shock crossed his face as the letters in his hand went flying. He tried to catch them in mid-air but succeeded in swatting them away like flies.

'Dear, dear, dear,' he said as he collected them from the ground, brushing away any dirt. Then he looked up, seeming to remember someone was nearby. 'Mrs Bramble,' he said, a crooked smile of recognition replacing his look of consternation. 'A good morning to you, too.' He thrust out his hand and

161

she took the proffered letter. 'Must dash, I've got a full bag today.'

'More haste, less speed,' said Mrs Bramble, shaking her head as she pocketed the letter, amused by the postman's scattiness as he hurried from door to door.

Her smile faded when the door to the Woodruffs' apartment opened and Miss Alice Woodruff emerged.

'Good morning,' said Mrs Bramble.

Miss Woodruff's brief frown made her appear irritated, but she greeted Mrs Bramble cordially enough.

'May I speak with you?' said Mrs Bramble in a way that suggested it was not a request.

Miss Woodruff hesitated. 'I'm afraid you'll have to walk with me. I have an errand to run in the village.'

'I'm not averse to a little exercise,' she said, falling into step beside the woman as they took the passageway towards the main gate. 'Although I see your limp is quite pronounced.'

Miss Woodruff huffed irritably. 'I turned my ankle yesterday and it is a little stiff this morning,' she said, using her cane for assistance rather than relying on it for total support.

Mrs Bramble raised an eyebrow. 'I'm sorry to hear that.'

'It's but a trifle.' Miss Woodruff waved away any concern with her free hand, drawing Mrs Bramble's attention to her gloves.

'Your handwear is rather elegant, Miss Woodruff,' she said as they turned through the main gateway arch and onto the bridge. 'If I may say, pale blue suits you.'

'They are old, but ...' Miss Woodruff, her face cold and stiff like polished stone, glanced sideways at the housekeeper keeping pace with her. 'You wanted something?'

Mrs Bramble noted the terse response, all pretence of cordiality evaporated.

'I do,' she said, keeping a wary eye out for Cole. 'The

inspector from Scotland Yard is still very busy with his interviews, so I wanted to follow up on something he said to me yesterday.'

'Oh?'

'It appears he is in possession of a document listing the investors in a business.' Mrs Bramble looked for signs of recognition. 'The name of your late father is on the list.'

Miss Woodruff's eyelids fluttered, her lips pressed together as though underlining her nose, and she gave Mrs Bramble a sidelong glance. 'My father invested in many businesses. Do you know which one?'

'I was speaking to your mother about this very topic when you returned home yesterday morning. She said the investment had turned sour and the whole affair had caused some resentment between your family and that of Sir Philip Chafford.'

'I don't see ...' Miss Woodruff stopped, allowing herself more time to reply as the two women continued to make slow progress towards the gate in the perimeter fence giving access to the street. 'Unfortunately, Sir Philip was more adept at persuasion than my father was in resisting and he often found himself talked into ventures he knew little or nothing about.'

'Mining being one of them?'

Miss Woodruff looked away. 'Indeed.'

'Do you know who else invested in the Blue Eland mining company?' said Mrs Bramble, throwing the name down to gauge the reaction.

Miss Woodruff's head snapped back. 'I do not.' A quick reply this time, with another flutter of eyelashes. 'We have a solicitor in London who handles all of my father's affairs, now transferred to my mother, of course.'

'Of course.' She changed tack. 'Is Mildred around? I haven't set eyes on her today.' She noticed no obvious reaction to this question.

'She was at home earlier, but I believe she may be out for a walk with a few of the other servants. As you know, it's something they do each week when able.'

'Ah, that will be it.'

'Hmm,' said Miss Woodruff, now looking as disinterested as it was possible for one person to be.

'I have to get back,' said Mrs Bramble as they stopped at the gate. 'I'll pass the details of our chat to the inspector.'

'Then I'll bid you good day,' said Miss Woodruff, turning to walk away.

'Oh, one last thing.' Mrs Bramble watched her turn back. 'I take it you won't have heard of a gentleman by the name of Dr Peregrine Frizzell?'

Mrs Bramble thought she saw a flicker of recognition, but Miss Woodruff made a show of pulling a lace handkerchief from her sleeve and dabbing her nose. A distraction, perhaps?

'Should I?' came Miss Woodruff's clipped response.

'Perhaps not.'

'Hmm,' said Miss Woodruff again, and Mrs Bramble watched her go, convinced Miss Woodruff knew more about her father's affairs than she was prepared to let on, although her disinterest in Mildred had seemed genuine.

# 23

After resisting the urge to follow Miss Woodruff to the river and scan the embankments for signs of the housemaids, Mrs Bramble returned to her empty apartment, hoping Kitty's magic was working on Mildred, the Woodruffs' maid.

'Oh!' She jumped as a head popped around the door of the parlour.

'I do beg your pardon, Mrs Bramble,' said Joan, coming into the room, wiping her hands on a cloth.

Mrs Bramble put her hand to her chest as though to calm her racing heart. 'Joan, you caught me unawares. I'd forgotten you were here.'

'Sorry 'bout that. I didn't mean to make you jump.'

'I'm sure you didn't.' She gave the cook a concerned look. 'Are you well?'

Joan curtsied. 'Still feeling a bit dicky, but I'm on the mend.'

'No need to curtsey, Joan.' Mrs Bramble smiled. 'We may both be women, but I'm afraid neither of us are considered ladies.'

'Unfair, is that.' Joan shook her head sadly. 'In this day and age.' Then she looked up, bright-eyed. 'I'm making a pie for you and Rosie. Chicken. Least I could do for looking after me. Rosie said it'd be all right by you.'

'Of course,' said Mrs Bramble. She was used to Rosie's cooking but knew that none of the grace-and-favour ladies would employ bad cooks. 'And you can stay with us until Lady Emelia needs you again, which I'm sure will be quite soon.'

Joan went to curtsey again but seemingly remembered and nodded instead. 'I could do you a sandwich for your lunch, if you'd like?' A cloud seemed to darken her features. 'Miss Franklin was partial to a sandwich. Never seemed to have time for a proper meal, that one.' She glanced at the clock. 'I almost forgot – when Rosie went out, she said she might not be back for a while and told me to tell you she'd come looking for you if she had any news. Don't know what she meant, but there 'tis.'

'I know exactly what she meant,' said Mrs Bramble, moving towards the door. 'You haven't seen Inspector Cole and Reverend Weaver, have you?'

'No, Mrs Bramble. I was in the land of nod a long time – knocked right out, I was – and I haven't seen no one but you and Rosie since I woke up.'

'Ah, not to worry. I'll have the sandwich later, if I may?'

Mrs Bramble left by the front door and strode straight across the courtyard, no longer concerned about whom she might encounter. One of the many niggles that had been eating away at her for many hours had given her a notion, and a talk with a certain few of the ladies might help to throw more light on the conundrum.

As she passed through George II's Gateway, she stopped dead. The green door to her left led to Lady Ives' apartment and she fancied the knowledge had dislodged a thought elsewhere in her brain. She waited a few seconds to pin it down and remembered the 'Wet Paint' sign from the night before. She looked to see where she might have kicked it, but it had gone.

In that perverse way that draws people to confirm things for themselves regardless of the potential consequences, like checking a plate is hot having been told it is, she touched the door with her fingers to see if the fresh paint was wet or dry. It had the not-quite-smooth, not-quite-sticky feel of the recently dried and her fingers came away clean, but something Lady Madeleine had said came back to her.

In spite of funny looks from a group of visitors who bundled through the gateway chattering like troop of macaque monkeys, she bent to inspect the door and found what she was looking for. The smudgy imprint of a finger marred the glossy finish near the door handle.

She still wanted to speak to Mrs Ewan, but with a host of activities designed to keep boredom at bay for high-born ladies of leisure, there could be no telling who was where at any given time of the day. Coffee mornings, luncheons, afternoon tea, high tea, dinners and suppers, not to mention opportunities for gardening, walking in the Privy Garden, card schools, croquet and tennis kept them occupied. It seemed as though most of the ladies of the palace almost never stayed in their own apartments.

While still bent over, her face near the handle and keyhole, the door opened and she looked up to find Lady Ives looking at her with a quizzical expression. She couldn't help observing the woman's nose to be a more suitable colour for her face today than the alcohol-fuelled beacon it had been during Lady Venetia's gala.

'Mrs Bramble,' said Lady Ives, surprise in her voice. 'I espied you crossing the courtyard and hoped I'd catch you, but I did not expect to see you in such a position when I opened the door.'

Mrs Bramble's cheeks coloured as she tried to cover her embarrassment at being found snooping. 'I saw you'd had your door painted but noticed a blemish and thought it might be as a result of shoddy workmanship.'

'Really?' Lady Ives looked towards the handle. 'Oh, I didn't notice, so never mind.' She glanced over her shoulder and back at Mrs Bramble. 'Have you a spare moment to look at something for me? I would like your impartial opinion.'

'I—' Mrs Bramble tried to decline but found herself being steered into the stairwell and ushered upstairs.

Lord knows what the woman wanted, but it was a long time since she'd set foot inside this apartment and the invitation aroused her curiosity.

A pungent tang, one she'd experienced recently, stung her nostrils as they climbed, increasing to an unpleasant intensity at the top. She followed Lady Ives into a room in which wallpaper decorated with delicate flowers hung above waist-high wood panelling. It looked like it should have been a parlour or bedroom, but the smell was strongest here and the paraphernalia on show explained everything.

Drawings and paintings adorned the walls, some framed and some not, like an art gallery undecided about what constituted a masterpiece worth displaying. Many tubes of oil paint in a variety of colours, two with their lids left off and thus inviting the air to dry them out, lay in several open boxes. More tubes lay on the shelves of two six-foot tripod easels. A splay of artist's brushes, with the hairs uppermost, stood in one old jam jar like a display of tropical flowers. Another jar held a similar cluster of brushes, this time with the hairs facing down, submerged in two inches of a dirty brown liquid Mrs Bramble assumed was paint-thinning turpentine; the source of the smell. As an artist's studio, it had everything you could want.

'Here you are,' said Lady Ives, indicating a half-finished painting secured to the nearest of the two easels. 'What do you think of this one?'

Whatever Mrs Bramble had expected, it hadn't been this. She'd had no inkling Lady Ives had taken up this particular pastime, assuming it took time and patience and the type of character Lady Ives had never struck her as having. The painting itself was a mish-mash of browns, reds and greys with a splash of blue, a single glance at the view through the windows giving Mrs Bramble the one clue as to the subject. She squinted, attempting to get a greater sense of what the erratic and haphazard marks might be trying to represent.

'It's a study of Clock Court?' said Mrs Bramble speculatively.

'Splendid.' Lady Ives clapped her hands. 'And what about this one?'

Feeling like she had passed some kind of test, Mrs Bramble turned her attention to the second easel. This painting, with its delicate blue sky, grey-brown paths and layered foliage in hues of green, although looking so much better because she'd seen the other poor effort first, did leave her impressed.

'It's rather good,' she said. 'Even though it's not finished, I can tell it's the Pond Garden.'

'Yes,' said Lady Ives, clapping her hands. 'I told Mrs Ewan she was better than she realised and should have more confidence in her ability. She's a natural, don't you agree?'

'Well . . .' Mrs Bramble didn't know what to say.

She wasn't sure about Mrs Ewan being a natural, but the fact that it came from her hands surprised her even more than learning Lady Ives was an artist – of sorts. The paintings did explain the flecks she'd seen on the dresses of the two ladies, and the odour she had smelled in Mrs Ewan's apartment. Perhaps that was why she had kept rubbing her fingers. Maybe the turpentine used to thin the oil paint and clean brushes and fingers had dried her ageing skin, causing irritation and itching.

'Will Mrs Ewan be painting today?' asked Mrs Bramble.

169

'I'm afraid not. She's meeting Mrs Woodruff in the Privy Garden for a stroll.'

After recent disputes, this surprised Mrs Bramble, although perhaps the two ladies did have something in common. She had received complaints about both Mrs Ewan's and Mrs Woodruff's reception of what some of their neighbours in Master Carpenter's Court considered excessive visitors.

'Are they friends again?' said Mrs Bramble.

Lady Ives smiled. 'We're all friends. We may argue and complain, but we are no different to one big family living in one big house. Siblings and friends are bound to quarrel from time to time, aren't they?'

Mrs Bramble managed a wan smile in response. She would prefer to have them be one big *happy* family to make her life easier, rather than one forced to rub along together with the friction and hotspots the situation so often caused. An extended version of the less-than-happy one she had grown up in.

'I'd best see if I can catch Mrs Ewan while I can.' Mrs Bramble gave a respectful nod. 'I'll see myself out, Lady Ives.'

# 24

Mrs Bramble found her way through the orangery to the Privy Garden without further incident and began her search for Mrs Ewan and Mrs Woodruff, but it soon became clear she would not enjoy instant success. Having once been the preserve of palace residents, the Privy Garden had been opened to everyone the year before and proved popular with the general public. A number of palace ladies and their companions had also chosen this time of day to take their health-giving constitutionals, making the garden particularly busy.

Despite Mrs Ewan's unique dress sense recalling the Elizabethan style, often recognisable from a distance, she favoured the current fashion for austere simplicity and dark colours when venturing out to the palace gardens and beyond, as most of the ladies did. One avenue for displaying individuality was through the type, size and colour of parasols they owned, carried open whether necessary or not – a practice Mrs Bramble saw as ridiculous.

Bonnets and hats represented another, and these could be worn towards the front or back of the head, tilted to one side, befeathered, covered in ripples of silk or adorned with flowers. Most of the elderly ladies seemed to favour holding them in place with ribbons tied under the chin, while the younger ladies preferred long hatpins to secure them.

In addition, the baroque garden of William III's reign had become lost as the topiary trees and shrubbery went unclipped and took the opportunity to flourish unbounded. Verdant foliage and bushes lined the paths and filled flower beds both established and recent, forming pathways, screens and shady spots where those seeking private conversation or quiet contemplation could saunter.

All of this made finding the two ladies a most complicated affair and left Mrs Bramble with two choices. She could either wait for them to return, which could take an age if they had not long arrived, or enter the garden in search of them. Time was ticking away, she had other duties to perform and, in her opinion, the investigation could not be left in the sole hands of Inspector Cole.

This made up her mind for her and she stepped forwards, taking the main avenue stretching in a straight line to the far end of the garden. She politely greeted ladies she recognised, trying to look purposeful rather than engaged in leisure or surveillance, and huffed in frustration every time she passed a couple who looked promising but turned out to be strangers. A number of benches placed throughout the garden offered comfort if one wished to tarry longer, but Mrs Ewan or Mrs Woodruff occupied none that she passed.

Mrs Bramble paused in a large open area, a circular pond with a fountain at its centre. Being halfway along, this marked the crossing point of a shorter path, forming the arms of a cross, but still no one resembling the ladies she sought stood out. Two smaller paths, not part of the original layout, ran parallel to the main avenue back to the orangery, but she left those for later.

*If I wanted to be out of earshot, where would I go first?* she pondered, and looked towards the gates and railings separating the garden from the Thames towpath. *Down by the river*, she decided.

Another open circle marked the furthest point from the palace, away from the throngs of visitors who couldn't be bothered to venture beyond the spectacle of the fountain. Two old ladies pausing there would appear to casual observers as taking in the fresh air while appreciating the river view.

Mrs Bramble walked cautiously along the tree-lined avenue in that direction, slowing as she approached the open area where a large circle of grass displayed a white marble statue of the Greek god Apollo at its centre. A couple conversed over by the ornate railings, one partially obscured by the statue's plinth and the other Mrs Bramble recognised by the pale green parasol she carried. Both wore dark bonnets with bright feathers, tied under their chins with ribbons.

As she took the circular path skirting the grass, the other person came into full sight. Mrs Woodruff put her parasol to one side and leaned in as she spoke to the partially deaf Mrs Ewan in a way that suggested she would prefer to do so than raise her voice and be overheard. Despite this, so engrossed were they that Mrs Bramble was able to move within earshot without either of them noticing.

'It sounded like a man to me,' said Mrs Woodruff.

'To me, too, dear,' Mrs Ewan agreed.

'Then again, I heard the tapping of a cane ... Like the one you use.' Mrs Woodruff raised her eyebrows accusingly.

'Well, don't look at me.' Mrs Ewan put her hand to her chest to avoid any confusion about who she meant. 'As I told the inspector, I heard the murderer outside as he arrived.'

The conversation intrigued Mrs Bramble. Why was Mrs Woodruff still accusing Mrs Ewan when the inspector had made his favoured theory known? What could she have to gain by continuing to cast aspersions to the point where she almost seemed to be trying to convince her grace-and-favour neighbour that she, Mrs Ewan, must have committed the crime? The cause couldn't be lingering animosity over the issue of excessive visitors, which they had in common, or the saga of whether the installation of a bath should be paid for by the Crown or the individual, could it?

'It must have been one of the entertainers.' Mrs Woodruff raised her nose haughtily. 'Funny people, entertainers.'

'A rum lot, I'm sure.'

'What about the music hall fellow?'

Mrs Ewan scoffed. 'Dreadful suit and poor jokes, but that doesn't mark him as a murderer.'

'It does in my book.'

'Oh, come now, Flora.'

Mrs Bramble had to agree with Mrs Ewan. All the entertainers had been gathered in the Great Watching Chamber at one end of the Great Hall, chaperoned during the show and accounted for at the conclusion of the evening's entertainment. Not one of them had the opportunity to sneak off. In any case, they could not have broken into Mrs Chafford's apartment because the palace gates had been closed after they had been escorted to their accommodation beyond the walls.

She gave a small cough to alert the ladies to her approach and they jerked apart, trying to conceal guilty expressions.

'Mrs Bramble,' said Mrs Woodruff, the light flashing off her Blue John ring as she nervously scratched the mole on her upper lip. What brings you to this end of the garden at this time of day?' Her tone made it sound like an accusation.

'I am glad I found you two ladies together,' said Mrs Bramble, catching a faint whiff of turpentine from Mrs Ewan, even in the open air. 'Inspector Cole is still pursuing his inquiries in a most haphazard way and I need to clarify something on his

174

behalf.' Her expression of innocence never wavered as the white lie tripped off her tongue.

'I'm sure the inspector will speak to us if he needs to,' said Mrs Woodruff.

Although true, Mrs Bramble pressed on anyway. 'The inspector is quite busy, making more work for himself than is strictly necessary, in my book, but that is men of importance for you.'

The ladies nodded in agreement.

'I would be surprised if the inspector even bothers to leave the palace walls, let alone venture this far into any of the gardens.'

More knowing nods from the ladies.

'What is it we can do for you and the inspector, Mrs Bramble?' asked Mrs Ewan.

Mrs Bramble glanced back along the avenue towards the fountain and the palace beyond as though about to speak conspiratorially. 'You both heard someone passing through Master Carpenter's Court at the time the murderer was abroad. Is there anything you remember today that you may not have recalled yesterday?'

'Such as?' said Mrs Woodruff. 'I spoke to you and the inspector and told the both of you everything I knew.'

'As did I,' said Mrs Ewan.

'And very helpful that has been,' said Mrs Bramble. The ladies looked affronted, but she hoped they would remain co-operative. 'Perhaps if I explain. Mrs Ewan, you said you saw a figure in the courtyard but could not make out who it was.'

'Correct.'

'And you said they wore ... a dark cloak, was it?'

'That is also correct. I am sure it was a cloak.'

'No top hat, bowler or flat cap?'

'Oh, I don't know.' Mrs Ewan looked surprised at her lack

of detailed recall. 'Definitely not a top hat. I would have noticed. Maybe something flatter ...' She didn't sound hopeful.

Mrs Bramble paused for a second. Mrs Ewan had seen someone, no question, but a court would convict on points of accurate fact. If whoever it was had not been wearing a top hat of the kind a gentleman might wear, maybe it had not been one of Miss Franklin's usual visitors. Although less unusual these days for a businessman to wear a bowler, Mrs Ewan had noticed the inspector wearing one upon his arrival, so would have recognised the rounded profile.

'They also carried an umbrella,' said Mrs Bramble. A wearer of a flat cap might suggest something underhand, given the time of night, but that seemed less certain if they carried an umbrella.

'I believe so,' said Mrs Ewan.

'Believe, or know?'

'Are you questioning my integrity, Mrs Bramble?' Mrs Ewan frowned and looked down her nose.

'Not at all, Mrs Ewan. I didn't mean to imply anything of the sort,' said Mrs Bramble, still hoping to keep the woman amenable. 'As you know, the lighting is not good in the courtyard, so I wanted to confirm your recollection.'

'Hmm.'

The non-committal response left Mrs Bramble unconvinced. 'Is there a possibility the figure you saw may have been a woman?'

'Good Lord, no.' Mrs Ewan seemed almost amused by the suggestion. 'A *lady* would not have been out alone at that time of night.'

*Puts me in my place*, thought Mrs Bramble. She turned to Mrs Woodruff, who returned a furtive glance.

'Mrs Woodruff, you told me you heard a person pass through the courtyard three times, tapping a cane as they went.'

'I did,' said Mrs Woodruff, twiddling the silver Blue John ring on the little finger of her right hand.

Mrs Bramble noticed a green tinge to the red inflammation on the skin beneath the ring.

'Can you think of an explanation for why you heard it three times? Wouldn't you expect the murderer to arrive once and depart once?'

'I suppose. I hadn't given it that much thought.'

From the conversation she had heard on arrival, Mrs Bramble knew that to be a lie.

'It *was* a cane you heard, I suppose?'

'What do you mean?' Mrs Woodruff looked confused.

'Could it have been an umbrella, like Mrs Ewan stated?'

Mrs Woodruff scoffed. 'I shouldn't think so.' She held up her parasol as illustration. 'An umbrella is not a sturdy instrument at the best of times, whereas a cane is solid. They make quite different sounds when tapped on a stone floor ...'

She hesitated and Mrs Bramble saw something pass across her face.

'But now you mention it, it could have been an umbrella, I suppose.'

She averted her gaze and Mrs Bramble took this as a sign of another lie.

'Do you think it could have been a woman, Mrs Woodruff?'

Mrs Woodruff gave her a sharp look and shook her head. 'Don't be ridiculous. Ladies are not in the habit of striding about late at night dressed like men. In addition, the tapping of canes noisily on stone floors for the fun of it would not have been thought inconsiderate by most of the so-called gentlemen I have met.'

Whoever the prowler had been, Mrs Bramble doubted *for the fun of it* had featured in their thinking.

'I'm sure you are correct,' Mrs Bramble said, not wishing to push her luck.

As the astronomical clock in the palace chimed the quarter-hour, she conceded nothing more could be gleaned from these ladies and her thoughts turned elsewhere.

'Do you happen to know where Lady Madeleine is, by any chance?'

'I have no idea,' said Mrs Ewan.

'Nor I,' said Mrs Woodruff. Her lip curled. 'Why, are you going to interrogate her, too?'

'Only about her cockatoo,' Mrs Bramble lied.

# 25

Mrs Bramble left the two ladies to their post-mortem of the conversation and took a side path running parallel to the main avenue to avoid being further waylaid about domestic issues. Along here she spotted a gardener tending one of the flower beds. Although unsure of his name, she recognised him from around the palace and a thought crossed her mind.

'Good day,' she said.

The gardener stopped work and popped his head above the foliage, wide-eyed and curious to see who had greeted him.

'Oh. Mrs Bramble. Good day to you, too. Can I help you?'

'Perhaps.' She glanced up and down the path to check for eavesdroppers. 'I know there are a number of you dotted here-abouts, but do you know who might have provided Dr Kemp with rat poison?'

'Rat poison?' The gardener gave the wispy beard on his chin a stroke. 'You'd be best off speaking to Billy, I reckon.'

'Billy?'

'He sees to most of the rats and mice around the palace, so he'd know all about poisoning 'em.'

'And where can I find Billy?'

'It's gone quarter past, so I'd try the Wilderness if I were you, 'cause he might be tending to the cherry trees. It ain't easy keeping all the pests off the fruit and vegetables, let me tell you. Full-time job, it is, and that's not even counting the rodents, rabbits and moles.' Another stroke of the chin. 'Yep. Billy's your best bet.'

Mrs Bramble thanked the man, watched his head disappear back behind the foliage and set off towards the Wilderness.

The Wilderness was once Henry VIII's vast orchard before Charles II converted it into a pleasure garden for his courtiers. Situated on the north side of the palace beyond the Tudor tennis court, it now provided a less formal area to be enjoyed by all. Mrs Bramble knew the wide open-air paths around the buildings to be the quickest and easiest route, and hoped striding with apparent purpose would deter potential interruptions and afford her a better chance of reaching her destination unhindered.

No such luck.

Mrs McGowan and her perpetual companion, Miss Cameron-Banks, waddled out of the east entrance facing the Great Fountain Garden and spotted her immediately. Arms linked, and as in step as soldiers changing the guard at Buckingham Palace, they took a line to intercept.

'Mrs Bramble,' said Mrs McGowan as both she and her companion blocked the way.

'Ladies,' said Mrs Bramble, brighter than she felt but a lot less luminous than the piercing blue of Mrs McGowan's eyes. 'Out for your daily constitutional?'

'Indeed,' said Mrs McGowan with a pout. 'Some enjoy spacious accommodation' – the jibe did not go unnoticed by Mrs Bramble – 'but when one has been allocated a pokey hole in which to exist—'

'One has to stretch the legs,' Miss Cameron-Banks interjected, 'when one can—'

'And take the fresh air where one can get it. We heard about—'

'—that dreadful incident. Not to mention—'

'—last night's to-do. The murderer came back, we hear?'

Both ladies raised their eyebrows and leaned in, hoping to hear more. Not having the energy to engage in a long conversation, Mrs Bramble took half a step backwards. *They* may have been ladies of leisure, but she was not and certain things needed attending to.

'I believe Inspector Cole has the investigation progressing,' said Mrs Bramble with a steely gaze. 'Would it not be better to see what transpires rather than speculate about what may or may not have occurred last night? After all, *we* were asleep in our beds, were we not?'

'Of course,' said Mrs McGowan with a sweet smile. 'I only ask because you are at the beating heart of the palace.'

'Hardly so, Mrs McGowan,' said Mrs Bramble. 'The palace superintendent would have something to say about that.'

'Talking of whom, my brother may be returning to these shores from Africa in the not-so-distant future and will wish to speak with the superintendent about our circumstances.' She tilted her head to indicate her companion.

'Circumstances,' her companion repeated on cue.

A jolt went through Mrs Bramble like a lightning strike. 'Africa?'

'South Africa, to be exact,' said Mrs McGowan.

'Your brother is called Perry?' She recalled a conversation from the previous day.

'That's correct.' Mrs McGowan frowned.

'Short for Peregrine?'

'Mrs Bramble. Are you quite all right?'

Mrs Bramble touched her forehead in realisation. This shed

a different light on these women and the murder of two nights ago. 'Frizzell is your maiden name?'

'The family name, yes. McGowan is my married name.'

'I never knew.'

'Why should you?' said Mrs McGowan, giving Mrs Bramble a look of suspicion. 'It is of no consequence to you or anybody else.'

Mrs Bramble composed herself and shook her head. 'No, of course not. All I meant was, it is remarkable how close together we all live in this place without ever knowing much about the people around us. But you are correct; everyone's business is their own.'

Mrs McGowan's smile didn't touch her eyes and without the customary concluding pleasantries, she turned towards the garden to continue her walk, jolting her surprised companion in the process. Mrs Bramble watched them go, Miss Cameron-Banks falling in step with Mrs McGowan, before resuming her own journey.

So, Mrs McGowan's brother, Perry, was Peregrine Frizzell, investor and manager at the Blue Eland Gold & Diamond Mining Company. This fact alone justified adding the two ladies to the list of potential suspects. After all, if the mine was failing, putting the company on the verge of collapse and its investors in danger of bankruptcy, it could be why he was returning home. If the Frizzells blamed the Chaffords, that would be a motive for murder.

Mrs Bramble found it difficult to imagine Mrs McGowan or Miss Cameron-Banks committing murder, and never with a letter opener, but that didn't preclude them from having employed someone to do so on their behalf. Maybe Peregrine had taken matters into his own hands, perhaps literally.

She emitted tuts and huffs of annoyance as she wove in and out of tourists who seemed incapable of adhering to one side of the path, walking in a straight line or looking where they were going, their lack of attention and consideration for other pedestrians preventing her from concentrating. Her greatest irritations were the telegrams she had sent, which had yet to elicit replies, and the post-mortem on Miss Franklin, about which she had heard nothing further. In a modern industrialised world where fast travel and communications connected all corners of the British Empire, it often seemed to her that the slow pace of the Middle Ages had not been entirely left behind.

She turned left through urn-topped stone columns supporting sturdy wooden gates giving access to the area known as the Wilderness and stopped. It was a big area to search, with paths going off in three directions and no gardeners in sight. *Is it worth it?* she wondered. She needed to get back to the palace, to be in view even if not in fact doing palace work, but a quick look around wouldn't go amiss, seeing as she had come this far.

Her choice of the path straight ahead soon proved fruitful. The handles of a wheelbarrow came into view to one side, before the deep tray and single wheel, and the soles of a workman's boots as he kneeled among the foliage.

A clump of leafy green weed, not unlike flat-leafed parsley but with a white root resembling an immature parsnip, arced back with a spray of soil and landed in the tray amid other clumps.

'Excuse me,' said Mrs Bramble.

'Don't touch!' the gardener snapped. He stopped and squatted on his heels, a muddy trowel in his gloved hand.

'I had no such intention,' she said, taken aback at his abruptness.

'Oh, my apologies,' the man said. 'Didn't mean to shout.'

'No need to do that,' she said at the sight of him touching the peak of his flat cap. 'I'm not a society lady.'

'A lady nonetheless.' He smiled.

He had the handsome face of a man in his early thirties and the muscley arms of a man not unused to physical work, but Mrs Bramble didn't flinch, being used to ruggedly handsome soldiers far more practised in the art of insincere flattery.

He inclined his head towards the wheelbarrow. 'It don't belong in a place like this. Some thinks this is chervil, but I know it ain't and it won't do you any good, so I gotta weed it out and get rid. Thought you were after some for your soup.'

'Of course not,' she said, because it seemed the most non-committal response. 'I'm looking for Billy.'

The man smiled. 'You've found him.'

'Excellent.' She returned his smile. 'My name is Mrs Bramble and I am Lady Housekeeper at the palace.'

'Ah,' he said. 'Knew I'd seen you round and about, but we don't mix too much with the insiders.'

Although true, she also remembered seeing him before. 'One of the men in the Privy Garden said I might find you here.'

'Did he now? What business did he have telling you that?'

'I have a question he couldn't answer but said you might.'

Billy wiped his hands on a rag. 'You can ask.'

Mrs Bramble kept her smile fixed in place, despite being irked by the casual offer of permission to speak when she had no intention of doing anything other than giving voice to her question.

'Someone told me you are the man to see about getting rid of garden pests.'

'I might be. What's the problem?'

She ignored the question. 'Do you remember supplying Dr Kemp with rat poison?'

He swept off his cap and scratched his head. 'Kemp? Aye, I do, as it so happens. I'd hurt my eye tending to the cherry trees a few weeks ago and it felt like something had taken up

184

residence in there. He passed by on his palace rounds, so I asked if he could get it out for me.

'He obliged but said he had a mouse infestation at his surgery and offered to waive his fee if I could sort it out. I ain't got a minute to myself at this time of year, or any time, if truth be told, but we came to an arrangement.

'He's a smart man, so I gave him a small amount, told him how to use it in safety and let him get on with it.' He donned his cap and looked at her. 'Why? He ain't poisoned himself or his patients, has he?'

'No, thank goodness, nothing like that.' Mrs Bramble's inclination to keep Dr Kemp on her list was waning, but a small doubt still lingered. 'What type of poison was it?'

Billy eyed her quizzically. 'That's a strange question for the Lady Housekeeper to ask.'

Mrs Bramble gave him her best benign smile but said nothing.

He shrugged. 'Paris Green, if you must know.'

'Oh, I've heard of Paris Green.'

'Got to watch yourself because of the copper and arsenic in it. If you're not careful, you can end up making yourself ill instead of killing rats.'

'Is it the only rat poison you use?'

Billy shook his head. 'We use several types, including arsenic on its own if need be, so they won't get used to it. If they gets used to it, it don't work so well. We try to hide the traps so the delicate ladies and visitors don't see them. A dead rat is just as frightening as a live one to some folk.'

'I'm sure it is,' she said, having seen worse things in her life than rats. 'Well, Billy, I thank you. You've been most helpful.'

'I'm glad to hear it.' He smiled and touched his cap in salute. 'Please give my regards to Mildred, if you see her.' He winked. 'And you know where to find me if you need me.' He smiled again and she left him to his weeding.

185

She mulled over the corroboration of Dr Kemp's account of how and why he had acquired the rodent poison, and the uncovering of an interesting fact. The common form of arsenic was available throughout the palace if one cared to look for it. With its odourless and tasteless properties being common knowledge, surely arsenic presented a would-be murderer with a more effective method of poisoning than the highly detectable Paris Green.

With this knowledge weighing in Dr Kemp's favour, a chess piece slid across her mind into position.

Time to question the ladies again.

# 26

Mrs Bramble made her way back through the palace on the lookout for Lady Madeleine, making sure she was seen to be attending to her duties. Her heart sank when she saw Inspector Cole in the cloister by the Tudor servery, a flustered-looking Reverend Weaver at his shoulder.

'Mrs Bramble,' said Cole. 'I'm so glad I caught you.'

'I'm glad I'm easier prey than the murderer,' she replied icily. 'I take it he hasn't been unmasked?'

Cole removed his bowler and swept his fingers back through his thinning hair in obvious irritation. 'I have questioned everybody, twice, with this idi—' He paused and replaced his bowler. 'With Reverend Weaver as my constant shadow.'

'I'm sure you make a great team,' she said, employing her sweetest smile and seeing Weaver smirk.

'I admit, the reverend's knowledge of the palace is indeed useful.' He inclined his head at Weaver in thanks. 'However, his procrastination, hesitation and deviation from the task at hand, not to mention his flights of fancy, are a waste of my time and most distracting.'

Weaver's smile became a toothy grin. 'The pleasure is all mine, Inspector.'

Cole gave Weaver a sidelong glance as though unsure

whether his behaviour was innate or by design. He looked back at Mrs Bramble. 'It seems you are ahead of me every time, despite our agreement that you should stick to your job and let me do mine.'

'That was your agreement, Inspector,' she said with as much innocence as she could manage. 'It is my royal duty as Lady Housekeeper of Hampton Court Palace to speak to the grace-and-favour residents, address their concerns and see to their needs, so far as they come within my remit.'

'And what is your remit?' he almost growled.

'Between the palace superintendent and me, as I'm sure he will confirm, pretty much anything and everything that occurs within the grounds and confines of the palace.'

Cole gritted his teeth and shook his head, a conflicting expression of defeat and determination on his face. 'Where's the damn sergeant? I've been looking for him all morning.'

'Catching up on his beauty sleep, I shouldn't wonder, seeing as you dismissed him after keeping him up all night.'

Cole's cheeks coloured. 'How the devil did you know ...?'

'As I said, I'm the Lady Housekeeper. I know everything that goes on here. Except who the intruder was, of course. That's your job. Word gets around in a place like this and if facts and results aren't forthcoming, the ladies and staff tend to make up their own minds.'

'And false stories.'

She stared at him as if to suggest the blame rested with him. 'I hear the sergeant performed admirably but being left alone, at night, in this rabbit warren of a palace, hampered him.' She knew other palace police would have been patrolling elsewhere, but the inspector did not because he hadn't bothered to use the sergeant or his resources to the best advantage. 'Were your lodgings comfortable?'

Cole said nothing and paced away a few feet. She could see

his shoulders rise and fall as he took deep breaths, suspecting with some amusement he might be counting to ten. He wheeled around and paced back, his anger under control.

'Was anything taken last night?' she asked, as though commenting on nothing more important than the weather.

'No,' said Cole. 'Lady Emelia's housemaid has been checked.'

'One blessing, at least.'

'May I ask, what else have you found out since we last spoke?' he said.

Mrs Bramble saw the conflict within the inspector and the effort it took for him to ask nicely and decided giving him something wouldn't hurt.

'I have another potential suspect. One of our ladies, Mrs McGowan, has a brother called Perry. Her maiden name is Frizzell.'

'Perry,' Cole said, his expression changing slowly as the penny dropped. 'Peregrine Frizzell.'

She nodded. 'The manager of the Blue Eland mining company, mentioned in the files I gave you.'

'So, we have another one who might have borne a grudge against Miss Franklin about the failing investments.'

'Exactly.' Mrs Bramble put her hand in her pocket and pulled out the business card. 'I found this in a book in Miss Franklin's study.'

Cole took the card and studied the front and back. 'The Gunpowder Club. I've heard of it but never had cause to be interested.'

'I believe all the investors met each other there. I'm not sure that's significant in any way, but you never know.' Mrs Bramble reached into her pocket. 'And there's this.' She produced her handkerchief and unwrapped it to display the bloodstain and hatpin. 'I found it this morning, discarded on the ground by the door to Lady Emelia's apartment, and I also noticed the keyhole displayed fresh scratches and a smear of blood. I suspect last night's intruder used this to pick the lock, pricking a finger in the process, and dropped it when confronted by the sergeant.'

Cole frowned as he pocketed the evidence. 'You could not have given me these earlier?'

'You are the first policeman I have seen all day.'

Cole sighed. 'Anything *else*?'

'I have a few things running around in my head but nothing I can be sure of,' said Mrs Bramble. 'Nothing worth sharing with you at present.' She raised an eyebrow. 'Do you have anything for me?'

Cole jabbed a thumb over his shoulder. 'I'm sure Reverend Spy will fill you in. I'm going to get something to eat.' He put up his hand to stop Weaver from following. 'I prefer to dine alone with my thoughts, Reverend. For pity's sake, please allow me five minutes to myself.'

Mrs Bramble and Reverend Weaver stepped to the side out of the way of a group of palace visitors, one of whom was with child and pretty far along. She held the arm of her husband, both holding their heads high as though proud of their achievement. When Mrs Bramble turned back, Cole had walked off alone.

'Reverend Spy,' said Weaver with a crooked smile. 'I like that.'

'How has he been?' said Mrs Bramble.

'Tetchier by the minute,' he said. 'He threatened to arrest me and lock me in the village cells at one point, but he knew some of the ladies wouldn't have spoken to him had I not been there to introduce him.'

'The poor man, he's only doing his job.' Mrs Bramble chuckled. 'Did you find out anything else?'

'He's spoken to everyone and anyone, which has been quite

exhausting, but I have no idea whether he feels any closer to apprehending the murderer than first thing this morning.' His eyes widened. 'Oh, he spoke to Lady Venetia about her gala entertainments evening and was satisfied she and those around her are in the clear.

'Mind you, he can't seem to shake himself from the idea that an outside burglar broke in and murdered Miss Franklin and came back last night to finish off Lady Emelia. He spoke to her again, too, but all she said was that she stands to inherit all the money, or what's left of it, plus the investments her late husband left in the hands of her sister.'

'It all goes to her?'

'Apparently so.' His eyes widened further. 'I say, Mrs Bramble, does that put her at the top of the list again?'

'Money is a great motivator and motive for murder, but Lady Emelia seemed content to allow her sister to deal with all the financial affairs she had no interest in or aptitude for. Why would she kill her now? Don't forget, Lady Emelia, Rosie and Joan corroborated each other's account of what happened when they got back from the Great Hall, and I witnessed the study door locked with the key inside.'

'It's quite the conundrum, isn't it?' said Weaver.

'Could the inspector at least be correct about the murderer climbing through the window? After all, it was left open, which you'd be likely to do if you were intent on escaping quickly that way.'

Mrs Bramble pondered this for a moment, unable yet to discount the possibility fully, despite growing evidence to the contrary. 'In my opinion, given what we've learned and the number of people who would still have been about at that time, I think it unlikely.'

'Then I suppose discovering the solution must be rather like looking at a pond,' said Weaver. 'If you stare at the surface

191

long enough, eventually you'll focus on the fish swimming below.'

Mrs Bramble narrowed her eyes. Maybe Weaver had something and the answer really could prove rather simple.

'Do you want me to stay with the inspector after his lunch?' said Weaver.

She shook her head. 'That won't be necessary. I gave him almost all of the physical evidence I found and he has spoken to everyone I have. I hold high hopes our conclusions will tally.'

'In which case, what do we do next?'

'Another word with Lady Madeleine wouldn't go amiss, and I hope Lady Emelia might be able to shed more light on the mysterious Mr Peregrine Frizzell.'

# 27

As Mrs Bramble entered Master Carpenter's Court with Reverend Weaver, she spotted Miss Alice Woodruff entering the apartment she shared with her mother. Lady Madeleine's cockatoo, Sunny, could be heard screeching, 'Strumpet, strumpet,' but the time had not long ticked into early afternoon and as such lay outside any agreement reached about curtailing the bird's behaviour. No one answered the bell pull at Lady Emelia's apartment, so Mrs Bramble rang at Lady Madeleine's. A moment later, the maid let them in and showed them through to the parlour.

'Good day again,' greeted Lady Madeleine. 'It's always pleasant to receive visitors, even if it is the same ones over and over again.' Her genuine smile negated any suggestion of sarcasm. 'Do sit.'

Weaver accepted the invitation and lounged back on a two-seat settee, his mouth forming an O of surprise as he sank into copious cushions.

'What can I do for you this time?' said Lady Madeleine, picking a seed from her dress as Mrs Bramble perched on the edge of the cushion next to Weaver.

'More of the same, I'm afraid,' said Weaver apologetically from the depths of the soft furnishing.

That was true in a way. In Mrs Bramble's experience, allowing a short period for reflection before asking the same questions in a different way often elicited extra information from the innocent and compounded the lies of the guilty.

'Inspector Cole is on his own and still needs our help to follow up on certain aspects of his investigation,' she said. Although not an outright lie, neither did it represent the whole truth.

Lady Madeleine sat a little straighter. 'I'll do anything I can to help, of course.'

'Thank you. When we spoke yesterday morning, you said you had seen a figure wearing dark clothing in the courtyard at about nine o'clock the previous evening. Is there any other detail you can remember? Anything at all?'

'I'm not good with details, I'm afraid,' said Lady Madeleine. 'Not with these eyes.'

'What about something a little more obvious, such as a hat?' said Mrs Bramble. 'A topper, perhaps, or maybe featuring a lower profile like a bowler or a cap.'

'Not a top hat, but I wouldn't say as flat as a cap, either, or even a bowler.'

'What about a lady's hat?' said Weaver. 'They come in all sizes and can be mistaken for all sorts pinned atop piles of hair.'

Lady Madeleine gave him a look of pity as he tried and failed to sit forwards.

'You may be correct, Reverend, but your guess is as good as mine in this instance.'

Mrs Bramble narrowed her eyes. The testimonies of each witness had started to match the recall of others and make more sense. 'The figure carried an umbrella, you said before, but could it have been a walking stick or cane?'

'It could have been either, I suppose,' said Lady Madeleine.

She pouted. 'Come to think of it, he leaned heavily on whatever he held because the tapping on the stone ground was quite noticeable.'

'Not an umbrella, then?' said Weaver, gripping the end of the settee's arm for leverage.

'I really couldn't say. You're confusing me now.' She put her hand to her forehead for dramatic emphasis. 'All I can say for certain is, I saw someone in dark clothing, maybe wearing a cloak but not a top hat, carrying something sticklike and tapping the metal ferrule as they passed, followed by a knock-knock on a door, repeated.' She looked surprised at her sudden recall of this detail. 'Doesn't sound like the actions of a burglar or a murderer at all, does it?'

Mrs Bramble had to agree, but the coming and going, although witnessed by a few, had enough elements of concealment about it still to mark the mere presence of the figure as suspicious.

'I'm sure there's a simple enough explanation,' said Mrs Bramble.

The more she discovered, uncovered and corroborated, the more she felt certain a burglar or gentlemen business caller lay outside the scope of a rational solution. Inspector Cole's supposed experience as a Scotland Yard detective, a band of men revered around the world as the finest of their kind, should have counted for something. But after all the information she had collected and presented to him, she marvelled at his continuing reluctance to entertain alternative explanations.

She stood up to leave and the maid appeared, offering her hand to Weaver as he tried to extricate himself from the settee. Mrs Bramble extended hers, too, and he grasped it as they hauled the flustered reverend to his feet in a shower of cushions, apologies and thank-yous.

'Sorry for bothering you,' said Mrs Bramble. 'We appreciate your time and patience.'

'Not at all, not at all,' said Lady Madeleine. 'As I said, I'm glad to have someone to talk to other than Sunny; he doesn't say much at the best of times.'

The maid rolled her eyes at this and showed them to the front door.

Outside in the courtyard, they stood taking stock.

'I'm not sure Lady Madeleine added anything to what we already knew,' said Weaver, still smoothing the creases from his settee-crumpled jacket. 'Do you?'

'On the contrary, every little detail adds to the picture.' She glanced up at the Chaffords' apartment and noted the curtains still closed, signalling that it remained unoccupied. 'We're getting there, Reverend, but it's time we visited Lady Venetia's apartment, I think. For another talk with Lady Emelia.'

At the south-east corner of Fountain Court, Mrs Bramble and Reverend Weaver entered the stairwell at ground level, signalling the start of a long trek up many flights of stairs to the grace-and-favour apartments on the top floor.

A thin rope, hung from a winch bolted to the third-floor balustrade, dangled down the entire height of the stairwell and terminated in a hook. It was to this a basket laden with produce had been affixed, ready to be hauled up without the need to exert oneself further by lugging it up several flights of stairs. Far too many, complained Mrs Bramble as they trudged up stone step after stone step for what seemed like an eternity, holding onto the wooden handrail atop ornate ironwork for much-needed support.

Each floor was lit by a gas lamp to supplement the light dribbling down the stairwell from a skylight at the top and they stopped for a breather on the upper landings as the climb took its toll. The ceilings were much higher here than in Master Carpenter's Court and Mrs Bramble's knees complained at every step of the climb. She suspected she could have been across the river to the village by now for the same effort.

'Let me get my puff back,' she said as they paused on the third floor, fanning her face with her hands.

Weaver, short of breath himself but trying to conceal the fact, tried to smile but produced more of a grimace just before he tripped up the last step. With a cry, his hands shot out, searching for anything solid. He grabbed the balustrade one-handed next to the winch, which succeeded in spinning his body around until he came to rest on the floor with his legs splayed and his fingers still gripping the handrail.

Mrs Bramble went to his rescue, helping the blushing reverend to his feet, but she had no intention of brushing the dust from the seat of his trousers, a task she left for him to do. She made a note to speak to the maid about cleanliness.

Before they were ready to ring the bell outside Lady Venetia Merritt's apartment, the door opened and her housemaid rushed out, so focused she appeared not to notice them, and grasped the winding handle of the winch. The swinging basket drew higher at each turn, the ratchet clicking, and it took but a few seconds before it reached the top. The maid unhooked the basket and turned back.

'Oh!' she cried, covering her mouth with her free hand.

Weaver stepped back in alarm, recovered and moved forwards with concern. 'Are you all right, my dear? I'm afraid we've caught you unawares.'

'Goodness, Mrs Bramble, Reverend Weaver. I'm sorry.'

'It is us who should apologise,' said Mrs Bramble. 'You were absorbed in your duties and we made you jump.'

'True enough.' She patted her chest. 'My heart's going nineteen to the dozen. Don't get many visitors up here at this time of day, see.'

'Understandable.' Mrs Bramble smiled to calm and comfort the young woman. 'Is Lady Venetia at home?'

'I'm afraid not,' said the housemaid. 'Her Ladyship went for a late constitutional a while back, but she shouldn't be much longer, if you'd like to wait?'

Lady Venetia's absence was an added bonus for Mrs Bramble. She had no desire to speak to her while cornered in her apartment with no avenue of escape without appearing rude. Draughts and the inability of households to heat their apartments was a hot topic here in the baroque part of the palace and Lady Venetia had voiced strong opinions on the subject.

'Actually, it is Lady Emelia we have come to see, if she is still here?' said Mrs Bramble.

'You're in luck,' said the maid. 'Lady Emelia and Rosie are still here, but they're preparing to leave.' Her shoulders hunched defensively as her gaze flicked left and right as though searching for eavesdroppers. Then her voice lowered almost to a whisper. 'I heard what happened. Dreadful, truly dreadful. In this day and age, too.' Her piece said, she straightened up and stepped towards the apartment. 'If you'd like to follow me, I'll tell Her Ladyship you're here,' she said, looking a lot brighter.

The housemaid showed them to a high-ceilinged withdrawing room adorned with gilt-framed oil paintings on delicate blue plasterwork set above wood-panelled dados. Large windows flooded the room with light and afforded views across the Privy Garden to the River Thames. Chairs, settees and tables had been arranged in haphazard fashion on the large floor carpet, which had been positioned crookedly. There was no contemplation of the aesthetics, a fact that bothered Mrs Bramble's sensibility.

The baroque apartments had always seemed to her to be

far too large to be cosy in winter, as Lady Venetia attested, and a waste of space all in all. They did put those in Master Carpenter's Court to shame in terms of grandeur, which may have been the reason Lady Emelia had yet to return home, but Mrs Bramble considered her own apartment very comfortable. Although she had to admit that Reverend Weaver's rambling three-floor dwelling in one half of the Seymour Gate held its attractions.

The door opened and Lady Emelia swept into the room, opal pendant at her throat, looking a lot livelier than the last time Mrs Bramble had seen her. She and Weaver stood but retook their seats when waved to do so.

'Mrs Bramble and Reverend Weaver, what brings you to see me here?' said Lady Emelia.

She looked relaxed and Mrs Bramble could detect no outward sign of nervousness or distress. Her night spent here must have done her a world of good.

'Inspector Cole is still pursuing his inquiries, but I fear he may be following the wrong path,' said Mrs Bramble.

Lady Emelia looked no more than interested. 'How so?'

'In spite of his best efforts, he has been unable to discover the identity of the figure seen in the courtyard, or even establish that the person was a prowler at all.'

Lady Emelia's eyes narrowed almost imperceptibly. 'What has that to do with me?'

Mrs Bramble still detected no undue concern. 'Like everyone in the palace, I had not met the inspector before yesterday, so any impressions we have of him are based on our limited interactions with him over two days. I have no idea if he plays his cards close to his chest or wears his heart on his sleeve and can only base my judgement on what I see and hear.

'In my opinion, given that caveat, the inspector is turning away from the possibility that the person who murdered Miss

Franklin was an outside intruder and is returning to the possibility that they were already in the palace.'

'A domestic servant or workman, do you mean?'

Mrs Bramble gave a slight tilt of her head. 'Or a lady resident ...' She paused as the penny dropped.

'Me?' Her hand reached up to fiddle with her pendant. 'I am suspected once again?'

In Lady Emelia face, Mrs Bramble saw the first signs of doubt and concern, a not unreasonable reaction.

'We are not certain,' said Weaver, clasping his hands as if in prayer, 'but it does seem as though the inspector has returned to his first impression of the case since the break-in last night.' He raised a questioning eyebrow. 'Nothing was taken, I hear?'

'Rosie tells me so, and I trust her judgement.'

'Unusual, don't you agree? That someone would take the trouble to break in a second time but leave everything untouched.'

'Fortunate, I'd say. The sergeant chased him off.'

Mrs Bramble nodded her agreement and an awkward silence descended.

'Not that it carries any weight, but I am not convinced the inspector's current reasoning is sound,' said Mrs Bramble. 'A pile of financial papers found in your study listed a number of investors in a South African mine. It appears the mine has proven barren, leading to the possible failure of the venture and all that entails in terms of loss of investment capital, even bankruptcy.'

Lady Emelia's eyes looked dark as she considered this. 'I still don't know why that would taint me as someone who would kill her sister. A sister, I may add, who ran our business affairs since my husband died so tragically early.'

'Can you think of any reason why the inspector suspects you over and above any other person?'

200

'I cannot.' Lady Emelia gave a defiant tilt of her chin, looking down her nose at Mrs Bramble and the reverend. 'The death of my sister does not improve my position nor my financial standing. It does not win me a better apartment in this palace, nor does it secure my long-term future. In fact, it makes my lot materially worse for having lost my beloved sister and the one person on whom I could rely to keep us on an even keel. There is nothing beneficial to me about my sister's passing.'

Mrs Bramble could see tears forming in the woman's eyes. Although that could be the result of the net closing in, the plea of innocence sounded genuine and plausible.

'Are there any other papers your sister had in her possession? Something someone may have wanted. By that I mean, could there have been a document which, if discovered, would point the finger at someone who might have been driven to commit murder?'

Lady Emelia considered this, shook her head and shuddered. 'There seemed nothing untoward leading up to that ghastly moment when you and I discovered my sister, and no reason I can countenance why anyone would want to murder her.' She looked imploringly at Weaver. 'A failing business venture cannot be sufficient motivation to warrant taking a life, can it?'

Weaver's eyes held a sadness born of truth. 'Your Ladyship, I'm afraid the wickedness of man leads to unspeakable deeds for reasons the rest of us find unfathomable. Men have died for pennies. Less, even.'

Mrs Bramble experienced a wave of irritation, not because of Lady Emelia's answers but because there had to be something else. Assuming for a moment the burglar last night also murdered Miss Franklin and was not two different people altogether, why had they risked returning to the scene of the crime so soon? Perhaps they had been discovered while looking for something on that first night and had killed Miss Franklin out of fear and panic. Maybe something incriminating had been left behind and they had to return to retrieve it, or even failed to find what they sought the first time and had returned to search again.

No other items but the files had been hidden beneath the floorboards. The papers in the files had been numbered and catalogued in date order on a list at the front. Nothing had been removed, so could she have missed an important document within those cardboard covers or did it still lie undiscovered somewhere in the study?

Lady Emelia and the reverend had continued conversing, but Mrs Bramble broke into their exchange.

'Do you know a Dr Peregrine Frizzell?' she said.

Lady Emelia was taken aback by the interruption. 'I don't believe I do. Should I?'

Not wishing to lose her train of thought, Mrs Bramble ignored the question. 'Did Miss Franklin ever mention him?'

'As I said, she handled all of our business affairs.' Lady Emelia frowned. 'Who is the fellow?'

'He is the manager of the mine in question and also an investor. Of all the investors, he is the one we know least about.'

Lady Emelia's eyes widened. 'Is he the one who came for Philomena?'

Mrs Bramble said nothing. It was possible but unlikely, given there were others who may have been vengeful and in far better positions to seek and gain some kind of satisfaction. She decided a change of direction might bear fruit.

'When was the last time you spoke to Mildred?'

'Mildred?' Lady Emelia gave Mrs Bramble a sharp look at the sudden switch. 'As I believe I already told you, I haven't spoken to her since all the unpleasantness of a few months ago. I wish to have nothing more to do with the girl, and in any case, she isn't in my employ.'

'But she did come to your door two nights ago?'

'Not to see me; to see Rosie. She spoke to the girl and sent her packing, I hope.'

Even the most moral person, whether high or low born, has the capacity to lie if a situation puts them in a difficult position. Mrs Bramble's days in the army had taught her that and she had expected one of two answers. While neither provided proof, consistency often indicated truthfulness and deviation could suggest an attempt to cover up some incriminating confrontation or altercation, but the easy response reinforced her belief that Lady Emelia did not seem the type to take a life. The inspector was wrong about a random burglar and he was wrong about Lady Emelia, she was sure of it.

Preparing to ask another question, she stopped when Weaver leaned forwards, his hands in front of him with fingers interlaced, elbows on his knees.

'Do you think the Woodruffs should have dismissed Mildred?' said Weaver.

'Of course,' said Lady Emelia with a slight smile of surprise, as though a stupid question had been asked. 'If it had been Rosie or Joan, they would have been gone in an instant.'

'But surely one is innocent until proven guilty and no one provided evidence even suggesting her guilt?'

Lady Emelia's cold laugh matched the room's chill air. 'The missing items are valuable but small enough to secrete anywhere in her room, or the whole palace, in fact.'

'So, you still don't believe her innocence?'

'Certainly not.'

Mrs Bramble realised Weaver was exploring how deep Lady Emelia's animosity towards Mildred ran. Could it have been reciprocated to the point of murder?

'Even so, I can't see Mildred as capable of this terrible deed,' said Weaver.

'Any servant is capable, I would say,' said Lady Emelia, airing her prejudice with an almost proud glance at Mrs Bramble. 'They are a different breed, although Rosie and Joan have been with me for a long time and I trust them as completely as one ever can a domestic servant.'

'What I cannot grasp' — Weaver clasped his hands together for emphasis — 'is why would Mildred want to kill Miss Franklin? The whole affair died down months ago and a lot of water has flowed under the bridge.'

'That may be so, but my sister and I knew her for what she was and the girl had an axe to grind. There is no accounting for the bearing of grudges, is there?'

The irony was not lost on Mrs Bramble, but Lady Emelia gave a dismissive wave of her hand.

'If Flora had sent her packing at the moment of suspicion and accusation, my sister might still be alive.' Lady Emelia pouted.

Weaver cocked his head like a dog listening to a strange sound. 'You blame Mrs Woodruff?'

'Yes ... no, not really.' Lady Emelia shook her head. 'All I'm saying is, that girl should have had an eye kept on her. I don't feel safe knowing she is still allowed the freedom to roam about this palace unsupervised.

'When I heard about what happened last night, I was dreadfully worried, but a house is never as secure as when you are at home and can bolt the doors on the inside. Nothing may have been stolen, but she will come for me. You mark my words.'

'So you *do* think it was Mildred,' said Weaver.

Lady Emelia nodded. 'Let's say I shall ensure Rosie pushes home every bolt in the apartment tonight, which should keep us safe and sound.'

'We heard you intended to return to your apartment today,' said Weaver.

'I cannot impose on Lady Venetia for another night. Has Joan recovered her health?'

'I saw her earlier and she is doing well.' Mrs Bramble remembered the pie awaiting her. 'I suspect she will have returned to your apartment by now.'

'Excellent,' said Lady Emelia. 'She is the best cook I've ever employed. Been with us for years.'

'We'd best be getting along,' said Mrs Bramble, eager to seek out Kitty and discover what had been said between her and Mildred. As she and Weaver rose to leave, she hesitated as though something had occurred to her in that moment. 'Would you object if I popped by later to have another quick look in your study?' The sharp glance from Lady Emelia convinced her even more that another search might prove beneficial. 'I would hate to think the inspector and I had overlooked some detail that may serve to explain all this.'

Lady Emelia fixed her with a cool eye. 'If you must.'

Mrs Bramble returned an equally cold smile. 'Considering the manner of your sister's death, I most certainly *must*. I fear the murderer may very well kill again.'

# 28

After leaving the Fountain Court apartments by the same stair-well – an altogether easier undertaking going down – Mrs Bramble strode along the cloister and through the Wren colon-nade.

'Why do you want to look at the study again?' said Weaver as he struggled to keep up the pace. 'Do you also suspect Lady Emelia now?'

'Not at all, but there must be something I've missed,' said Mrs Bramble. 'Nothing was taken, so the intruder must have been looking for something.'

'Like what?'

'Papers, a letter, a last will and testament, another file.' She held out her hands. 'Something.'

'What if there isn't anything?'

'Then we will need to look elsewhere.' At the south-west corner of Base Court, Mrs Bramble rapped on the door to her own apartment. 'I have a jigsaw puzzle in front of me and a picture is forming, but some of the pieces are still missing. I'm hoping my two telegrams yield favourable responses, because time is running out for Lady Emelia. The inspector's patience won't last for much longer and he *will* arrest her.'

Kitty opened the door and let them in. She had returned from her walk with the other domestic servants and was having a cup of tea with Lady Emelia's cook, Joan, who seemed back to her old self. Eager to hear Kitty's report, Mrs Bramble waved away the offer of tea and asked Joan to stay. Having been poisoned herself, she was not at the top of the suspects list and whatever Kitty had to report might have a bearing on her safety, too, and that of her mistress.

'She didn't want to say anything at first,' said Kitty. 'She's a loyal one, is Mildred, and she didn't want to speak out of turn about the Woodruffs. Rosie kept coming over and butting in, talking about whether Lady Emelia could afford to keep her on, which was most annoying. I had to keep quiet until she went off again. Mildred did let it out bit by bit, though, and I've managed to piece it together.

'She said Miss Woodruff is courting someone in London. Goes there every Tuesday morning and comes back Wednesday morning. I asked her if she knew who it was and she said it was an MP, but she didn't know his name.'

'How does she know this?' said Mrs Bramble. 'Has he visited her?'

'No, she always goes to see him. Always stays in the Savoy hotel, as far as she knows.'

'Is he married?' asked Weaver, his brow creased with a dis-approving frown.

'Nothing like that,' said Kitty. 'It's all above board, or so I'm told. Out in the open.'

Mrs Bramble sat forwards. 'If what Mildred says is true, and I have no reason to doubt it, Miss Woodruff was where she said she was on the night of the murder and there is no issue.'

Kitty hesitated and made a face. 'There is, I'm afraid. Mrs Woodruff took right against the MP from the off, which is why he's never visited her here.'

'Mothers can always sense trouble,' said Weaver. 'They always protect their young.'

'And she was right, too. Having been party to the telegram messages sent between them, Mildred said he's got himself caught up with that big scandal.'

Mrs Bramble knew of only one big scandal doing the rounds and her eyebrows rose. 'The Baccarat betting scandal? Involving Queen Victoria's son, Prince Edward?'

'That's the one. The MP plays cards at the Gunpowder Club, but he's often invited to other games elsewhere.'

'That is important news, Kitty. Do go on.'

'Well,' said Kitty, 'Mildred said Miss Woodruff intended to cast her beau adrift in light of the scandal.'

'For what reason? To save face?'

'There's more to it than that. The gold and diamond mine hasn't got any gold or diamonds in it, so the Woodruffs, although not facing impending ruin, might be plunged into financial hardship for a while. Mildred said they can get through it with their other investments, but not if they are tainted by the scandal. He may be an MP and all, but Miss Woodruff couldn't risk the affair being scrutinised because of the reputational ruin.'

Weaver sat back and blew out through puffed cheeks. 'That puts a different complexion on things.'

'It does,' said Mrs Bramble. 'We need to know when the affair ended and check whether or not Miss Woodruff was with the MP on Tuesday night.'

'I heard Miss Franklin have a bit of a row a couple of weeks back,' said Joan, having listened in silence up to that point. 'Would've been a Tuesday evening.' They all turned to look at her and her cheeks flushed. 'I'm not saying it was with Miss Woodruff – can't have been, can it? – but they'd had words before.'

'Do you know what about?' said Mrs Bramble, intrigued.

'It always involved the gold mine Kitty mentioned, but I

couldn't hear this time. I thought they might've found something and were squabbling over it, but I don't know anything else. If it don't affect me, I don't pay it no mind.'

Mrs Bramble and Weaver glanced at each other. Another piece of the jigsaw had been moved closer to its place. Having thanked Kitty for her sterling work, Mrs Bramble and Reverend Weaver escorted Joan back to Lady Emelia's still-empty apartment. Joan let them in and headed straight upstairs to the kitchen.

'You do what you have to, Mrs Bramble,' said Joan. 'I must get on 'cause I've been neglecting my duties. I can't be doing with getting ill.'

Mrs Bramble thanked her for the chicken pie and let her go.

'Anything wrong?' said Weaver as Mrs Bramble stopped with her hand on the study's doorknob.

'Not at all.' She bent and looked through the keyhole for a moment, espying the spindly-legged table, two easy chairs and a drinks cabinet before straightening up with a 'hmm.' She unlocked the door and stepped inside.

Weaver followed and closed the door behind them.

'What are we looking for?' he said, scratching his head.

'Anything relating to the gold and diamond mine, of course.'

'Such as?'

Mrs Bramble pursed her lips and gave him a stare. If she knew what she was looking for, she'd have a good chance of finding it. As it was, it could be anything and could be anywhere. It might not be here at all but locked in a solicitor's safe.

Weaver gave her a soppy grin and turned to rummage through the bookcase.

Taking the bureau first, Mrs Bramble searched in, underneath and behind the drawers and writing flap, racking her brains about where she would hide her most important document given the same circumstances. Not that she ever had important documents – other than those pertaining to the palace and its residents. She'd never had a secret to conceal but had always been intrigued by those who did. Whether political, criminal, financial or romantic, the keeping of secrets was an art form in itself, often practised by those incapable of keeping a confidence. Then there were some who would kill to preserve or expose one.

Weaver had already moved on from the bookshelf by the time Mrs Bramble gave up on the bureau. They both ran their hands around and underneath the furniture and lifted the edge of the carpet. Frustration prompted Mrs Bramble to return to the compartment beneath the floorboards, the last place left. Weaver watched with interest as she bent on one knee, drew back the carpet, lifted the two sections of wood and felt inside the cavity.

Mrs Bramble's hand came out empty. She frowned.

'What now?' said Weaver.

'I was certain we'd find something else,' she said, trying adjoining boards for signs of loose fitting.

She had been convinced something remained to be discovered, but they had searched every inch of the study. Miss Franklin could have hidden anything in her bedroom, but why would you do that when you've a good study and a secret hidey-hole at your disposal?

Then it dawned on her.

'Could you light that paraffin lamp for me, please, Reverend?'

Weaver did as asked and passed it to Mrs Bramble, who went down on both knees this time. She placed the lamp to one side and put her head as close to the floor as she could. Tutting, she moved the lamp an inch at a time to change the angle of illumination but came up empty-handed again. Changing position, she repeated the manoeuvre in the opposite direction and gave a triumphant, 'Ha!'

'Have you found something?' said Weaver.

'I believe so.' Mrs Bramble probed inside up to her elbow and withdrew her hand, but this time her fingers clutched a folded sheet of paper.

She replaced the wood pieces and smoothed out the carpet before allowing Weaver to take her hand to assist her back to her feet. They sat in chairs near the table and she unfolded the paper.

'It's from Dr Peregrine Frizzell to Miss Philomena Franklin, on plain writing paper dated two months ago.' She glanced at Weaver. 'It takes about three weeks for a ship to sail to England from Cape Town.' She scanned the typed writing:

The cluster of several nuggets of gold weighing just over 100lb in total found last year in a deep shaft is the only find in the entire mine. Tunnels excavated along what was hoped might prove to be a lucrative seam produced no evidence of precious metals or gemstones.

It is my conclusion, and those of expert miners, that the nuggets were an isolated outcrop. As a consequence, my recommendation is for Blue Eland to abandon the project as soon as possible, cut its losses before the situation gets any worse and sell all assets to the highest bidder.

If I do not hear from you by the end of next month, I will have to take matters into my own hands.

She read through the letter again, aloud this time.

'Sounds like a threat,' said Weaver. 'What about the nuggets?'

'It says here they are to be cut up and sold separately from the assets, with half the proceeds going to Miss Franklin and half to Dr Frizzell, as per some agreement drawn up with Sir Philip Chafford before his death.'

211

'A private arrangement to cheat the other investors?'

Mrs Bramble sat back. 'It seems Frizzell and Chafford had high hopes for the mine but devised this little contingency measure in case the venture did not prove as lucrative as expected.'

'If that's not a motive to murder, I don't know what is,' said Weaver. 'Does it say how much they're worth?'

'It talks about troy ounces and troy pounds, whatever they are . . .' She ran her finger down the page. 'Ah, here we are. One pound in weight is worth roughly sixty pounds sterling, which is more than an average man's pay packet for the year, and they found a hundred, making six thousand pounds. As you say, Reverend, worth killing for if someone found out.'

'Do you think this is what the intruder was looking for?' said Weaver. 'Perhaps one of the investors or widows wanted to prove business fraud and theft.'

'It's a possibility, but which investor?' Mrs Bramble ticked them off on her fingers. 'Lady Emelia is Inspector Cole's primary suspect, but instead of motive, he is basing his suspicions on opportunity and method. It appears Miss Woodruff was in London on the night of the murder but her mother did give voice to their gripes. Like everyone else, Mrs Ewan stands to lose money, but she seems most caught up in domestic disputes.

'Dr Kemp appeared unconcerned when I spoke to him. He invested a small amount in the mine but has investments spread over other concerns so is protected. Dr Frizzell invested the same amount as Kemp but is getting paid to manage the mine. Being in South Africa, it would be easy for him to steal all the gold and disappear should he so wish.'

'Don't forget, people saw Miss Franklin as a woman with the temerity to operate in a man's world, and Dr Frizzell has all that gold at his disposal,' said Weaver. 'If he is a vengeful man who did not receive the response he had hoped for from Miss Franklin, can we rule out the possibility that he travelled back to England to kill both her and the wife of his former business partner, Sir Philip?'

'Hmm,' said Mrs Bramble, unsure about Weaver's hypothesis. 'That leaves Frizzell's sister, Mrs McGowan. I admit, I haven't questioned her extensively on this matter, but I have seen no evidence that she knows anything about the state of the mine or any secret arrangement. She seems quite proud of her brother, in fact.'

'What about Miss Cameron-Banks?'

Mrs Bramble shook her head. 'The argument against Mrs McGowan also holds true for her companion. Doubly so.'

'In which case, we are no nearer to uncovering the identity of the murderer now than we were on discovery of the body.'

'On the contrary.' She gave him a knowing smile. 'We know enough to narrow the field, but I need to establish a few more facts to be certain.'

Weaver scratched his head as if to say he hadn't a clue what was going on but had trust in her.

She became serious. 'But we will have to move fast once I receive replies to my telegrams. I fear the inspector will do something rash like arrest the wrong person out of frustration. If that happens, it will be so much harder to reverse his decision.' She turned the letter over to check the reverse before putting it in her pocket. 'I'm afraid I must ask you to become his shadow once again and to let me know the minute he makes his move.'

# 29

Mrs Bramble watched Weaver hurry off in search of the inspector. She knew she was several steps ahead of Cole in the game as a whole, but he followed a different path to her. She had spoken to everyone at least twice and wasn't sure there was much else to be gleaned from them. She had searched the study several times and was convinced it would yield no more secrets. Dr Kemp still had to report on his post-mortem of Miss Franklin's body and his analysis of the brandy, if he could be trusted, but in any case, the pharmacist, Mr Pittman, had done a first-rate job with the hot toddy.

She stood rooted to the spot in the middle of the courtyard, at a loss as to what to do next.

'Rubbish,' she heard Sunny squawk, and turned, knowing she'd find Lady Emelia and Rosie returning to their apartment, both laden with bags no doubt containing apparel and personal items they'd taken for their brief stay at Lady Venetia's.

'Lady Emelia,' greeted Mrs Bramble. 'I'm glad to see the inspector hasn't yet been so rash as to arrest you.'

'I'm sure it's not for want of trying,' said Lady Emelia. 'Rosie and I narrowly avoided being apprehended leaving Lady Venetia's apartment, but of course, Inspector Cole doesn't know the palace like us residents do.'

*And like the intruder so obviously did*, thought Mrs Bramble, nodding her agreement. 'I've not long escorted Joan back to your apartment. She is fully recovered.'

'That is good news,' said Lady Emelia. 'I have to say, in confidence, Mrs Bramble, that for all its apparent opulence, I do not desire Lady Venetia's apartment, which is cold, uninviting and somewhat impersonal. How she can live with all those paintings of places she has no affinity for and people she is no relation to defeats me. Nor do I covet her domestic staff. Rosie is dear to me and Joan's skill far surpasses anything I have consumed these past hours, not least in the realm of meat pies.'

Mrs Bramble's stomach growled as the chicken pie awaiting her for dinner came to mind.

'Do not think me rude, but I am going up,' Lady Emelia continued. She glanced at her bags. 'I desire to know all that has happened in my absence from this court and have a mind to call on Lady Madeleine but wish to divest myself of this burden beforehand.'

'Lady Emelia,' said Mrs Bramble with a slight nod, watching as Rosie gave a twitch and a slight dip, which she guessed must pass for a curtsey.

They watched Lady Emelia disappear through the front door and Rosie waited for it to close before turning back.

'What is it, dear?' said Mrs Bramble. 'Is something the matter?'

'I remembered something, is all,' said Rosie, her eyes flicking left and right to look past Mrs Bramble's shoulders. 'Might be nothing, but who knows?'

'Indeed.' Mrs Bramble smiled.

'I was thinking earlier, about the brandy.' Rosie hesitated.

'Go on,' Mrs Bramble encouraged.

'Why was it there? I mean, I know Lady Emelia doesn't drink it, and I never saw a decanter in the study before, and I clean it every day.'

215

'Maybe Miss Franklin bought some to keep handy for her frequent business guests.'

'Ah, that's what I thought at first.'

Mrs Bramble said nothing, waiting for Rosie to spit out what she wanted to say.

'What if someone put something in the brandy and brought it to Miss Franklin as a present?'

'Someone, who?' said Mrs Bramble, intrigued by Rosie's eagerness to help.

Rosie hesitated and looked over her shoulder at the front door before speaking. 'Lady Emelia.'

A jolt went through Mrs Bramble from her back to her chest. Of all the things Rosie could have said, that wasn't what she expected. 'What makes you say that? I understood you liked working for the Chaffords.'

'I do. I did. Until today.' Rosie looked scared and clutched her midriff. 'I heard Lady Emelia tell Lady Venetia something had been amiss for a while and she had become more and more worried something might happen to Miss Franklin. I never saw anything, mind, but it's made me worried Lady Emelia might have poisoned the brandy, got impatient when Miss Franklin didn't drink it and stabbed her instead.'

Rosie looked upset, although her eyes held no tears, and Mrs Bramble gave her a comforting hug. 'Why would she want to kill her own sister? Hmm?'

'They never got on, Mrs Bramble,' Rosie muttered. 'At each other's throats, they were.'

Mrs Bramble held Rosie at arm's-length. 'Siblings are like that sometimes. Don't forget, we all found the body together, behind a locked door.'

Rosie frowned and looked confused. 'Oh, yeah. I'd forgotten. Must've been a burglar, after all. Still don't make no sense to me, though.'

'Nor me,' said Mrs Bramble. 'If the brandy did make Joan ill, I'm sure it had nothing to do with Lady Emelia. You heard her singing your praises and those of Joan not ten minutes ago, so why would she have given the brandy to Joan for her to cook with if she knew it contained something bad? Lady Emelia would surely have realised something flavoured with the brandy would end up on her own plate.'

Rosie looked crestfallen, but Mrs Bramble wasn't convinced the apparently innocent but misplaced accusation of murder against her employer was the cause.

'I'm sure you are in no danger, but you should bolt your windows and doors tonight, for your peace of mind if nothing else.' Mrs Bramble gave her a smile of encouragement. 'You'd best be getting along.'

'Yes, Mrs Bramble.' Rosie repeated the half-curtsey and disappeared into the apartment.

Mrs Bramble pursed her lips. The time had come to chivvy Dr Kemp into completing his post-mortem before it was too late to prevent Lady Emelia from being arrested.

Mrs Bramble did not get far before her next unscheduled encounter.

'Ah, Mrs McGowan,' she said, with a nodded greeting to Miss Cameron-Banks. 'What a coincidence. I was just thinking about your brother, Dr Peregrine Frizzell. I believe he is an investor and manager at the Blue Eland Gold & Diamond Mining Company in South Africa, is he not?'

Mrs McGowan frowned, her blue eyes narrowing. 'He is, but I don't recall mentioning that fact.' She pulled off her thin, navy-blue gloves, finger by finger.

Mrs Bramble smiled. 'Lady Emelia may have mentioned it to Inspector Cole.'

'Maybe so, but why was he on *your* mind.'

'*Your* mind,' repeated Miss Cameron-Banks.

Mrs Bramble became serious. 'My late husband served as a soldier in the army for several years and I as an army nurse. We were both in South Africa for a time and I found it a very beautiful country. The mention of Dr Frizzell and South Africa brought back many memories, both happy and sad.'

'Ah, I see,' said Mrs McGowan, raising her eyebrows knowingly at her companion. 'It is a small world.'

'Small world,' her companion agreed.

Mrs Bramble left a beat before asking, 'Has your brother returned to England yet? You mentioned he planned to visit.'

Mrs McGowan's expression softened. 'As I believe I mentioned earlier, I hoped he would return soon, but I am yet to receive word of his exact intentions.'

'Intentions,' echoed Miss Cameron-Banks.

'I'm sure it won't be long. As you said, it's a small world and getting smaller every day, what with railways and fast ships.'

'Indeed. And it is in railways that Perry made his fortune.'

'Mining and railways? I wouldn't have put those two professions together.'

Mrs McGowan chuckled. 'Conditions abroad can be challenging and they always need mining engineers to design tunnels, cuttings and embankments. The mine was an opportunity for Perry to get back to doing something he loved and could not let pass. It does seem as though he has enjoyed himself.'

'Enjoyed himself.' Her companion nodded.

'He is very passionate about his work, but we've always been close and I do miss him, as I know he misses me. He is a gentle man in a harsh profession and he told me in the letter I received earlier this week that he misses home very much and wished to return. So, I am hopeful.'

'Let us hope it is not too long before you are reunited.' Mrs Bramble smiled again. 'Well, I mustn't keep you, ladies. Good day.'

'Good day,' the two women replied together.

Mrs Bramble watched them waddle off as usual, feeling somewhat melancholy. The time spent with her husband in the army hadn't been so bad. Not the fighting, that had been horrendous, as had the aftermath with its quota of dead, dying, wounded and maimed to take care of. The bits in between, such as travelling to new places, meeting new people, eating new food and being with her husband – those were the precious moments. If she'd known how few years they would have together, she'd have made even more of them than she had at the time. Now, only the sadness and heartache of loss remained, and thoughts of what might have been: a home of their own; children, perhaps.

She sighed and her attention returned to the present as she continued towards her apartment.

Supposedly, Mrs McGowan believed her brother would be returning home soon but at this moment was still in South Africa. However, the delay in receiving a letter sent from so far away, travelling aboard a standard sailing ship rather than one of the fast tea clippers like the *Cutty Sark*, did not preclude the possibility that he had arrived in the country having boarded a ship at the same time and beaten his letter home.

She had no authority to ask for passenger lists and so many ships sailed every day from every port in the British Empire that there was no way she could discover whether or not Dr Peregrine Frizzell had landed in England in recent days. Except ... Weaver had sent a telegram to South Africa on her behalf and the eagerly awaited response had yet to be received.

Mrs Bramble gave a tug on the bell pull outside the Woodruffs' apartment and waited for it to be answered. Having made it all the way back to her own front door, something Mrs McGowan had done, a simple and insignificant act, had sparked off another train of thought, forcing her to return to Master Carpenter's Court.

The door opened and Mildred stood there with her hazel eyes narrowed in a slight look of puzzlement.

'I didn't expect to see you again so soon, Mrs Bramble,' said the housemaid. 'People seem to be getting around a lot today, and no mistake.'

'That they are,' agreed Mrs Bramble, smiling at the under-statement. 'May I come in?'

Mildred hesitated. 'Both the mistresses are out at present. Is it something I can help with?'

Mrs Bramble cursed herself. She had returned in haste without preparing what she might say to Mrs Woodruff or her daughter, never mind Mildred. She grasped for an excuse, and the crossing of swords with Lady Venetia Merritt and her ward the day before about their leaky pipe came to mind.

'There have been reports of leaky pipes in the palace and I fear some may need replacing,' said Mrs Bramble, looking up as though searching for drips.

Mildred frowned. 'Shouldn't the plumbers be looking out for that?'

Thinking quickly, Mrs Bramble said, 'There are far too many pipes and not enough plumbers, dear. It's a very big palace, so we all have our part to play to make sure it remains habitable, for us if no one else.'

'I s'pose,' said Mildred.

'There is access to the roof, is there not?' said Mrs Bramble, knowing there was.

'Yes, Mrs Bramble. I sometimes takes the washing up there to dry off or give it an airing, but it's not washday until to-morrow.'

'Excellent. Show me the way.'

'I don't recall seeing no leaks.' Mildred stood her ground.

220

'Are you able to call back later when the mistresses are home?'

Mrs Bramble gave her the look of the world-weary. 'Mildred. I am just as busy as you – busier since all this business with Miss Franklin and now Inspector Cole – and I haven't the time to pick and choose when I can or cannot perform my tasks for the day.'

'Is it about ...' Mildred's eyes narrowed. 'Again?'

Mrs Bramble knew she meant the accusation of theft that remained unproven but still hung over her. 'Pipes, dear,' she lied. 'Pipes. If there are any that need replacing. I'm sure your mistresses would prefer them to be identified before they got to leaking. You must have plenty to be getting on with, so if you'd be so kind as to take me to where I can get onto the roof, I can have a quick scout about while you get on.'

Mrs Bramble employed her best unwavering stare and watched the housemaid shrink from her.

'Follow me,' said Mildred after a quick glance along the courtyard.

Mrs Bramble complied as the housemaid led the way up the flight of stairs to the Woodruffs' apartment and stopped in the hallway.

'It's at the top of the stairs,' said Mildred, opening a door to a tight stairway giving access to the second floor. 'On the landing between the bedrooms where us domestic staff sleep.'

'You get along, dear,' said Mrs Bramble with a smile. 'I need to catch my breath and I don't want to be the cause of you being reprimanded because you haven't completed your duties.'

Another fib. Mrs Bramble was more than fit enough to negotiate another set of stairs without pausing but did not want Mildred peering over her shoulder while she did what she had come to do – snoop.

Mildred hesitated, sort of half-nodded, half-curtsied, and

turned to leave. Mrs Bramble waited for her to disappear through a door at the far end of the hallway before beginning her search in the nearest room, which turned out to be a water closet.

The next room on the far side contained baskets with spools of coloured thread and balls of wool, boxes of sewing and knitting needles, various apparatus for the stretching of cloth, some of which displayed half-completed works of embroidery, and other related accoutrements. The room looked too well appointed to be a staff workroom for the mending of clothes and suchlike, so Mrs Bramble concluded that Mrs Woodruff, perhaps even Miss Woodruff, enjoyed knitting, sewing and decorative needlework. This wasn't unusual for ladies of elevated status and had been a popular pastime at the palace since the days of Henry VIII.

With no time to tarry, she peered into every nook and cranny that looked as though it might be a good place to conceal something, but none hid what she sought. A wooden tray at the edge of a desk contained a number of receipts for various spools of thread and a note to a shop in the village, signed by Miss Woodruff.

She was about to leave, when the handwriting caught her eye. It wasn't the style that attracted her interest but the pressure used in the writing of the note. The ink had flowed evenly as the pen passed over the paper, making delicate marks on the surface. She took out the letter from Frizzell, studied the signature and turned the paper over. The reverse showed a continuous indentation as though the writer had pressed hard; unnecessary when using an ink pen. A quick reread of the letter also revealed a flaw in the typeface. The tittle – the small dot above the lower-case 'j' – was missing.

While digesting the possible significance of the unusual indentation and missing tittle in the same letter, Mrs Bramble put the letter back in her pocket and moved to the room on the nearside of the water closet.

This proved to be a storage room with several shelves for domestic sundries. It also doubled as a laundry room, where dirty clothes and bed linen piled in wicker baskets awaited washday, which Mildred had said was tomorrow. After a quick listen to ensure Mildred's duties still occupied her elsewhere, Mrs Bramble rummaged through each basket but came up empty-handed. With a frustrated snort, she returned to the hallway. This kind of snooping was not her forte and she felt guilty for engaging in such intrusive subterfuge, but she had convinced herself the situation demanded it.

The rooms further along the hall where she could hear Mildred working remained out of bounds for now, which left the two rooms upstairs that served as the staff quarters.

Mrs Bramble took the narrow stairway and closed the door at the bottom behind her, not only to afford her more privacy while searching but also to serve as a warning should curiosity get the better of Mildred. On the second-floor landing, a small stepladder had been hooked over brackets affixed to the windowsill. This gave access to the roof via a double window big enough to accommodate all but the largest person, as long as they were agile enough to negotiate the five steps.

She listened at the top of the stairs for a few seconds before opening the window and making as much of a meal of it as possible with all the noise that entailed. Satisfied, she turned her attention to the bedrooms.

The first room, tiny in comparison to those downstairs, held little of interest. Whitewashed plaster covered the ceiling and walls, a small rug lay over part of the polished wooden floor and plain green curtains hung from a rail above the window, as limp as the sails of a becalmed ship. A wardrobe with a single door, a chest of drawers on which sat a porcelain ewer placed inside a matching bowl, and a bed with a tiny table next to it constituted the totality of the furniture. It took two minutes to search.

Mrs Bramble struck gold in the second room, at last finding what she had been searching for but half-hoping not to find, cursing herself for the decision to search everywhere else first. Being a mirror image of the first room, it contained the same furniture, but the ewer had been placed beside its bowl atop this chest of drawers. The bowl held a small amount of cold water, in which soaked a left-handed, cream-coloured lady's glove, a dissolving spot of red visible at the end of the forefinger. *Miss Woodruff's favourite pair*, thought Mrs Bramble, the ones she had seen her wearing until recently when a pale blue pair made an appearance.

It had been during Mrs McGowan's removal of her gloves during their most recent encounter that Mrs Bramble had made the connection between the hatpin, the cry of pain from the burglar and Miss Woodruff's change of gloves. She noticed a few white grains around the edge of the bowl and guessed the water contained salt, a remedy often effective for drawing out various stains from clothing, including blood.

But why did Mildred have it in her room rather than downstairs in the laundry room? The dropped railway ticket reported as belonging to a woman had led her on one path, to Miss Woodruff, but now?

Mrs Bramble left the bedroom and made a noise closing the windows and pretending to climb down the stepladder. She then stomped downstairs and opened the door to the hallway. Mildred approached from the far end, wiping her hands on a cloth.

'Was everything shipshape and Bristol fashion, Mrs Bramble?' she said.

'I'm sure the pipes will last a good while yet,' Mrs Bramble replied. 'Always good to check, though.' She gave her best neutral smile, the one she had employed so often in the past when badly wounded soldiers had asked her if they were going to be all right and avoiding a straight answer had seemed the kindest option. 'I can see you're busy, so I'll show myself out.'

As she descended the stairs, her pulse raced with the knowledge of what she needed to do next.

# 30

Mrs Bramble pulled the front door closed at the same moment Rosie appeared in the open doorway to Lady Emelia's apartment on the opposite side of the courtyard, shaking the dust from a mat and giving it whacks with a long-handled carpet beater.

'Have you seen Inspector Cole or Reverend Weaver?' asked Mrs Bramble, her heart beating hard at the news she had to report.

'I've been busy upstairs, Mrs Bramble,' said Rosie. 'You look flustered. Is everything all right?'

Mrs Bramble strode over and lowered her voice. 'I have information to impart and need to find him immediately.' She glanced back at the Woodruffs' front door. 'I know you have your duties, but I want you to keep a close eye on that front door and come find me if Mildred leaves.'

'Mildred?' said Rosie, wide-eyed. 'You think she did for the mistress, after all?'

'That remains to be seen, but until I fetch the inspector, I don't want her disappearing.'

Mrs Bramble left Rosie to her surveillance and hurried back to Base Court, looking for Inspector Cole and Reverend Weaver. For the first time in two days, she hoped for an encounter with any of the ladies on the off chance they knew where her quarry might be.

She tutted in frustration every time she turned a corner or entered another courtyard, cloister, passageway or stairwell with no sign of the duo. *Why are men never around when you want them and always there when you do not?* she thought, then chided herself for being uncharitable.

Having soon completed a full circuit of the palace with no success, and with her feet beginning to ache with all this unusual running around, she entered Clock Court from Anne Boleyn's Gateway and had to steady Mrs Ewan to prevent her from keeling over.

'You gave me quite a turn,' said Mrs Ewan with her shrill voice, leaning on her cane and clutching her necklace, seemingly for comfort.

'My sincere apologies, Mrs Ewan,' said Mrs Bramble. 'I am in quite the hurry to find Inspector Cole. Have you seen him on your travels around the palace?'

'I have, as a matter of fact.' Mrs Ewan drew herself up to her full height with the realisation that she knew something Mrs Bramble appeared not to. 'Reverend Weaver has been looking everywhere for you because—'

'Mrs Bramble!'

Weaver ejected from the opposite gateway in much the same way as a cuckoo from a Swiss clock, but tripping, bumping into people and dancing around couples as he covered the distance across the courtyard. He stopped short of bowling the two women over and bent double, hands on knees, taking gasps of air. After three gulps, he stood up.

'Mrs Bramble, I've been trying to find you.'

'So it seems,' said Mrs Bramble. 'And I, you.'

He took another gulp. 'Inspector Cole was speaking to ...'

He flinched, noticing the other woman standing there for the first time. 'Oh, hello, Mrs Ewan.'

Mrs Ewan chuckled. 'Reverend.'

'Where was I? Oh, yes. The inspector was speaking to Mrs Ewan' – he nodded to her – 'and Mrs Woodruff, and suddenly decided enough is enough.'

'Enough is enough?' echoed Mrs Bramble. 'What does that mean?'

Mrs Ewan's expression darkened. 'It means he's gone to arrest Lady Emelia for the murder of Miss Franklin.'

'Good Lord!' exclaimed Mrs Bramble. 'No-no-no, he's wrong. How long ago was this?'

'Fifteen minutes at the most,' said Weaver. 'He went to find the sergeant first. "In case there is any unpleasantness," he said.'

Mrs Bramble turned on her heels and headed for her apartment, Weaver following erratically in her wake like an unmanned cutter towed behind a navy frigate under sail. She rang the bell and Kitty answered the door within a few seconds as though waiting in earshot for such an eventuality. She stepped into the hallway, bade Kitty and Weaver to follow, and went through to the parlour, where she found a pen and some paper.

'Kitty, my apologies, but I have an urgent task for you in the village and it demands subterfuge on our part,' said Mrs Bramble as she wrote.

'Anything you ask, Mrs B,' said Kitty.

'I need you to go to the post office straight away and send a telegram. You must ensure this message is not altered in any way before it is sent.' She handed the paper to Kitty.

Kitty read the note and looked up in surprise. 'You want to send this as though Inspector Cole had written it?'

'I beg your pardon?' said Weaver, puzzled.

'If the telegram is sent under my name, it will be ignored. A Scotland Yard detective inspector should get an immediate response.'

'But what about Cole? Won't he have something to say about fraud or forgery?'

'Not if the answer is as I suspect,' said Mrs Bramble, hoping her confidence and suspicions were not misplaced. 'Cole will know I have interfered again the moment he receives a reply, because I must now give him the letter from Dr Frizzell to Miss Franklin that we found in the study, which I believe to be a fake.'

'You've lost me,' said Weaver, shaking his head.

'Don't worry,' said Mrs Bramble while giving Kitty a few coins. 'I know what I'm doing.'

She hoped she did know as she hurried Kitty on her way and followed her out with Weaver.

As Kitty disappeared through the main gate, they took the north-west passage linking Base Court to Master Carpenter's Court, the quickest way to Lady Emelia's apartment. They turned into the courtyard and strode to the front door, which was open but with no sign of Rosie. Mrs Bramble glanced at Weaver, the blood thumping in her ears, and started up the stairs.

She found the scene in the drawing room not unlike a stage tableau. Lady Emelia was sitting on a chair, her face as pale as a china doll and her hands limp in her lap, iron cuffs linking her wrists. Cole and the sergeant were standing either side of her as though about to pose for a formal photograph. Rosie, one arm across her middle, leaned against the frame of the far doorway for support, her face flushed with shock.

'Ah, Mrs Bramble,' said Cole. 'All is well. We have our culprit.'

'Culprit?' said Mrs Bramble, gathering her wits. 'You make

Lady Emelia sound like a petty street thief when she is neither a thief nor a murderer. This is a foolish move, Inspector, when the—'

'I fear you forget who you're talking to,' said Cole, his eyebrows raised in surprise at his judgement being questioned in front of others.

'Lady Emelia is no more the murderer than you or I.'

'And you can prove that, can you?'

'I believe I can.'

'Be my guest.'

Mrs Bramble glared at Cole and ushered Weaver into the room. Of the three men present, she believed Cole to be going through the motions to preserve his reputation as one of Scotland Yard's finest. The sergeant was doing his best in circumstances he had undoubtedly never encountered before. Weaver she considered a very good friend but ineffectual in most situations beyond religion or the confines of the Chapel Royal. In essence, featherbrains. She pointed to the window, beyond which lay the courtyard.

'The Woodruffs live across the way and I found a crucial piece of evidence when I visited there half an hour ago.'

'You did *what*?' said Cole, his face tight. 'What evidence?'

'A glove.'

'A glove?'

'I found the left-hand glove from Miss Woodruff's favourite pair, soaking in salty water to remove a stain from one of the fingertips.'

Cole scoffed. 'Why is that evidence?'

'Because I believe it to be a bloodstain,' she said triumphantly, her buoyancy waning when Cole failed to comprehend. 'As a housekeeper who was once an army nurse, I am used to seeing such stains and the remedies employed to remove them. The burglar whom the sergeant saw breaking in the night after the murder used a hatpin to pick the lock, the one I found outside and gave to you. I believe the hatpin belonged to Miss Woodruff but had been stolen along with the gloves to be used in the burglary.'

'Stolen by whom?'

'Their housemaid, Mildred. I had an inkling about the gloves when I saw Miss Woodruff wearing a different pair instead of her usual and she said her favourite pair had gone missing. I had no wish to think badly of Mildred, because no evidence of theft had been found the last time, but curiosity drove me to look for them in the Woodruffs' apartment. It was in Mildred's quarters that I found the glove. If you hurry, it will still be there as evidence of Mildred's guilt.' Mrs Bramble turned to Rosie. 'Did you keep watch on her like I asked?'

'I tried as much as I could, but Lady Emelia told me to put her things away,' said Rosie. 'Next thing I know, the inspector and sergeant hammered on the door.' She looked sullen. 'They could've just rung the bell like everybody else.'

Mrs Bramble stepped to the window and looked down at the courtyard. 'If you hurry, Inspector, you may still catch her inside, if your entry into this apartment did not frighten her away.'

'Fine,' said Cole through clenched teeth. 'But she stays cuffed until we've checked.'

Lady Emelia looked up crossly at being called 'she', but Cole and the sergeant had already headed for the hallway.

'Look after Lady Emelia,' Mrs Bramble cast over her shoulder to Weaver as she hurried after the two policemen.

By the time she had reached the courtyard, Cole had already pushed open the unlocked door of the Woodruffs' apartment, peering inside the stairwell for any imminent danger. She caught them as they advanced up the winding steps, pausing at every creak. Her first thought was that the unlocked door signified Mildred's hurried flight to avoid being apprehended, a view reinforced as they stood in the silent hallway.

Cole and the sergeant checked every room for signs of the Woodruffs and their housemaid, satisfying themselves no one remained on this floor, leaving the staff bedrooms until last.

Cole led the way again, calling for Mildred to show herself and telling her, 'Don't be a silly girl.'

No answer came — the reason soon clear.

As the three of them crammed onto the small landing at the top of the narrow staircase, with the roof ladder still affixed to the windowsill, Cole pushed open Mildred's bedroom door and took a sharp intake of breath. The sergeant swore, apologised for his language, then swore again in a whisper.

Mrs Bramble held onto the door frame for support as a wave of shock rippled through her and sank her heart. She pressed her lips to a thin line and shook her head in sadness at the sight of Mildred lying face down on her neatly made-up bed in her small but tidy room.

Although one could be forgiven for thinking at first glance that she was merely sleeping, her unnatural stillness and the blade buried in her back bore witness to the fact that the maid was very much dead.

# 31

A gold-plated letter opener, with a single tiny sapphire set into the pommel of the rosewood handle, protruded from Mildred's back between her shoulder blades. Her black maid's dress disguised the colour of the blood, but there was no mistaking its presence in a sodden patch glistening in the light from the window, a scarlet stain spreading across the counterpane.

Cole checked her neck for a pulse and shook his head.

'Send someone for Dr Kemp,' he said to the sergeant. 'And come straight back.'

'Yes, sir,' said the sergeant, and he left to carry out the order.

'She was alive and kicking and tending to her duties not half an hour ago,' said Mrs Bramble.

A wave of sadness and guilt passed through her. Had she been wrong about Mildred? Had her earlier actions prompted whoever did this to do so in revenge?

'Who would dare to do this in broad daylight, right under our noses?' she said as Cole checked the room, inspected the bowl with the soaking glove and stepped outside the room to look at the windows over the stepladder.

'Even if you were right about Mildred, it seems we still have a murderer at large in the palace.' He rattled the windows to check the catches. 'But they didn't get in this way. Must have been let in through the front door, because it wasn't forced.'

'Meaning she knew her attacker,' said Mrs Bramble, the possibilities already cycling through her mind.

'Or she answered the door to a stranger and he barged his way in,' suggested Cole.

Mrs Bramble shook her head. 'It's difficult enough getting up the stairs from the ground to first floor, and you saw how narrow and steep the stairs are to get up here. It would have been impossible for anyone, man or woman, to force Mildred up here against her will without her kicking them down the stairs or screaming her lungs out for help.'

Cole moved to the bedroom window, checked those catches, too, and looked at the ground below. 'No entrance this way, either, which leaves one question: who did Mildred know who would have visited her at this time of day?'

Despite Cole's disapproving glare, Mrs Bramble moved closer to the bed in the hope that some clue to the murderer's identity had been left by accident.

'It could have been anybody,' she said, peering at the bed-side table and along the floor at the edge of the bed. 'Ladies often call on other ladies. Delivery boys and the postman do their rounds. Dr Kemp visits to dispense medical care and medicine. And domestic servants call on each other to borrow ingredients all the time – not to mention the inevitable but occasional romantic liaisons among staff.'

'That doesn't help,' Cole growled, as though it were her fault the palace supported so many people.

She ignored him and scrutinised Mildred's lifeless form. 'Most of the palace workers and domestic servants are engaged in their duties most of the day, which makes it difficult for anyone unfamiliar to go unnoticed without someone challenging them.'

'But not impossible for a stranger to slip past while backs

are turned.' Cole inspected the bedroom door. 'This wasn't forced, either.'

Seeing Mildred lying there brought back so many memories from Mrs Bramble's nursing days and she had to turn away. 'If you are a stranger to the palace, roaming in the dead of night brings its own difficulties, but calling on the off chance during the day is fraught with danger. You can't tell when the mistress of the house is in or out, or how many domestic servants or pets they might have.'

'Pets?' Cole laughed. 'What have they got to do with it?'

'Lady Madeleine has a cockatoo who is not the quietest or sweetest-sounding bird she could have chosen. Despite being against the rules, several of the ladies keep dogs that tend to yap at all and sundry.'

Cole frowned. 'If you're right and the residents, their staff and their pets form a mutually beneficial network of lookouts, the murderer must be known to all living in this court, and I believe whoever killed Miss Franklin also killed Mildred.'

Mrs Bramble looked up. 'Because the same kind of weapon was used?' she scoffed.

'Exactly,' said Cole, his expression reinforcing his belief he was right.

'But not the *same* weapon.'

Cole's eyes narrowed. 'Meaning?'

'The silver letter opener used on Miss Franklin was a re-placement because her usual one had gone missing.'

'The one Lady Emelia accused Mildred of stealing?'

Mrs Bramble nodded. 'The one used to kill Mildred, Inspector.'

'You mean this . . .'

She nodded again. 'After all I've seen since the death of Miss Franklin, finding the glove was the piece of evidence that convinced me most that Mildred must have been the murderer.

235

Now, I can only assume she must have known something, perhaps even who the real murderer is, and whoever killed her did so to keep their identity from being revealed.'

'I should interrogate Lady Emelia again as soon as the doctor arrives,' said Cole, writing in his notebook. 'Given her animosity towards her sister and her grudge against Mildred, finding the former with a silver letter opener from the study in her back and the latter slain with the same bejewelled letter opener she had been accused of stealing, the evidence discovered thus far all points to Lady Emelia having sought murderous revenge on the both of them.'

'That doesn't make sense,' said Mrs Bramble, her fears Cole would revert to his original but flawed conclusion suddenly realised. 'Why use the one weapon that would cast suspicion back on yourself?'

'Women are an irrational and illogical breed, Mrs Bramble.' Cole tilted his head back and looked down his nose at her. 'Who knows what goes through their minds at times like these?'

This left Mrs Bramble speechless and she could do nothing more than glare at him. Cole seemingly noticed the silence and looked back quizzically, his cheeks colouring, no doubt at the realisation of what he'd said and to whom he had said it.

'I—' began Cole.

The clomping of boots on the narrow stairs announced the return of the sergeant and his flushed face appearing at the door interrupted Cole.

'I hope you don't mind, Mrs Bramble, but I've sent young Kitty to fetch Dr Kemp,' said the sergeant.

'Perfectly fine,' said Mrs Bramble.

The sergeant turned to Cole. 'I didn't think you'd want me to leave Lady Emelia alone by sending Rosie.'

Cole raised his eyebrows. 'Initiative, Sergeant? How refreshing.'

He went down another notch in Mrs Bramble's expectations. Sarcasm to one's staff or the lower orders while in the presence of witnesses was never justified in her book.

They left the sergeant at the front door to prevent anyone from entering before the doctor arrived and returned to Lady Emelia's apartment. She hadn't moved an inch since being placed in handcuffs, although cups of tea provided by Rosie now stood on the table nearby. That Lady Emelia's had been half-drunk perhaps accounted for the return of colour to her cheeks, a state that didn't last long as they entered the room.

'Your Ladyship, why did you kill the Woodruffs' housemaid?' blurted Cole.

Lady Emelia's mouth dropped open and her eyes widened in both surprise and shock. Rosie stepped back to the doorway at the sound of the accusation and Weaver rose from his chair with his hand held out as though trying to halt a runaway coach-and-four.

'I-I didn't,' said Lady Emelia. 'How could I when I was in handcuffs?'

'It appears you've gone off half-cocked, Inspector,' said Mrs Bramble.

He looked at Lady Emelia. 'Care to tell Mrs Bramble where you were when I arrived with the reverend and arrested you?'

'In my study,' said Lady Emelia, puzzled.

'There, d'you see?' said Cole, looking at Mrs Bramble as if no more needed saying. Then he realised what had been said. 'Wait – what? No, I meant where had you been before that?'

'Oh, why didn't you say so? I had been out to see Lady Madeleine, but she wasn't at home so I thought I might call on Lady Ives instead, but she was out, too.'

Cole looked around in triumph. 'I had deduced that not only was she the one most likely to have wanted her sister dead, but she was also the one person who had the motive, means and opportunity. I was on my way here to make my arrest, but I arrived too late to prevent her from killing Mildred, too. The housemaid, Rosie, confirmed she and her mistress arrived back from their stay at Lady Venetia's and spoke to you at the front door.'

'That is correct,' said Mrs Bramble.

'Lady Emelia left here soon after, having told Rosie to put away her things, and returned sometime later, giving her ample opportunity to call on Mildred and kill her,' said Cole. 'By her own admission, finding witnesses to her movements will be nigh on impossible, because the ladies she claims to have visited had not been at home.'

Mrs Bramble closed her eyes and rubbed the bridge of her nose. How many times would she meet so much stubbornness? She admitted she had her flaws, as did everyone, but time and again in her life she had come up against those who regarded their own opinions as unimpeachable truths. Matrons in certain hospitals, sergeant majors and lieutenant colonels in various army regiments, Scotland Yard detective inspectors – she had butted heads with them all.

Once the level of confidence required to carry out their duties got to the stage where those around them felt unable to question their decision, challenge their authority, mistakes could happen. In her experience, infections had spread, soldiers had been sacrificed and criminals had evaded justice.

'I fear you are being far too dramatic, Inspector. If you can bear to wait for Dr Kemp's post-mortem results, I'm sure we can shed doubt on your convictions, if not prove Lady Emelia's innocence altogether.'

Cole looked at his watch and pursed his lips as Mrs Bramble continued.

'I also sent three telegrams asking for information from various parties and I expect replies imminently. They should help clear up other aspects of this case that have been bothering me and lead us closer to who the real culprit is.'

Cole took a deep breath and emitted a long sigh. 'Given yet another post-mortem will be needed and Dr Kemp does not appear to be the fastest of workers, I suppose I have no choice but to retain my room at the inn for one more night. Meaning you have until midday tomorrow, after which I must take Lady Emelia to London. Her handcuffs can be removed for now, but she is to remain under house arrest.'

'I am still here, you know,' said Lady Emelia in a huff.

Cole ignored her. 'The sergeant will remain on station to ensure she does not flee. Unlike last time.'

'There was no last time,' Lady Emelia protested.

'I agree,' said Mrs Bramble. 'The person who fled from the sergeant is not the person sitting in front of you.'

'Ha,' Cole scoffed.

Mrs Bramble drew the letter from her pocket. 'Something bothered me and I couldn't rest until I had satisfied my mind.'

'Of course you couldn't.'

She ignored his half-sneer. 'I felt sure a piece of the puzzle was missing, so I went back to Miss Franklin's study and looked again underneath the floorboards, where I first discovered the Blue Eland files, and found this letter tucked away.'

Cole's expression transformed into an angry frown, but Mrs Bramble handed him the letter and continued before he could launch into another dressing-down.

'It is from Dr Frizzell to Miss Franklin about a supposed discovery of a small pocket of gold.' She noticed Lady Emelia's mouth drop open as Cole unfolded the sheet. 'As you will see, he reports no other gold has been found and recommends any profit from the nuggets, the discovery of which appears not to have been disclosed to other investors, be shared between the two parties and the mine sold to cover any outstanding debts.'

Cole finished reading. 'Quite apart from the collusion be-tween Miss Franklin and Dr Frizzell to commit business fraud, this proves Lady Emelia had motive because she would benefit from Miss Franklin's death.'

'If the letter is genuine, which I believe it isn't.'

'You can prove that?' said Cole.

'Not yet, but I hope to very soon and you will look pretty foolish if you take Lady Emelia to London before I have the full picture.'

'Before *you* have?'

'Sir,' said the sergeant from the doorway. 'Sorry to inter-rupt, but Dr Kemp has arrived. With two men to remove the body.'

'Right,' said Cole, striding from the room. 'Sergeant, remove Lady Emelia's handcuffs but keep her under house arrest until I say so. That means keeping a close eye this time.'

'I should come, too,' Weaver blurted, stepping forwards as they made to leave. 'To pray for Mildred's soul.'

'Of course,' said Mrs Bramble, cutting off Cole's objection before it could be uttered.

'If you must, but I should warn you,' said Cole, giving Weaver a cold look that made the reverend visibly pale. 'Unlike last time, there is a lot of blood.'

240

# 32

Standing in Mildred's tiny room at the top of the Woodruffs' apartment, Mrs Bramble noticed the overriding smell of carbolic soap emanating from Dr Kemp, suspecting he'd probably had his hands inside a cadaver not twenty minutes ago. The inspector and reverend appeared to smell it, too, for they sniffed and wrinkled their noses against the strong odour. Kemp did not appear to be in the best of moods and this was borne out by his first exchange with Cole.

'How am I supposed to complete my post-mortem if I keep getting called back to the palace every five minutes?' said Kemp. 'I'm not some high-paid London consultant who can swan about issuing edicts and orders to a plethora of junior staff. I have actual work to do.'

'As do I,' said Cole, 'and I have officers above me who demand swift results, even though I am often at the mercy of others.'

The two men glared at each other like stags about to lock antlers.

'Do you intend unearthing more bodies, Inspector?' said Kemp.

'I sincerely hope not, for both our sakes,' said Cole. 'How goes your post-mortem, now you've mentioned it?'

'It is almost complete. I have restored the body as best I

can and have only to conclude some tests on a few samples I extracted earlier before I can provide you with the answers. As long as there are no more interruptions. The written report will follow in due course.'

'Good to hear, Doctor.' Cole looked at Mildred's body. 'Your verdict here?'

Kemp bent to examine the body in much the same way as he had with Miss Franklin's the previous morning. 'She has no wounds I can see to indicate a fight or even scuffle. If she had been taken by surprise, from behind, say, I would expect marks around the throat and neck, perhaps bruising to the arms and wrists, or maybe signs she had been struck an incapacitating blow to the head. None of these are present, and there are no lesions, lacerations or anything to suggest a violent death other than the letter opener in her back. I fear we have been here before, Inspector.'

'Indeed,' said Cole. He glanced at Mrs Bramble. 'What d'you say now? Still think Lady Emelia is innocent?'

'Mildred was a housemaid and must have known many people she would willingly let in,' said Weaver, interrupting his own muttering of prayers.

'That's as maybe—'

'Of course,' Mrs Bramble interrupted Cole. 'Although very few would be allowed up to her bedroom. I suggest Lady Emelia would not have been one of those since this is the Woodruffs' apartment, where she held no authority.'

Cole's jaw muscles tensed as he clenched his teeth. 'If there is something being withheld from me, I swear to God—'

'Please leave any communication with the Almighty to me, if you please,' said Weaver. 'This may be no more than a crime scene to you, Inspector, but it also represents the tragic loss of another of God's children, whether or not it transpires she had strayed from the path of righteousness.'

242

Cole rubbed his tired-looking eyes with a finger and thumb. 'Is there anything more you can tell us at this moment, Doctor? About the stain on this glove, perhaps?'

Kemp took a wooden tongue depressor from his bag to prod the finger of the glove and agitate the surrounding liquid.

'Doesn't look like ink or paint,' he said. 'I would hazard a guess and say that it's a bloodstain. No real way of telling, of course, but people scratch and cut their fingers all the time. I know I do when I'm gardening.' He delved inside his bag again and drew out a sling for a broken arm, and a pair of tweezers. 'If Mrs Bramble could carefully extract the glove and roll it in this clean sling, I will take it with me to have a closer look. No promises, though.'

Mrs Bramble did as he requested. Despite its soaking, the glove retained the stubborn remains of the suspected bloodstain and she allowed as much liquid as possible to drain back into the bowl, noticing a slight but unfamiliar tinge. After laying the glove on the clean white sling, she rolled it up and gave it to the doctor.

'I have men waiting to take the body back to my surgery for another post-mortem, but it'll have to wait until tomorrow morning,' said Kemp. 'I'll cancel my surgery appointments to ensure expediency.'

Cole nodded. 'Much appreciated. When can I expect you to be finished with Miss Franklin?'

Kemp looked at his pocket watch. 'If I return to my surgery without delay, I'd say within the hour.'

Cole tutted and pushed past the others. Mrs Bramble waited for his footsteps to recede down the narrow staircase and listened for the door closing before she turned to Kemp.

'Apologies for asking, Doctor, but is the brandy in the decanter one of your outstanding tests?' said Mrs Bramble.

'No, as a matter of fact,' said Kemp. 'I completed that out

of curiosity and can confirm the brandy does contain a high concentration of arsenic, as you suspected.'

'Thank you, Doctor. I look forward to your further analysis with keen interest.'

'It's rather strange . . .'

Mrs Bramble's ears pricked up. 'How so?'

'Well,' said Kemp. 'Rummaging around inside a dead body during a post-mortem can reveal information one never expected.'

'Such as?'

'I don't wish to be specific at this juncture, another test to do and whatnot, but surprises may lie in store.'

Mrs Bramble narrowed her eyes. 'What are you saying, or not saying?'

Kemp rubbed his chin. 'It's all a bit strange, but I am forming the opinion that Miss Franklin did not die from the wound the letter opener caused in her back. Nor did she die from being poisoned by brandy laced with arsenic, of which I found no trace in her.'

This came as a bit of a surprise – not that the stab wound hadn't killed her but that she hadn't drunk the poisoned brandy. Not even a sip. Given the fact that Dr Kemp had been most of the way through his post-mortem at the time of Mildred's murder and he had reported the presence of arsenic in the brandy, as confirmed by Mr Pittman, the chemist, any lingering suspicion she had that the doctor had killed either of the two women had dissipated.

'As for Mildred—'

'There does seem to be a lot of blood,' Weaver interrupted Kemp, placing one hand over his mouth and the other on his stomach as though trying to keep its contents contained as he looked over at the body.

'Indeed,' agreed Kemp. 'I had suspected Miss Franklin's

clothing may have mopped most of it up, so to speak, but that was not the case. As you can see here, the blood *has* soaked Mildred's clothing, which is an initial indication, unlike Miss Franklin, that exsanguination as a result of the wound appears to be the cause of death.' He held up a finger to make a point. 'Something only my post-mortem can confirm.'

'Understood, Doctor,' said Mrs Bramble. 'We'll let you and your men get on.'

Mrs Bramble led the way down to the main floor of the apartment and then down the main stairs to the ground floor, hearing Weaver stumble and slip a few steps before recovering. They emerged into the hallway, she with determination on her face and he with an embarrassed flush, passing Kemp's two men on their way up to collect Mildred's body.

'Curious about the letter openers, is it not?' said Weaver.

They left the apartment and stood in the courtyard, Mrs Bramble taking in the cool air to clear her head. Her mind turned its attention to the gloves she had found in Mildred's room. Until that discovery, she had suspected Miss Woodruff of being the murderer because being pricked with the bent hatpin outside Lady Emelia's apartment seemed like a finger-post pointing the way. But, finding the gloves being treated with salt solution upstairs and not in the laundry room had seemed too odd to be anything other than damning evidence against Mildred.

The stabbing to death of the young woman did not necessarily contradict her conclusion Mildred murdered Miss Franklin, but it did throw everything in disarray. She supposed the bowl might have been in the way in the laundry room and at risk of getting knocked over, hence Mildred's decision to take it somewhere safer. They were Miss Woodruff's favourite pair, after all. Did that shed the light of suspicion back on Miss Woodruff?

245

'Mrs Bramble?'

'Sorry, Reverend,' she said, realising Weaver was speaking to her. 'You were saying?'

'I said, what was all that about another test and something strange being found – in relation to Miss Franklin, I mean?'

'A very good question and I think I know the answer, but it means you might have to get your hands dirty.' She chose not to elaborate.

'Good-o,' said Weaver, rubbing his hands together. 'Always glad to lend a helping hand.'

'But first, we need another word with Lady Madeleine, right away.'

'Of course.' His smile faded and became quizzical. 'About her cockatoo?'

'All in good time,' she said, 'although time is a commodity in short supply because Inspector Cole is not a patient man. He won't stay another night to await Mildred's post-mortem if he believes he has his murderer. We have less than an hour before Dr Kemp returns with his post-mortem report on Miss Franklin. Less than an hour to catch the real killer and prove Lady Emelia's innocence before Cole carts her off to Newgate Prison. If you search for Lady Madeleine through Base Court and I take the route past the kitchens, we can cover more ground on our search. Let's meet at Fountain Court.'

'What do I do if I see her? I cannot force her to comply by dragging her to you.'

'Tell her I'm looking for her with important information, then come to find me as quickly as you can.'

Mrs Bramble turned without waiting for an acknowledge-ment and sidestepped around two ladies before entering the cloister. A few pieces of information had been swilling around at the back of her mind for some time but were now coalesc-ing, forming something more cohesive and solid.

She popped into the Tudor kitchens, more on the off chance than with any real expectation of seeing Lady Madeleine, before continuing along the cloister. Of course, she might be visiting one of the other ladies for tea and gossip, although they tended to call it information and intelligence, there being no actual difference apart from the terminology used. She had very little time to solve the case but had every confidence the disparate strands were twisting and plaiting together at last. Although she had been mistaken so very recently, this time she felt it in her water, and that was rarely wrong.

Her circuit through the cloister passed mercifully un-hindered, but without any sign of Lady Madeleine, and intersected with Weaver's at the north-west corner of Fountain Court, where he reported no sign of their prey. Frustrated, they turned back into the cloister and had just passed the door to the Chapel Royal, when Mrs Bramble heard her name called. She turned to find Lady Madeleine, squinting and still picking random seeds from her cuffs, emerging with Lady Ives, who continued to worry at the flecks of oil paint on hers.

After an exchange of formal greetings, Lady Ives announced, 'We have offered prayers for the soul of Miss Franklin. It seemed the fitting and Christian thing to do, under the circumstances.'

The insinuation that Weaver's involvement in the murder investigation had come at a cost to his pastoral duties did not go unnoticed by him, as indicated by his cheeks colouring.

Lady Madeleine was more direct. 'We had hoped to see you in the chapel, Reverend, but as you and Mrs Bramble seem to be in the know, has the inspector made any more progress?' Her face wore an expectant look as though waiting for a medical test result or the conclusion to a gripping tale.

'The sorry affair has taken quite a turn,' said Mrs Bramble, pausing for dramatic effect. 'I'm afraid there has been another tragic death.'

'Not another?' said Lady Madeleine, her hand covering her mouth when Mrs Bramble responded with a solemn nod.

Lady Ives emitted a mew of distress and Weaver took her elbow to steady her as she swayed at the revelation.

'Thank the Lord I live above Anne Boleyn's Gateway,' she said, as though anywhere in the palace other than Master Carpenter's Court was safe.

'I know this has come as a shock, but I need to ask you one more question, Your Ladyship,' said Mrs Bramble. 'On behalf of the inspector.'

Lady Madeleine pouted and stuck her nose in the air. 'If you must.'

'Thank you. When we spoke before, you mentioned seeing a figure in the courtyard and hearing a noise.'

'I did.'

'Please, can you tell me again what noise that was?'

Lady Madeleine glanced up, recalling. 'I heard the tapping of a cane on the flagstones.'

'And ...?'

Lady Madeleine thought again for a second. 'He knocked on a door. I suppose it must have been the Chaffords' apartment. I heard it twice, in fact.'

'Twice, as in two knocks?'

'Yes, two knocks, but repeated.'

'Two knocks and—'

'Another double knock, yes.' Lady Madeleine gave a short, sharp sigh of annoyance. 'I beg your pardon, but what is this? I cannot believe the inspector will be concerned about whether I heard one knock, two knocks or a rat-a-tat-tat.'

'On the contrary, Lady Madeleine. I believe what you have told me will be of great interest to him.'

Mrs Bramble watched her draw herself up to her full height with the pride of knowing she had provided information crucial to the success of the investigation.

'I can't see what bearing it has, but if it helps, it helps, I suppose. Is that all?'

'For now.' The two ladies looked discomfited as Mrs Bramble looked at each in turn and said, 'Lady Madeleine, Lady Ives,' in parting.

She watched them glide away without discernible bobbing up and down, as though on wheels, chattering as they went, and filed away this latest snippet of information. Like other parts of the jigsaw puzzle, it was a piece that had sat at the back of her mind for a while, her thoughts passing over it now and then in the hope that it would soon fit into the whole picture.

This time, it did.

# 33

'What now?' said Weaver. 'I didn't understand the significance of that exchange.'

'No time to explain,' said Mrs Bramble. 'We need to get to the Wilderness before anyone else speaks to Mildred's sweetheart.'

'Her what?'

Mrs Bramble had already set off back to Fountain Court, leaving Weaver playing catch-up again. She swept out through the main entrance to the East Front and turned towards the Wilderness, her long skirt swishing as her stride lengthened. The desire to get to the bottom of the whole affair far outweighed any criticism that could be levelled at her later for neglecting her own duties and avoiding unnecessary conversations with any of the ladies. If her mission had not been so important and time so pressing, she might have smiled as Weaver, being unfamiliar with the need for such haste and rarely having found any cause to break into a run in his entire existence, trotted to keep up.

As he drew level with her shoulder, she turned in through the gate to the Wilderness, causing him to overshoot. He retraced his steps, tripped as he came through the gate and stumbled up to her as she stopped at the place where Billy had been removing the weeds earlier.

'What are you looking for?' panted Weaver.

'Not what, who,' said Mrs Bramble, her head and gaze swivelling as she searched for someone to consult.

A gardener appeared on the grass from behind a cluster of nearby trees, leather-gloved hands gripping the handles of a laden wheelbarrow as he turned to trundle it away.

'Wait there, sir!' she called.

The gardener's head turned, his expression one of surprise at being shouted at, and he set the wheelbarrow back down on the grass. Weaver seemed to baulk at walking across the soft ground in his soft shoes, but Mrs Bramble had no such qualms about striding on the grass in her shiny boots. The situation demanded it.

'It's not often I get hailed as a sir,' said the gardener with a grin as she approached.

'It's not often I have need to shout in public,' she said gravely, 'but I have urgent need to find Billy.'

'Why, what's the rogue done now?'

'He has done nothing wrong, but I have to speak to him to clear up a little misunderstanding from earlier.'

'Ah,' said the gardener, nodding while his now-serious face belied any suggestion he understood. 'In that case, you might find him in the Kitchen Garden. They've got a problem with rabbits getting at the vegetables, so he took himself off to have a look at it, to see what he could do.'

'Thank you,' Mrs Bramble threw back over her shoulder, having already begun walking away towards the other side of the Wilderness.

She passed the bemused Weaver, who turned to follow her again, and strode towards the double gate set into the far wall. This led to a path running alongside a trellised wall in the Tiltyard and through a pair of brick pillars at the far end that gave access to the walled Kitchen Garden.

She spied Billy on the far side of the garden and set off along the gravel-strewn earthen path towards him. Bent double, he looked for a moment as though he were vomiting, but as she got closer, she could see he was wrestling with a length of netting, trying to affix it to a wire frame positioned over the tops of leafy vegetables.

'Billy,' she called.

Billy's head bobbed up and he stood straight as she approached. 'Hello again, Mrs Bramble. Don't see you for days and now you can't keep away. Not that I'm complaining.'

Mrs Bramble saw his grin soon fade when she failed to reciprocate.

'I am so sorry for interrupting your work twice in one day,' she said as Weaver caught up. 'I need to ask a question about your earlier task, the one you were engaged in when I spoke to you before.'

'Oh yes?' He took off his cap, scratched his head and replaced the cap.

Mrs Bramble took time to consider the best way to ask. 'I know you told me why those weeds in the Wilderness needed removing, but I'm interested to know how that came about.'

'Blimey,' said Billy. 'You came all the way out here to ask me that? And with the reverend, too.' The gasping Weaver flapped a hand in greeting. 'I'm not sure what you mean, though.'

'My apologies,' said Mrs Bramble. 'My question was unclear. I meant, did you see the weeds and decide to dig them up, did someone else tell you to remove them, or did some other reason prompt you?'

'Oh, I see. We knew it was there but weren't in no hurry to get rid because it was doing no harm. We had more pressing jobs to deal with, like stopping the rabbits getting to this crop, but I walked past it the other day and saw a piece had been cut off.'

Mrs Bramble's heart gave an extra half-beat. 'Cut off or picked?'

'If a few leaves had been picked I wouldn't have noticed. No, it looked like a small sprig had been cut with a knife and I was worried someone had mistaken it for chervil. To be on the safe side, if anyone asks nicely, we'll usually give them a handful of fresh herbs from here to take with them.' He winked. 'Especially a pretty girl.'

Satisfied, Mrs Bramble nodded, but her heart weighed heavy at the next task she needed to perform, as though a stone had lodged there.

'I'm sorry again for needing to ask you that question before the other reason I came to see you. I hope you can forgive me.'

'Nothing to forgive,' said Billy with a smile, but it faded again at the sight of her solemn expression.

'I take it from our earlier conversation you and Mildred are sweethearts?' she said, watching Billy's eyes narrow with suspicion.

'We're stepping out together,' Billy confirmed. 'It's all above board.'

'I am sure it was,' said Weaver.

'She told me we were lucky because the master of the house where her friend, Rosie, worked had been very strict about not allowing his servants to have men friends. She'd had a bit more freedom since he passed away.'

Weaver stepped forwards and placed a comforting hand on the gardener's shoulder.

'Hold on, I don't understand.' Billy glanced at Weaver's hand and up to his face. 'What d'you mean, was?'

'We are the bearers of bad news,' said Weaver.

Billy took a step back.

Weaver's hand dropped to his side. 'Mildred has gone,' he said.

'Gone? Gone where?' Billy looked back and forth between the two. 'You're mistaken,' he scoffed. 'I saw her just this morning. She wouldn't just up and leave.'

Mrs Bramble shook her head. 'He means Mildred has passed away, Billy.'

'No-no-no.' Billy put his hands on his head, his face ashen. 'She can't have.'

'I'm afraid it's true,' said Weaver.

'I don't believe you.' Billy lowered his hands and wiped them on his trousers, a flash of anger in his eyes. 'If she don't want to see me no more, she can tell me herself.' He stepped forwards.

Weaver held out his arm to stop him from passing. 'Billy,' he said firmly. 'She's in the hands of God now.'

'But I need to speak to her.'

Weaver pulled Billy into a hug, the young man making no attempt to hide the tears that suddenly streamed down his cheeks as the fight seemed to leave him.

'What would He want with her so soon?' the young man managed to say as his face crumpled. 'She's too young.'

Mrs Bramble offered silent thanks when Weaver did not respond with the usual *God moves in mysterious ways* placation.

'She never had a day sick, so what did I do to make Him take her from me?' Billy sank from Weaver's embrace to a crouch as though his legs could no longer support the weight of grief. His bottom lip quivered.

'You did nothing wrong,' said Weaver.

'How?' said Billy through a half-suppressed sob. 'Was it peaceful?'

Mrs Bramble would have given much to render the next blow unnecessary, but it would have been crueller in the long run to withhold it.

'We believe someone murdered her this afternoon,' she said. 'While she worked alone.'

A few seconds passed when the airy songs of birds in the nearby trees seemed at odds with the silence of the three people in the garden as the gravity of those words pressed down on them.

Billy stood slowly, his grief turned to shock. 'That's not God takin' her, is it? Who would do such a wicked thing?' He wiped the tears from his cheeks with the sleeves of his jacket. 'She wouldn't hurt a fly, so why would someone want to hurt her?'

'That is for Scotland Yard to establish,' said Mrs Bramble, choosing not to divulge her own part and that of Weaver in the investigation. 'There is a detective here already, investigating the murder of Miss Franklin. It is suspected the perpetrator may be the same.'

Shock turned to anger as Billy balled his hands into tight fists. 'I'm a peaceful man, Mrs Bramble, Reverend, honest I am, but if I catch him, I'll kill him before the gallows can take him.'

'Understandable sentiments,' said Weaver, placing a calming hand on Billy's shoulder again. 'But it won't help Mildred now and would send you to the gallows instead. Please heed my words, Billy, when I say this matter is best left to the inspector. We will keep you informed of any news and try to keep you out of the investigation as best we can. Does she have kin that you know of?'

Billy shook his head. 'Her mother died giving birth to her and her father died of a broken heart. At least that's what she said the orphanage told her.'

Weaver gave Billy's shoulder a reassuring squeeze. 'Under the circumstances, I would be happy to help with any, um, arrangements regarding Mildred.'

'Thank you, Reverend.' Billy's hands relaxed, his shoulders sagging as more tears welled. 'Can I see her?'

255

'Not yet, I'm afraid.' Mrs Bramble shook her head, a lump forming in her throat as she witnessed the young man's heart breaking in front of her. 'She is with Dr Kemp, but I shall let him know to tell you when you can.'

'We'd not been courting for long, but we were sweet on each other. Who'd want to take that from us?'

'As I said, Inspector Cole is on the case and making progress, so we should trust in justice to run its course.'

The young gardener watched Mrs Bramble for a long few seconds and she felt his gaze searching her soul before he gave one small nod.

'Good man,' said Weaver, patting Billy on the shoulder. 'Will you join with me in reciting the Lord's Prayer?'

Billy bowed his head and mouthed the words that Weaver spoke, looking up with a forlorn expression at the *Amen*.

'I will come and see you later on or tomorrow morning,' Weaver promised him. 'Grief can play tricks on the mind, so please reassure me you will not be alone this evening.'

'I lodge with an old bloke, so I cannot escape company,' said Billy.

'Right. Good, right,' said Weaver.

Mrs Bramble touched Weaver's elbow as a signal they should depart and they left the young man alone at the centre of the Kitchen Garden, looking devastated and defeated. As they re-entered the Tiltyard, a heart-wrenching wail echoed from behind.

# 34

Although the mere conveyor of such devastating news, guilt settled on Mrs Bramble like a thick blanket at the sound of Billy's anguished cry. If she had taken more time to consider the information at hand, perhaps she would have followed the right path and prevented the murderer from taking another victim. If she'd listened to her instincts, maybe the loss of the young woman's life could have been avoided. She'd had her suspicions elsewhere, after all.

'The inspector will wish to speak to the young man to obtain his information at first hand, will he not?' said Weaver, scuttling alongside Mrs Bramble as they entered the Wilderness.

'Of course, but not yet. You can be sure Inspector Cole would see Billy as another candidate for his prime suspect, but I saw and heard nothing in that garden to give us cause to set him off on another tangent. It would have done well for Cole to witness Billy's genuine grief but that can't be helped now. It can do no harm to let the young man digest the devastating news and come to terms with it, at least for an hour or so. By that time, I hope the intelligence he has given us will be mere supporting evidence and of little other consequence.'

'Given *us*?' said Weaver in surprise. 'You give me too much credit, for I have little or no idea about the significance of what it is people are telling you, never mind how it all fits together. All I can do is hope you know what you're doing.'

'I always hope so, too, but one can never be sure.'

'Where are we going in such a rush?' said Weaver, lagging behind again.

'We still have Lady Emelia to save, and what little sand we have left in the hourglass is fast running through.' Mrs Bramble turned towards the palace.

'But what else can we do?'

She wondered the same thing. The replies to her three telegrams, each of which would provide a vital piece of information, had yet to come back. If the responses were as expected, Billy's answers would help to forge another link in the chain she was constructing.

'I worry about Inspector Cole,' she said.

'Why so?' said Weaver, panting again.

'Once his theory about an opportunistic burglar or some invading stranger had been proved a nonsense, he became dead set against Lady Emelia. His experience has been so soiled and stained by the mire he wades through every day in London that his reasoning is tainted by it. He measures everyone by the same yardstick and cannot see past the wronged wife of a secretive husband, the rivalry of distant but superficially cordial sisters, and the potential for fatal revenge.'

'He is wrong, of course?'

'Of course.' She turned in through the entrance to Fountain Court. A fresh idea had wormed its way to the front of her mind and she needed to follow it to its conclusion. 'And in furtherance of proving such, we must find Alice or Flora Woodruff.'

'Again?' said Weaver from further behind. 'Whatever for?'

Mrs Bramble stopped in the cloister to allow him to catch up.

'The letter I found is not all it seems,' she said.

258

Weaver arrived at her side.

'It's not?' He looked at her with a puzzled frown. 'Um, which one are we talking about?'

She lowered her voice so passers-by could not hear. 'The one from Dr Frizzell to Miss Franklin about the nuggets of gold.'

'Ah, of course.' The frown lines on Weaver's forehead deepened. 'Why is it not?'

'I have a theory, but in this case the proof of the pudding is not in the eating but in another piece of correspondence I hope the Woodruffs will have retained, as I'm sure they must.'

'About what?' said Weaver as she set off again through the cloisters leading towards Master Carpenter's Court.

'It doesn't matter as long as it came from Dr Frizzell.'

'Why?'

'Ah, Mrs Woodruff,' said Mrs Bramble as she entered the courtyard, spotting the woman speaking to the sergeant. 'I am so glad I caught you.'

'Caught me?' Mrs Woodruff rounded on Mrs Bramble. 'Caught me? This, this' – she waved a hand at the palace sergeant guarding the door to her apartment – 'so-called policeman won't let me inside my own home to collect my things and insists on keeping me waiting in public like a commoner, probably because they think I killed Mildred. Why would I do that to my own maid? As far as I can tell, that so-called detective from Scotland Yard is doing nothing more than running around like a headless chicken, accusing all and sundry the moment anything new comes to light.'

'Believe me, Mrs Woodruff, I am as concerned as you.'

'Unless Kitty has been stabbed to death in your apartment, I do not believe you can be.'

Mrs Bramble pressed her lips into a thin line to contain the angry retort that threatened to burst from her at the insensitive remark.

Mrs Woodruff fiddled agitatedly with her silver Blue John ring, the mark on her finger now angry and raw. 'The inspector is in there now, rummaging through my personal things in search of clues to prove my guilt.'

'He will find nothing of the sort,' Weaver reassured, giving Mrs Bramble a look of concern. 'He cannot possibly suspect you of murdering your own housemaid when you could have dismissed her or had her arrested.'

'I had no reason to do either of those things.' She glared at the sergeant for emphasis.

'I'm sorry,' said the sergeant to all of them. 'The inspector is inside as we speak but I can't tell you anything because he didn't tell me.'

Mrs Bramble groaned inside. 'Does the man never take heed or learn?'

'I wish to move apartments forthwith,' said Mrs Woodruff, cutting off any reply the sergeant may have been about to make, and with a stern look at Mrs Bramble. 'I cannot continue to live where a life has been so brutally taken.'

'That will be difficult to accommodate, as I'm sure you are aware, but I will speak to the palace superintendent and see what we can arrange.'

'Nothing temporary, except for a day or two.' Mrs Woodruff raised her nose in defiance. 'After which, it must be a permanent move.'

Mrs Bramble bit her tongue. Even after the tragic deaths of two residents in the courtyard, Mrs Woodruff had joined the ranks of those trying to manoeuvre towards what they considered to be better apartments. Yes, Mildred had lost her life inside Mrs Woodruff's home, but a housemaid's bedroom was not a place any mistress of the house would ever venture anyway. Employers tended to treat domestic servants like

260

children who should be seen and not heard, and when out of sight they remained out of mind.

'I am sure Mrs Bramble will do everything she can,' Weaver soothed. 'In the meantime, my door is always open should you wish to avail yourself of my pastoral ministering, and the chapel is there for prayer and quiet reflection, of course.'

'My sanctuary has been violated,' said Mrs Woodruff with a pout of petulance. 'A cup of tea will not resolve the matter. Nor will brooding in silence.'

Weaver looked crestfallen.

'Sergeant,' said Mrs Bramble. 'May I be permitted to enter and speak to Inspector Cole?'

'I'm afraid not,' said the sergeant. 'The inspector mentioned your good self by name as someone who should not be allowed to enter.'

'But I found the body,' she complained.

The sergeant shrugged apologetically, so she turned to Mrs Woodruff.

'Is there anything inside that could help further the inspector's investigation, perhaps something he may not easily recognise and therefore fail to see is connected?'

'Such as?' said Mrs Woodruff, frowning.

Mrs Bramble did not wish to antagonise her into withdrawing, but more minutes had ticked by, reducing Lady Emelia's time as a free woman every second. 'A letter, perhaps.'

Mrs Woodruff scoffed. 'I have many letters.'

Mrs Bramble bit her tongue again. 'This would be a letter from Dr Peregrine Frizzell, manager and investor in the Blue Eland Gold & Diamond Mining Company, in which you, too, have an interest.'

'That again?' Mrs Woodruff huffed. 'I have papers, of course, but why would one of those be of interest to you or the inspector? I make no secret of my dislike for Lady Emelia, due

261

to the actions of her late husband and sister, but how could any letter from Dr Frizzell be of use?'

Mrs Bramble decided it could be beneficial to reveal a little more. 'One may contain a particular identifying mark the inspector would find interesting.'

'Would this letter prove Lady Emelia's guilt?'

'No, but it might help to prove Miss Woodruff's innocence.' This was a lie, but it would fill in a missing part of the tale. Mrs Bramble watched with satisfaction as shock registered on the woman's face at the suggestion that her daughter was a suspect. She threw her a lifeline. 'The police always need to eliminate suspects from their inquiry and, as I said, it may help towards that goal.'

The sergeant cleared his throat to get their attention.

'Mrs Bramble, if you have information of benefit to the inspector, I consider it my duty to allow you inside to speak with him.'

Mrs Bramble noticed the flush to his cheeks. He knew such an action in violation of the inspector's expressed instructions would result in another dressing-down, but she hoped the limit of the detective's jurisdiction and influence would be insufficient to jeopardise the palace sergeant's career.

'Thank you, sergeant,' she said and entered before his fear of the inspector made him reconsider.

She found the inspector upstairs in one of the day rooms and watched him open the door of a waist-high cupboard in polished teak set against one wall. He looked inside and closed it again, his expression remaining blank. She had no idea what he was looking for and from his continuing cursory glances in, under and around various items of furniture, she suspected he didn't, either.

He turned his attention to a writing desk containing several drawers and slots for papers and stationery but with no lockable flap like the one Miss Franklin had used. He leafed through a pile of correspondence extracted from a drawer, tutted and went to put them on the desk.

'Having no luck, Inspector?'

'Christ almighty!' Cole jumped and spun on his heels, scattering the papers across the desk. 'How the devil did you get in?'

Mrs Bramble suppressed a smile at Cole's unexpected reaction. 'Mrs Woodruff is remonstrating with the sergeant about being excluded from her home and I'm afraid I took advantage of the distraction.' It was another lie but a small white one, to shield the sergeant from Cole's ire.

Cole huffed, gathering the papers back into a pile. 'Well, I'd be grateful if you could leave. I have official business to complete.'

'It looked to me as though you were poking around on the off chance of finding something useful.' Cole threw her a sidelong glance but said nothing. 'I see you've found some correspondence. Any letters with indentations?' she continued, hoping to pique his interest.

It worked and the inspector paused for a second. 'What kind of letters?' He picked up the top letter to study it.

'From Dr Frizzell in South Africa.'

'Frizzell?' said Cole. 'There are several.' He looked at the pile. 'What do you mean by indentations?'

Mrs Bramble stepped inside the room for the first time and approached the desk. 'A signature, pressed into the paper to make a strong mark.'

'I don't recall seeing such a signature.' He flicked through the pile, studying the signatures. 'Is it an important letter? What should I be looking for?'

'I don't know whether the contents of the letter are in themselves important, but if there is such a signature, it may prove useful.'

263

Cole looked her square in the eyes. 'If this is another of your theories, I could do without the time-wasting. Please return downstairs before I have the sergeant remove you.'

'You do know he is not actually under your command?' She met and held his gaze. 'In any case, my theory, as you call it, may prove to be inconsequential, but we have a duty to explore every avenue, do we not?'

'*We* do not,' he said flatly. '*I* do.' He resumed flicking through the papers.

She watched with growing irritation at Cole's lack of attention to detail and at his disregard of her suggestions.

'Just an idea, but would turning them over help with revealing a heavy-handed signature?' She saw a brief hesitation and felt petty satisfaction at having irked him.

Cole turned the papers over but found nothing. With a smirk, he offered the pile to Mrs Bramble. 'Be my guest.'

She had already seen from Cole's handling of the letters that the one she hoped to find was not among them. She cleared her throat theatrically as he tried a larger pile of papers taken from the next drawer. With another glance of irritation, Cole split the pile in two and handed her one half. She turned them over and examined the back of each one, becoming more frustrated at the lack of any sign of a heavy pen.

Cole smiled when she sighed and placed the pile on the desk. About to concede she may have been mistaken, an admission likely to bring her discomfort alongside Cole's I-told-you-so satisfaction, she saw the smile fall from his face. He turned over the letter in his hand and turned it back again.

'How did you know?' he asked.

'I didn't for certain, but it was the simplest explanation.'

'For what?'

She ignored the question. 'May I?'

Cole placed the letter in her hand. 'What does it mean,

264

beyond the obvious that Frizzell is heavy-handed with a pen.'

She took it and noted the deeply imprinted signature. 'This is not his usual way,' she said, selecting another piece of correspondence. 'Look.'

Cole inspected the signature on the other letter. 'A light touch.'

She nodded. 'Frizzell never presses hard. Nobody has need to, because ink should flow naturally from pen to paper. A light scratching, maybe a blot or a run here and there, is all one should expect from even the most inexperienced signatory. Do you have the other letter I gave you on your person?'

'I have.' He reached inside his jacket and took out the letter from Dr Frizzell to Miss Franklin.

'Compare the two signatures, if you will. Are they similar?'

Cole looked from letter to letter. 'They are, but I still don't understand your reasoning.'

'I suggest you keep hold of all three of these letters for now,' she said, intending to play her cards as close to her chest as she could for as long as she could. 'They may prove useful when the time comes to expose the true identity of the murderer.'

'Ha!' Cole scoffed. 'I don't know why you think this absolves Lady Emelia. All this does is indicate Miss Franklin and Miss Woodruff were in league, as their investment in the mining company already confirmed.'

'I agree, that would be the obvious conclusion to make, but I sent a telegram earlier today, the response to which I hope to receive any moment and the contents of which I expect to enable us to draw an entirely different picture.'

'Mrs Bramble,' Cole said with exasperation. 'If I have told you once, I have told you a thousand times, I am a detective and you are a housekeeper. Although I appreciate you bringing certain facts to my attention, as I would expect any God-fearing, law-abiding member of the public to do, that does not make you my subordinate officer. Nor does it elevate you to the role of private detective.'

'Of course not, Inspector,' she said sweetly. 'As I have explained before, I am performing my duties in relation to the safety, security and advantage of the residents in this unique, royally sanctioned community, no more.' She glanced at a clock on the mantelshelf. 'In furtherance of which, I would like to request one more thing of you.'

'Yet another?' said Cole. 'Just the one more, is it?'

'I believe Dr Kemp said his post-mortem report would be ready within the hour,' said Mrs Bramble, ignoring Cole's sarcasm. 'That was almost half an hour ago. If you, the sergeant and Lady Emelia would be so kind as to meet me and Reverend Weaver in the Large Oak Room in forty minutes, I am confident we can help you to bring your case to a satisfactory conclusion.'

Cole bowed his head and pinched the bridge of his nose as if to stave off a headache. 'Please tell me there is nothing else you've been doing you shouldn't have or that you've discovered but not informed me of?' He looked up to see Mrs Bramble at the door, already leaving.

'Bring all the evidence we have accumulated, Inspector,' she said, stepping outside. 'And rest assured, you have as much information at your fingertips as I do. Almost.'

'Almost?' Cole said, rushing to the door.

But she had already gone.

# 35

Mrs Bramble extricated Reverend Weaver from the continuing altercation between Mrs Woodruff and the sergeant, and steered him along the passage towards Base Court. She had no time to answer his questions, even after Rosie had answered the door to her apartment and they all stood in her parlour.

She fetched a piece of notepaper and a pen, and wrote as she said, 'Reverend, I must ask for your assistance once again. Twice or thrice, in fact – and yours, Kitty.'

'Of course,' said Weaver, waiting for instructions like an excited puppy. 'Whatever you require.'

'Kitty, the dustcart still comes once a week and is due tomorrow morning. Am I correct?'

'Yes, Mrs B,' confirmed Kitty. 'I've already taken today's rubbish out to the dustbins.'

'In which case, Reverend, I need you to visit Dr Kemp and tell him Inspector Cole requests his presence in the Large Oak Room of this palace at five o'clock. He should bring his full report of the post-mortem on Miss Franklin.

'Afterwards, go straight to the post office and ask whether any telegrams for me have been received this afternoon. If not, please wait for as long as you can but no longer than five o'clock.' She handed him the note. 'Take this. It contains instructions to the postmaster to give you any telegrams addressed to me so you can deliver them to me yourself.'

'Good Lord,' said Weaver. 'Whatever for? Where will you be?'

'Kindly also ask if anything has been received for Inspector Cole,' she said, ignoring his question. 'He may be loath to divulge that information, but ask anyway. His manner may reveal the answer.'

'I will use my best persuasions,' said Weaver.

'I need everyone involved in this terrible affair to assemble in the Large Oak Room for five o'clock,' she continued. 'I am fortunate that several of the ladies who have found themselves under suspicion will already be there in anticipation of the weekly game of whist and I shall leave it to the inspector to eject anyone else not required.

'He and the sergeant will be escorting Lady Emelia, so the last one on my list is a gardener named Billy. Kitty, I need you to fetch him as quickly as you can. You might find him in the Kitchen Garden and you'll have to get him to hurry. I shall see to Rosie and Joan myself, to ensure they comply.'

'Yes, Mrs B,' said Kitty. She frowned. 'Have you forgotten Lady Madeleine?'

'I have not forgotten,' said Mrs Bramble with a smile, pleased to have such an astute young woman with such insight and reasoning as her maid. 'I will call on Lady Madeleine myself, once Lady Emelia has left the courtyard.'

'You said you had three things for me?' said Weaver, eyebrows raised.

'I did,' said Mrs Bramble. 'But I'm afraid the third may not be a pleasant task.'

'If Job could survive God's trials, I'm sure a little unpleasantness can be endured.'

She smiled at him apologetically. 'On your journey back

268

from the post office, I need you to make a detour to the palace dustbins. As Kitty confirmed, they are due to be emptied tomorrow, so we need to recover a vital piece of evidence today.'

'From the bins?' queried Weaver, not looking as enthusiastic as before.

'I'm afraid so,' said Mrs Bramble.

She had considered giving this one to Kitty or taking it herself but needed both to remain presentable for dealing with the palace ladies. As questionable as the palace chaplain's behaviour might first appear to anyone coming across him rummaging through the rubbish bins, he was a respectable man of integrity and propriety, so she hoped and believed the perceived lapse of decorum, however odd, would be chalked off as eccentricity and soon forgotten.

Weaver grimaced, obviously not of the same mind, as she began to relay her instructions.

Mrs Bramble watched from the cloister as Kitty set off on her mission to fetch Billy and Weaver turned towards the main gateway on his way to the village. She had assigned Kitty the easier task but hoped Weaver's more difficult mission would bear fruit, too. If it didn't, her whole line of reasoning would fall under close scrutiny, however close to the truth it may be. Cole would expect and accept nothing less than solid evidence before he would even consider releasing Lady Emelia. The whole case was far more complicated than he accepted but in the end it came down to simple reasoning.

The astronomical clock had not long struck half-past four and Mrs Bramble dared not set about her work just yet. Part of her plan required the element of surprise, a certain theatricality, so she had to wait for the inspector and the others to be clear of Master Carpenter's Court. As for the reverend, she hoped he wouldn't trip head over heels on his return and deposit the telegrams in the cold-flowing Thames or lose them among the palace rubbish.

When the pair disappeared from sight, she hastened along her usual covered route, towards the Large Oak Room that had once been King William III's private dining room. It now served as the venue for the grace-and-favour residents to meet, dine, play cards and put on much smaller entertainments than the one held by Lady Venetia in the Great Hall two nights ago.

She espied a uniformed guide, one of many employed by the palace for the benefit of visitors, as he attempted to herd a small group of tourists along the Wren colonnade. Feeling some sympathy for the harassed-looking man who did not appear to be having much success, she commandeered him and noted he seemed both relieved and grateful in equal measure.

They arrived no more than a minute later at the Large Oak Room, which, as its name suggested, was clad from floor to ceiling in highly polished, light-oak panelling, apart from the near end where a curtain hung across to conceal the stage area employed during the performance of plays.

Lit from above and the sides by modest but effective chandeliers and wall-mounted candelabra, from the far end by two tall windows, and on occasion by the warm glow from logs crackling in the fireplace, it was perhaps a little grand for the type of gathering Mrs Bramble had in mind. What it lacked in modesty it made up for by having enough space to sit without being on top of one another while still being small enough for everyone to be seen and heard. It also had the added benefit of privacy, its location sufficiently out of the way to avoid attendees being overheard or interrupted by casual passers-by.

A fireplace with a marble surround, mantelshelf and hearth took up a large space on one side of the rectangular room and an expansive carpet covered most of the polished wooden floor. A number of straight-backed utilitarian dining chairs and green baize-covered tables usually stood in a line along the opposite side, waiting to be arranged into the next suitable configuration, Four of these had already been moved away from the wall and positioned in a diamond pattern in the centre of the room, one chair having been placed along every side, ready for the sixteen card players to arrive. Each table had been positioned far enough apart from the next to allow its players uninterrupted and unoverlooked play but not too distant to prevent congeniality between tables. She walked around, touching the back of each chair as she spoke the name of a potential occupant, and stopped at the table nearest the window.

'Take the other end,' said Mrs Bramble, moving two chairs and grasping the edge of the table.

The guide did as commanded and helped to move it away from the others. 'Anything else?' he said.

Mrs Bramble stood with hands on hips, frowning in concentration, trying to think if she had forgotten anything. Now wasn't the time to lose faith in her abilities and she almost fancied she heard her husband behind her, whispering in her ear. *You are the most capable woman I've ever met, Lydia Bramble. What are you doing, doubting yourself?* She glanced over her shoulder, ready to smile, but was disappointed to realise her husband hadn't returned to her.

'I would be most grateful if you would stay here while I attend to some business,' she said, turning to the guide. 'I must insist you do not let anyone in except those I have mentioned. When the ladies arrive, ensure they sit at those two tables. The one at the far end is reserved for the servants, the window end is for Inspector Cole and the sergeant.'

'Are you sure?' said the guide, looking amused. 'A table for the staff? What will the ladies say? This all seems a bit informal for mixed company.'

271

'Theatrical, I'd prefer to say. And deliberately so.'

Inspector Cole would need convincing, so the more she could beguile him with logic wrapped up in storytelling, the more chance she had of saving Lady Emelia's life and unmasking the real murderer.

An important part of what was to come rested on her ability to persuade Lady Madeleine to accompany her to the Large Oak Room for five o'clock and convince her to bring Sunny in his travel cage. She knew the cockatoo had been out of his larger cage fewer times since he'd arrived than the number of fingers contained on one hand, and out of the building only once during its refurbishment. But the rooms in Lady Madeleine's apartment were far too small for the kind of gathering she had in mind for this evening. Mrs Bramble knew Lady Madeleine kept a covering for his travel cage in case of emergencies and she prayed it would keep him quiet, but there was no telling whether the disturbance of being moved would cause him to scupper her plans.

Leaving the guide to guard the room, and hearing the astronomical clock strike a quarter to the hour, Mrs Bramble hastened back to her apartment to collect the boxed ceramic dish given to her by Mr Pittman, the pharmacist, and the sample of hot toddy contained within the old tonic bottle. She made it over to Master Carpenter's Court in time to see Inspector Cole and the sergeant depart with Lady Emelia. Moving swiftly to the Chaffords' front door, she pulled the bell handle, hoping to catch Joan and Rosie at home. Rosie soon answered, surprise flickering across her features before she recovered.

'Lady Emelia left not long since,' she said. 'With Inspector Cole and the sergeant.'

'It doesn't matter. I'll not be stopping,' said Mrs Bramble. 'It's you and Joan who interest me. Is she in?'

'She is, Mrs Bramble,' said Rosie, throwing a glance behind her at the staircase.

'Please fetch her down. Inspector Cole has gathered a number of ladies and we are to attend, but first we must collect Lady Madeleine and her cockatoo.'

'Sunny? Whatever for?'

'All in good time. I'm sure the inspector has no desire to be kept waiting.'

Rosie gave a polite nod before hurrying up the stairs and returning a few minutes later with the worried-looking cook.

'What does he want with the likes of us?' said Joan. 'If you don't mind me asking.'

'Maybe he wants to assure us everything is all right.' Mrs Bramble smiled in what she hoped was a comforting manner. 'The deaths of Miss Franklin and Mildred are bound to have affected us all in one way or another.'

'It won't end well for us,' said Joan, shaking her head. 'Not if Lady Emelia goes to the gallows. I mean, where would we go? This isn't just where we work, it's our home, too.'

'I wouldn't go worrying yourself, if I were you. I'm sure all will be revealed in good time, which is running short, in fact. Follow me, please.'

Mrs Bramble took the few paces across the courtyard to Lady Madeleine's front door, where a quick tug on the bell pull brought the maid to answer. Lady Emelia's two servants waited downstairs while Mrs Bramble went upstairs to the apartment and stood in the sitting room, trying to explain her intentions and why those involved both Lady Madeleine and Sunny.

'I've never heard anything so ridiculous in all my life,' said Lady Madeleine.

Knowing some of the conversations the palace ladies frequently indulged in, Mrs Bramble doubted that very much but held her tongue.

273

'I can assure you, the other ladies of this court are already gathering in the Large Oak Room. The police are already there and Dr Kemp will join us as soon as he—'

'I am supposed to be playing whist in five minutes,' Lady Madeleine interrupted.

Despite the interjection, Mrs Bramble could see the mention of the other ladies and the doctor beginning to sway Lady Madeleine. Declining on principle was one thing, missing out on what must be an important gathering was another.

'I must stress, this is not a trial but still a chance to uncover a number of truths,' she continued, pressing home her advantage. 'Your witness testimony and the information both you and Sunny possess are invaluable to the inspector in his efforts to ensure the path of justice is straight and true.' She put one hand behind her back and crossed her fingers, negating any suggestion of a lie in the eyes of God while accepting that her words insinuated that Cole was the instigator of what she had planned.

Lady Madeleine pouted. 'I have no wish to subject Sunny to any kind of charade.'

'Not even to save Lady Emelia from the gallows?'

She watched another change in the woman's milky eyes as the realisation that she might hold the fate of another human being in her hands hit home. Mrs Bramble knew she could have saved herself the bother of a verbal sparring session by invoking the name of Inspector Cole earlier and suggesting it was he who had demanded the gathering, but experience had taught her that quiet cajoling always worked better with certain ladies in the palace.

Lady Madeleine's shoulders relaxed as she capitulated. 'If it is for a short while, as you suggest, I suppose it would do no harm.'

'Most gracious of you, Your Ladyship. I'm sure the inspector will be most appreciative of your efforts to assist Scotland Yard with their murder in—'

'Yes, yes,' Lady Madeleine said, waving away the flattery.

Under close instruction, Mrs Bramble found Sunny's travelling cage and waited for Lady Madeleine to coax the chattering cockatoo to the door of his spacious home. He eyed them both suspiciously and she held her breath as further encouragement lured him into the much-reduced confines afforded by the domed enclosure.

As she enveloped the cage with a purpose-made cover to keep Sunny quiet, Lady Madeleine said, 'We had better make haste,' as though the cause of any delay could be laid entirely at Mrs Bramble's door.

Mrs Bramble led the way downstairs, supporting the cage with two hands and marvelling at the combined weight of bird and bars. For a travelling cage, it didn't seem as portable as one might like, and halfway down she regretted not utilising the strength of Dr Kemp, Billy or the sergeant. Although not unfamiliar with the carrying of heavy items, she gladly handed over the squawking and shifting burden to Rosie and Joan, who did not seem at all pleased at taking over the task.

Lady Madeleine took Mrs Bramble's arm without further complaint and when the procession finally reached the throng of chattering ladies in the Large Oak Room, presided over by Cole and the sergeant, she allowed herself to be guided to a seat opposite Lady Emelia, on the same table as Mrs McGowan and Miss Cameron-Banks.

As per Mrs Bramble's instructions, the guide had steered the Woodruffs to the other table along with Lady Ives and Mrs Ewan. The human chatter filling the room decreased as Rosie and Joan set the covered cage on the floor next to the table near the inspector and Sunny screeched his usual repertoire of words. A moment after the servants took their seats at the end table reserved for them, the ladies resumed their speculation and the volume increased again. Sunny also seemed to grow bored with his own mimicking and reverted to squawking in protest.

'Can we hasten proceedings along?' hissed Cole, irritation evident in the jutting of his jaw. 'I have no wish to submit myself to an interrogation by these ... these ...'

'Refined ladies whose very existence has been threatened by an as-yet-unidentified assailant?' offered Mrs Bramble, seeing him glance towards where the bemused Lady Emelia was sitting.

'Not the choice of words I was searching for,' admitted Cole.

'I am expecting my housemaid, Kitty, at any moment. Reverend Weaver, too. But I'm afraid we cannot commence without Dr Kemp. His post-mortem report on Miss Franklin is one of the key pieces of information able to unlock this case for us all. Of course, other keys are in your possession, and mine, but I am afraid we must be patient.' She looked at the array of items on the table. 'I see you have produced everything, thank you.'

As requested, Cole had brought the bundle of mine company files, the three letters, including the two from Dr Frizzell, the bent hatpin, the broken box from Miss Franklin's study, the business card, the scrap of suicide note, the railway ticket and the two letter openers. Along with the toddy sample and ceramic dish in her pockets, these items and those expected would allow her to tell the story that culminated in the deaths of two women.

Miss Woodruff, her hair still tightly coiled and looking like a brown helmet, tapped her silver-topped cane on the carpet. 'Inspector, are we to be kept on tenterhooks for much longer?'

'I am told we await Dr Kemp, but he should be here shortly,' said Cole.

'Told?' said Mrs Ewan, the ruff around her neck quivering with its own indignance. 'By whom? Aren't you in charge?'

Cole threw Mrs Bramble a sharp look, which she ignored.

'Why are we sitting alongside domestic servants?' said Mrs McGowan haughtily, her nose in the air but with her piercing blue eyes trained on Cole. 'This is not the done thing.'

'I concur,' said Lady Madeleine, squinting to ascertain with whom she had agreed. 'No, it won't do at all.'

'Ladies,' said the sergeant, speaking for the first time since Mrs Bramble had entered the room. 'Everything is as it should be according to the wishes of Inspector Cole. I am sure we will get going soon, so I ask for your patience a short while longer.'

Mrs Bramble was impressed by the authority with which the sergeant spoke but could sense Inspector Cole's patience wearing as thin as the soles of his well-worn shoes.

'Now can we begin, for pity's sake?' implored Cole. 'That squawking creature is enough to get on anyone's nerves.' He grimaced at Sunny's covered cage, from which emitted occasional squeaks and whistles of disgruntlement. 'God alone knows why you've brought it here.'

'And soon everyone will know.' Mrs Bramble smiled.

Cole did not.

At that precise moment, relief came in the form of the guide's head peering around the door before he opened it fully to allow Dr Kemp to stride into the room. As Cole opened the large envelope offered to him by the doctor and removed a thin sheaf of papers, secured with a pin at the top left-hand corner, Mrs Bramble beckoned to the guide and instructed him to take Sunny's cage out to the anteroom. Kemp unrolled a cloth and showed her the still-damp but no longer sodden cream glove.

'As far as I can ascertain, I would say that stain on the finger is blood.'

With a satisfied nod, Mrs Bramble put it on the table and

277

took Kemp to one side as Cole flicked through the post-mortem report.

'Is it as I suspected?' she whispered, mentally keeping her fingers crossed for luck.

'It is,' said Kemp.

'So, the cause of death is ...?' Mrs Bramble nodded as he revealed his crucial piece of evidence. 'I was wrong to begin with, but that is by the by. I did not have all the facts to hand.'

'But you do now?' said Kemp.

Mrs Bramble smiled and gestured for him to take his reserved chair.

# 36

Mrs Bramble clapped her hands twice to gain attention. Dr Kemp looked up in mild interest, but the mouths of several of the ladies dropped open in unison at being hushed in such a fashion. Despite her office and title, after all was said and done, Mrs Bramble was still a woman from the working class. The ladies glanced at each other to express their distaste and glowered at Mrs Bramble, which she ignored as usual.

'Ladies and Dr Kemp,' she said. 'We asked you here this evening because it is time we brought this murder investigation to a close.'

Cole opened his mouth to protest at the use of 'we', but Mrs Bramble gave him a sideways glance and he closed it again.

'It is not two days since the tragic loss of Lady Emelia's sister, Miss Franklin, and fingers have been pointed, guided by fear. That is to be expected when there is so much unknown, but it is not helpful. We want answers, knowledge, certainty, justice, and I believe we can achieve all of that here in this room this evening.'

'Still playing the detective, I see,' said Mrs McGowan with a smirk. 'I'm sure we would all prefer you to give your full attention to your stated duties, given we all have requests for improvements to our apartments rejected almost daily.'

A hum of agreement went up from the ladies, but Mrs Bramble looked back at Mrs McGowan without flinching. She had wanted to wait until later before showing her hand, but putting the woman in her place, and the others by association, held much appeal.

'Since you and your brother are murder suspects, I would have thought you might be interested in hearing me out.'

Mrs McGowan opened her mouth to retort but her lips moved in silence, shock seemingly spreading with a flush across her features as the other ladies turned their attention to her.

'Mrs Bramble,' said Cole, frowning. 'If you please—'

'All in good time, Inspector,' said Mrs Bramble, relieved to see the door at the back of the room open and Kitty enter with Billy.

Billy fidgeted, clearly nervous at being in such company, as all heads turned to discover the identity of the latecomers. He squeezed and twisted the cap in his hands as though trying to wring it dry of water as he sat where Kitty directed and she sat next to him. He couldn't even lift his gaze from the carpet to look at anyone in the room, but Kitty could and she flashed a quick smile of reassurance at Mrs Bramble.

'Must we be addressed in such a fashion in front of servants?' said Lady Ives, with encouragement from Mrs Ewan sitting next to her.

Cole shook his head and sighed as the other ladies bristled with indignation. 'Ladies, I'm sure this will go so much smoother without interruptions. Mrs Bramble has her reasons and the sooner we hear them, the quicker we can return to our own concerns.'

Lady Ives pouted her displeasure but said nothing. Mrs Bramble noted that Mrs Woodruff and her daughter, both yet to comment on the proceedings, could not look at her for more than a second or two. They hadn't even glanced at each other in the last few minutes.

'I believe Inspector Cole and I have uncovered enough physical evidence and taken sufficient testimony from witnesses to unmask the real murderer,' said Mrs Bramble. 'I shall try to be as brief as I can but must emphasise that the sequence in which events occurred is very important to understanding how and why the two murders took place.'

She picked up the silver letter opener.

'When Lady Emelia's housemaid, Rosie, called for me on that fateful morning, I rushed to their apartment with my spare keys, ready to unlock the study in which Lady Emelia suspected her sister lay dead.' She held up the letter opener to show the gathering. 'When I entered the room with Lady Emelia and Rosie, we found the body of Miss Franklin with this plunged in her back, up to its hilt. Dr Kemp certified her death in situ.'

The ladies shifted uncomfortably on their chairs, the surreal presentation unfolding in front of them so very far from their everyday experience of genteel society with its specific rules of engagement and address. The servants sat unmoving and silent at the back table. They all displayed expressions of varying degrees of guilt, like a class of schoolchildren accused of committing a misdemeanour and under threat of collective punishment until the one true culprit could be exposed.

Mrs Bramble replaced the knife on the table. 'The inspector formed three theories based on his initial investigation. One, a burglar may have got in through the open window and killed Miss Franklin when disturbed by her. Two, a business or social dispute between Miss Franklin and one of her late-night callers may have escalated and ended in tragedy. Three, Mildred, housemaid to Mrs and Miss Woodruff, decided to end a long-running dispute by killing the person who had falsely accused her of theft and tried to get her arrested, or at the very least dismissed from her employment. I believe I can prove that none of these are true, but to do so I must take you through it step by step.'

'Is that necessary?' said Mrs Woodruff haughtily. 'Can we not be spared the gory details?'

'Guilty conscience, dear?' said Lady Madeleine, squinting in her direction.

Mrs Woodruff glared back, her lips forming such a thin line as to be almost invisible.

Mrs Bramble continued. 'Seventy-five residents attended Lady Venetia Merritt's gala evening, plus many domestic staff. Of those, some were also present before the dinner and some after the entertainment, but not all stayed for its entirety.

'Joan, Lady Emelia's cook, left her domestic duties early to help prepare the dinner, leaving Rosie, the housemaid, to tend to Lady Emelia's needs and finish her own chores. Miss Franklin was too busy to attend, so Rosie, as was usual in such circumstances, made her a sandwich before leaving to help with the serving.

'Lady Emelia stayed at the end of the gala to supervise the domestic staff in their clearing up, Rosie and Joan being two of those. Joan cleared up in the kitchen, left and went straight to bed. Rosie left shortly after and was followed a little while later by Lady Emelia who saw her in her apartment, knocking on Miss Franklin's study. No answer came, which I am told was not unusual whenever Miss Franklin was engrossed in her work, and both Rosie and Lady Emelia went to bed.

'In the morning, Rosie said Miss Franklin still wasn't answering and the study door was locked. Lady Emelia rose, checked the study door handle and peered through the keyhole. That is when she discovered her sister slumped over the bureau and sent for me to bring my spare keys.'

'Monkeys?' said Mrs Ewan, putting her hand to her ear to hear better. 'Are we on to pets again?'

'Door keys, dear,' explained Mrs Woodruff.

'Donkeys?' Mrs Ewan frowned and shook her head as if to clear it of confusion.

Mrs Woodruff rolled her eyes at the others.

Mrs Bramble let the exchange conclude, her patience being tested, before continuing.

'When we entered the study, I observed a smell of smoke in the room, although the window was open, and stepped on something that turned out to be the key to the study. One might think it had fallen from the lock when we entered, but if that had been the case, how had Lady Emelia seen through the keyhole?

'When the inspector arrived, he discovered that a box had been forced open, which often contained a large sum of money. A purse with a smaller sum had also vanished, which led him to believe a burglar had got in through the window and killed Miss Franklin. If that had been the case, why had the burglar not taken the expensive jewellery still on Miss Franklin's person, and why was the key on the floor?'

'Obviously, the return of Lady Emelia and Rosie disturbed the burglar,' said Lady Ives. 'In rushing to lock the door, he dropped the key and left before he could take the jewellery.'

'Which would tie in with the inspector's initial assessment. But when he could not find sufficient evidence to support his theory of a random opportunistic burglar, Lady Emelia became his prime suspect.'

'Relatives kill each other far more often than you would credit,' said Cole, as though that explained everything.

Mrs Bramble gave him a thin smile. 'The two women were well known for being civil towards each other but less than sisterly, a fact confirmed by Lady Emelia. I must admit I, too, entertained the notion that she had staged a burglary to cover the fact that she had killed Miss Franklin.

'She told me she had worried when Rosie reported her sister had not gone to bed, but I believe her concern had arisen long before that moment. I became suspicious about her account while searching the study, for four reasons. One, I looked through the keyhole of the study door to check and found that the bureau was not visible from that position. Two, the not-insubstantial key lay on the floor just inside the room. Three, a pen lay on the bureau's blotter as though it had been held by Miss Franklin at or around the moment of her death, but there was no evidence of any letter or note she might have written. Four, the window was open, even though the evenings and mornings recently have been chilly, and the room smelled of smoke, a fact Lady Emelia dismissed.'

'This all seems rather vague,' said Mrs McGowan.

'Vague,' echoed her companion, Miss Cameron-Banks.

'I agree,' said Mrs Bramble, wishing the ladies would refrain from interrupting. 'But on further investigation, I found this among the ashes in the fireplace ...' She held up the piece of burned paper. 'It is a scrap of what looks like a suicide note, written in green ink.' Mrs Bramble replaced it on the table. 'Miss Franklin had been left everything by her brother-in-law, Sir Philip Chafford, which must have rankled—'

'It did not!' Lady Emelia interjected. 'Philomena always had a head for business. Better than many men, I'd wager.'

Mrs Bramble looked at her sympathetically. 'A later search of the study uncovered a bundle of business files relating to the Blue Eland Gold & Diamond Mining Company, a company in which most of you have an interest.'

Lady Emelia looked surprised, while several ladies and Dr Kemp fidgeted again.

'They exposed the impending failure of that high-risk

investment in which Mrs Woodruff, Mrs Ewan, Dr Kemp and Mrs McGowan's brother, Dr Peregrine Frizzell, hold varying interests, but Miss Franklin had inherited Sir Philip's controlling stake. A trying situation, certainly, but not one that would cause a strong woman like Miss Franklin to contemplate suicide, because other successful investments protected her from ruin. Who, then, wrote the fake note on her behalf, only to burn it and stab her?'

'Lady Emelia,' said Cole emphatically. 'Those files and other evidence proves it.'

'Not so, Inspector.' Mrs Bramble tapped the pile on the table for emphasis, bringing a snort of irritation from Cole. 'Only part of the answer lies in those files. One of the papers discloses that several investments taken over by Miss Franklin from the late Sir Philip would pay out only in the event of death by natural causes, by accident or at the hand of another. Self-murder, suicide, the taking of one's own life, is a sin against God and any sums due from certain investments and life assurance policies would be forfeit.

'If Lady Emelia had discovered the failed investment, already knowing the terms of the investments and life assurances, would the frustration have been sufficient to tip her over the edge in a fit of temper and to commit murder?'

'Of course,' said Cole. 'I've seen men die for less. Sergeant, put the handcuffs back on Lady Emelia.'

'Wait.' Mrs Bramble held up her hand to stay the sergeant. 'There is another possibility.' She looked at the doctor. 'Dr Kemp, your findings, if you please.'

Kemp stood, smoothed his coat and cleared his throat. 'I can confirm the loss of blood from the wound in Miss Franklin's back would have been insufficient to lead to her demise.'

'What *are* you talking about?' said Lady Madeleine, looking

285

in the wrong direction at Cole as though it had been him talking. 'Stabbed people die, do they not?'

'Not in every case,' said Kemp, 'and I believe Miss Franklin was already dead when the point of the letter opener went in.'

Kemp sat as a hubbub of chatter erupted among the women, who talked to, at and over one another until Cole, rising annoyance displayed by the increasing colour in his cheeks, called for quiet.

Mrs Bramble nodded her thanks to him. 'It is possible that while the household still slept, Lady Emelia went to the study to check on her sister and found the door unlocked. Inside, Miss Franklin was slumped over the bureau, apparently unconscious. She liked strong drink and kept a cabinet of spirits, including brandy, for herself and visitors, so it may have seemed at first glance that she was drunk. It would be natural to check for a pulse, but Lady Emelia, finding none and spotting the suicide note on the writing flap of the bureau, may have put two and two together and come up with five.

'Believing her sister had taken her own life, Lady Emelia must have panicked. She knew the insurance company and some investments wouldn't pay out after a suicide, and feared ridicule and ruin. She decided on the spur of the moment to snatch up the letter opener and plunge it between her sister's shoulder blades to make it look like a bungled burglary had ended in murder.'

Mrs Ewan clutched her necklace for solace and Lady Ives fanned herself with a splay of playing cards. All eyes turned to Lady Emelia, whose expression held a mixture of embarrassment, disbelief and confusion. She opened her mouth to speak, but her lips formed no words and she looked imploringly at Mrs Bramble, as though willing her to end the humiliation.

'I suspected Lady Emelia knew about the note and must have burned it herself, because she made no remark about the smell of smoke in the room, despite my bringing it to her attention,' said Mrs Bramble. 'The quickest way to get rid of the distinctive aroma of burning paper was to open the window, but she couldn't risk waiting for it to dissipate, so she left it open, locked the study from the outside and slipped the key under the door to make it look as though the only way in, and out, was through the window.'

'Ridiculous,' said Cole, a deep frown making him look like a disgruntled bulldog. 'If Lady Emelia didn't kill her, who did?'

Mrs Bramble gave a small smile, confident that she was on track to supply a most shocking answer.

# 37

'Yes, Mrs Bramble,' said Miss Woodruff, speaking for the first time since the proceedings had begun. She pointed her cane at her. 'If the inspector is wrong, do tell us, who did kill Miss Franklin?'

'That's where the brandy and witnesses come in,' said Mrs Bramble, happy to oblige. 'We know Miss Franklin liked spirits, but Rosie said Lady Emelia hated brandy. Their cook, Joan, became ill on the day the body of Miss Franklin was discovered. Joan said she had made a hot toddy for her head cold by using a measure of brandy from a decanter Lady Emelia had taken from the study and given to her for cooking. Having once been an army nurse, I can recognise arsenic poisoning when I see it, and I did see it, as a grainy precipitate at the bottom of Joan's glass of hot toddy.'

The gathering erupted again, with raised voices and much finger-pointing, and it took several seconds for Cole to bring proceedings back under control.

'You may have been a nurse once, Mrs Bramble, but how can you be sure?' asked Mrs Woodruff.

'A fair question,' Mrs Bramble conceded. 'I gave the decanter to Dr Kemp to test for arsenic. I later discovered he had invested in the mining company, but the pit had turned

288

out to be barren and the company was in imminent danger of folding. All of its investors faced potential bankruptcy, so he had a motive for murder and I found I could not put my full trust in him.'

She held up the bottle of poisoned toddy for everyone to see before placing it on the table.

'For my own peace of mind, I poured Joan's cold remedy into a sterilised bottle and took it to Mr Pittman, the chemist in the village.' She pulled the box from her pocket and carefully removed the tiny ceramic dish, holding it up to show the underside. 'He kindly performed a simple scientific test, which left the silvery coating on this dish – proof that the toddy contained a lethal dose of arsenic, should anyone have drunk more than a sip.

'Dr Kemp restored my trust in him by explaining his modest investment in the company. Without knowing about Mr Pittman's test, he subsequently confirmed the lethal dose of arsenic present in the decanter. Joan is very lucky to be alive.'

Joan fidgeted in her chair.

'If you're saying someone poisoned Miss Franklin before Lady Emelia took the letter opener to her, who can it be?' said Mrs McGowan, looking at each of the gathered persons in turn.

'Who can it be?' her companion echoed.

'Miss Franklin was alive when Lady Emelia and her staff left for the gala, but we weren't sure if she died before or as they returned at about eleven o'clock,' said Mrs Bramble. 'However, we do know that several ladies from both in and around Master Carpenter's Court retired from the gala at the time the comedian went onstage. Among these ladies were those who have a financial stake in the mine and witnesses who both saw and heard an unidentified figure in the courtyard around nine o'clock.

'Lady Madeleine, who left early because she doesn't care for cheese or music-hall comedians, saw someone in the courtyard wearing dark clothing and carrying what she thought was an umbrella. Mrs McGowan also left because she doesn't like comedians and I understand Miss Cameron-Banks had eaten too much. They reported seeing nothing unusual.

'Mrs Ewan left after stating she'd had enough entertainment for one evening and saw someone wearing a dark cloak and something flatter than a top hat. That person tapped something on the ground that might have been an umbrella, but equally might not.

'Although Miss Woodruff did not attend the gala because of a trip to London, her mother, Mrs Woodruff, did but retired early because she had a headache, and she took her maid, Mildred, with her. She said she heard someone tapping a cane or perhaps an umbrella on the courtyard floor — three times during the late evening — and a double-knock on a door.'

'Do you believe the murderer was seen and heard by these ladies?' said Cole.

Mrs Woodruff went to speak, but Mrs Bramble held up a hand to forestall any repetition of her accusations against Mrs Ewan.

'Mrs Ewan uses a cane to aid her with walking, but there is no reason why someone who needs such support would walk up and down the same courtyard three times in quick succession,' said Mrs Bramble. 'Not after a long, tiring evening spent in the Great Hall.

'It is quite possible one of the tapping journeys heard by Mrs Woodruff *was* Mrs Ewan returning to her apartment. The other occurrences can perhaps be explained by a return railway ticket I found in the stairwell leading to Lady Emelia's apartment.' She lifted the ticket from the table and held it for everyone to see. 'This has been clipped for a journey to Hampton Court from London Waterloo, but the holder dropped it before they could use it to return to London.

'On the off chance one of the station staff might recall some-one asking about this ticket, I enquired there and was told a woman younger than I, having arrived at around a quarter to eight and lost her ticket, had bought a single ticket for the ten o'clock train to London. Their descriptions left a lot to be desired, but it seems she limped and carried a cane.'

'If we didn't know better, we would think that was indeed you, my dear.' Lady Madeleine smirked at Mrs Ewan.

'Outrageous,' snapped Mrs Ewan.

Mrs Bramble continued. 'Umbrella or cane? Top hat or something flatter? Could the prowler have been the woman who arrived from London, stayed an hour, dropped a ticket in the stairwell of Lady Emelia and Miss Franklin's apartment, and bought a replacement ticket for London?'

'Do you not think I would have known if it were a woman?' said Mrs Woodruff with indignation.

'Actually, I do, Mrs Woodruff. You have excellent sight and hearing, whereas Lady Madeleine has the misfortune to suffer from cataracts. Even so, Lady Madeleine described the prowler as having big hair, dark clothing, possibly a cloak and maybe an umbrella, walking stick or cane because she heard the tap-ping of a metal ferrule on stone. None of this contradicts the idea of it being a woman. She also heard a knock-knock on a door, repeated, but I shall come back to that.'

'Where is all this leading, Mrs Bramble?' said Cole. 'It seems very roundabout, I must say.'

A knock came at the door and the visitor guide entered. 'Apologies for the interruption, but Reverend Weaver asked me to give you these.' He handed over three telegrams before closing the door on his way out.

All tension left the muscles in her neck when she saw two of the telegrams addressed to her. 'I know who that is from,' she said as she passed the third to Cole. 'Please don't read it yet,' she urged as he went to open it.

Cole frowned and opened his mouth to argue but seemed to think better of it and slipped the telegram in his pocket.

Mrs Bramble opened and read her two telegrams, allowing herself the ghost of a smile before folding and pocketing the papers and resuming her story.

'Rosie said Miss Franklin argued with someone in her study two weeks ago about a man from London. This person, who may have been a woman, double-knocked on the front door and Miss Franklin answered it herself. Which brings me to the events of last night.

'Whenever I cannot sleep, I get dressed and wander through the palace to ease my thoughts and tire myself sufficiently to go back and get some rest. I did so last night and found myself in Master Carpenter's Court at exactly the time the prowler returned. They used a tool to pick the lock of Lady Emelia's apartment and enter while she and her housemaid spent the night at Lady Venetia Merritt's. Her cook stayed the night in my apartment to recover from her poisoning.'

Once again, the ladies exchanged glances of disquiet.

'Upon exiting, the prowler tried to relock the door but hurt their finger when disturbed by the sergeant, who had been posted on watch by the inspector.'

Cole shot a fierce look at the sergeant, who pretended not to notice.

'A chase ensued, but our quarry, wearing dark clothing and trousers, seemed to know the layout of the palace and was swift, even though they seemed to carried an injury to their leg or foot, and so managed to elude us. A subsequent search revealed a bent silver hatpin, fresh scratches on the escutcheon plate and signs of blood.' Mrs Bramble held up the hatpin and her bloodied handkerchief. 'At this time, I began to suspect Miss Woodruff of being the murderer.'

Miss Woodruff covered her mouth with her hand to stifle a cry of distress as the blood drained from her face.

'Now look here,' said Mrs Woodruff, getting to her feet. 'That is slanderous. You said the *man* wore trousers.'

'Please sit, Mrs Woodruff,' said Cole. 'Let us hear Mrs Bramble out and see if she has any justification.' He looked at Mrs Bramble with a hopeful expression. 'Do you?'

'I do. Witnesses heard the repeated double-knock, a safety signal Mrs Woodruff said her daughter often uses to announce it is her at the door and not some unwanted caller, and she also has an injury that is still causing her to limp. She knew her mother still kept her father's old suit in a wardrobe alongside his Royal Navy uniform, most useful to someone requiring a disguise. And she has changed her gloves.'

'Her gloves? What the devil has that to do with anything?' said Mrs Woodruff, glancing at her daughter's hands before glaring at the inspector.

Cole raised his eyebrows questioningly.

Mrs Bramble gestured towards the glove on the table. 'I found a cream-coloured glove from Miss Woodruff's favourite pair in Mildred's room, soaking in salty water to remove what in Dr Kemp's opinion and mine is a bloodstain. Alongside her long-running dispute with Lady Emelia over the alleged theft of a letter opener and other items and money, it seemed reasonable to assume a heated exchange had taken place leading to tragedy.' She shook her head. 'Not so. If you will indulge me further, I must deviate to the matter of green ink.'

'Ink now, is it?' said Cole, puzzlement joining all the other emotions displayed on his face. 'What on earth—'

'The scrap of suicide note is written in green ink,' explained Mrs Bramble. 'We found green ink blotches on the paper and all over the blotter pad, suggesting the pen had a faulty nib. Ink stains are notorious for being stubborn to remove, but both Miss Franklin's fingers and those of Lady Emelia showed no signs of such stains nor any signs of having been scrubbed clean.'

'They didn't write the note?' Cole sounded even more confused.

'They did not. The conclusion must be that the murderer wrote the note for Lady Emelia to find, to cover their tracks, not realising she would burn it and stab Miss Franklin with the letter opener. I looked for signs of green ink on the fingers of the suspect ladies and it surprised me that several had telling stains.'

Unease spread through the gathering as the ladies glanced at their fingers and then those of their seated neighbours.

'Lady Madeleine had a tinge at the end of her fingers when I spoke to her on her return from "popping in to see Lady Ives", as she called it, but this is easily explained.' Mrs Bramble ignored Lady Madeleine's glowering stare. 'During the nocturnal chase, I knocked over a sign outside Lady Ives' front door warning of wet paint. When I later inspected the door, I found a fingermark where Lady Madeleine must have touched the paintwork before it dried.

'While there, Lady Ives invited me in to offer my opinion on an oil painting she had completed and I discovered she had been giving art lessons to Mrs Ewan. This explained the green tinge to Mrs Ewan's fingers and the sharp smell of turpentine in her apartment. It also explained the small flecks of paint I noticed on her dress and that of Lady Ives.

'Mrs Woodruff also had a greenish discolouration, beneath a silver ring with a Blue John stone on her finger, along with red inflammation. One of the metals present in sterling silver is copper, from which many suffer an itchy rash when perspiration reacts with the metal. I suspect it is this that caused the green tinge and skin irritation.'

Smug looks had replaced the affronted expressions of the ladies sitting around the two tables, Mrs Bramble's deductions having discounted them from being the author of the suicide note.

But Mrs Bramble hadn't finished.

'One of the items I found in Miss Franklin's study is this ...' Mrs Bramble held up the business card. 'We know the potential ruin resulting from the failure of the gold and diamond mine could be a motive for murder and it transpires that all the investors first met at the Gunpowder Club. Dr Kemp admitted to being both a member and a minor investor, which, as I said, caused me to suspect him for a while, especially when he turned up to certify Miss Franklin's death dressed in a shirt with a green stain.'

'I had an infestation of vermin at my surgery and sought advice from one of the palace gardeners.' Dr Kemp indicated Billy, sitting at the back table, whose face turned red at the attention. 'In payment for removing a splinter from his eye, he gave me some Paris Green, used in the palace to kill rats and mice.'

'I did speak to Billy and he confirmed Dr Kemp's explanation,' said Mrs Bramble.

'This is all well and good, but what's your point?' said Cole, a tic betraying his rising irritation.

'My point, Inspector, is that of all the residents in Master Carpenter's Court, Miss Woodruff is the one lady who never allowed her fingers to be seen. Even when she arrived back from London and took off her coat and hat, she kept on her favourite cream gloves. I later noticed she had changed these to her less-favoured pale-blue pair.'

'Everyone is entitled to wear gloves and own more than one pair.'

'True, but ...' Mrs Bramble lifted the cream glove and showed it's pink stain. 'Not only can you still see the blood on the outside, but' – she turned it inside out – 'if you do this, you reveal the green stain of writing ink.'

Cole's mouth fell open as chattering broke out among the ladies.

Mrs Bramble held up her hand for quiet. 'On discovering the glove, I noticed an odd tinge to the salty water and realised much later what must have caused it. Whoever wrote the suicide note with the faulty pen also pricked their finger on the hatpin while attempting to re-lock Lady Emelia's door after breaking in. The hatpin is made of silver with a leaf design; far too fancy and expensive for a domestic servant.'

'It doesn't make sense,' said Cole. 'Why would Miss Woodruff write such a note?'

Mrs Woodruff stood indignantly but sat back with a bump when her daughter pulled her arm.

'Mildred could have stolen both the pin and the gloves,' Cole continued, his voice steady but lacking conviction.

'Maybe,' said Mrs Bramble. 'But I believe there is one witness who can identify the prowler. Lady Madeleine's cockatoo, Sunny.'

'What the—' Cole looked more exasperated by the minute.

'Sunny calls out insulting nicknames whenever he sees or hears certain ladies passing by – a fact confirmed by letters of complaint sent both to me and the Lord Chamberlain about this. Sunny was heard to squawk "strumpet" at around nine o'clock on the night of Miss Franklin's murder, and I heard this again on the night the sergeant and I chased the prowler.' She strode over to the door. 'I must ask you all to be absolutely quiet while we undertake a little demonstration because, as you will see, Sunny is a first-class witness.'

'Are we to play charades now?' said Mrs McGowan. 'Many have complained about the infernal creature's noise.'

'Infernal creatrure,' echoed her companion.

'I agree with Mrs McGowan,' said Cole. 'You can't expect justice to hinge on the squawking of a noisy pet.'

'It is a demonstration, no more,' said Mrs Bramble, appreciating the difficulty and legality of using a bird as a witness, but this wasn't a court of law and she hoped what happened next would be convincing nonetheless.

She waited for the chorus of discontent to die down and cease before asking the guide to bring Sunny back into the room. He set the cage on the table and retreated.

Raising the cover of the cage on the side facing away from the gathering, Mrs Bramble said, 'If I tap you on the shoulder, please be so kind as to walk behind the table, past the cage and back to your seat.'

She walked over to Miss Cameron-Banks and tapped her shoulder. The surprised woman threw a look of horror towards Mrs McGowan, who returned a nod of support, but she need not have worried. Sunny marked her slow walk behind the table with no more than a trill and a whistle.

Lady Emelia rose without looking at any of the other ladies and walked behind the table.

'Rubbish!' Sunny shouted. 'Rubbish!'

The ladies looked at each other in astonishment as Lady Emelia retook her seat, her face like thunder.

Lady Madeleine smirked.

Mrs Ewan went next and Sunny squawked, 'Wastrel,' as she passed his cage. 'Wastrel!'

Lady Madeleine chuckled, the other ladies looking concerned at what might be shouted at them. Miss Woodruff, the fourth and final person to be tapped, rose with reluctance from her chair before walking to the table, where she hesitated. Cole whispered a word of encouragement to her and she walked into the cockatoo's line of sight.

'Strumpet, strumpet!' Sunny shouted, and the ladies cried out in shock.

# 38

Mrs Bramble dropped the cover back over Sunny's cage and gestured to the waiting guide, who stepped forwards to take it from the room and resume his station outside the door. Cole strode over to Miss Woodruff, who offered no resistance as he pulled off her left glove, revealing the faint but telltale signs of green ink on her thumb and forefinger, and a distinctive, angry-looking red dot where a sharp object had pricked the end of her middle finger.

'I knew it,' said Mrs Ewan as Mrs Woodruff stood up in anger.

'Doesn't surprise me,' said Lady Ives.

Mrs McGowan countered with, 'Well, I—'

'—never,' finished Miss Cameron-Banks.

'Inspector Cole,' said Mrs Woodruff. 'This is preposterous, and you know it. My daughter is a genteel lady of refinement. You cannot believe the inane noises of an animal that has learned its manners from' – she struggled to find the appropriate words – '. . . from . . .' She sat down as though her legs could no longer support her.

'I must say, this defies all logic,' said Cole. 'Why the devil would Miss Woodruff want to kill Miss Franklin, let alone break in again the following night?'

'The answer is simple, Inspector,' said Mrs Bramble. 'Miss Franklin was desperate to keep the failing fortunes of the mine and other investments from Lady Emelia to shield her sister from worry and save the family from embarrassment. In turn, we discovered Miss Woodruff was courting an MP and travelled to London every Tuesday morning to meet him, staying overnight at the Savoy hotel and returning to Hampton Court every Wednesday morning.

'I sent a telegram to an old friend who works at the Savoy. She is stepping out with the doorman of the Gunpowder Club, where the MP is a member, as Miss Woodruff's late father had been, which is likely how they met in the first place. Although above board – the MP never visited or stayed with her at the Savoy – it was a courtship her mother held a deep disapproval of and forbade, but which Miss Franklin became aware of and knew had continued. And thus was the status quo maintained.'

The Woodruffs could not look at each other.

'Until ...' said Mrs Bramble, pleased to see she had everyone's undivided attention. 'The balance tipped when Miss Woodruff's beau became embroiled in the very serious Baccarat cheating scandal currently sweeping London society in which Queen Victoria's son, Prince Edward, is implicated.

'With her family's future prospects and security under threat, Miss Woodruff sought assurances from Miss Franklin about financial redress should the mine close. One can only imagine the fear and vitriol between two women with much to lose in terms of money, reputation and status, but I suspect Miss Franklin saw an opportunity to rid herself of the arrangement for good, resulting in the argument Rosie overheard.

'I assert that Miss Woodruff, as a result of the row, sought to take matters into her own hands in two ways. The first was simple: to attempt to distance herself from scandal by association, by ending the affair with the MP as soon as she could.'

'That would offer no guarantee of protection, even though their courtship, well known as it is in London society, would have been forgotten over time,' said Cole. 'Miss Franklin could have used her knowledge and influence to bring about reputational ruin by suggesting Miss Woodruff had been supportive of the MP's involvement in the cheating because the rewards would have eased her family's financial pressures.'

'Which is why the second way was to ensure Miss Franklin's silence, permanently.'

Cole looked thoughtful but unconvinced. 'Even allowing for the increasingly bitter nature of this relationship, how could Miss Woodruff have killed Miss Franklin when she was in London on the night of the murder?'

'A troubling question, I agree, but something bothered me about Miss Woodruff's return from London on the morning the murder was discovered. I was present when she arrived and her mother asked her for a snifter of brandy but was told they had none – a situation good servants would not allow – and I noticed an obvious space between bottles where another might stand. Or a decanter.

'The decanter of brandy found in Miss Franklin's study was laced with a fatal dose of arsenic. Billy confirmed that, in addition to Paris Green, arsenic is readily available to anyone wishing to acquire it in secret because it is used in rat traps all over the palace.'

Mrs Bramble noticed Billy shrink a little further on his chair at the mention of his name, as though fingers might be pointed and he be accused at any moment. She gave him a look of reassurance before continuing.

'I believe Miss Woodruff devised a plan to kill Miss Franklin by giving her the brandy, disguised as a peace offering, on the morning she left for London. Knowing Miss Franklin liked brandy but Lady Emelia did not, she could be almost certain the poison would not be drunk by the wrong person. In my experience, most people – ladies in particular – are not natural born killers.

'Despite having ended the love affair that evening, she must have become frantic with worry that her plan had not worked or her scheme had been uncovered. With the knowledge that most residents would be attending Lady Venetia's gala in the Great Hall, the solution she chose to achieve a modicum of peace of mind was to catch the next train from Waterloo to Hampton Court and recover the poison, whether it had worked or not, and return to London the same evening. Unfortunately for her, three events intervened.'

'I would say more than three,' piped up Cole, giving the sergeant another sharp look. 'But what evidence do you have?'

'The same as you, Inspector,' said Mrs Bramble, watching him bristle at the jibe. 'First, she turned her ankle on the steps of the Gunpowder Club, forcing her to accept the offer of the loan of the MP's silver-topped cane, another fact confirmed by my friend at the Savoy.' She indicated the cane held by Miss Woodruff. 'I noticed Miss Woodruff had a limp and saw that cane with its decorative embossed crest when she arrived home on Wednesday. This was the tapping heard by witnesses and it was Miss Woodruff's form they saw passing.

'Secondly, she called on Miss Franklin, absent-mindedly using her distinctive repeated double-knock in the process, and found the doors unlocked because Miss Franklin had never left the apartment and locked them. Entering the study, Miss Woodruff believed her poison had worked and decided to write the suicide note to deflect attention from any sugges-tion of murder. This took up too much time and those who had left the gala early could be heard returning.

'Upon hearing the tapping of a cane as Mrs Ewan arrived in the courtyard, and in fear of imminent discovery, Miss

Woodruff placed the note on the bureau but forgot the thing she had come for: the telltale decanter.

'Thirdly, having returned to the station intending to take the train back to London and maintain her alibi, she found her ticket missing and had to purchase another.'

'This is complete balderdash,' said Mrs Woodruff, but the strength and conviction had left her voice.

Her daughter said nothing, her face having lost all its colour.

'Another detail that convinced me the prowler had been Miss Woodruff was when I discovered Sunny shouted particular words whenever he saw or heard certain people,' said Mrs Bramble. 'When I spoke to Mrs Ewan, she complained that Sunny had squawked the word "wastrel" as she passed by, and then "strumpet" over and over again, but only *after* she had entered her apartment upon returning from the Great Hall. As you all witnessed, it is the word he shouts when Miss Woodruff passes.'

'Sergeant, the cuffs,' said Cole.

'One moment, Inspector,' said Mrs Bramble. 'There is a complication.'

'Dear God,' said Cole, running a hand back across his hair. 'Not another? You even said she went back to the scene of her crime the following night.'

'She did,' said Mrs Bramble. 'She had become convinced she had murdered Miss Franklin and, having been disturbed the night before, she needed to erase any evidence, but the decanter being unrecoverable dealt a serious blow. However, she had prepared a piece of misdirection, in the form of a fake letter from Dr Peregrine Frizzell to Miss Franklin, supposedly confirming that gold had been found. Then there was mention of the decision to close the mine and split the profit.'

Cole picked up the letter. 'This one?'

'The same. As we have heard, she ran out of time to complete her tasks and returned to plant it among the business files.'

'How on earth can you tell it's a fake?' said Lady Ives. 'It's typed.'

Cole cleared his throat and took a step forwards, apparently eager to share some of the limelight. Mrs Bramble let him take centre stage.

'You can see an indentation around the signature that does not occur when an ordinary ink pen is used.' He picked up the other two letters. 'These are letters from Dr Frizzell to all investors he sent some time ago. One has the same indentation, the other does not, proving someone traced over the signature to use on the fake letter. You will also see it is typed, whereas all the other letters in those files are handwritten. Why? To avoid comparison.'

'Miss Woodruff needed to expand the pool of potential suspects and how better to do that than to fake a gold strike?' said Mrs Bramble. 'The letter suggested a conspiracy between Miss Franklin and Dr Frizzell, which increased the number of suspects to encompass all the investors, including Frizzell himself.'

'No wonder you asked me about my brother,' said Mrs McGowan, a hard edge to her tone.

'To set your mind at rest, I sent another telegram, to Dr Frizzell in South Africa, asking two innocuous questions about the mine. Mrs McGowan expected her brother's imminent return, so he could not be ruled out until he replied to my telegram directly from Cape Town. That is the other telegram I received this evening, proving he is still there and could not have committed the murder.'

Mrs McGowan let out a little squeak and covered her mouth with the lace handkerchief she held in one hand. Lady Emelia put a comforting hand on her arm and gave her a reassuring smile. Mrs Bramble understood how Lady Emelia might feel some affinity with Mrs McGowan, having so recently been accused and subsequently cleared of her sister's murder.

'Can you prove my daughter wrote the letter?' said Mrs Woodruff.

Mrs Bramble turned to Cole. 'If you would be so kind as to read your telegram now.'

Cole unfolded the paper. 'It's from the Savoy hotel and reads: "Miss W did use typewriter. Stop. Can confirm lower-case 'j' damaged. Stop."' Cole checked the fake letter. 'The tittle – the dot over the "j" – is missing.' He looked at Mrs Bramble with a triumphant smile. 'Will you allow me to arrest Miss Woodruff now or not?'

Another hum of chattering rippled around the ladies, along with suspicious glances at each other and worried looks towards the inspector.

As she paused to take stock, a tingle of concern, one that had originated at the centre of her chest ten minutes ago, intensified due to the continuing absence of Reverend Weaver. Without the evidence he had been sent to find, the possibility that she might not be able to prove the murderer's guilt troubled her. Cole kept staring at the side of her head from one side and the sergeant did so from the other, but she refused to look at either. Once the ladies and Dr Kemp also became aware of the hiatus, the hum of conversation dissipated like morning fog and she began to feel uncomfortable.

As if on cue, a knock sounded on the door and Reverend Weaver stumbled in, apologising for his tardiness, his condition and for bumping the back of Dr Kemp's chair, depositing a long shred of brown-tinged cabbage on the doctor's shoulder. He carried a plate covered in waxed paper in one hand and held its contents secure with the other. The ladies nearest the door wrinkled their noses as Weaver passed by, but the smell

305

soon drifted across to everyone as he handed the plate to Mrs Bramble.

'Dear Lord,' said Lady Ives. 'What *have* you been doing?'

'The stench is awful, Reverend,' said Mrs Ewan, turning her head away.

'Have you bathed at all?' said Lady Madeleine.

Mrs Woodruff gagged and all the ladies now held handkerchiefs to their noses while attempting to wave away the aroma of rotting food with their free hands.

'You smell like a corpse,' said Kemp. 'No offence.'

'None taken,' said Weaver. 'I'm afraid the task Mrs Bramble set me took a turn for the worse when I knocked an entire bin over myself.' He chuckled. 'Clumsy oaf.'

'I am most grateful for your diligence, Reverend,' said Mrs Bramble, the tingling a thing of the past now she had what she needed in her hand. 'In answer to your question, Inspector, I'm afraid you should *not* arrest Miss Woodruff. She is not the murderer.'

# 39

'Damn and blast!' Cole threw the letters onto the table in exasperation, taking a big, calming breath and sighing. 'Excuse my language.' He held his hand up to the chattering ladies in appeasement. 'What in God's name is wrong this time?'

'Although a would-be murderer, Miss Woodruff was unaware that Miss Franklin had been poisoned by a substance other than arsenic,' said Mrs Bramble. 'Which brings us to the identity of the true murderer.'

This got the ladies' attention again, although she noticed that not one of them now looked suspicious or concerned, as though a weight of their own had been lifted.

'Please get on with it,' Cole snapped. 'If you really have done my job for me, which I won't ever admit to my superintendent, I'd like to hear it before my leg goes to sleep while standing here like a muttonhead.'

Mrs Bramble gave him a respectful nod, which seemed to irritate him more. 'Dr Kemp's post-mortem report may have established that the letter opener could not have been the cause of death, but it also proved that Miss Franklin took not one sip of the poisoned brandy.'

'I didn't see that.' Cole snatched up Kemp's report and flicked through its pages. 'She *didn't* kill Miss Franklin?'

'No.'

'I found no trace of arsenic in Miss Franklin's body,' confirmed Kemp.

'And Mildred?' Cole asked.

'Unlike Miss Franklin, I surmise the obvious loss of blood from the internal and external damage caused by the knife is indeed what killed her. Of course, I have yet to test for poisons.'

'And I suspect you won't find any,' said Mrs Bramble. 'Not if my deductions are correct, of course.'

'Of course.' Cole threw up his hands. 'Carry on, why don't you.'

In any other circumstance, Mrs Bramble might have needed to suppress a smile, but this was neither the time nor the place. The others present seemed to sense this, too, and a stillness descended as though the room itself held its breath.

'Outwardly, Lady Emelia's housemaid, Rosie, and Mrs Woodruff's housemaid, Mildred, were friends, but I witnessed an altercation between them while at Lady Venetia's gala. They waved it off as a tiff between friends, but I got the impression something else might lie deeper. After all, Rosie's mistress, Lady Emelia, had accused Mildred of theft, leaving her with a deep distrust of the girl, but no one ever presented any evidence and a simmering animosity had remained between them.'

Suddenly remembering the solicitor's letter folded in her pocket, she took it out, tore it open and read quickly. Nodding at the confirmation of her suspicions, she replaced it in her pocket.

'Following the discovery of Miss Franklin's body, Rosie told me she had posted a letter on her behalf to the family's solicitor the day after the argument she overheard. As all servants cannot help but do in fulfilling their daily service, Joan and

Rosie overheard talk about the South African mine and of serious money troubles. Joan also overheard another altercation in the study on a Tuesday evening, but I am inclined to think it was not Miss Woodruff this time because, in all likelihood, she had left on her weekly trip to London that morning.'

'So, who the devil was it, in your opinion?' said Cole, listening intently now. 'Mildred, I shouldn't wonder.'

'I thought so, too,' said Mrs Bramble, more to let Cole down gently rather than having any real conviction it had been Mildred. 'Rosie did admit to letting Mildred into the stairwell of the Chaffords' apartment on occasion while she fetched any ingredients Mildred wished to borrow, despite this going against the expressed wishes of Lady Emelia.'

'There you go, then,' said Cole, raising his chin for emphasis.

'In the course of my investigation' – she ignored Cole's sidelong glance – 'I had cause to speak to Billy about rat poisons used in the palace, as I mentioned earlier. I met him in the Wilderness, where he was working to clear a patch of weeds. That's when I discovered that Billy and Mildred were sweet on each other and she often visited him in the gardens or the Wilderness.'

'I can't see how the affairs of servants has any bearing on proceedings,' said Lady Ives.

'Hearing?' said Mrs Ewan. 'What about it?' She cupped a hand to her ear with a grimace of concentration.

Lady Ives rolled her eyes.

'It has a bearing because Mildred was being blackmailed,' said Mrs Bramble. 'By Rosie.'

'What the ...?' Cole's head whipped round and he stared at her.

The gasps from the ladies and Dr Kemp caused Rosie's already flushed cheeks to intensify their hue.

'It ain't true,' said Rosie, her eyes wide with alarm.

'I considered Rosie a prime witness at first but began to distrust her testimony as her stories changed and she gave me different information, even suggesting at one point that Lady Emelia had poisoned the brandy,' said Mrs Bramble. 'This could have been fanciful speculation on her part, but I'm sure it was an attempt at misdirection.'

Rosie shifted uneasily on her chair as Mrs Bramble picked up the jewel-handled letter opener.

'I believe Rosie knew Mildred was innocent of theft because she had stolen this letter opener herself, to sell when necessary. Maybe she threatened to plant it somewhere and have Mildred arrested and properly charged this time.'

'As intriguing as that may be, Mrs Bramble, why would she do anything of the sort and what has it to do with Lady Emelia?' said Mrs McGowan.

'What has it?' said her companion.

'However she engineered it, Rosie made Mildred do something on her behalf, but I'll come to that in a moment.' Mrs Bramble touched her pocket to assure herself she still had the letter. 'Mildred was seen speaking to Rosie at the door to the Chaffords' apartment earlier in the evening, before the servants left to work at the gala, and it took me a long time to realise why until Dr Kemp revealed his findings to me – in advance of writing his report, in fact.'

Cole's jaw muscles tightened as he shot Dr Kemp an angry glance.

'When we found Miss Franklin's body, Rosie ran to the water closet to fetch up. I've interviewed her a number of times over the past two days and she was sick again on a few occasions. At first, I put it down to the shock of seeing her mistress murdered, but I noticed something else. She was often breathless after climbing stairs and seemed to be holding her midriff, almost without thinking, and then it occurred to me.'

310

'Oh, dear Lord,' gasped Joan, looking at Rosie incredulously. 'You're with child.'

More gasps escaped from the ladies, mainly of disapproval, but in Lady Emelia's case, of shock at hearing that her trusted housemaid was both pregnant and a blackmailer. The hubbub flared briefly but died down at the sergeant's insistence and Mrs Bramble waited for silence.

'Soon after moving to the palace following the death of Sir Philip, the petty thefts of property and small sums of money began. Lady Emelia levelled her accusations at Mildred. However, I believe Miss Franklin had reason to suspect Rosie and somehow discovered the pregnancy because of it, although she had yet to show.

'Ordinarily, the revelation of an unmarried pregnancy would see a maid dismissed from her job and out on the streets, but Billy told me Sir Philip had been strict about who his staff associated with and Rosie hadn't been allowed men as friends. Miss Franklin knew this and feared that Sir Philip, the one man in the household, had to be the father.

'The altercation Joan overheard was not with Miss Woodruff about the mine, nor Mildred about the thefts, but a confront-ation with Rosie about paternity and how she should be provided for.'

'It's true,' said Rosie, defiantly meeting Lady Emelia's haunted gaze. 'Philip loved me and I've got letters to prove it. He'd have seen me right.'

'Of that I have no doubt,' said Mrs Bramble. 'I don't know the details of the demands and counter-offers, but it seems Rosie was dissatisfied and I doubt she had scraped together enough to survive if ejected from the palace. She needed money desperately and the desire for revenge grew like a canker. She could not face the rejection of what would soon be Sir Philip's son or daughter, Miss Franklin's nephew or niece, so I believe

311

she devised a plan. She would poison Miss Franklin and steal a large sum from her, hence the broken cash box and empty purse.'

A hubbub rose from the ladies and heads turned towards Rosie. Cole raised his hands for quiet.

'What about Miss Franklin's jewellery?' he said once order had been restored. 'Why didn't she steal that?'

Mrs Bramble gave him a knowing nod. 'Undoubtedly, Lady Emelia's return from the gala disturbed Rosie's endeavours. But in any case, the pearls would be far too difficult to sell without attracting attention. Rosie knew that Mildred and several of the ladies held grudges against Lady Emelia and Miss Franklin, and I believe she used these and the friction between the two sisters to deflect suspicion away from herself. Ultimately, to get away with murder by framing Mildred.'

'This is ridiculous,' said Cole.

'Exactly so,' agreed Mrs Woodruff. 'You have provided evidence to show Miss Franklin was neither stabbed nor poisoned with arsenic, so how on earth did she die, and under what circumstances?'

'All good questions, Mrs Woodruff.' Mrs Bramble gave her as reassuring a smile as she could muster. 'Billy was getting rid of the bushy weeds as quickly as he could, because although it looked quite pretty, reminiscent of the herb chervil to passers-by, a small bunch had been cut and he feared someone might become sick if they ate it by mistake. I suspect Rosie had seen it while out for a walk in the Wilderness and, having often helped in the kitchen, knew its true name. Billy was unaware Mildred was the one who had cut it, under instruction from Rosie, who didn't wish to be seen near it. That is what Mildred delivered on the night of the gala under the pretence of needing sugar.

'Joan was needed in the kitchens to prepare food for the

gala and left before she was able to cook anything for Miss Franklin. In any case, Miss Franklin was partial to a good sandwich and often preferred those if working in the evening. I'm sure she was more than satisfied when Rosie, the last to leave for the gala, brought her this two evenings ago.' She uncovered the plate to reveal half a beef and salad sandwich. 'I'm afraid I had Reverend Weaver rummaging through the palace bins before tomorrow's collection because I suspected something might be awry, and Dr Kemp's post-mortem confirmed it. Miss Franklin did indeed die of poisoning, from hemlock ingested in the salad of this sandwich.' She lifted the half-slice of bread to show them the chervil-like leaves of hemlock underneath.

'Hemlock?' said the sergeant. 'Good Lord. Didn't that disappear with the ark?'

'I'm afraid not.' Mrs Bramble shook her head. 'When Rosie returned after the ball, she found Miss Franklin dead as she'd hoped, but with the suicide note beside her written by Miss Woodruff. No doubt confused by the note, and hearing Lady Emelia entering through the front door below, she took the money but forgot about the sandwich remains. She closed the door and knocked, pretending to ask if Miss Franklin wanted anything. I dare say Rosie tried to retrieve the sandwich later but found the door locked by Lady Emelia and no key on the outside. Later the following morning, Lady Emelia innocently removed the bottle of brandy and gave it to Joan, while Rosie deliberately removed the sandwich and threw it away.'

'If what you say is true, and it seems so, what happened to Mildred?' said Mrs McGowan, her companion too dazed to echo her words. 'You're not suggesting ...?'

'I'm guessing, but it's not unreasonable to surmise that Mildred, accused of theft but not a thief, did not want to be accused of murder and perhaps threatened to expose Rosie for what she was. Did an altercation take place? Maybe – they'd already argued at the gala – maybe not, but Rosie stabbed her all the same, with the same gold letter opener Mildred had been accused of stealing but had actually been taken by Rosie. Rosie may have thought it poetic justice, but it was a strong indicator to me that whoever had killed Mildred had probably killed Miss Franklin, too.'

'Sergeant, the cuffs on the housemaid, if you please,' said Cole.

'It's a lie!' Rosie shouted as she leaped to her feet to flee amid uproar from the ladies. 'You've no proof.'

Kitty yanked her down again, holding her arm until the sergeant had secured his handcuffs around the young woman's wrists.

Mrs Bramble took out the solicitor's letter and showed the envelope to Cole. He extracted the letter and his eyes flicked back and forth as he read, handing it back to Mrs Bramble with raised eyebrows once he'd finished.

'Ladies, please!' said Mrs Bramble, and waited for their attention to focus on her again. 'Rosie, this is a letter from the family's solicitor in response to the one you posted on behalf of Miss Franklin two weeks ago. You feared being cast out and left destitute, but even without solid proof, Sir Philip having died soon after the moment of conception, it seems your argument succeeded in swaying Miss Franklin's opinion and she accepted your account.

'She also believed her brother-in-law would have wished to support you and his child, so provision has been made for you to receive a lump sum to tide you over, in addition to a small but regular income, representing far more money than you could ever have stolen.'

The fight left Rosie in a rush and she stopped struggling, her mouth open as if to speak but struck mute by the realisation of what she had heard. She slumped on her chair, deflated and defeated. Tears streamed down her cheeks, dripping on her housemaid's uniform, but the assembly had little sympathy for the young woman who had not only taken the life of another maid, but also one of their own.

Lady Emelia had gone as white as Rosie's apron at the revelation that her late husband had fathered the unborn child. The further realisation that her sister believed Sir Philip had loved Rosie enough to warrant providing lifelong support, at the family's expense, seemed to hit her harder. She stared at Rosie, but the maid kept her gaze downcast.

'Well, I never did,' said Mrs Woodruff, sitting bolt upright with a haughty expression now her daughter had been absolved of murder.

Miss Woodruff seemed to know she was not yet out of the woods and kept quiet.

'You took your time getting there, I must say,' said Lady Ives to Inspector Cole. 'Even with considerable assistance from Mrs Bramble.'

'Well, I——' began Cole, unable to say more, as Mrs McGowan stood up.

'And you had the barefaced cheek to suspect my Perry,' she snapped.

'Perry,' echoed her companion, also getting to her feet.

'I'd love a glass of sherry,' said Mrs Ewan, glancing around as though in hope of securing a glass.

'I can feel a letter to the commissioner of police in the offing,' said Mrs Woodruff, stopping as her daughter gave her arm a pinch.

Cole held his hands up for quiet. 'I'm sure you'll all get a chance to have your say – the sergeant will be taking statements in due course – but I must take my prisoner to Scotland Yard at the earliest opportunity. In the meantime, please address

315

your concerns to Mrs Bramble.' He turned to the sergeant. 'Sergeant, if you please.'

It took all of Mrs Bramble's strength to refrain from giving Cole a piece of her mind as he and the sergeant left the Large Oak Room with Rosie amid a cacophony of questions.

# Epilogue

A few days later, Mrs Bramble sipped her usual morning cup of Earl Grey tea, washing down the first of two slices of toast, buttered thickly and with a smear of marmalade. As demanded by Dodger, watching her expectantly through his green eyes with big black pupils, she prepared his buttered crust and placed it on the floor next to her chair.

The events of the past week could not easily be forgotten, but the palace was an institution that demanded a speedy return to normality and she for one would be glad of it.

Lady Madeleine, Mrs Ewan, Lady Ives and Mrs McGowan with Miss Cameron-Banks had all returned to their apartments with enough juicy gossip and tittle-tattle to fuel months of coffee mornings and afternoon teas. Dr Kemp resumed his busy life as general practitioner to both the village and the ladies of Hampton Court Palace, vowing to employ a proper rat catcher for his surgery in future.

With the sergeant acting as escort, Inspector Cole had returned to Scotland Yard with Rosie, having arrested her on suspicion of double murder. Lady Emelia, released into the care of Joan, who now had to double-up as housemaid until her mistress felt able to recruit another, had been in some distress to learn that if convicted, Rosie intended to 'plead the belly'. Using her pregnancy to stay the execution until after the birth made it highly probable she would be pardoned from execution and maybe escape any custodial sentence.

The Woodruffs had also retreated to their apartment, distraught after Cole had made it perfectly clear that he could not arrest Miss Alice Woodruff but considered her a would-be murderer whose plans had been thwarted only by Rosie getting there first.

Mrs Bramble felt a warm glow of satisfaction that in the end Inspector Cole had accepted every story she had told, every link she had made and every shred of evidence she had provided. She had even managed to persuade him to put a good word in for the sergeant, although it remained to be seen whether or not he would honour his promise. She suspected he would take the entire credit.

On her account, that was as it should be. She had no need for plaudits, nor any desire to be the centre of attention. Her previous life in the army, with her husband, had provided enough excitement, danger, happiness and sadness to last a lifetime. All she wanted was the life she had now, with all its petty squabbles about who should have the biggest apartments, who should pay for maintenance – she watched Kitty rub Dodger's ear as he strolled past – and the legitimacy of keeping pets. She threw a glance at the telegram Kitty had just propped against the marmalade pot and smiled wryly at the thought of what new gripe lay inside.

Reverend Weaver had taken a bath at the earliest opportunity to expunge the stink of rotten vegetables from his body and nostrils, fearing he had his work cut out persuading his flock that the tragic events of the week had gone according to God's holy plan. As she opened the telegram, she chuckled at the thought of seeing him dotted with cabbage scraps, recalling his subsequent delight at being rewarded for his

318

part in catching Rosie by being asked to officiate at a special Holy Communion service at the Tower of London. Weaver, of course, had accepted the invitation immediately and Mrs Bramble undertook to discover how he had fared last night in the Chapel of St Peter ad Vincula.

She had not long to wait.

'Here we go again,' she said as she read the telegram, drawing a surprised glance from Kitty. 'I'm afraid we'll be needing our travelling coats. It seems, inexplicably, that our good friend Reverend Weaver has been arrested for murder.'

# Acknowledgements

It's not every day that one gets asked to write a cosy crime mystery for a major publisher like Orion Fiction, especially with the backing of a significant organisation like Historic Royal Palaces. There was a lot to consider in undertaking such a commission, but even though I knew the scrutiny would be high when it came to being accurate and sensitive to the history of Hampton Court Palace, it was both a pleasure and a privilege to say yes. Then came the hard work, which inevitably involved more people than just me as the author. These demand recognition.

First, I must thank my wife, Jane, who encouraged me to accept the challenge, and our two daughters, Laura and Holly. They suffered daily interruptions as I wittered on, talking us (me) through troublesome plot points towards the right solutions. No real hardship, you might think, but while my mind was focused on dealing with structural edits, their minds were focused on final preparations for Laura's wedding!

Secondly, authors are often referred to as 'the talent', but that does not tell the whole story, because other talented individuals do so much both before and after the first draft is written. Therefore, thanks go to my fantastic agent, Nelle Andrew, and all at Rachel Mills Literary, who continue to believe in me when sometimes my own belief wanes, and Leodora Darlington, Publishing Director of Orion Fiction, who had faith enough to entrust me with this project. Thank you as well to my project editor, Anshuman Yadav, and copy editor, Claire Dean, and all the unnamed stars at Orion Fiction who will have had a hand in bringing this project to fruition, turning my words into a book and making it fly.

At Historic Royal Palaces, I must thank Clare Murphy, Polly Putnam and Karey Draper, who took the time to give me a private tour of Hampton Court Palace, especially areas within the grace-and-favour apartments rarely seen by members of the public; and Sarah Kilby, who treated me gently during an interview for *Inside Story*, the Historic Royal Palaces membership magazine.

Finally, thanks go to Peter Atkinson, a friend from primary school, since when we have had many adventures together. His amateur dramatics experience came in very useful during a research visit as I filmed him hurrying around Hampton Court Palace in search of a fictional intruder. The scene was playing out in my head, not those of casual observers, so we inadvertently entertained many visitors with our actions that day!

It only remains for me to say that this is a work of fiction set in a real environment. Although I have tried to be accurate where possible, I admit to playing fast and loose with both history and reality for the purposes of entertainment. If anything has piqued your interest, there are many books about Hampton Court Palace, including a few about grace and favour, but I have to say there is no substitute for visiting this magnificent set of historic buildings, gardens and parklands for yourself.

# Credits

N.R. Daws and Orion Fiction would like to thank everyone at Orion who worked on the publication of *Murder at the Palace* in the UK.

**Editorial**
Leodora Darlington

**Copy editor**
Claire Dean

**Proofreader**
Holly Kyte

**Audio**
Paul Stark
Louise Richardson

**Contracts**
Dan Herron
Ellie Bowker
Oliver Chacón

**Design**
Jet Purdie

**Editorial Management**
Anshuman Yadav
Snigdha Koirala
Charlie Panayiotou
Jane Hughes
Bartley Shaw

**Finance**
Jasdip Nandra
Nick Gibson
Sue Baker

**Marketing**
Corrine Jean-Jacques

**Production**
Katie Horrocks
Ruth Sharvell

**Publicity**
Ellen Turner

**Sales**
Catherine Worsley
Esther Waters
Victoria Laws
Rachael Hum
Ellie Kyrke-Smith

Frances Doyle
Georgina Cutler

**Operations**
Group Sales Operations team

**Rights**
Rebecca Folland
Tara Hiatt
Ben Fowler
Alice Cottrell
Ruth Blakemore
Marie Henckel

# Help us make the next generation of readers

We – both author and publisher – hope you enjoyed this book. We believe that you can become a reader at any time in your life, but we'd love your help to give the next generation a head start.

Did you know that 9 per cent of children don't have a book of their own in their home, rising to 13 per cent in disadvantaged families*? We'd like to try to change that by asking you to consider the role you could play in helping to build readers of the future.

We'd love you to think of sharing, borrowing, reading, buying or talking about a book with a child in your life and spreading the love of reading. We want to make sure the next generation continue to have access to books, wherever they come from.

And if you would like to consider donating to charities that help fund literacy projects, find out more at **www.literacytrust.org.uk** and **www.booktrust.org.uk**.

THANK YOU

*As reported by the National Literacy Trust